W9-BNU-414

For my sons:
Alan, Iain, and Andrew

Acknowledgments

My thanks to my wife, Vicki, to Russ Galen and Tara Wynne, to the team at Random House, and in particular to Liz Scheier.

The nightmare roared out of the darkness.

He had to get clear. If he stayed, he would die, incinerated in the hellish blast of a runaway fusion plant, his body vaporized into a ball of incandescent gas expanding into space. Panic tore him apart, and he started to run. Hammer missiles and rail-gun slugs ripped the heavy cruiser's fabric, and the huge ship died around him. Beneath his feet, the tangled bodies of dead spacers carpeted the deck, but the harder he ran, the less progress he made. He was getting nowhere: unable to breathe, lungs afire, legs refusing to work properly, mouth open in a soundless scream. And there, in front of the lifepod, between him and safety, stood Detective Sergeant Kalkov, eyes bulging, face a hate-twisted mask drifting in and out of flame-shot smoke, jeering at Michael's frantic efforts to get away, the knife that had killed him held in an outstretched fist, dripping blood to the deck.

The nightmare ended the way it always did.

The ship exploded in a searing flash of white, a ball of raw energy, and he woke up, his body wrapped in tangled sheets. For a long time, he lay there sweat-soaked, chest heaving, heart racing, the face of the Hammer police sergeant he had killed during his escape after the loss of the *Ishaq* still burning in his mind's eye.

Forcing himself out of his bunk, he went over to the washbasin to clean the sweat off his face, the water so cold that it stung. He peered at himself in the mirror.

"You look like shit, Lieutenant Michael Helfort," he said aloud. His face stared back from wide-set hazel eyes sunk deep in gray-framed sockets and underscored by dark bags. His skin, normally tanned to a rich brown, stretched ashen and washed out, tightened by stress across well-defined cheekbones, his lips clamped shut, thin and bloodless. His hair, overlong and unruly at the best of times, spiked into a tangled mess, sweat-darkened from brown to black.

It was true: He looked like shit. He sighed despairingly. He decided not to waste time trying to sleep. Invariably it eluded him after the *Ishaq* nightmare, so he hunted around the net to see what the holovids offered; he preferred to watch the dross they churned out. Even that was better than picking over the ghosts from his past.

Here we go, he thought finally. One of the better news channels had a segment dealing with a report from one of the Federation's think tanks on Space Fleet. Should be worth a look, he decided; comming micropayment—he was in no mood for advertisements—he pulled the item off the net. When the program anchor, Thad Horung, appeared, he put his feet up to watch.

". . . and our thanks to Johanna Morgenstern for that report from the Frontier Planets," Horung said. "Their refusal to support the Federation in the war against the Hammers will continue to be a major headache for this government, and we will of course keep you up to date with any developments there.

"Now we turn to the Tesdorf Institute. Yesterday it released its analysis of the long-term effects the Comdur disaster will have on Space Fleet. In a moment, I will talk with retired admiral Orenda Pekefier"—Michael groaned out loud; the woman was self-centered, opinionated, and bombastic, traits he did not enjoy—"about the key issues the Tesdorf Institute has identified. But first, what are those issues? Ashokan Mokhtar takes up the story."

The holovid cut to Mokhtar, a tall and impeccably dressed man standing in front of an imaginative re-creation of the Comdur disaster, all fireballs and tumbling Fed ships. Michael winced; it bore little resemblance to the awful day when Hammer missiles carrying antimatter warheads destroyed the Federated Worlds' fleet at the Battle of Comdur.

"Thank you, Thad," Mokhtar said. "The Tesdorf Institute's report is an impressively detailed document. Reading it through"—you liar, Michael mouthed; an underpaid research hack had that thankless task—"one issue stands out, the radical changes forced on Space Fleet by the loss of so many experienced personnel at Comdur and, in particular, the development of what we understand Fleet is calling dreadnoughts. These—"

Shocked, Michael sat bolt upright. The fact that dreadnoughts existed was one of the worst kept of Fleet's many secrets. In itself, talking about them was not a problem. But spelling out in detail what Fleet had done to convert its heavy cruisers to dreadnoughts: massively upgraded ceramsteel armor, crews cut to a handful of spacers, their air groups, landers, and marines removed, all unnecessary equipment torn out to reduce mass? For the Hammers to discover all that would be a major disaster. Even they could work out what the enhancements had created: a warship orders of magnitude tougher and more maneuverable than any conventional heavy cruiser, a warship—the only warship in humanspace—able to withstand antimatter weapons, the Hammer weapon that had wreaked such havoc at Comdur.

All traces of tiredness gone, Michael listened intently to Mokhtar.

". . . ships are essentially heavy cruisers with skeleton crews. No surprises there—we know Fleet is critically short of experienced spacers after their losses at Comdur—except for one very disturbing fact. Sources inside Fleet have confirmed that some of these dreadnoughts will carry no human crew at all, a development the Tesdorf Institute says is . . . and I quote . . . 'deeply problematic for the future of Space Fleet, prejudicial to the security of the Federated Worlds, and potentially a breach of the Dakota System Treaty, which prohibits the use of self-replicating machines.' Those are very serious charges, and we will explore them with Admiral Pekefier in some depth. Clearly, Fleet faces these and many other challenges at the present time, one of which must be whether or not Admiral Martha Shiu is the woman to lead Space Fleet at this critical time. The institute also identifies . . ."

By the time Horung wrapped up the segment, Michael was relieved to see that the Tesdorf Institute had no inkling that the dreadnoughts were such a breakthrough: game-changing ships intended to shift the strategic balance away from the Hammer of Kraa back to the Federated Worlds. Pekefier had spouted a great deal of verbiage about the implications of reducing crew size, the risks created by Fleet operating unmanned cruisers, the Dakota System Treaty, and so on, but that was all. Most of what the institute said was ax grinding by somebody unwilling to accept that conventional starships with large crews might no longer be the future of space warfare, a well-placed and senior Fleet officer most likely. Clearly, Pekefier knew nothing substantive about dreadnoughts, nor had she worked out the threat they posed to the Hammers. As far as she was concerned, dreadnoughts were just heavy cruisers with no crew. So much for your much-prized insights, Admiral, Michael thought as he listened to her rambling on.

And yet, buried in all that talk was the real issue, a truth that Horung and Pekefier had missed.

Michael understood the concerns of the Tesdorf Institute's anonymous source: Dreadnoughts were a problem . . . for some. They required much smaller crews; that meant a smaller Space Fleet. They threatened too many vested interests. They jeopardized too many entrenched positions. They imperiled the aspirations of too many ambitious officers, of whom Fleet had no shortage. So why would anybody be surprised by the response they evoked? Of course so many reacted viscerally. Dreadnoughts tore away the assumptions that underpinned the careers thousands of officers had spent decades constructing. For them, and with morale already at an all-time low after Fleet's disastrous defeat at Comdur, dreadnoughts became part of the problem, not the solution.

But since when had the concerns of Fleet's aspirants, ambitious and petty, self-centered and self-serving, ever been important? Surely only one thing mattered: defeating the Hammer of Kraa?

The dreadnoughts had to work. And when they did, they would be the only ships in the Fed order of battle capable of surviving an attack by Hammer missiles carrying antimatter warheads. If dreadnoughts worked, they would buy the Feds precious time, time to reverse engineer the antimatter weapons he and *Adamant* had captured from the Hammer ships *McMullins* and *Providence Sound*. With antimatter weapons the Feds could take the fight back to the Hammers, beat them on the field of battle, and bring down the most brutal, most repressive government in human history.

That was the dreadnoughts' destiny.

His was to be the captain in command of *Tufayl,* the first dreadnought to enter service; the dreadnought's destiny was his, too.

"Ah, Lieutenant. Please take a seat."

Michael Helfort sat down, even if sitting in front of one of Fleet's most senior psychiatrists was the last place he wanted to be.

Surgeon Captain Indra peered at him, much the way a researcher scrutinized a laboratory rat. "Right, Lieutenant," she said. "Let me tell you why I've asked you to see me, and we'll take it from there. Okay?"

"Yes, sir."

"Good. To be blunt, you're here because my staff thinks you are not as well as you pretend to be, and I have to say I agree with them."

Michael nodded. Burying the ghosts of the past was easy; keeping them buried was not.

If he read her right, Indra was about to rip away the screen he had built with such care to conceal the fear and self-loathing that festered inside his brain. If she ruled him unfit for active service, the one thing that drove him on—the promise, driven by a cold-burning resolve, to make the Hammers pay for all the death and destruction they had inflicted—would vanish.

What would he do with his life then?

"Let me see," Indra continued. "We graded you P-4 immediately after your escape from Commitment. No surprises there after what you'd been through. Now, . . . yes, we upgraded you to P-1 once you finished postcombat stress deprogramming."

Michael nodded. "That's right, sir. P-1, fit for active service. I have since been posted to *Tufayl* as captain in command." Michael tried to keep any pleading out of his voice. He needed, he wanted, the *Tufayl* . . . badly.

"Ah, yes. *Tufayl*. First of the dreadnoughts, I think?" Indra said.

"Yes, sir. She is."

"Interesting idea," Indra said. She looked at Michael directly. "Let's get to the point. You've not been straight with us, have you?"

Miserably, Michael shook his head. "Guess not, sir," he said, tired of the lies all of a sudden. "The same nightmare. Every night. It's bad."

"Ah, yes," Indra said. "We were pretty sure there was something there. Problem was, you were good at covering it up. Too good."

"So how did you . . . you know, how di—"

"Did we work it out?"

"Yes."

"Don't take this the wrong way, Lieutenant, but we've been watching you for a while. Admiral Jaruzelska was concerned; she asked us to have a good look at you. And when we did, it became clear to us after a while that whatever you are, you're not P-1 . . . Show me your hands!" she snapped.

Startled, Michael did. Indra nodded. "It's that obvious, Lieutenant. Once you know where to look," she said, her voice soft, "it really is."

Numbed by despair, Michael stared at his hands. They trembled, and no matter how hard he tried, they refused to stop. "Does this mean I'll lose the *Tufayl*?"

"Not necessarily," Indra replied with an emphatic shake of her head. "I know how badly Fleet needs you and the dreadnoughts. Admiral Jaruzelska was quite forceful in that regard, I have to say," she added wryly, "so I'll give you two options. You can be honest with us and work with us to get your postcombat stress under control. I can't say it will ever disappear, and since neurowiping is not an option, I can't make you forget what you've been through. But we can help you manage it. If you won't cooperate, you can keep doing what you have been doing—covering the problem up—in which case we can't really help you much, I'm afraid. One thing I can tell you for certain, though. If you won't work with us, you'll be downgraded to, let me see . . . yes, at best, P-2, more likely P-3. In fact, never mind 'will.' As of now, that's what you have been graded."

"P-3?"

"Yes, P-3, unfit for combat duties. You are not stable enough to take the stress of combat. You'd be risking the lives of your fellow spacers. But it does not have to be that way."

"So there's a chance I can be P-1 again?"

"Yes, most certainly . . . if you're honest with us. I cannot guarantee it, of course, because in the end it's up to you, but your exposure to stress after the loss of *Ishaq,* although extreme, was relatively short. You're young, you're strong, and you're fit. So yes, you can be P-1 again. But if you're not open with us, postcombat stress will continue to be a problem for you, and much as you might want to be the captain in command of *Tufayl,* it'll never happen. We've analyzed the simulator exercises you've been doing for the admiral, and postcombat stress is affecting your performance. Transient episodes of indecision, loss of concentration, a lack of mental resilience, and more. Do I need to go on?"

Michael shook his head. "No, sir, you don't. It has to be the first option. And I'm sorry. I didn't mean to play games. I was sure I'd get over it. I really was."

The concern on Indra's face was obvious. "I know you were, Lieutenant, so there's no need to apologize. Everyone thinks they'll get over it. We see it all the time. Now," she said, her tone brisk and businesslike, "we have a job to do. Your boss says the world won't end if we keep you for the day. So unless there's somewhere else you'd rather be?"—Michael shook his head—"No? Good. Let's get started. What we will do first is . . ."

*   *   *

After a long day with Indra's people, Michael walked slowly back to his quarters. His mind felt strangely empty, hollowed out, scoured by the postcombat stress team as they probed back to a time before the Hammers.

Not that Michael had forgotten anything. He remembered everything he had been through as if it had only just happened: *DLS-387* fleeing for its life after the Battle of Hell's Moons, *Ishaq*'s loss in a Hammer ambush, the dead, empty eyes of Doctrinal Security's Colonel Hartspring as he ordered yet another savage beating, the escape from the Hammer prisoner-of-war camp, the look of terror on Detective Sergeant Kalkov's face when he slipped the knife up into the man's heart, the DocSec trooper whose throat he had cut so effortlessly, the death of Corporal Yazdi, *Eridani*'s short but brutal war, the catastrophic defeat of the Fed Fleet at Comdur. It was all so fresh, just thinking about what he had been through threw his heart into overdrive.

Today was just the start. Indra wanted him back to do it again and again. When all the emotional baggage he had picked along the way up had been identified, labeled, sorted, and analyzed, Indra's team could start the painstaking business of training him to control all he had been through. He had no illusions. It was not going to be easy; worse, the nightmares would still be there—Indra said they came from a place so deep in his brain that they would never leave him—but at least she held out the promise that much of the soul-destroying load he had been carrying all these months would be lifted.

It had to work. He needed to be fit enough to return to active duty. He had a job to do. He had promised to make the Hammers pay for all the pain they had inflicted, and taking *Tufayl* and the rest of the dreadnought force into battle was the first step in keeping those promises.

"Captain, sir, officer in command."

Lieutenant Commander Kaya, *Penhaligon*'s captain, snapped awake. "Yes?"

"Flash pinchcomm signal from Fleet, sir. Your eyes only."

"On my way."

"Kraa damn it," Kaya mumbled as he climbed out of his bunk, what now? Fleet had been on his back from the word go, the entire patrol an endless sequence of "hurry up and do this" orders sending *Penhaligon* chasing one shadow after another. But a flash precedence signal—usually reserved for enemy contact reports and other urgent traffic—well, that was a first. After a brief struggle with a reluctant shipsuit and pair of uncooperative boots, he made his way to *Penhaligon*'s combat information center.

Kaya's irritation soon vanished. He read the signal one more time just be to be sure he understood it. He half smiled. He did, and it was just what the crew of the *Penhaligon* needed: a short, sharp operation. He glanced around the combat information center. The on-watch crew avoided his eyes with studious care. Kaya's smile broadened; he was pleased to see the hungry anticipation on their faces. Bored they might be, but by Kraa, they wanted action just as much as he did.

Kaya picked up the old-fashioned hand mike, flicking a switch to patch it into the ship's main broadcast. "Lieutenant Yasuhiko to the combat information center," he said, his voice booming through every compartment on the ship. "Ops planning team to the wardroom. I say again, ops planning team to the wardroom."

The commander of *Penhaligon*'s marine detachment arrived promptly. Kaya watched Lieutenant Yasuhiko stride into the combat information center. The marine was a lean, dark-faced man dressed in an immaculate dark-green ship-suit and well-used combat boots polished to a soft shine. Kaya liked and respected Yasuhiko; he trusted the man to get things done and done right the first time.

Yasuhiko weaved his way through the combat information center's maze of workstations. He snapped to attention in front of his captain. "Sir?"

"Have a look at this," Kaya said as he authorized Yasuhiko's access to the pinchcomm signal. Yasuhiko flicked his microvid screen down to read the message; he did not take long.

"Seems straightforward enough, sir," Yasuhiko said, pushing his microvid back up. "Kraa knows, we've practiced deepspace boarding operations often enough. The target, this VIP, Professor Saadak. Someone that important will be in the ship's knowledge base, as will the *Galaxy Queen*. I'll download the files and get my boys started. We don't have a huge amount of time. But a body snatch from a Fed mership should not be too difficult. Unless . . ." He shrugged his shoulders.

"Unless Fleet intell—" Kaya stopped himself in time. Ambitious captains never criticized Fleet. Anyway, he did not need to say any more. There wasn't a Hammer spacer or marine who had not been screwed around by poor intelligence at some time or other.

Yasuhiko worked it out, anyway. He grinned, his mouth a predatory slash of hungry anticipation. "Maybe this is the one they get right, sir."

Kaya smiled back. "I hope so. Go to it. I'll see you in the wardroom after you've briefed your team." Yasuhiko's lust for action showed, and Kaya was happy to see it.

"Sir!"

Yasuhiko turned and left. Kaya climbed out of his seat to follow him, suppressing an urge to laugh out loud at the look on the officer in command's face. The young lieu-tenant in charge of *Penhaligon*'s on-watch crew struggled not to ask him what the signal actually said. Kraa! The man was hopping from one foot to the other, a pained grimace betraying his frustration. Kaya patted him on the shoulder when he walked past.

"Patience, my son, patience," he whispered. "All good things . . ."

"Captain, sir. Comsat jammer on station, on standby, all systems confirmed nominal."

"Roger." Kaya nodded his satisfaction. *Penhaligon*'s patrol might have been a long and fruitless one so far, but that had not diminished the professionalism of his crew. Which was all very well, but if the spooks had gotten it wrong—an all too common event, he would have to say—all that professionalism would be a complete waste of time and energy. He settled down into his seat to await his target's arrival.

The wait was a short one.

"Command, sensors. We have a positive gravitronics intercept. Estimated drop bearing Red 30 Up 10. One vessel. Gravity wave pattern suggests pinchspace transition imminent. Designated hostile track 456001."

"Command, roger." He turned to his operations officer. "Activate comsat jammer."

"Ops, roger, activating. Stand by . . . jammer nominal. All mership distress, calling, and data frequencies are jammed."

"Command, roger."

"Command, operations. Drop datum passed to assault landers. Stand by . . . landers on vector to intercept."

"Roger."

Surreptitiously crossing his fingers, Kaya forced himself to relax. The comsat jammers were new and worryingly unreliable, like all new equipment. Worse, they were in short supply; *Penhaligon* carried only the one. He would have been much happier with three or four out there to guarantee that a barrage of electronic noise would overwhelm his hapless target's bleatings for help. Provided that his only jammer worked, nothing the *Galaxy Queen* transmitted would make it through to the satellites that sent ship arrival and departure data back to the FedWorld Traffic Coordination Center back on Terranova. So his fingers were crossed for good reason: If the jammer failed even for a few seconds, the game would be over—even the dumbest mership captain could identify a Hammer warship—and the damned Feds would know what *Penhaligon* had been up to; considering there was an armistice in force . . .

"Command, sensors. Estimate drop datum at Red 30 Up 12, range 15,000 kilometers."

The encounter geometry might have been better, but not by much, Kaya realized exultantly. Clearly, the mership captain did not trust his own navigation: *Galaxy Queen* was about to drop into normalspace a long way short of Setianto Reef. That would give the assault landers plenty of time to intercept the mership before she crossed the reef's gravity rip and jumped back into the safety of pinch-space.

"Command, sensors. Track 456001 dropping. Datum confirmed Red 30 Up 12, range 13,000 kilometers. Vector consistent with the flight plan filed by *Galaxy Queen*."

"Command, roger."

A transient flare of ultraviolet announced the target's arrival; Kaya sat back to watch the operation unfold. Truth was, he did not have a lot to do. Success—or failure—now lay in the hands of Lieutenant Yasuhiko and his marines.

"Command, sensors. Hostile track 456001 has dropped on datum. Stand by identification . . . sir, ship is positively confirmed as FedWorlds registered mership *Galaxy Queen*."

"Confidence?"

"One hundred percent, sir. Optical beacon is squawking correct ship ID, confirmed by hull registration, dentology, and radio frequency intercepts. Target is *Galaxy Queen*."

"Roger that," Kaya said. It would not do for Yasuhiko and his marines to tear the wrong ship apart in their hunt for the hapless Professor Saadak. Embarrassing for Fleet but terminal for his career.

"Command, sensors. Target vector confirmed nominal for transit of Setianto Reef en route to Surajaya system."

"Command, roger. All stations, target confirmed. Immediate execute Golf One. I say again, immediate execute Golf One. Assault Leader acknowledge."

Yasuhiko's response was instantaneous, his voice a model of calm, controlled confidence. "Assault Leader acknowledge. Executing Golf One. Closing *Galaxy Queen*."

Lieutenant Yasuhiko hung twenty meters off the *Galaxy Queen*, the mership's hull flaring a brilliant white under the assault lander's high-intensity arc lights. Despite the best efforts of his suit's environmental control unit, he sweated heavily inside his bulky ceramic armor while he waited for the clock to run down. He always did before combat. In front of him, the marines of Team One under the command of Sergeant Kambon hung clustered around the main passenger air lock, black shapes crisp against the ship's hull.

With five seconds to go, Yasuhiko took a deep breath and gave the order. "All teams, Assault Leader. Stand by on three . . . go, go, go!"

Utterly focused, Yasuhiko scrolled through the holocam feeds from his assault team commanders' helmets as his marines exploded into carefully choreographed action. He nodded, satisfied the operation had gotten off to a good start. He turned his attention back to the team he would follow into *Galaxy Queen*.

Sergeant Kambon had things well in hand. He fired the high-energy photonic cutting charges fastset to the hull. A brilliant white flash punched a large hole around the air lock, and the hatch in its titanium frame tumbled into space, driven out by the pressure of air inside the ship. A plasfiber igloo air lock was fastset around the gaping hole in *Galaxy Queen*'s hull. Yasuhiko followed the assault team in; he sealed the igloo's hatch onto its plasteel ring behind him and pulled a large red handle, the scream of high-pressure air dumped to repressurize the air lock lobby audible even through his armored helmet.

Sergeant Kambon waved two marines—the smallest members of the team for obvious reasons—into the gaping hole in *Galaxy Queen*'s hull to place the next set of photonic charges.

No sooner had they gone in then the two marines were

back. Behind them, the inner air lock hatch blew out with another flash, the igloo creaking when the back blast hit. Air from the overpressured air lock blew the door out into the access lobby, its titanium frame skidding along the deck.

A hail of indiscriminate low-velocity fire greeted the door's arrival, rounds ricocheting off the air lock walls and out into space, passing through the plasfiber igloo with a soft popping *pfffft* before self-sealant stopped up the holes. One lucky shot punched a marine right in the center of his ceramfiber chest armor, the impact of the round leaving him winded but otherwise unhurt.

"Damn," Yasuhiko grumbled to himself. Ever the optimist, he hoped that they would get in unopposed. Hard vacuum and bullets—even low-velocity ones—were a combination he did not enjoy.

Sergeant Kambon was wasting no time. "Flashbangs," he said before the shattered air lock door even came to rest. Together, the marines pitched small gray cylinders into the ship, where they bounced and skittered off bulkheads and decks before exploding with an eye-watering flash and a splintering crack that hurt even inside an armored assault suit.

When the flashbangs went off, the marines followed up with smoke and knockdown gas grenades, the entire access lobby turning into a murky scene from hell as the assault team erupted from the air lock, a tidal wave of black armor charging unstoppable through the smog. With the *Galaxy Queen*'s defenders lying semicomatose on the deck, it was all over in seconds. When the air cleared, Yasuhiko examined the neat row of plasticuffed bodies laid out on the lobby floor with some satisfaction, the corridors leading off the air lock lobby secured by black-suited marines while behind him a hand-operated inner air lock was fastset into place.

Sergeant Kambon's report was a formality. "Assault Leader, Team One. Air lock Papa-1 and access lobby secure." Kambon sounded a touch smug. Fair enough, Yasuhiko thought. Kambon's team had been first into the ship and by a good ten seconds; already backup teams cycled through the makeshift air lock to take up their positions for the final assault, black combat space suits dumped in favor of lightweight assault armor, the discarded suits looking uncomfortably like dead bodies strewn with careless abandon across the field of battle.

One by one, the rest of the assault teams reported in, and Yasuhiko gave the word.

Hammer marines erupted in ten different directions at once. To a casual observer, their movements would appear random; in fact, Yasuhiko coordinated the attack with great care to keep the *Galaxy Queen*'s crew off balance, pinned down, and, if unreasonably stubborn, attacked from behind, above, or below, but never head on unless there was no other way.

Not that it was easy. Taking a mership in deepspace never was, and even an inexperienced commercial spacer could inflict serious damage on an assault-suited marine if he kept his head and aimed for the weak spots in the marine's body armor. The only real problem faced by Yasuhiko's marines was the personal security detail assigned to protect the VIP. Not that he had any real concerns; a handful of well-trained but lightly armed men—but these were Feds, so Professor Saadak's security detail would include women, too, no matter how dumb it was trusting women in such an important job—might be professionals, but they only could delay the inevitable.

Galaxy Queen had been designed to work the minor trade routes, of which humanspace had thousands connecting lesser planets and orbital habitats to the major systems. She carried no more than two hundred passengers—this trip, fewer than fifty—so her living spaces were compact and easily contained. In the end, the ship was too small, the Hammers too numerous, and Yasuhiko's control of the operation too good for the outcome to be in any doubt. Despite the desperate efforts of the *Galaxy Queen*'s crew and the target's security detail, the operation was over and Yasuhiko's marines had their VIP in custody barely twenty minutes after the first air lock door blew out of the hull. Success came at a cost, though—the marine assault teams had suffered two dead and eight wounded—but in the wider scheme of things, that was acceptable. Things were much worse for the Feds. Their futile attempts to keep Yasuhiko's marines at bay had cost the lives of Saadak's security detail—every last one of them—along with five of *Galaxy Queen*'s crew. So be it; Yasuhiko did not care. They were only Feds, after all.

While the assault teams rigged demolition charges, Yasuhiko stood back to watch his men struggle with the plasticuffed VIP his marines had come to abduct. Professor Saadak, a tall, stylishly dressed woman with the foulest mouth Kaya had ever come across—that was saying something; he had been a Hammer marine for more than ten years—protested every step of the way as she was dragged to the air lock, the air ripe with abuse and threats of revenge, her objections silenced only when she was manhandled forcibly into a body bag for transfer back to the *Penhaligon*.

Lieutenant Commander Kaya watched dispassionately as demolition charges ripped the *Galaxy Queen* apart, the explosive release of energy when her main fusion plant lost containment vaporizing the mership's massive bulk. A microsecond later the mership had disappeared, a cloud of ionized gas all that remained to mark the *Galaxy Queen*'s passing, fast breaking up into writhing skeins of white-hot matter twisting uselessly away into space. By the time the next mership dropped into normalspace to transit Setianto Reef, the gas would have expanded and cooled beyond detection, all evidence the *Galaxy Queen* had ever been anywhere near Setianto Reef vanished.

Kaya grunted. Things had gone well. *Penhaligon* would jump; once well clear of Setianto Reef, she would drop back into normalspace. The *Galaxy Queen*'s passengers and crew would have their neuronics sterilized and short-term memories neurowiped before they were loaded into the mership's hijacked lifepods and dumped to await rescue, leaving not one clue that the Hammers were responsible for the outrage.

All but one passenger: the unfortunate Professor Saadak, the woman all this effort had been about. Hammer intelligence would enjoy debriefing her. It wasn't often they laid their hands on a deputy secretary from the Federated Worlds' defense ministry. And not just any old deputy secretary, either. No, the professor was the ministry's deputy secretary for finance, no less. Kaya understood why the intelligence boys wanted to get their hands on her: What she did not know about where Fed defense spending went would not be worth knowing. She would be a gold mine.

A broad smile split Kaya's face. It was almost too good to be true. By Kraa, the Feds would shit themselves when they found out. But not half so much as the morons who had decided it was fine for someone as important as Saadak to travel on a Fed mership without a warship escort, her security assured by a small personal protection squad carrying nothing heavier than low-velocity machine pistols. What in Kraa's name were the stupid Fed bastards thinking?

Kaya stifled an urge to spit on *Penhaligon*'s immaculate deck. Bloody Feds! "Arrogant" did not even begin to describe them. Even though the Hammers had handed them their asses at the Battle of Comdur, they still acted like they owned humanspace. Well, they didn't, not anymore. Chief Councillor Polk only had to give the order, and the Hammer fleet—the only fleet in humanspace with antimatter weapons—would destroy every last one of them, and their home planets while they were at it.

With the armistice keeping the Feds and Hammers apart looking more and more fragile, Kaya was confident that it was only a matter of time before Polk gave the order for the Hammer fleet to resume offensive operations. For him, that order could not come soon enough.

Confident that he had done his bit to make it happen, Kaya ordered *Penhaligon* to turn and run for home.

Unseen, Dreadnought Squadron One—ten ships arrayed in an extended line abreast across hundreds of thousands of kilometers of space—coasted in toward Commitment, the distant home planet of the Hammer of Kraa Worlds. All around the ships, countless millions of stars hung in great cascading sheets, diamond-sharp pinpricks of light strewn in careless profusion across the black of deepspace. For a moment, Michael Helfort forgot himself, overwhelmed by the sight, its glorious extravagance in stark contrast to the wretched self-serving schemes that preoccupied most of humankind most of the time. Michael stretched to ease stress-tightened muscles, wondering just what the hell the point of it all was. The cosmos did not care whether the Federated Worlds or the Hammer of Kraa came out on top, that much was for sure.

"Command, Warfare." The steady voice of the artificial intelligence responsible for battle management dragged Michael's attention back to the job at hand.

"Command," he replied.

"Threat plot is confirmed. Hammer task group designated Hammer-1 has four heavy cruisers, six light cruisers, plus escorts and multiple auxiliaries. The Hammer task group's orbit is nominal for Commitment nearspace defense. Mission prime directives met. We are go for the operation."

"Command, roger. Wait."

Michael stared at the threat plot. Warfare might be happy with the tactical situation, but he was not. The problem was the Hammer task group his ships had been sent to attack. For a force tasked with nearspace defense, it had too many auxiliary ships. With plenty of support and maintenance platforms in Clarke orbit to support the Hammer warships protecting Commitment planet, auxiliaries would be an unnecessary complication, something no half-competent commander would want in a task group intended to stop a Fed attack in its tracks, yet there they were. Why?

The Hammers were up to something: There had to be a reason why the commander of the Hammer task group had been saddled with a bunch of thin-skinned and poorly armed auxiliaries. What that reason might be, Michael had no idea, and neither did Warfare. Without any better ideas and with nobody else to talk to, he would take all the time he had in the hope of finding out. If the threat plot looked the same when it came time to launch the attack, so be it. He would have done his best, and all the admirals in the Federated Worlds Space Fleet could not ask for more than that.

"Warfare, command," Michael said. "We'll maintain formation until 22:00 and then jump as planned."

"Warfare, roger."

Michael sat back, frustrated. The dreadnought concept was all very well in theory, even if it had been forced on a reluctant Fleet by the appalling loss of spacers at the Battle of Comdur. But the simple fact remained that artificial intelligence worked only up to a point. When it came down to it, AIs were no substitute for the human brain, of which the ten heavy cruisers of Dreadnought Squadron One had only his to call on. Not enough, he was sure; he had a horrible feeling that his brain could not get the job done on its own. Not for the first time he wished he had a combat information center crewed by real live spacers to talk to before making the hard decisions. But it was not to be—too many good spacers had died at Comdur to allow Fleet the luxury of deploying fully crewed warships—and he might as well get used to that fact.

Eyes half closed, Michael began the slow and tedious process of reviewing the raw sensor data spilling through his neuronics. His only hope—the faintest of faint hopes—was that he would get lucky and uncover whatever it was the Hammers were up to.

*   *   *

"Stand by to drop."

Michael started, his attention dragged away from a nearly obsessive review of the threat plot. It was a good thirty minutes out of date, the time the dreadnoughts needed to jump clear of Commitment and reverse vector to make a single, slashing run back through Hammer nearspace before heading for home and safety, having, he hoped, consigned the Hammer task group to Kraa, that damned god of theirs. He offered up a silent prayer that—please, just this once—things would go his way.

The week had consisted of an endless stream of tactical simulations, and a bad week for him it had been. Sadly, if his instincts were right, things would not improve. Each and every tactical simulation exercise was marred by mistake after mistake, all his. It was humiliating. Despite his best efforts, controlling the *Tufayl* and the nine other heavy cruisers of Dreadnought Squadron One had been like trying to juggle soap bubbles: at best impossible, at worst a complete disaster, a point of view expressed that very morning with some vigor by Vice Admiral Jaruzelska, director of the dreadnought project and his boss.

He breathed in slowly to steady himself. Going into combat a raggedy-assed bundle of nerves would not improve his already slim chances of turning the squadron into an effective fighting force. Jaruzelska had made it clear: Failure was not an option. The Hammer of Kraa would tear the Federated Worlds apart if the Feds did not come up with an effective counter to their dammed antimatter missiles. Dreadnoughts were the only answer at hand, the only ships tough enough to have any chance of surviving an antimatter missile attack. There was no choice; they had to work.

"Command, roger," he acknowledged, mouth dry with tension, stomach tightening into a twisted ball of acid. "Warfare. Confirm weapons free. You have command authority."

"Warfare, roger. Weapons free. I have command authority."

Michael settled into his shock-resistant seat. He commed the AI to tighten his safety straps and waited for the *Tufayl* and her sister ships to drop out of pinchspace, one last check confirming that the ten dreadnoughts under his command were fully operational.

"Command, Warfare, stand by, dropping . . . now."

In an instant, space-time turned itself inside out, the ten dreadnoughts erupting into normalspace, intense flashes of ultraviolet radiation marking their transition from pinchspace.

Michael held his breath as alarms told him his laboriously assembled threat plot was worthless. By the time they jumped and reversed vector into Hammer space for the attack, the Hammer task group he had been sent to destroy had split into two and opened out. A single glance told him that much, but what did it mean? Which of the two groups presented the real threat? Desperately, Michael scanned the torrent of data pouring in from the dreadnoughts' sensors even though he knew full well he could never make sense of it before *Tufayl*'s AIs did.

The warfare AI entertained no doubts which of the two groups of Hammer ships posed the greater threat. "Command, Warfare. Primary threat axis is Red 10 Up 3, Hammer auxiliaries and escorts designated Hammer-2. Stand by . . . missile salvos away."

While *Tufayl*'s hydraulic launchers dumped a full missile salvo outboard, Michael ignored the rest of the AI's report, acting on adrenaline-fueled instinct alone. The AI had to wait; maneuvering the dreadnoughts into position to survive the inevitable Hammer counterattack could not. He had to act. Everything told him that Warfare had made a terrible mistake. Struggling to bring order out of chaos, the warfare AI had ordered the dreadnought squadron to turn toward what it believed to be the primary threat: Hammer-2, the Hammer ships directly up-sun. Michael scowled with frustration, certain he had spotted the AI's mistake. The sunward ships consisted of the auxiliaries along with a handful of light escorts, screened by decoys pumping out enough electromagnetic radiation to fool the unwary into thinking they were heavy cruisers. Was Warfare dumb enough to fall for it?

Yes, it was.

Michael swore out loud. Auxiliaries did not have the fire-power to kill a dreadnought. The real threat was the cruisers in the second group of Hammer capital ships—task group Hammer-1—now sitting 40 degrees off *Tufayl*'s port bow; already they had launched their Eaglehawk long-range anti-ship missiles toward the dreadnoughts. The bastards were close; it would not be long before they flung rail-gun salvos at his ships. If he did not get them before they turned to meet the attack . . .

He hesitated for a second. Should he split his forces? Should he attack both Hammer task groups? No, he decided. Go for the primary threat, deal with the rest later.

"Command override. All ships, come left, emergency turn to threat axis Red 40 Up 3. Close and engage task group Hammer-1," Michael said, his voice half choked by stress. Warfare's order to ignore the Hammer cruisers was plain wrong: They orbited closer; they carried missiles, rail guns, and long-range antiship lasers. Of course they posed the pri-mary threat!

"Command, Warfare. Roger," the AI replied calmly. "Re-designating targets . . . stand by rail guns."

Michael forced himself to sit back in his seat. There was nothing more he—or any other human—could do now. Close-quarters battle management was the one thing AIs ex-celled at. Making tactical decisions based on the avalanche of data generated by ship sensors tracking thousands of in-coming missiles and rail-gun slugs and at the same time controlling the outgoing counterattack was simply too much for any human. To sit still was an effort, yet Michael forced himself to do exactly that, to watch the squadron's defensive weapon systems soak up the Hammer attack, missile after missile erupting in brilliant balls of white flame as medium-range missiles and lasers hacked them out of space. But some made it through, triggering the dreadnoughts' close-in defenses: a triple layer of lasers, short-range missiles, and chain guns working desperately to keep the Hammer missile attack out, the problem greatly compounded when a rail-gun salvo blasted its way through to smash into his ships, timed to arrive a few seconds before the surviving missiles hit home.

Michael braced himself; the *Tufayl* bucked and heaved under the impact of multiple missile and rail-gun slug strikes. "You'll have to try harder than that, you sons of bitches," he murmured while the *Tufayl*'s reinforced frontal and flank armor shrugged off the attack with contemptuous ease. "Now it's our turn."

He watched intently as the dreadnoughts finally turned their bows onto the threat axis. The instant they did, all ten ships let go with everything they had, the *Tufayl* reverberating with the characteristic crunching metal-on-metal thud of the rail guns punching slugs and decoys—hundreds of thousands of them—toward the Hammer cruisers at more than 3 million kilometers per hour, the shape of the swarm designed to force the Hammer ships to move where the slug density was greatest, where the ship-kill probabilities were highest.

"Command, Warfare. Missile launch from auxiliaries of task group Hammer-2. Stand by . . . missiles are Eaglehawks."

"What?" Michael suppressed a momentary flash of unease. Eaglehawks? That made no sense. "Command, confirm." The auxiliaries of task group Hammer-2 had just done something they were not—supposedly—capable of: launching Eaglehawk missiles. According to every technical intelligence report he had ever read, Hammer auxiliaries did not carry the Hammer's heavyweight antistarship missiles. In theory, they posed no real threat. So how were they able to launch Eaglehawks?

"Confirmed, command. Task group Hammer-2 has launched Eaglehawk missiles. Stand by . . . Hammer-1 is jumping."

Michael watched in despair as brief flares of ultraviolet light signaled the cruisers of task group Hammer-1's jump into pinchspace, his missile and rail-gun salvos arriving too late to do anything but rip uselessly through the knuckles of tangled space-time left by the ships' departure. This does not look good, he said to himself. Hammer capital ships did not make a habit of abandoning their posts in the middle of an attack, but that was what they were doing. Why? He had been so sure that they posed the main threat to his ships, that they would stay to slug it out.

Something cold and clammy slimed its way into Michael's chest and squeezed his heart hard. Without understanding why, he knew something bad was about to happen. Now his only option was to jump his own ships to safety, and he would be dammed if he was going to run away. He had come here to fight, and while he faced Hammer ships, fight he would.

"Command, Warfare. Missile salvo from Hammer-2 assessed to be low-density attack consisting of multiple Eaglehawk ASSMs plus decoys. Vectors and salvo geometry are nominal for antimatter attack. Insufficient time to complete turn onto threat axis. Probability of mission-abort damage is high and rising. Recommend emergency jump into pinchspace. Repeat, recommend emergency jump into pinchspace."

Michael did not give himself time to think. "Negative, negative," he shouted. "Expedite turn to threat axis and engage."

"Warfare, roger. Expediting," Warfare replied calmly. "Hammer missiles are inside our mission abort damage radius . . . missile detonation imminent."

"Goddamn it," Michael whispered. He slumped back, the sweat-soaked shipsuit under his armored combat space suit suddenly ice-cold. With shocking clarity, it became all too obvious. Apprehension washed through him, and his stomach acid-churned, sour and unsettled. He had walked right into the trap set for him and his ships. Pride and stupidity had stranded him there, and now it was too late; he had to wait and pray that his ships would ride out the Hammer attack.

Inside the Hammer missiles, traps holding the warheads' antihydrogen payload collapsed. Antimatter annihilated matter, releasing a tsunami of gamma radiation into space.

Tufayl and her sister ships did not stand a chance. For all their reinforced armor, the dreadnoughts were too close to withstand the prodigious wave of energy released by the missiles. Impulse shock waves bludgeoned the ships with lethal force, battering critical systems to the point of failure and beyond. Seconds after the attack, the enormous fusion plants powering the dreadnoughts' main propulsion power plants lost containment, transformed into blue-white flashes of raw energy that consumed the ships from end to end, leaving nothing but a few shattered fragments of ceram-steel armor and writhing tendrils of ionized matter to mark the passing of ten once-powerful ships.

There was complete quiet, the command holovid flash-ing "SHIP DESTROYED" in letters that flooded the combat in-formation center with bloodred light. Then the holovid displays that curtained the combat information center went blank and the lights came on.

Michael stared, stunned, unable to move. The weight of yet another failure was close to unbearable.

"All stations," a disembodied voice announced. "This is control. End of exercise. Hot wash-up in Conference Room 4 in thirty minutes. Control out."

"Shit, shit, shit. What a bloody disaster," Michael mut-tered. The day had been bad enough without having to sit through the humiliation of a debrief chaired by Vice Admi-ral Jaruzelska, the Fleet's most respected, experienced, and successful combat commander.

Why me? he asked himself, throwing off his safety straps. He forced a body stiff with tension and stress to its feet. All he had ever wanted to be was an assault lander pilot, not some damned cruiser captain, a job he had not asked for, a job he was beginning to think he should not have. He smiled for an instant, his mouth twisting into a grim gash devoid of any humor. Well, look on the bright side, he told him-self dispiritedly. After today's performance, there was every chance he would not be *Tufayl*'s captain designate much longer.

Someone else would have to make dreadnoughts work.

*   *   *

"So, to sum up, the critical command error occurred here, at drop plus fifteen seconds, a mistake compounded by the warfare AI's failure to communicate effectively with the command. The Hammer capital ships in task group Hammer-1 were too close to our ships to deploy antimatter missiles. Conventional chemex and tacnuke-armed missiles were their only options. That made them the lesser threat. The auxiliaries and their escorts in Hammer-2, on the other hand, orbited far enough away to launch and survive an antimatter attack, and that is exactly what they did once our ships committed to the attack. After missile launch, command had the option to jump to safety but elected to ride out the attack. That was the wrong decision, and as a result . . ." The analyst's voice trailed off; she appeared somewhat embarrassed.

Michael squirmed in his seat. In the cold light of day, it was all so easy, so damn obvious. Why was he so stupid? His head slumped onto his chest, the shame nearly unbearable.

Vice Admiral Jaruzelska's voice cut through the hush. "Okay, folks. I think that'll do. I want department heads back here, Monday morning, 08:00. We'll review lessons learned from this week and your recommendations for improvement. No top of the head stuff, either. Detailed proposals. I'll also com you a list of specific areas I want checked. Any questions?"

There were none, and the meeting broke up, the mood subdued and—to Michael's mind at least—the atmosphere heavy with the smell of failure.

Jaruzelska called Michael over.

"Sir?"

"My office in ten."

Unable to speak, Michael nodded. For all his could-not-care-less bravado, he did care. He wanted to be the one who transformed dreadnoughts from a bright idea into the weapon that would drive the Hammers into the ground. But maybe he was not the one; maybe Jaruzelska was keeping him back to tell him just that.

*   *   *

Jaruzelska waved Michael into a seat in front of her desk. She stared at him for a long time before speaking.

"Been a bad week, Michael," she said at last.

"You might say that, sir."

"Ridden you pretty hard, haven't we?'

Michael nodded. "Yes, sir, you have," he said, unable to conceal a sudden bitterness.

"Well, I think it's time for me to own up."

"Own up? I don't underst—"

Jaruzelska's hand went up, cutting him off. "You weren't supposed to. You see, Michael, the point of this week was to see just what one of the best tactical brains in Fleet was capable of unaided. And you showed us. Quite understandably, you saw this week's sims as just one failure after another, and it's true. They were. But we saw the week differently. For us, the sims shone the spotlight on the things we need to do to make dreadnoughts work."

Jaruzelska paused; she studied him thoughtfully. "So let me ask you something, Michael," she continued. "There are thousands of lieutenants in Space Fleet. Know how many come even close to you?"

Michael shook his head. What a dumb question. After one of the worst weeks of his life, probably most.

Jaruzelska half smiled. "None that I know of," she said, "none. You are one of the few spacers I've ever met who can hold an entire engagement in his head. All those ships, not to mention missiles, rail-gun swarms, decoys, and all the rest." She shook her head. "We don't know how you do it, Michael, but you do. Problem is, there's no point in watching you do well, there's no point designing tactical exercises we know you can cope with. Success doesn't teach us squat. What does teach us something is failure, watching you make a complete dog's breakfast of things. Thanks to you, we know how to help you become the best damn squadron commander this side of deepspace."

"Shit, sir! You might have told me!" Michael said, his face twisted into a grimace of pained frustration. "Oh, sorry, sir."

In his limited experience, admirals—even the good ones—did not appreciate overly familiar junior officers.

Jaruzelska let it pass. She nodded indulgently. "Don't worry about it, son. Would not have worked if we'd told you. Anyway, I have some good news for you. The first thing is to give you what every cruiser captain has sitting alongside him."

"Operations and threat assessment officers?" Michael replied, looking doubtful. "Far as I know, warfare officers are thin on the ground after Comdur, so where will we find them?"

"We don't." Jaruzelska smiled broadly. "We're bringing two cruiser AIs out of retirement to do the job. What you have been missing, Michael, is not AIs to make decisions; I know you've got plenty of those, and I've never met an AI that's not ready, willing, and able to make decisions . . . never mind whether they're right or wrong. No, what you've needed is the advice and support the two senior warfare officers sitting alongside their captain have always provided. Problem is you can't have people. So instead of real live spacers, you'll have two AIs. Proven ones, ones with a lot of combat experience. They'll never be as good as real people, but they'll be one hell of a lot better than two empty chairs."

Michael considered the idea for a while; he nodded slowly. "Sounds good, Admiral. Hope it works."

"We think it will. In fact, I'm kicking myself we did not pick it earlier. Anyway, we'll find out."

"Can't wait, sir," Michael said with a conspicuous lack of enthusiasm at the idea of spending more time in the simulators.

"Cheer up, my boy. It'll work. Right, moving on," she said, her voice brisk. "I'm giving you a week's leave. I suggest you go see a certain junior lieutenant I know you're fond of. Personnel will have your travel authority. Okay?"

"Yes, sir," Michael said, looking much happier, the prospect of seeing Anna Cheung again bringing a touch of color to his cheeks, even if the chance of the two of them meeting up stayed the same as always: pretty close to nil. "Thanks."

"Ah, yes. One more thing. *Tufayl*. Fleet had scheduled her handover for October 2. But Commander Watanabe tells me that we can take her out of the yard's hands early. So, Lieutenant Helfort, it's dress blacks for you. Commissioning ceremony, 09:00, Thursday 21st. Okay?"

Michael gulped. He had been so sure that Jaruzelska was about to sack him. "Yes, sir. So does that mean I'm still—"

"Still captain in command? Well, let me see," she said, eyes dancing mischievously. "I talked with Surgeon Captain Indra last night."

"You did, sir?" Michael tried not to sound too hopeful.

"I did. You've been making good progress, so she's regraded you P-2. Provided you continue to improve, she intends to grade you P-1, so I don't think there's much doubt that you will be fit for active service."

"Jeez, sir. Thanks. I can't tell you what . . ." Michael ground to a halt, unable to speak.

Jaruzelska shook her head. "You don't have to. Now go. I'll see you Monday week. You know what? I think we might get you straight back into the sims."

Michael smiled ruefully. "You don't say, sir. I'll look forward to that."

"You should," Jaruzelska said with unexpected intensity, "you should. Because I think we're close to making dreadnoughts perform the way we want them to. So enjoy your leave. You'll see some changes by the time you get back. So go. I've work to do."

"Sir," Michael said as he left, already writing the vidmail to Anna to tell her to pull every string she could pull to organize some leave. More in hope than expectation, he fired the vidmail off. He had checked *Damishqui*'s tasking, and things did not look at all promising. The armistice between Feds and Hammers might be holding, but there were always more missions to perform than ships to perform them, so Anna's ship, like every ship in the Fleet, was kept busy.

But maybe the Fates would work for him, just this once.

Utterly content, Michael sat alone on the deck of the Palisades, the family's weekender high in the western foothills of the Tien Shan Mountains. The house provided the perfect place to sit and pretend—for a few precious minutes—that the rest of humanspace with all its cruel stupidities did not exist. Beer in hand, Michael gazed out across the valley of the Clearwater River, the ground far below invisible through a gray murk below the clouds scudding overhead. It was a wet, blustery day. He did not care. The weather might be crap, but it was still perfection. He knew it was all a chimera, but he was grateful for it, though it would have been better if Anna had been there in person. How good would it be to have her—

The insistent chiming of his neuronics smashed his daydreams to dust. "What now?" Michael muttered aloud while he accepted the incoming com.

It was his agent, Mitesh, the face of the artificial intelligence that of an older, wiser Michael. A Michael with wrinkles and a bad haircut, the family always said, teasingly. The AI's computer-generated avatar had the good grace to look apologetic. "I know you said no callers, Michael, but I'm pretty sure you will want to take this pinchcomm."

"Goddamn it, Mitesh, Anna is the only person I want to hear from, so . . ." His voice trailed off. "Ah, yeah, right," he said after a moment.

A smug grin split Mitesh's face. "Precisely, not that you ever told me that. Quite the opposite, in fact. What you actually told me was—"

"Okay, okay, I know what I said." It was Michael's turn to look apologetic. "Sorry about that."

Mitesh smiled. "Don't worry about it. So may I tell Miss Anna that you'll take her call?"

"Miss Anna! Jeez, she'd love that." Michael laughed, shaking his head. "You're a real smart-ass! Makes her sound like some sort of feudal grande dame. Put her on."

"Patching her through."

After a short pause, Anna's face blossomed in Michael's neuronics, her avatar the most faithful of faithful renditions, thanks in large part to an indulgent father's extravagant gift of the best avatar software in all of humanspace. In Michael's view, it was money well spent. Anna seemed real; she might have been standing there right in front of him. She was stunning, her beauty a testament to the Chinese, Asian, African, and European gene pools of Old Earth, not to mention a great deal of expensive geneering spanning many generations.

The breath caught in his throat at the sight of her. Anna's face was a dark honey-gold set under fine black hair that dropped to frame sharply defined cheekbones dusted with pink, a firm nose fractionally too large—geneering was still far from an exact science—above a generous mouth quick to smile. But it was the eyes that always grabbed him: large and set wide, infinitely deep green pools that dragged him in and down.

Anna groaned in mock despair. The ability of her eyes to mesmerize Michael was a long-running private joke. "Michael, for chrissakes, pay attention," she said in no-nonsense tones. "There's been a change of plan."

"Change of plan?" Michael's focus snapped back to the here and now. He sat up. This sounded promising. Had the fates delivered for once?

"Yup, change of plan," Anna said with a smile of pure happiness. "You're in luck, sailor boy. Good old *Damishqui* is cactus. One of our primary fusion plants has dropped offline, and nobody seems to know why. We've been diverted to Suleiman to get the problem fixed. The engineers say we'll be in the yard for at least a week, and after much groveling, my boss has given me leave. So, let me see . . . yes, I'll see you tomorrow morning your time, so make sure you're at

Bachou to pick me up. I can't stand here talking. This call is costing me a fortune, and I've got a flight to catch. I've commed you my itinerary. 'Bye."

Euphoric, Michael stared open-mouthed while Anna's avatar disappeared. Well, he said to himself, sometimes things went his way, an all too rare occurrence for a Fleet officer.

He commed Mitesh.

"Yes, Michael?"

"You followed all that?"

"I did. I'll keep an eye on things and let you know when to leave to pick her up."

"Thanks, Mitesh."

"But while you're on the line"—Mitesh winced at Michael's exaggerated groan—"I've been swamped with requests for interviews."

"Let me guess," Michael said, his voice twisted with resentment, the euphoria blown away in an instant. "All provoked by the latest trashvid documentary?"

"That's exactly why. You watch it?"

"No way, Mitesh," Michael snarled. "That's the fourth doco on the *Ishaq* business, and if this one was anything like its predecessors, why would I?" He stopped to recover his mental balance. "I suppose you did."

"It's in my job description, Michael," Mitesh replied primly, lips stiffening into a thin line.

"So it is. And?"

"Well, let me see. How best to put it? Yes . . . it was sensationalist drivel based loosely on what actually happened, sprinkled with interviews from people who weren't there, seasoned with opinions from so-called experts who could not find their ass with both hands, the whole tawdry brew spiced with exaggeration, innuendo, more than a few outright lies, and—"

"Enough, Mitesh, enough!" Michael said, laughing despite himself, "I get it, I get it. It was garbage."

"Garbage? You can say that, though I'd prefer to call it two hours of brain-numbing pap. There were some good things about it, though."

"Oh, yeah?" Michael shook his head in despair. "Do tell, Mitesh."

"The Hammers received a good kicking, and you came out well. Man of the moment and all that. Nice shot of you in your dress blacks. Mmmm, all those medals, command hash marks, unit citations, wound stripes. I do so love gold on black. The girls will be—"

Michael's laughter stopped Mitesh's increasingly camp account in its tracks. "Stop, Mitesh, stop!"

"Well, you asked," Mitesh protested.

"I did," Michael said with a heartfelt sigh. He hated the scrutiny; for as long as he could remember, he had avoided the spotlight—public speaking scared the crap out of him—yet here he was, getting it in spades. "Jeez, Mitesh. Why the hell won't they just leave me alone?"

"You know why, Michael. The average Fed needs heroes just like everybody else, and you're the poor sap who just happens to be the man of the hour. So live with it. It will pass. Just do your duty and let the trashpress get on and do their thing. They'll get bored eventually and start looking for someone else, someone new."

Michael sighed again. Easy for Mitesh to say but hard for Michael to endure. Exhausted by the relentless attention, he had given up going out in public. Hell! The trashpress even turned that simple decision against him. "The Hermit Hero—What Is He Hiding?" had been one of their headlines, followed by hundreds of words before providing the answer: nothing!

"All right, Mitesh. Enough on those scum. No to the interviews, of course."

Mitesh's face tightened in disapproval. "That's a bad call, Michael. Ignoring the trashpress means letting them tell your story the way they want to. You need to tell your own story. They're beginning to get cranky. You should talk to them before they turn on you."

"No," Michael said, "no, I can't."

"Can't? Not a word I associate with you, Michael," Mitesh said tartly. "But it's your life."

"Yes, it is. Anything else?"

"No. I'm working through the vid, and if there are any errors of fact, I'll lodge a formal complaint with the Mass Communications Tribunal. I'll com you if I do that; otherwise I'll leave you be."

"Thanks, Mitesh," Michael said, grateful for Mitesh's unflagging support. Mitesh might be nothing more than the product of some fancy AI engineering, but he was a true friend.

Sunday, September 10, 2400, UD
Bachou Municipal Airport, Ashakiran

"Golf India 55, this is Bachou Tower. You are cleared for takeoff on runway 25. On departure, you are cleared to follow flight pipe Green 66 Bravo."

"Golf India 55, cleared for takeoff on runway 25, pipe Green 66 Bravo. Roger."

Michael glanced across at Anna. "Ready?"

Anna nodded. "Let's go."

Michael held the flier on the brakes, his seat shuddering while its mass driver came up to full power, steam ripping the air apart behind the compact little machine. Satisfied that all was the way it should be, he released the brakes, the acceleration driving him back into his seat as the flier gathered speed rapidly. He lifted the nose up sharply, Bachou's small airport fast disappearing behind them.

"In a hurry, are we?" Anna asked, looking across at him, batting her eyes.

"You know me. Places to go and all that," Michael said with a smile. He held the flier nose up, climbing steeply under full power, the blue of the sky above deepening when they burst through the surface haze filling the valley of the Clearwater River.

"You don't change, do you?"

"More than you know, Anna," he said, trying to sound flippant and failing.

Concern clouded Anna's face. "You okay?"

"Yeah, think so. It's been pretty rough. Long days. Pressure, pressure, pressure. Jaruzelska's one tough woman. But I'll be fine. And the Fleet postcombat trauma guys have been great. So I'll survive."

"Hope so," Anna said. "Suppose you still can't tell me what these damn dreadnoughts will be used for?"

Michael shook his head. "Sorry, no. I'm not trying to be cute. We haven't been told yet. But soon, I hope."

"It's hard not knowing what the bastards have you lined up for. Whatever it is, it'll be mayhem. You and trouble seem to go together, Michael Helfort."

"Yes, we do," Michael said with a frown, "but don't blame me. Blame the Hammers."

Anna sat quietly for a while. "The Hammers," she said at last. "Does anyone understand those sons of bitches? I sure as hell don't."

"Nor me," Michael replied with a shake of the head. "Something tells me it will not be long before we're at their throats again. If I were them, I'd tear up the armistice. Go back on the offensive. Hit us while we're still trying to rebuild the Fleet after Comdur, shut down all our interstellar trade routes, force us back to the negotiating table."

"Hell. That's a cheery assessment. Can they do that, shut us down, I mean?"

"Don't know for sure, but they should try. What can they lose? If they sit around waiting for something to happen, we'll eventually have a Fleet that can take them on—who knows, maybe with antimatter weapons—and we're back to where we were before Comdur. Lining our ships up, loading the marines, and counting the days down until we can invade Commitment to rip their Hammer hearts out," he said, his voice rising, shaking with vicious intensity.

He paused for a moment to recover his self-control. "Sorry. Got a bit carried away." He threw a quick glance at Anna, her face radiant in the early-morning sun. "I must stop taking it so personally. I really must."

"You have every reason, Michael," Anna said, her voice softened by concern.

He nodded. He had. "So," he said after another long pause, "what about us?"

"What can I say?" Anna said, shrugging her shoulders. "Nothing's changed. You're right about the Hammers. There's no chance they'll sit around scratching their asses while we take our time rebuilding the Fleet. So the armistice is a dead man walking. It can't be long before it falls over. That means *Damishqui* will be in the thick of things, and those dreadnoughts of yours, too. I'm damn sure they won't leave you doing endless sims."

Michael frowned and shook his head. "No, they won't."

"So, like I say. Nothing's changed. I love you, you love me, but until the Hammers are beaten, I cannot commit, and you can't; you shouldn't, either. Michael"—Anna touched his arm, so softly, it was more a caress—"don't push it. I know you want me to commit, but I can't. Not until this is over. Just take it a day at a time, and with a bit of luck we'll both come through. Then we'll do the whole commitment thing, I promise. Marriage, house, day jobs, kids . . ."

Her voice cracking, Anna turned away, but not before Michael saw the tears.

"Enough," she said after a while, head still turned away as she wiped her eyes. "I've just been on the commair flight from hell, so all I want is a shower, a decent cup of coffee, and some breakfast. So let's just leave it at that. Wake me up when we get close to the Palisades."

There was nothing more to say. Soon Anna was asleep. They flew on, the flier's cabin quiet, the only noise the soft hiss of air across plasglass.

For all the progress Michael was making with the post-combat stress deprogramming, Detective Sergeant Kalkov's jeering face still haunted him, the nightmare grinding its way to the same terrifying conclusion. Thanks to Indra's team, the nightmares troubled him less, but they came all the same, and tonight was one of those nights.

Shocked awake, Michael knew better than to lie there thrashing around in a futile attempt to get back to sleep. Quietly, he slipped out of bed. Throwing on coat and shoes, he made his way out of the house, leaving Anna dead to the world, a shapeless lump in the bed, exhausted by a brutally tough day climbing the rock walls behind the Palisades. Outside, the air was cool and crisp; dawn was hours away, the night dark under a moonless sky, clear, still, and star-studded.

Aided by the low-light processor embedded in his neuronics, Michael followed the narrow track, climbing fast but carefully until he reached a solid mass of rock that reared up out of the heavily timbered spine of the ridge, an island of granite in a sea of green. Scrambling up the scree that skirted the outcrop, he sat down where he always did, a small, comfortable heather-filled cleft slashed into the base of the huge rock. It had long been one of his favorite places, a place he used to clear his mind.

He needed to. He had hoped Anna would help him sort things out, but she had not. The exact opposite, in fact. He was more confused than ever by the competing demands that fought for supremacy in a badly conflicted mind: the irreconcilable demands of love, duty, family, and honor.

He loved Anna, and she loved him: He owed it to her to stay alive.

There was a war on: Walk away from his duty as a serving Fleet officer? Unthinkable.

His family had suffered more than any family should, at times his parents wracked to the point of utter despair: He owed it to them not to get himself killed.

That left the demands of honor. He had made promises, and he was old-fashioned enough to think that promises should be kept once made; otherwise, why make them? The problem was that every single one of those promises involved making the Hammers pay for all the pain they had inflicted . . . on him, on the family, on the crews of *DLS-387* and *Ishaq,* on the Fed Fleet at the Battle of Comdur.

Michael was no fool. He knew that keeping those promises did little to increase his life expectancy, but what else was he to do? Walking away from them would make his mom and dad happy, Anna, too, probably. But he could never live with himself if he did. Jeez, what a mess, he said to himself. Soon Anna would be on her way back to *Damishqui,* and he to Comdur, doing what he always did—going with the flow, hoping for the best, and trusting that fate would allow him to deliver on his promises without getting killed in the process.

He pushed back against the rock and stared up at stars strewn in profligate confusion across the sky. He was there a long time, the warmth seeping out of his body, his mind churning without getting anywhere before a combination of cold and tiredness drove him to his feet.

Time to get back, he said to himself.

He scarcely made it off the scree slope before, through the treetops, a tiny, fleeting flicker of black smeared a path across the stars. He stopped, staring up. Whatever it was, it felt wrong—why he was not able to say—so, without thinking, he slid under the cover of a small overhang of rock.

Unable to see much, Michael chided himself for jumping at shadows when, with scarcely a soft hiss to mark its passing, a black shape leaped from the darkness below the ridge and shot overhead before disappearing back into the night. What the hell, he wondered, was an unlit flier doing this far from civilization in the middle of the night?

He had a bad feeling about this; whatever the flier was up to, it was probably nothing good. Had the flier spotted him? If it had done a high-level reconnaissance, it might have picked up his infrared signature. He hoped he had moved before they had.

Every instinct told him not to risk it, to get as far away as possible, to ask questions later. But he could not: Anna was back in the house asleep, and he refused to take the chance that the flier was just out joyriding the night away, even if that was the most rational explanation. Gambling that the flier would take its time before turning back, he started to run through the trees back to the house.

He had gone less than a hundred meters when the slashing hiss of a flier with its noise-reducing shroud deployed brought him skidding to a halt; he turned to see what was happening. The flier had returned, but this time the black shape, nose high in the air to kill its forward momentum, headed for the rock outcrop. Slowing into a hover, it spewed superheated steam into the cold night air, the blast driving pebbles skittering and tumbling into space while it came in to land.

Michael did not wait to see what would happen next; it was not hard to guess. The flier was small; assuming the pilot stayed where he was—he certainly would if he had any sense—the chances were that three, maybe four people would be on his heels before much longer. He ran, his mind desperately trying to work out how he could get himself and Anna safely off a ridge of rock bounded on all sides by cliffs he would think twice about climbing down even in broad daylight. Any way he looked at it, he and Anna were trapped, their escape route cut off by assailants certain to be well armed and invisible under chromaflage capes.

He sprinted down the track and did the obvious thing: commed a desperate call for help to the Bachou police. Find somewhere safe to hide, the cops said; an armed response team was on the way and would be there inside an hour. "We'll all be dead by the time they arrive," Michael said tersely before he cut the com. His next was to the sleeping Anna. To Michael's frustration, she refused to wake up, but finally she responded, sleepy and confused, far too slow to understand the seriousness of the situation. Suddenly she worked it out. Snapping awake, she listened without a word while Michael laid out the only plan he could think of.

Michael broke out of the timber. He ran past his flier sitting silent on the landing pad and across the track that dropped into the valley in a series of horrific hairpin bends cut into sheer walls of rock. No escape that way, not on foot; too exposed, he decided. Pity they did not have a mobibot: He and Anna would have been well on their way to safety. Without stopping, he commed the flier's fusion microplant to go online—shut down for most of the week, it would be a good ten minutes before it was flight-ready—and prayed that they would live long enough to use it. He prayed even harder that overconfidence would persuade the new arrivals not to disable it.

Without stopping, he ran straight into the house.

"Anna! Anna!"

"Here, Michael," Anna said, no more than her head visible in the gloom, the rest of her body unseen below a hunter's chromaflage cape. She shoved a second cape and a thin-bladed ten-centimeter kitchen knife into his hands. "Now, if you think I'm going to *mmmfff*—"

Michael placed his hand across her mouth. "Anna," he hissed, "I know you're marine-trained and I'm not, but we don't have time to argue this. I love you, so trust me. If it's me they are after, and I'm damn sure it is, it's up to me to deal with it. Let me find out what they're up to, then we can decide what happens next. Okay?"

Anna's mouth tightened into a slash of disapproval; she nodded, anyway.

"Good," Michael whispered, relieved that she was not going to argue the point. "No neuronics for the next ten minutes; they are bound to have scanners running. Set them to standby so they think we're sleeping. Done that?"—Anna nodded again—"Good. Ten minutes from now, that'll be at 03:55 exactly, turn them on for ten seconds, I'll update you, and we'll take it from there. If you don't hear from me, go back to standby, wait another five minutes, try again, and so on. "

If I'm still alive to com you, that is, Michael wanted to add, his stomach churning with fear.

Anna nodded again.

"Good. Go!" A fleeting kiss, a quick hug, and Anna left, a shapeless blur under her chromaflage cape disappearing into the darkness.

Michael ran out of the house and sprinted hard up the track. Past the lander and he was back into the trees; he kept moving along the path for as long as he dared, gambling that whoever these people were, they would take their time to get close to the house. Why would they hurry on what ought to be a simple job? Provided that they had not picked up his infrared signature from the bluff, they would think he and Anna lay in bed asleep, alone in an unlocked house with no security alarms in the middle of nowhere, with no place to run.

Michael prayed that the attackers—he had no doubts, none at all, that they had come there to kill him—assumed exactly that. The more they believed this was going to be a quick and easy operation, the less prepared they would be when he tore their guts out.

Renewed fear banded Michael's chest; for a moment he struggled to breathe. He and Anna would have been the softest of soft targets. He just hoped that was what the bad guys reckoned.

An easy job. Remote location. A slow, careful entry. Locate the bedroom. Find the bed. Two shots to his head, two to Anna's. Couple more for luck. Confirm they were both dead. Withdraw. Fly away. How difficult could it be?

Far enough, he decided. Ahead, the ridge narrowed to a neck that brought the cliffs in close on both sides, forcing the path to negotiate a way through a small tangle of boulders. The attackers were compelled to come this way; they had no choice.

Carefully, Michael positioned himself off the path, his ambush position screened by the boulders at his back. His attackers would have to turn around to see him when they came past. Arranging the chromaflage cape to leave just his eyes exposed, he settled down, knife in one hand and a large rock in the other.

The wait seemed a long one, though it probably was not. Michael was relieved when a faint chink of stone on stone broke the stillness. His heart was racing now, the adrenaline pouring into his bloodstream. All of a sudden, the tiny patch of dirt and rock visible through the slit in his cape became the only thing that mattered in the entire universe. Michael slowed his breathing, exhaling softly downward to minimize the heat signature rising from his body. Please do not turn around, he prayed, his body poised to explode into action; please keep moving.

The first attacker drifted into view, a distorted blur. It appeared to be a man, a worryingly big man, broad-shouldered, tall, dressed in a commercial chromaflage cape—not a good one, thankfully; Michael's neuronics had no trouble locking on to him—and carrying a small machine pistol sticking out from under his cape and clearly visible, a bulky silencer screwed to the muzzle. Sloppiness like that could get him killed, or so Michael hoped. Head and gun swinging from side to side, the man walked past Michael and on down the track. Michael stopped breathing, but the man never turned to check behind him. Anxiously, Michael waited; there had to be someone backing up the man on point.

There was, and he was not far behind. Backup was a chromaflaged blur in the darkness, his machine pistol visible, swinging slowly from side to side, just like Point's. Thankfully, he did not look back. More sloppiness. These two were rank amateurs; they deserved to have their asses kicked. But he had a problem. The two men were in sight of each other, so he would get only the one chance. He had another problem. Should he wait to see if there was a third member of the team?

"Shit, shit, shit," he muttered. The longer he waited, the closer the attackers got to Anna. But if he went too early and there was a third man, he risked a shot in the back.

Michael decided to go with what he knew. He needed to

make his move. If he waited and found himself with three men to deal with, his chances of rolling them up one after the other without being detected were nil.

Steeling himself, he stood up; with infinite care, he eased himself onto the path behind Backup, a quick glance back confirming that there was no third man. Reassured, Michael knew he had to get this right. He did not have the luxury of wasting time. The second he neutralized Backup, Point's neuronics would go ballistic, telling him there was something seriously wrong with Backup's health. If Michael did not have Backup's machine pistol pointing at Point when he turned around to see what was up, things were going to get difficult.

Michael closed the gap, but something must have warned Backup. The man started to turn, but Michael was ready for him. He moved quickly, his arm already up, the rock in his right hand slashing down brutally hard and fast, hitting the side of the man's head with sickening force, the impact barely audible. For a moment, Michael worried that he had not done enough. But he had: Backup crumpled slowly to the ground with a soft "*ooohhhh,*" folding forward from the waist, twisting when he fell. Michael lunged for the machine pistol but could not tear it from Backup's hands before the man hit the ground, dragging Michael down with him, the pair landing on the track in a confused jumble of arms and legs, the dead weight of Backup pinning him to the ground.

Point glanced back, his confusion obvious. "Jed," he hissed, "what're you doing, you dumb son of a bitch?"

For an instant, Michael wondered why the man did not shoot. At that distance, he could not miss. Belatedly, the reason dawned on him. Point could not see him. He would think he was looking at the unlucky Jed, a crumpled shape on the ground under a chromaflage cape. Michael snatched his chance.

"Aaahhh," he moaned softly, waving his free arm at Point. "Aaaahhh . . . shit . . . sorry . . . tripped . . . head."

"What's up?" Point whispered. "For chrissakes, you clumsy sack of shit. We don't have time for this. We need to kill Helfort and get the hell out of here." He moved a few steps back along the track toward Michael.

Michael had not been lying there wasting time. Concealed under Backup's body, he worked frantically to get the man's fingers off the trigger guard.

Point stopped. Michael's heart did, too, when the attacker's gun swung up.

"Hang on," Michael mumbled. "Hurts . . . head." His fingers closed around the trigger; with a convulsive heave, he rolled Backup's dead weight off his arm and pulled the gun clear. The instant it came free, he fired one-handed, the machine pistol firing with a stuttering *phuttt*, rounds stitching a wavering line through the air before hitting Point's body, knocking him backward off his feet and onto his ass.

"Oh," Point said softly, sounding puzzled.

With a frantic shove, Michael pushed himself away from Backup, rolled off the track, and fired a second burst. The rounds struck Point high across the chest, pushing the man onto his back, arms thrown out wide. He did not move.

"Shit," Michael muttered, trying to control a sudden trembling before vomiting violently into the bushes. Jeez, Michael, he chided himself, wiping his mouth; finish the damn job first. He checked the time, astonished to see that less than ten minutes had passed since he and Anna had split up. Galvanized into action, he stripped both bodies of their capes, taking their small backpacks and Point's machine pistol. Backup groaned, forcing him to waste more time while he dug around in the backpacks, hoping to find plasticuffs to tie the man up. Thankfully, he did; the hit team might be sloppy, but they came prepared. With Backup trussed and both bodies rolled off the path behind a boulder—Michael resisted the temptation to tip them over the edge of the cliff—he set off, running hard and turning on his neuronics.

On time to the second, Anna's neuronics came back online. "You safe?" he said.

"Yes, Michael. Wha—"

"Listen, don't talk. Two of the attackers are down. There may be more. I've taken their guns. Meet me at the house. Now! And turn your neuronics off."

Michael ran fast, feet pounding down the track and onto the road. Relief swamped him when he saw Anna's slight shape, a blur crossing the yard to the house, and then he was in her arms.

"Oh, Michael, what the hell is this all about?" she said, her voice shaking, pushing him back to talk.

"Hit team, I think. Bunch of fucking amateurs, thankfully. They're after me," he said, lungs heaving. "Two options. Stay here and wait or go back up the track to the flier"—he waved a machine pistol back the way he had come—"and see if we can get away. Who knows, we might be able to take out a few more before we go."

Anna shook her head in despair. "No wonder trouble keeps finding you. You bloody well go looking for it." Her voice hardened. "But I don't like people who creep through the night carrying guns, and I certainly don't like the idea of them getting away, so if you want to have a go, I'm with you."

Michael hugged her again. "Right," he said, "I agree. Let's teach the murderous bastards a lesson. You stay back 10 meters or so. Keep me in sight at all times; close up if you lose me. Watch your six o'clock. Keep the gun under your cape and look behind as much as you look around. If you see anyone who's not me, shoot the sonofabitch," he said handing her a machine pistol and a pair of spare magazines. "Know how to use one of these, sweetheart?"

"Smart-ass!" Anna snorted scornfully, grabbing the gun. "Just try me."

"Good. If things get too hot, we'll go left off the track and hide. The damn cops can sort things out. If they ever get here," he added. "Let's go."

Moving fast while still staying quiet, the pair moved off. They reached the flier pad without incident. Stopping short, Michael waved Anna to the ground while he wormed his way off the path and forward to the edge of the clearing. He moved slowly, careful not to make any sudden movements, scanning the low scrub that bordered the landing pad. The pad was clear; he beckoned Anna up to join him.

"Anna," he whispered, "pad looks okay, but if there's more

of them, this is a good place for them to be, over there, just off the path back toward their own flier. I'll work my way to ours and power up. Don't move until I call you over. Keep an eye on the scrub. Let me know if anything moves. Neuronics on now."

"On? You sure?"

"We have to take the chance. We need to be able to talk to each other. They'll know something's gone wrong."

"Roger that."

Michael eased his way around to put the lander between him and where he thought the bad guys might be before setting off through the short grass that covered the pad. He was dangerously exposed. If the bad guys caught him out here, he was finished. It took an age to cross the ground, his skin crawling at the thought of the damage a burst of machine pistol fire would inflict on his unprotected body, but finally he was at the flier. Trembling with a mixture of fear and excitement, he had stopped to recover when Anna commed him.

"Michael. Three o'clock from the flier. Where we thought. There's someone there."

He stopped and lay unmoving. With great care, he checked the scrub. No movement, none of the rippling blurry distortion of a chromaflage cape, nothing. "Anna, I can't—"

He saw movement, just a flicker. Anna was right.

"Okay. Let me indicate it to you." Michael commed the image to her neuronics overlaid with a scarlet target icon. "Is that it?"

"Yup, that's the one. Small bush left of the pair of boulders."

"Okay, on my mark, hit it hard while I go for the flier. On three. One, two, three!"

With ruthless efficiency, Anna fired two quick bursts into the small bush; she was rewarded by a scream of agony, and then a chromaflaged shape burst out of hiding before collapsing onto the ground, unmoving.

With a convulsive leap, Michael was in the flier, ordering the mass driver to power up. It was a lifetime before the flier's AI confirmed that yes, it really was him, and yes, he was authorized to pilot the flier, and another lifetime until the engine was flight-ready. Michael sat hunched down in the pilot's seat, waiting for the ax to fall on his naked neck. "About bloody time," he muttered when the AI confirmed that the flier was good for takeoff.

"Anna. Flier. Go!" he commed. He did not wait for her, feeding power into the mass driver, the air around the flier erupting into a confused cloud of steam billowing up into the night. He lifted the flier into hover, holding it half a meter off the ground until Anna burst through the murk and threw herself into the passenger seat alongside him. The instant she was in, Michael rammed the mass driver to full power. The flier bolted upward, and he pulled it onto its tail, forcing the little machine backward off the ridge before turning it into a stomach-churning drop nose first into the valley below and away from the ridge, accelerating hard.

"Holy shit," Anna said, her voice shaking while she struggled to strap herself in, "where the hell did you learn that little stunt?"

"I just made it up," Michael replied, throwing her a grin, easing off on the power.

Anna shook her head. "Now what?"

"Well, the baddies are still on the ground—well, those still breathing, that is. So I think we'll pay their flier a visit. If we can disable it, they can't get away. It's time you were my door gunner. Get the window open. Here, take my gun, too. Make sure you've full magazines and get the silencers off if you can. Hate to waste good muzzle velocity. Think you can manage one in each hand?"

"Oh, yeah," Anna said with a wolfish smile.

"Thought so. Ready."

"One second," Anna muttered while she forced recalcitrant silencers off. "Okay, ready," she said, twisting in her seat, both guns out the window.

"Right, here we go. Hold on," Michael said, pulling the flier back into a steep climb and turning until the rock outcrop lay right ahead of them, on it the squat shape of the killers' flier. "Okay, there it is. I'll make one run low and fast, and then we're out of here."

"Roger that."

Level with the top of the outcrop, Michael pushed the flier's nose down and brought the mass driver up to full power. Shaking under the acceleration, the craft rocketed past the massive pile of rock, the hostiles' flier clearly visible against a star-studded sky. Anna let go with both barrels; the cabin reverberated with the appalling racket of unsilenced machine pistols and filled with the acrid stench of burned propellant. They drove out hard across the ridge and over the valley before Michael, throttling back, pushed the flier into a slow turn, straining his eyes to see how the opposition fared. He was disappointed to see nothing but darkness, his night vision degraded by muzzle flash.

"What do you reckon?"

"Not sure," Anna said, busy changing magazines. "It all happened a bit too fast. One more pass uphill of them, a bit slower this time, and we'll get clear to wait for the cops."

"You sure?" Michael replied. "I don't think that's a good idea. Come on, I think we've done enough."

"No bloody way, pal," she said fiercely. "Don't chicken out on me. These fuckers came to kill us. I'll be damned if we let them get away. So let's do it."

"Okay," Michael said, resigned. He banked the flier back toward the bluff. "In we go."

The flier turned hard and started its run in. Once again, the outcrop and the flier stood out, looming black shapes against the stars, growing fast as Michael fed power to the mass driver, punching the craft forward.

"Slow down, slow down," Anna yelled. "Not so fast, Michael."

He ignored her. This was getting dangerous. They had had the advantage of surprise the first time. This time the bad guys would be expecting them. With less than a hundred meters to run, he was proved right when guns opened up from broken ground upslope of the bluff, muzzle flashes lighting up the ground around what had to be two shooters.

"Steady!" Anna called.

A burst of ground fire found its mark, slicing through the windscreen and into the cabin roof. "Shit!" Michael flinched away from the blizzard of plasglass that filled the cabin, stray shards slashing cuts into his face. He wiped away the blood dripping into his eyes. He pushed the mass driver to emergency power, the cabin once again filling with muzzle flash and racket and acrid smoke as Anna emptied her guns into the attacker's flier, a metallic *phock phock phock* telling him that they had been hit again.

The noise stopped. "Oh, shit," Anna said, her voice barely audible over the noise of air ripping through the shattered windscreen.

Michael paid no attention, his attention focused on getting them safely away. He steadied the flier on vector away from the Palisades and handed control over to the AI, ordering it to get to Bachou. He turned to Anna.

She lay back in her seat, head slumped to one side, hair thrashed wildly across her face by the blizzard of cold air pouring into the flier's cabin. Michael commed on the cabin lights, shocked by what he saw. Her skin was pale under thin skeins of blood from plasglass cuts, her mouth a tight, pain-twisted slash. Michael's stomach lurched. "Anna," he said frantically, shouting to make himself heard over the noise of the air buffeting the flier, "what's up? Tell me!"

"Not sure. I think one of them hit me." Her voice was faint.

"Where, Anna, where?" Michael yelled. Desperately, he threw off his straps and knelt in his seat to get closer. "Where are you hit?"

"Up here, I think." Feebly she pointed to her chest, high up on the right-hand side. Michael's heart skipped a beat; he saw the blood spreading across her chromaflage cape. He reached up to the overhead stowage to grab the first-aid kit.

"Nothing anywhere else?" he said.

"Don't think so."

Michael patched into her neuronics. She had a single wound to the shoulder; that was the good news. The bad news was that her shoulder was a mess and she was bleeding internally. Quickly, Michael packed the entry and exit points and commed Bachou Hospital. In seconds, the trauma AI connected to Anna's neuronics and downloaded her vitals. The AI's air of calm confidence did wonders for Michael's state of mind, and it soon had him ransacking the first-aid kit for the unholy mix of drugs and nanobots it wanted pumped into Anna. The AI kept him so busy that the flier's announcement that they were about to land at Bachou caught him by surprise.

He left the flier's AI to it. Hands shaking, heart racing, and racked by guilt that he had allowed this to happen to Anna, he was in no fit state to pilot a flier. The instant they landed, the system took over; the paramedics had Anna out, in a trauma tank, and on her way to the hospital before he even left his seat. Not that he wanted to get out; he was exhausted, at a loss what to do next. He had trouble believing what he and Anna had just been through. Not even two hours ago, she had been in bed asleep and he had been lying on his back looking at the stars, wondering how to keep his life under control. It was total madness, he realized with a sudden flash of anger. What the hell was the world coming to?

A soft cough interrupted his thoughts.

"Michael Helfort?"

It was a tall rangy man in plain clothes. "Yes?" Michael said.

"Lieutenant Hartcher, Bachou police. I think we need to talk. You okay?"

"Yeah, think so. Minor cuts," he said, wiping eyes gummy with congealed blood. "But I need to get to the hospital."

"Yes, you should. You need to get checked out first, and we can get an update on Ms Cheung's progress. I've spoken to the hospital, by the way; the surgeons are ready to start work on her when she arrives, but the initial report from the paramedics is that she should be fine. The trauma tank has her stabilized. Your parents are already there. Miss Cheung's are on their way. You okay to go?"

"Yeah, think so," Michael said, voice shaking.

He forced himself to follow Hartcher as the policeman headed for a small mobibot. Michael swore softly: The instant he showed himself, a small but determined group of holocam-toting media brushed aside the police holding them back and made straight for him. Ignoring Lieutenant Hartcher's protests, they surrounded him, the questions thrown so thick and fast that he had no idea who wanted to know what.

"I'm sorry, folks," Michael said, raising his voice to cut through the racket, hands up in a vain attempt to keep the holocams out of his face. "There's nothing I can say. I need to get to the hospital. There'll be a statement from my agent later. Thank you."

Following Hartcher's lead, Michael dropped his head and barged a way though the milling mob, the media's strident demands for answers ignored while he fought his way to the safety of the mobibot.

"Let's go over it again one more time."

Michael stared at Hartcher. It had been a long day, and postcombat fatigue had set in with a vengeance, the energy draining out of his body as adrenaline burned off. But no matter how many times he told the police lieutenant what had happened, the man always wanted to hear it one more time. Something inside snapped. He shot to his feet, his chair skidding back into the wall. "Enough, Lieutenant! Enough! Tell you what, I'll just give you my complete neuronics records. Uncut, unedited, the lot. Will that do?"

Hartcher's eyebrows shot up, his surprise obvious. "We normally have to go to court for those, but if that's what you want to do, fine. Com them over, but before you do, let me just confirm that you have understood the caution I gave you earlier."

"Yes, yes, yes," Michael snapped. "I know my rights."

"Don't tear my head off, Michael," Hartcher said patiently. "People died today, and by your own admission, you killed at least one of them. You and Ms. Cheung might be facing homicide charges."

Michael glared at Hartcher. "Justifiable, don't you think, Lieutenant?"

Hartcher shook his head. "Maybe, maybe not. It's not for me to say. You know that. It's a matter for the prosecutors and for the courts to decide if it ever gets that far. Anyway, com me your records and we're done."

Michael did, cursing his stupidity. If he gave Bachou police access to his full neuronics records, they would see every thought, emotion, and sensation, everything his brain had experienced during the attack. His mind would be laid bare for total strangers to poke and peer at, its every secret open to their examination. It was a deeply unsettling idea. No wonder there was a flourishing black market in full neuronics records; no wonder pornovid stars made so much money. What he was doing was something no sane person should ever do for free. He gave himself a mental shake; what was done was done. There was no point wasting any more time agonizing over it.

Hartcher nodded. "Okay, received. Thanks. You can go. I'll arrange a mobibot to take you back to the hospital. We'll need to talk to Ms. Cheung, of course, but that can wait."

"Of course."

"By the way, the hospital's been in touch. The surgery's gone well. Ms. Cheung will be fine. A bit stiff and sore until the nanobots finish putting her shoulder back together again, but otherwise okay."

Overwhelmed for a moment, Michael was unable to speak, unable to forgive himself for risking Anna's life. He just nodded.

"Come on, Mr. Helfort," Hartcher said. "Let's get you back to the hospital."

Anna's eyes flickered, two bottomless pools of green staring unfocused up at the ceiling; her skin, normally honey-gold below pink-dusted cheeks, was a dirty, washed-out gray.

"Welcome back, Anna," Michael whispered. "How are you feeling?"

It was a while before she answered. "Tired," Anna said finally. "Sore. What the hell happened?"

"Well, we nailed the bad guys, crippled their flier, and left them for the police to pick up. That's the good news. Bad news is they managed to get a round into your shoulder. Did a bit of damage."

"Oh," Anna mumbled. "Since I'm talking to you, I assume I'll be okay."

"That's what the doctors are saying. Give it a few weeks, and *Damishqui* will be expecting you back."

"Bugger *Dami*—" Anna's eyes rolled back up into her head, and she was asleep.

Four hours later, Anna woke up to demand a bowl of ice cream, then another and another.

"Jeez, Anna! Enough already," Michael protested even as he commed the foodbot for more.

"Up yours, Michael," Anna said. "I've got one hell of a sore throat, and ice cream is ten times better than those damn drugbots."

"It's on its way," Michael said, stoic in the face of Anna's determination.

When the ice cream arrived, it did not last long. "Mmm, that's better," she said, pushing the bowl away.

"Feeling better?"

"Am."

"Your folks called. They'll be here first thing in the morning."

Anna rolled her eyes. "Oh, great. Something tells me I'm in for the mother and father of all lectures. Wish they'd stop treating me like some sort of china doll."

"Well, you are small and perfectly formed, apart from your nose of course, so what's the . . . ow!" Michael yelped when Anna backhanded the empty ice cream bowl into his temple. "Temper, temper," he said, rubbing the side of his head. "That hurt."

"It was supposed to; you deserved it. You are a rude bastard," she said. "Shit, shouldn't have done that. My shoulder's killing me." Anna lay back. After a while, she reached out and folded his hand into hers.

"Anna," he said, his voice faltering. "Anna, look, I—"

"Michael, Michael, Michael," Anna said. She squeezed his hand gently. "You don't have to explain. You are the single most accident-prone man in humanspace. Being around you is like standing next to an unexploded Eagle-hawk missile." She shook her head, her eyes filling with sudden tears. "Loving you is a hundred times worse, and not a day goes by without me asking why I do. But here I am."

"Anna—"

"Shh," she said, lifting her hand to Michael's lips. "You know what? You are what you are, and I might as well get used to it."

Michael had no idea what to say, so he said nothing. He squeezed Anna's hand hard, watching her slip away into unconsciousness.

Michael stayed with Anna while she slept, her face framed by jet-black hair stark against white linen, the faintest of faint blushes of pink across high cheekbones marking the start of her return to health.

For a long time he sat there. His vigil was interrupted when his mother stuck her head through the door. "How is she?"

"Hi, Mom. She's fast asleep."

"Good. Come on, Michael. You're no good to her dead on your feet. We're going home. Dad has supper for you. We'll be back first thing tomorrow to meet Anna's parents. The hospital will call you if there are any developments."

A sudden wave of exhaustion swamped him. Kissing Anna on the forehead, he raised his hands and conceded defeat. "Okay, okay. Let's go."

Monday, September 18, 2400, UD
Dreadnought Project Conference Room,
Comdur Fleet Base

Vice Admiral Jaruzelska called the weekly project meeting to order.

"Morning, everyone. Michael?"

"Sir?"

"You look like a sack of shit, but since you've managed to turn up for work, may I assume you're okay?"

"Gee, thanks, sir," Michael said over the laughter. "But

yes. Bit battered, bit bruised, but I'll be fine, which is more than I can say for the opposition."

"Quite," Jaruzelska said drily as laughter turned to cheers. "More to the point, how's Anna?"

"Recovering well, sir, thank you. She'll be fine."

"Glad to hear it. Bad business," Jaruzelska said, her face grim. "Police making any progress?"

Michael shook his head. "No, sir. Dead end. All they know is that the attackers were a bunch of lowlifes recruited from the gutters of Torrance City. Someone they had never seen before threw them a load of money and told them to get on with it. The operation was thrown together in a rush, which was why we escaped. With more time to prepare . . ."

"Know what? I'd still bet good money you'd get out alive, Michael," Jaruzelska said with a broad smile. "You have a knack in that regard, I have to say."

Michael squirmed in embarrassment. Jaruzelska stopped to let a good-natured mix of cheers, boos, and clapping fade away.

"Okay, okay. Before I hand over to the chief of staff to cover the routine items on the agenda, I want to brief you on the results of our meeting with the brass back at Fleet." Jaruzelska paused for a moment. "I'm sure you know that Captain Tuukkanen and I met with the chief of the defense force and the commander in chief. You also know that this was an important meeting, one we asked for to get rid of the roadblocks in our way. Right up front, you need to know that while we had some wins, we also had some losses."

Jaruzelska paused again while a soft murmur of concern washed across the room. Her hand went up. "Nothing to get too oxygenated about, folks. Project's on track, and the time line for Dreadnought Squadron One to go operational still stands. But our plans for the follow-on squadrons have changed. Captain Tuukkanen will be distributing a detailed report of what those changes are, together with the things we need to do in response. But in essence, the changes are these. First, there won't be the six dreadnought squadrons I recommended, but three."

A soft groan filled the room. Like everyone else present,

Michael knew of Jaruzelska's firm view that sixty dread-noughts was the minimum number needed to take the fight back to the Hammers and, more important, to defeat them and their antimatter weapons.

Jaruzelska ignored the disquiet. "Second, Fleet has down-graded the specifications for the ships of the follow-on squadrons. These will be designated Block 2 dreadnoughts. They will be heavier and slower, but at least they will be dreadnoughts. Obviously, only the ships of the First Squadron will have the full Block 1 dreadnought conversion."

This time there was not a sound. "Oh, shit," Michael mur-mured. That was two losses for Jaruzelska.

"Third, I have agreed with Fleet that our crew numbers for the Block 1 dreadnoughts are too low. So rather than the crew of ten we suggested, we'll be going with a crew of fifteen. That's the largest crew we can accommodate with-out compromising the Block 1 design specifications. Crew levels for the Block 2 dreadnoughts are still under review, but I anticipate a final complement of around thirty or so. Michael?"

Taken by surprise, Michael snapped upright in his seat. "Sir?"

"Given we're commissioning the *Tufayl* on Thursday, this is something we need to get on to right away. Drafting the right people will be difficult . . ."

In his head, Michael finished the sentence for her: ". . . which is why I proposed a crew of ten in the first place, you idiots." Sometimes he wondered whether the people who ran Fleet had any brains at all.

". . . so I want you along with the systems engineering and tactics people to get together when we're finished here to work out where real, live human beings can be most use-ful. We all know that Fleet is desperately short of spacers after Comdur, and especially those with navigation and warfare qualifications. There is no point asking for people they don't have, so don't. Okay?"

"Sir."

"Good. Next, command and control. Today Fleet will be

announcing the formal establishment of Dreadnought Force effective this Thursday. It will also announce my appointment as commander. That means—"

Jaruzelska stopped when the room erupted, all of them coming to their feet, clapping and cheering. This was good news. Fleet canceled projects all the time. Forces in being could not be canceled—not easily, anyway—and that meant, for all the hostility they aroused, dreadnoughts were here to stay.

Slowly, the noise died down, and Jaruzelska was able to continue. "I was about to say," she said, "that means the future of dreadnoughts is assured, but I guess I don't have to. I think you just worked that out for yourselves."

Jaruzelska joined in the laughter sweeping the room, but the good humor did not last long. "Fleet will also be announcing the appointment of Rear Admiral Van Perkins as Deputy Commander, Dreadnought Forces. He will join us in October."

In a flash, the mood in the room changed. Michael swore silently. The political fix was in. Perkins was no friend of dreadnoughts, though to say that was a more than charitable view of his unforgiving opposition. Just how in the hell having someone like Perkins—combat-proven commander though he was—around would make anyone's life better, how it would make dreadnoughts work, he could not begin to imagine.

"Now," Jaruzelska continued, "those are the key points from my meeting. Before I hand over to Captain Tuukkanen, let me make one thing crystal clear. I will expect everyone posted to Dreadnought Force to be committed—nothing less than body and soul—to making dreadnoughts work. No, not expect . . . I demand that everyone posted to Dreadnought Force be committed to making dreadnoughts work, and I can assure you there will be no exceptions. None."

Sullen silence turned to stunned amazement. Michael whistled softly; Jaruzelska was being dangerously frank in response to the question everyone wanted an answer to:

How committed would Perkins be? Afterward, Michael would swear that a surge of fierce loyalty to Jaruzelska had nearly overwhelmed him, and, not for the first time, he marveled at her ability to get the best out of her people.

"Okay, folks. That's it from me. Captain Tuukkanen?"

"Thank you, Admiral," Jaruzelska's chief of staff said, striding to the podium. "Turning to less exciting matters. First up . . ."

Wednesday, September 20, 2400, UD
Dreadnought Project Conference Room,
Comdur Fleet Base

Michael's head hurt.

When he was not having the stuffing kicked out of him in the sims, he sat in interminable meetings like this one, called to work out how best to meet Fleet's demands that the Block 1 dreadnoughts carry an extra five crew members. He wondered about Fleet's priorities sometimes: all this management effort over such a trivial matter just to placate the antidreadnought faction. It was nuts. But at least this meeting—unlike far too many he had been forced to attend—promised a result without spawning working groups, assessment teams, cross-functional impact studies, and all the other bureaucratic paraphernalia so loved by Fleet staffers.

The meeting's chair, Commander Andraschi, a systems engineering commander Michael did not know well, had the floor; thankfully she was summing up. "We're agreed. We can ask for extra personnel all we like, but if Fleet cannot supply them, we're wasting our time. That leaves us with landers. The marines were least affected by Comdur, so we have plenty of them along with assault landers and their pilots. Adding a lander will give our dreadnoughts capabilities—

limited, I know—that they would not otherwise have. A single heavy assault lander with command pilot and minimal crew takes the complement to fifteen."

She turned to Michael. "This is your show. Can you live with that?"

"Can, sir," Michael said. "Beggars can't be choosers, and we have more than enough landers to go around." It was true; more by luck than by good judgment, the planetary assault vessels carrying the Fed marine expeditionary force tasked with the invasion of the Hammer Worlds had been out in deepspace when the Hammers attacked Comdur. An idea hit him. "Hang on a minute, sir. If I'm to carry one, why not a Block 6 lander? They're pinchspace jump-capable. And that," he added, eyes lighting up, "is a capability well worth having."

Andraschi glanced at everyone in turn. "Anybody see a problem with that? No? Me neither. A lander's a lander's a lander, after all, and I think the admiral will agree. If she does, I can't see Fleet arguing the point. Right, enough talk," she said firmly. "Decision made. The final report will recommend a Block 6 lander with a crew of five."

"Thank you, sir," Michael said, pleased with the win, even if it was a small one.

"Right, we're done here, I think. We all have more than enough to be getting on with."

While the meeting broke up in a welter of noise, Michael's neuronics pinged. He accepted the call. It was the personnel office.

"Lieutenant Helfort, sir, Warrant Officer Morriset, Personnel. I thought you'd like to know that your crew has arrived. We've just finished processing them. They'll be ready for you in Conference-3 in five minutes, if that's okay."

"Thanks. I'll meet them there."

"No worries, sir."

After he dropped the call, Michael forced air into lungs tight with anticipation. All of a sudden things were turning serious. Within a matter of weeks, he would be a full-blown captain in command, responsible for taking a warship and its crew into action against the Hammers and—far more important—for bringing them back alive.

Taking another deep breath, he set off for Conference-3, his spirits rising with every step. It would be good to be part of a team again, and even better, he would have Chief Petty Officer Matti Bienefelt as his coxswain. If the world's largest spacer could not keep him—and *Tufayl*—on the straight and narrow, nobody could. After all he and Bienefelt had been through together—in *DLS-387,* in *Eridani,* in *Adamant* when they captured the Hammer cruisers *McMullins* and *Providence Sound* along with their precious outfits of antimatter warheads—it would be good to have her back onboard.

His executive officer was another matter. Junior Lieutenant Jayla Ferreira, barely months out of Space Fleet College, was one of the lucky few able to return to active duty after her first ship, the light cruiser *Sailfish,* was badly damaged at the Battle of Comdur. He hoped she was half the spacer Matti Bienefelt was.

"Attention on deck!" his new executive officer barked when Michael entered the room, and the ship's company of *Tufayl* leaped to their feet, snapping to attention. "Dreadnought *Tufayl* all present and accounted for, sir," she said, hand to forehead in an impeccable salute.

"Thank you. Take your seats, everyone." Michael paused until the crew of *Tufayl* settled down. Nine faces stared back at him. Matti Bienefelt he knew, of course; as for the rest, all volunteers, he knew only what their service records told him. On paper, they appeared solid—Jaruzelska's ruthless selection process had seen to that—but only time would tell how good they really were.

"Right, I'll be as quick as I can," Michael said. "Welcome. *Tufayl* is a special ship, the first of a special squadron. I need a special crew, and you're that crew. *Tufayl* is the toughest ship in the Fleet, and she's tough for a reason. It's tough because we will get the missions other ships cannot carry out. *Tufayl* is tough for another reason. Those Hammer bastards beat the crap out of us at Comdur, no doubt about it"—

an angry rumble filled the room, forcing Michael to raise his voice—"but now it's our turn. It won't be easy, and it sure as hell won't be safe, but it'll be the dreadnoughts that turn this war around, and you'll be there every step of the way."

Michael waited until the noise died away. "Finally, you and me. I may be the youngest skipper in the Fleet, but I do have some experience in that regard." He stopped to let the sudden burst of laughter run its course. "But I cannot get this done without you," he continued, "without all of you. I am here for you, any time of the day or night. Of course," he said, flicking a quick look at Ferreira, "give the executive officer a chance to fix things first"—another burst of laughter—"but if she can't, I'm here."

"I'll be knocking, sir. You can count on it. You owe me a beer, for one thing," a voice said in a poor but passably menacing imitation of a Hammer accent.

Michael laughed. "Chief Petty Officer Bienefelt! You'll have to do better than that. And yes, I owe you a beer. I hadn't forgotten. Okay, okay, settle down. I'd also like to say that unlike other heavy cruisers—sorry, dreadnoughts—you all have unrestricted access to Prime. I think you'll like her, though she prefers to be called Mother, so that's what I suggest you do. I've always believed the primary AI to be the closest thing a warship has to a soul, so I'd encourage you to talk to her. She's been around awhile, so there's not a lot she hasn't seen. Bit like Chief Bienefelt, I'd have to say."

"Bet she's prettier," said an anonymous voice. Chief Chua, the senior spacer responsible for *Tufayl*'s main propulsion, Michael decided while he waited for the laughter to die down.

"Okay, okay. One last thing, and this is probably the only difficult thing I have to say to you."

He forced himself to breathe properly; he had not been looking forward to this part of the welcome talk.

"Some people think," he continued, "that dreadnoughts are the spawn of the devil. If you don't know that already, you soon will. You can expect people to give you a hard time, maybe even a very hard time, just because you've been posted to *Tufayl*. All I can ask you is to deal with it the best way you can, and please note that does not mean beating the crap out of anyone dumb enough to say they don't approve of us. Right, I'm done here. Once again, welcome aboard. XO, carry on please."

"Sir! Attention on deck!" Ferreira called while Michael left.

Thursday, September 21, 2400, UD
Offices of the Supreme Council for the Preservation
of the Faith, city of McNair, Commitment planet,
Hammer of Kraa Worlds

". . . there's nothing I can say. I need to get to the hospital. There'll be a statement from my agent later. Thank you."

Sour-faced, Chief Councillor Polk watched the blood-spattered figure of Michael Helfort barge its way through the media scrum and climb into a mobibot before driving off. The holovid cut back to the network anchor, an immaculately dressed young woman looking for all the world like one of the impossibly beautiful models who filled the trashvids his wife liked to spend her life watching.

"That was the scene this morning at Bachou Airport after an extraordinary night for young Michael Helfort and his girlfriend, Anna Cheung. Now we turn to Professor Nikolas de Witte for his assessment of the wider implications of this incident. Welcome, Professor."

"Good to be here, Amelie."

"First of all, the question everybody is asking. Who was behind this attack?"

"Well, Amelie, I think that's pretty obvious," the professor said, his voice a studied mix of gravitas and concern. "This is the work of the Hammers; there can be no doubt about it. I think—"

I really do not give a shit what you think, you pompous cretin, Polk thought savagely. He skipped the holovid back, pausing it at a frame of Helfort walking across the tarmac toward the onrushing media. Anger surged through him. By Fed standards, Helfort was an ordinary-looking man: not tall but heavily built, broad-shouldered, with penetrating hazel eyes set wide in a face tanned dark below windblown brown hair. Ordinary or not, Helfort was making a fool out of him and out of the Hammer of Kraa, and Polk did not like it one little bit.

To worry about one Fed out of billions was beyond stupid. Polk knew that, but Helfort represented everything he hated about the Feds. Even Helfort's understated good looks offended him. Testament to generations of geneering—an abomination long proscribed by the Faith of Kraa—Helfort radiated the same effortless air of arrogance and superiority all Feds gave off. Polk could not help himself; that was the one thing about the Feds that irked him more than anything else.

He laughed mirthlessly. Helfort's looks annoyed him even when splashed with blood from wounds inflicted by Hammer agents. But a bit of blood was not enough. If the chief councillor of the Hammer of Kraa Worlds could not deal with a single lowlife Fed, the damn job was not worth having. He flicked off the holovid and called his personal secretary.

"Singh!"

"Sir?"

"Councillor Kando in town?"

"He is, sir."

"Right. I want him in my office. Now!"

Polk's eyebrows were arching so far up his forehead that they nearly disappeared into his steel-gray hairline. He shook his head in disbelief.

"So, just let me sum up, Councillor," he continued, acid-voiced. "An unarmed man, asleep in his bed, aided and abetted by his girlfriend, held off an entire hit squad before killing two of them, hog-tying one more, disabling their flier, and

leaving them for the local police to pick up. Oh, yes, everyone's worked out who was behind the attack, so guess what?
We are being blamed for it! How am I doing so far, Councillor Kando? Have I understood it right? Kraa! Incompetent
does not even begin to describe it. What a shambles."

"Sir," the councillor for intelligence protested, "I think
I should point out—"

"No, Councillor!" Polk snapped angrily. "I think I should
point out that a bunch of temple novices armed with feather
dusters could have done a better job than your covert operations people. Covert operations, my ass! Brain-dead clowns,
more like it!" Polk said, voice betraying his frustration and
anger. "How much did this mess cost us . . . no, no"—Polk's
hand went up—"don't tell me, I don't want to know."

"But Chief Councillor—"

"Shut up! Shut up, Councillor. I've had enough of this
little toe rag. I am sick and tired of having his exploits rubbed
in my face by the Fed trashpress. Sick of it, do you hear?
So"—Polk's finger stabbed out across the desk at Kando's
face—"let's try again, Councillor Kando. Get your people off
their fat, overpaid backsides. I want them to organize a proper
operation. Funding no object. Just get it done. This is personal. I want Helfort dead. Understood?"

"Yes, sir."

"I hope you do, I really hope you do. Get out!"

Monday, October 2, 2400, UD
Secure Repair Facility Golf Five, Comdur Fleet Base

"All stations, stand by for the cold move."

The voice of *Tufayl*'s executive officer was steady.
Michael was impressed. It was time for the dreadnought to
go to work, for Ferreira to take the ship out of the yard's
hands and into orbit around Comdur. True, he would be
sitting there watching every step of the way, but by long-

standing Fleet tradition, cold moves—moves handled by hydraulic rams and space tugs without any assistance from the ship's engines—were always controlled by the ship's executive officer, her sole assistant the ship's maneuvering AI. Cold moves: easy to say, hard to execute. *Tufayl* was an enormous ship, certain to be unwieldy and uncooperative, and more than a few executive officers made a complete hash of them.

With another reminder to himself to stay out of Ferreira's way, Michael stood back to watch, offering up a short prayer that Junior Lieutenant Jayla Ferreira would do as good a job in reality as she had in the sims. Around him, the rest of *Tufayl*'s crew did not even come close to filling the combat information center. For such a large ship, it carried a ridiculously small crew: Carmellini and Lomidze, his two warfare spacers, Faris, his comms man, four engineers— Fodor, Chua, Lim, and Morozov—and of course the un- mistakable shape of Chief Bienefelt, *Tufayl*'s coxswain, made ten, including him and Ferreira. The extra spacers forced on him by Fleet—in retrospect he was glad they had insisted on increasing his crew; a pinchspace jump-capable heavy lander would be a real asset—were yet to join them. The process of digging out people who met Jaruzelska's high standards was proving to be a prolonged one.

Ferreira turned to him. "For your information, sir. We are ready in all respects to move."

"Roger. All yours, Jayla. Dent my shiny new ship and I'll dent your skull."

She grinned, a mix of excitement and nerves obvious. "I won't, sir," she replied. "All stations, this is Command, stand by. Dockmaster, this is *Tufayl*."

"Dockmaster."

"Release docking clamps and initiate cold move."

"Roger . . . clamps released, moving now."

With that, a faint shudder ran through *Tufayl* as hydrauli- cally rammed cradles started the dreadnought on its way from the zero-gravity repair facility at the center of the asteroid that hosted Comdur Fleet Base. Ahead lay a 300- kilometer ascent through rock tunnels to the surface for handover to the space tugs that would take *Tufayl* up into parking orbit.

"Captain, sir. Cold move complete, ship is in orbit, orbit is nominal. Tugs detached. Propulsion fusion plants are coming online, all systems nominal. We will have full power available in twenty minutes."

"Thank you. Nice job," Michael said, much encouraged by Ferreira's flawless execution of an evolution that had brought more than a few executive officers undone in the past and even more encouraged that *Tufayl*'s fusion plants were not about to blow his ship apart. Start-ups from cold were tricky, which was why Fleet standard operating procedures insisted that they take place well away from ships and base facilities.

"Thank you, sir," Ferreira said, her relief obvious.

"Okay, Jayla. What's next?"

"Final planning meeting for our shakedown cruise in thirty, sir."

"Okay. I'll see you there. I'm going walkabout. Chief Bienefelt, walk with me."

"Sir."

With *Tufayl*'s coxswain in tow, Michael set off. Leaving the combat information center, he went forward to the ship's main drop tube, which took him two decks down into the cavernous air group hangar. Michael took a look around. It was the largest compartment on board. Spanning the full width of the ship, it stretched close to 200 meters long fore and aft. Once *Tufayl* would have stored an entire air group there: fifty-six landers and space attack vehicles, packed in tight.

Now it hosted the diminutive shape of a single light assault lander. The sight unnerved Michael, the hangar's emptiness a powerful reminder of how much change the disaster at Comdur had forced on the Federated Worlds Fleet.

Bienefelt broke into Michael's thoughts with a soft cough. "Take it you didn't bring me down here to look at all this empty space, sir?"

"Uh, no. Sorry, Matti. I know you're busy. I just wanted a chat."

"Knew you might, sir," Bienefelt said with a chuckle.

"I'm that obvious, eh?" Michael replied. "Yes, two things. First, thanks for agreeing to be my coxswain. I know it's not the best posting from a personal point of view. How does Yuri feel?"

"Well"—Bienefelt's face reddened—"well, he, er . . . well, uh . . . he says he loves me and as long as I come back, he can wait," she said, finishing in an embarrassed rush.

"He's a good man, Matti. He'll be there when this is all over."

"I know he will, sir."

Michael stared right at Bienefelt. "I can't tell you how good it is to have you here. We go back a way."

"We do, sir, we certainly do. Life is never dull with you around."

"Seems to be that way, and something tells me all this"—he waved a hand at *Tufayl*—"is going to keep things interesting."

"Don't think that's in any doubt."

"No, it's not. Second thing. The troops. What do you think of them so far?"

Bienefelt considered the question a while before responding. "With one exception, they're solid. They'll do the job and do it well. But . . ."

"Come on, Matti, Spit it out!"

"Well, sir," Bienefelt said, measuring her words carefully. "I'm a bit reluctant to leap to judgment because it's early days yet. But Carmellini bothers me. He's outstanding on paper, but something's not quite right there."

"Carmellini. Thought it might be him. He came to us from *Retribution*?"

"He did, but he wasn't onboard when the shit hit the fan at Comdur. He missed that little fiasco. He was absent on compassionate leave."

"So, what is it? Survivor's guilt?"

"Yes. That's my best guess, sir. *Retribution* suffered the

second highest casualty rate on that day. Few *Retribution*s came home, and most of those that did will never return to active duty. You can understand why he's feeling guilty."

"Damn," Michael muttered. "Something must have gone wrong. Fleet's pretty good at treating postcombat stress"— something he knew from firsthand experience, he realized with a twinge of guilt—"and it's had plenty of practice over the years. Carmellini must have slipped past the assessment teams."

"Pretty sure that's what's happened. They had their hands full."

"So what do we do? Send him back?"

"No, sir," Bienefelt replied, shaking her head. "Not yet, anyway. I think I'd like to hang on to him. See if we can pull him out of it."

Michael considered that for a moment. "Sure you don't want to refer him to the postcombat stress people?"

"No, sir. I have spoken to them, though. They've done the hard work for us, and we know what we have to do to make sure he doesn't slip back."

"What does Lieutenant Ferreira think?"

"Actually, sir," Bienefelt said, "the XO picked it up first. She's already spoken to me about Carmellini. She told me to take a week and get back to her. I assume she would have briefed you if she was still worried," she added diplomatically.

Michael smiled. It was good to find out the two key members of his crew had picked up on a problem before he had. Even better, he sensed that Bienefelt respected Ferreira. He hoped so; it meant he had the makings of a good crew and a good ship.

"I'll leave it with you, Matti. Off you go. I'll see you at the shakedown cruise briefing. I'm going to see if the engineers have fixed that damned heat transfer pump. "

"Sir."

It had been a long day but a good one. *Tufayl* was a living ship again, back in space where she belonged, one more step along the road to the day when she would go into ac-

tion against the Hammers. A welcome beer in hand, he
commed Mother, the AI in charge of the hundreds of AIs—
big and small—that made the dreadnought work.

"Yes, Michael?" Mother said, her face by long-standing
tradition that of a middle-aged woman.

For a moment Michael was a child again, talking to his
own mother, which was probably why the primary AIs of this
world looked the way they did: relics from a long-lost male-
dominated past intended to reassure insecure and lonely
male officers that however bad things might seem, there was
still hope. That summed up Anna's view and that of every fe-
male spacer he had ever met. Sadly, Michael knew that what
Anna said held more than a grain of truth.

"What do you think? This going to work?"

"*Tufayl* or dreadnoughts?"

"Both, I suppose."

Mother took her time before answering. "The short answer
is yes," she said finally, measuring her words carefully. "I've
been back through every engagement this ship has ever been
in, real and simulated. I've found only a handful where having hundreds of spacers around made a significant difference
to the outcome. I hate to say this, Michael, but apart from
fixing defects or repairing battle damage, all those spacers
mostly just get in the way, not to mention the mass of all the
systems needed to keep them alive. No, there's no reason
why they won't work."

Michael nodded. Admiral Jaruzelska had made the same
points to him more than a few times.

"There is one caveat, though," Mother continued. "I agree
with the admiral. I've studied every operation since the *Tufayl* entered service, focusing on the interaction between the
captain and the operations and threat assessment officers.
One thing is obvious. Without their support, the job of command in combat is too hard."

"Even with a warfare AI as good as ours?"

"Yes. Warfare is not there to provide advice. It is there
to manage close-quarters combat, to execute command-
approved plans, to do what it's told basically. Expecting any
more of it is a waste of time."

"Don't I know it," Michael said. "So you think it's a good idea, sitting two AIs alongside me?"

"Yes, I do. And you're getting two good ones."

Michael's eyebrows shot up. "Oh? You know who they are?"

"I do," Mother said a touch smugly. "Us AI's have our ways of finding things out. Seems we are getting the operations AIs from *Kuibyshev* and *Kaladima*."

Michael's eyebrows lifted even farther. "*Kuibyshev* and *Kaladima*? Shit! They decommissioned them, what, ten years ago? I know the AIs are kept current, but are they up—"

"Up to it?"

"Well, yes, that, too, though I was going to say up to date. A lot has changed since they went through the Third Hammer War."

"Not as much as you think, Michael. Space warfare is space warfare, and they've spent thousands of hours in Fleet's StratSim simulator since the *Kuibyshev* and *Kaladima* were scrapped. I don't think you'll find them out of touch. They'll do a good job."

"I know," Michael conceded, "and if Admiral Jaruzelska had a hand in their selection, I'm sure you're right."

"We'll see. Oh, yes, one more thing. They both know your parents."

Michael groaned out loud. Was there anyone—human or AI—in the Federated Worlds Space Fleet who did not know his parents?

"Get me another beer before I have you turned off," he said to Mother even though it was not her job to summon the drinkbot.

"Yes, Michael," Mother said meekly.

Cruelly lit by the glare from banks of overhead lights, the interrogation room was a bleak and unforgiving place, its fittings limited to three chairs and a simple metal table, all bolted to a stained plascrete floor pierced by a small drain.

The sole occupant of the room sat facing the door, her hands cuffed to the metal table. Professor Saadak was a pitiful sight: dirty blond hair hanging in matted strands, forehead slashed by an angry cut, its crust of dried blood black in the harsh light, eyelids puffy over half-closed eyes, skin gray and stretched tight. Unmoving, she stared into the distance.

The woman started in shock when the door crashed open, head snapping back, hands twisting in a desperate, futile attempt to push her body away from the table. A man in dark gray coveralls came in and sat down; he ignored her. The woman gave up her struggle; without a word she watched the man arrange his data pad on the table.

The silence dragged on and on; still the man just sat.

Without warning, he stood and reached across the table. Working quickly, he pulled her sleeve back, ignoring her frantic efforts to stop him. He pulled a small gas-powered hypo gun from a coverall pocket; Saadak flinched when he fired it into her arm.

"You bastard, Balluci," she said, her voice a harsh croak, "bastard, bastard, bastard . . ." Her voice trailed off. For a minute she sat motionless. She sat up with a start, her pupils closing to pinpoints and her hands steadying as the drug seeped into her system. She whimpered, soft moans of agony, eyes casting left and right in a frantic search for a way out of her suffering.

"All right, Professor Saadak, I think we're ready to talk," Interrogator First Class Balluci said, "so let's get started.

Remember, you can finish this by telling me the truth, first time, every time. I can give you something to ease the pain. I know that drug's a real bitch."

"I've told you everything," Saadak said, trembling, "everything I know."

"Not true, Professor. You still refuse to give me access to your neuronics."

"I can't," she cried, "I can't. I've told you over and over. I can't give you access. My neuronics are blocked, and you aren't authorized to—"

Balluci moved so fast that Saadak had no time to react. He lunged across the table, and his open hand smacked her head savagely to one side, a scream of drug-enhanced agony racketing off the wall of the room. She slumped forward, head shaking from side to side, tears dripping onto her jumpsuit, hands clawing uselessly at the metal tabletop.

Balluci waited until she lifted her head, peering at him from pain-filled eyes. "You know what, Professor?" he said.

"No," Saadak croaked, "what?"

"I think we believe you on the neuronics thing. So let's move on. Tell me about your defense research and development programs. Did you have oversight of their budgets?"

"Yes, I did," Saadak said, utterly beaten.

"Okay. Let me ask you . . ."

Four hours later, the man behind the one-way mirror allowed himself to be convinced. The woman had nothing more to tell them. If it was in her brain—pity they had not cracked her neuronics—Balluci would have dug it out. He was one of the best, even if he was beginning to get too fond of the physical side of the business; the woman was a mess. Everything Saadak said confirmed that the Feds were conducting the basic research; she knew of no funding for antimatter warhead production. All of that meant the Feds had a long way to go before they managed to weaponize antimatter. It would be even longer before any antimatter weapons made it into frontline service in useful numbers.

He put a holovid call through to his boss. His masters would be happy to hear what he had to say.

With a lurch, the universe turned itself inside out and *Tufayl* dropped into normalspace, back where she belonged. With one eye on the navigation AI while it computed the vector for Comdur, Michael heaved a sigh of relief. It had been a hard seven days. Shakedown cruise, my ass, he said to himself. Shakedown it certainly had been, cruise it had not. The pressure was relentless, crisis after crisis thrown at them to test the ability of the *Tufayl*'s tiny crew to react to and contain the problems deepspace operations might toss at them.

All the time, standing back in the shadows, ship riders from the staff of the flag officer for space training watched everything and missed nothing; at times, their postexercise debriefings verged on the brutal as they dissected the mistakes made by Michael and his team. It was an unforgiving process, not least because any failure by one of *Tufayl*'s crew was his failure. He might be in command of the most advanced warship ever produced by humans, but some things never changed.

He was glad it was over, happy to know he would soon see the back of the last of the ship riders.

"Command, sensors. Threat plot is confirmed. Plot is green."

"Command, roger. Warfare, weapons tight. I have command authority."

"Warfare, roger."

"All stations, command. Stand down from general quarters. Revert to cruising stations, ship state 3, airtight integrity condition x-ray. Engineering, restore artificial gravity. Jayla, you can stand down. I'll take the ship in."

"You sure, sir?" Ferreira asked.

"Yup. Just get those ship riders off my ship the instant we're in orbit."

"Yes, sir," Ferreira replied with a huge grin. "I'll see to it."

Michael sat alone in the combat information center, asking himself the same question over and over again: Had *Tufayl* done well enough? Did she have her precious Operational Readiness Certificate?

"Command, navigation. Confirmed vector is nominal for Comdur parking orbit."

"Command, roger," he replied. He triple-checked the navigation AI's vector calculations. Comdur's defenses were formidable; they tolerated no mistakes. To stray off vector risked an encounter of the terminal kind: If space mines missed them, autonomous defensive platforms armed with ASSMs and antiship lasers came next. If they did not get them, space battle stations—newly commissioned and nervous after the Hammers wiped out most of their predecessors—would. Michael knew he was justified in keeping a close eye on his navigation AI.

Satisfied all was well, Michael allowed himself to settle back while he watched *Tufayl*'s painstaking transit through Comdur's defenses.

"*Tufayl,* Space Training Control."

"Space Training Control, *Tufayl,*" the navigation AI responded.

Now what? Michael wondered.

"*Tufayl,* Space Training Control. Stand by to receive shuttle with one pax for you. Chop vidcomm channel 36, contact shuttle Mike Romeo 4466."

Michael overrode the AI. "Space Training Control, *Tufayl.* Authenticate Kilo Mike Alfa Quebec." After a week suffering at the hands of vindictive ship riders, Michael did not trust the people who managed the minutiae of space training. Who knew what stunt the bastards might try to pull even at this late stage? He would not put it past them to have packed the shuttle with marines for a last-minute boarding exercise.

"*Tufayl*, Space Training Control. I authenticate Lima Lima Yankee Golf."

"*Tufayl*, roger. Chopping vidcomm 36. *Tufayl*, out," Michael acknowledged, relieved that the vidcomm message was genuine and that the shuttle was not some last-minute test of *Tufayl*'s operational readiness. He and *Tufayl* had had just about all the shaking down they could take.

He would find out soon enough who was important enough to warrant sending a shuttle all the way out to meet *Tufayl*. In the meantime, he would do what all prudent captains did when entering Comdur nearspace: make sure his ship's vector was precisely where it was supposed to be.

Thirty minutes later, a gentle bump announced the arrival of the shuttle. Michael forced air deep into his lungs to control a sudden attack of nerves. The shuttle brought him a visitor he had never wanted to meet. He watched the coxswain pipe the side, the shrill squealing of bosun's calls greeting the new arrival while he scrambled out of the plasfiber boarding tube.

Michael saluted Rear Admiral Van Perkins, the newly appointed deputy commander of Dreadnought Forces. Perkins—tall, buzz-cut blond hair, florid complexion—snapped to attention to return Michael's salute.

"Admiral Perkins, sir," Michael said formally, "welcome aboard."

"Thank you, Captain," Perkins replied, piercing blue eyes looking Michael right in the face. "Pleased to be aboard this fine ship."

Michael smiled politely as they shook hands. The man might outrank him by a country mile, but at least Perkins had not forgotten his manners. "Can I introduce my executive officer, sir? Junior Lieutenant Ferreira."

Ferreira stepped forward to shake Perkins's hand. "Welcome to *Tufayl*, sir. And welcome to dreadnoughts."

"Lieutenant," Perkins said.

Michael wondered if anyone else noticed how the man's mouth tightened at the word *dreadnoughts*.

"Shall we go, sir?" Michael said. "I should get back to the CIC."

"By all means. Lead on, Captain."

Setting off, Michael shoved the admiral out of his mind. Only a fool took Comdur's defenses for granted, and no admiral in humanspace would distract him from getting *Tufayl* safely inside them.

An awkward silence followed while the pair made their way down to *Tufayl*'s combat information center. Michael did not care. Once back in the command seat, he kept his eyes on the command holovid, much more concerned to keep an eye on *Tufayl*'s transit through Comdur's defenses.

"Captain," Perkins said. "I see you are on vector, so may we go to your cabin? I would like to debrief you on your shakedown week."

Michael was on the point of agreeing, when something in Perkins's eyes stopped him. Shit, he said to himself. Was this a test? "Happy to, sir, but would you mind if we dropped into parking orbit first?"

"Not at all," Perkins responded, seemingly oblivious to the fact that a mere lieutenant had just refused an admiral's request. "I'll be staying with you, so that's fine."

"Thank you, sir. Appreciate that," Michael said gratefully.

"Can I get you a drink, Admiral?"

"A beer, thanks."

Michael waited until the drinkbot handed Perkins his drink before speaking. "Well, sir," he said, "once again, welcome to dreadnoughts."

Perkins nodded. "Thank you. The Flag Officer, Space Training"—Michael's heart skipped a beat; had they found some fatal flaw in *Tufayl*'s performance? Was that why Perkins had shown up so unexpectedly?—"asked me to pass on his congratulations. Not the best week they've ever seen at space training, but pretty good considering how few spacers"—he waved a dismissive hand around Michael's day cabin—"these things carry. You'll get your Operational Readiness Certificate tomorrow. Oh, yes. Admiral Jaruzelska asked me to say well done."

Michael slumped back in his chair, the relief washing through him. "Thank you, sir," he said, "thank you very much." Fatigue did not allow him to say much more. All he wanted was for Perkins to drink up and leave. When the man did, he could turn in. He needed to catch up on a week's lost sleep—badly.

It took Michael a while to get rid of Perkins, but at long last the admiral was piped over the side for the shuttle transfer back dirtside. It had been an interesting session, and not in a good way.

Perkins's message was pretty simple, even if cloaked in enough euphemism, equivocation, understatement, and ambiguity to give the man all the wiggle room he would need if Jaruzelska found out what he was saying. Perkins's message was nearly subliminal, to a point where Michael struggled to work out what the message actually was. But despite having little sleep for a week, he did work it out in the end, and when he did, it shocked him.

Perkins did all the talking: The dreadnought concept was dangerous, it did serious damage to the Fleet, and it risked the long-term security of the Federated Worlds. Michael's job was to stay in line and follow orders. Under no circumstances was he to offer the dreadnoughts any support or encouragement. Once the dreadnought heresy was consigned to the trash can of history, Perkins would see to it personally that Michael received the recognition an officer of his talent and potential so richly deserved.

Michael had been stunned and unsettled by Perkins's veiled insubordination, and his response had been perfunctory in the extreme. He had said nothing more than "yes" or "no" throughout. Not that Perkins noticed; he seemed more than happy to interpret Michael's reticence as agreement.

Wrong, Rear Admiral Perkins, Michael said to himself while Perkins left the ship. Admiral or not, Perkins would find out that Michael's taciturnity was not consent. With or without Perkins's support, he vowed to make dreadnoughts work.

Friday, October 13, 2400, UD
Offices of the Supreme Council for the
Preservation of the Faith, McNair

The weekly Defense Council meeting over, Chef Councillor Polk beckoned Councillor Jones over. Polk waited until the room cleared before speaking, his face dark with anger and frustration.

"Kraa damn it!" Polk said with a snarl. "I am sick and tired of this council telling me what I can't do. When"—his hand smacked down with a dull thump—"will you tell me what I can do? All I hear is excuses!"

"Well, sir, as you know," the councillor for war said warily, "our antimatter warhead stocks are limited. We expended most of our inventory in the Comdur attack. We need to conserve what few missiles we have left. And there is an armistice in force."

"Yes, so? That sounds to me like more of the same, Councillor Jones," Polk hissed venomously. "So tell me. What the hell is the point of stockpiling missiles? The bloody things are there to be used, for Kraa's sake. As for the armistice, what do I care? It's just a bit of paper. I signed the damn thing. I can unsign it if I want, and I will."

Polk pushed himself back in his seat. "I've had enough of this, Councillor," he said. "I want the armistice torn up. I want offensive operations against the Feds resumed. I want them hounded back to the negotiating table. I want them forced to make the concessions we need. Kraa! We have antimatter weapons, and the damn Feds don't. How much simpler does it get? So brief Fleet Admiral Jorge. Tell him I want to see an options paper from him for next week's Defense Council meeting. It is time to take the offensive."

"Yes, Chief Councillor," Jones said glumly.

The captain of the mership *Pasternak* had been cursing sotto voce for a good hour, a steady stream of profanity that derived its considerable color and diversity from a long career as a mership officer. Not that cursing made the slightest difference, even though it did make him feel better. Fact was, he was well and truly screwed, and no amount of swearing would change that.

With only a fraction of a second left to run before *Pasternak* was scheduled to leave pinchspace, the ship's error-prone navigation AI lost lock, precipitating an emergency drop into normalspace. Now, rather than tying up alongside a planetary transfer station to off-load passengers and cargo, the ship was coasting through farspace at a leisurely 150,000 kph on vector for Ashakiran.

That was the good news. The bad news was that Ashakiran was a depressingly long way away. It would be days before they decelerated into orbit around the second of the Federated Worlds' home planets, and nothing would make it happen any sooner. The only way of getting home any faster would be to trust the navigation AI that had dropped *Pasternak* into the shit in the first place; since that risked emerging inside Ashakiran itself, he was not going to chance it.

That left *Pasternak* a long way out in farspace, very much on its own. It was not a good feeling. He hoped that the armistice with the Hammers still held. Ashakiran Farspace Control, though sympathetic, refused his request that a Fed warship—ever hopeful, he had asked for at least three—be sent to escort him in. So there they sat in farspace, alone and defenseless should a wandering Hammer warship happen to pass by, a tiny bubble of life sitting at the heart of a sphere of electromagnetic radiation that expanded at the speed of light screaming "Defenseless mership; come and get me." Anyone who imagined the Hammers would stick to the terms of the armistice when presented with a soft target like poor old *Pasternak* was a damn fool. They would have to be saints, and he had never met a Hammer who came even close.

He hated the idea that he might end up having to beg some Hammer spacer to spare his ship thanks to a useless navigation AI. It would be just his luck if one of the worst trips in his long career ended in being captured by those bastards.

He was not happy, his crew was not happy, and worst of all, the self-loading cargo—a bunch of arrogant, overbearing xenobiologists returning from a field trip to Kanaris-IV with a mountain of equipment and thousands of samples—were not happy. "Miserable jerks," he mumbled under his breath. What else did they expect from a clapped-out mership? Why did the penny-pinching bozos think the *Pasternak* charter was so cheap in the first place?

Pasternak's captain fidgeted in his seat, trying hard not to think about how quickly the profit from the trip—never huge to start with—was disappearing. If there was any left at all by the end of the trip, it would be a miracle. Why did he bother? he wondered despondently while he made himself settle down to wait.

Five minutes later, a wall of gamma radiation from two antimatter warheads fired hours earlier by a Hammer cruiser smashed into the aging mership's hull. The radiation ripped through the mership and raced away toward Ashakiran planet. Less than a nanosecond later, the fusion plant driving *Pasternak*'s main propulsion lost containment; the hellish energy released by the fusion plant's failure expanded in a huge blue-white ball of ionized gas.

The ship had ceased to exist.

Alone in his cabin, nursing a welcome coffee, Michael Helfort sat thinking about the day.

He was drained of all energy and saturated by fatigue; only willpower kept his body and mind going. The week had been long, full of relentless, grinding pressure while he struggled to achieve the impossible. More than that, it had been a solitary week; all the old clichés about the loneliness of command were right on the money. Apart from Mother, there were few people he could talk openly to. The spacers seconded from fleet development to work on the dread-nought project were senior to him by ten years or more, and his peers—those who had escaped alive after the Hammers trashed much of the Fleet at Comdur—worked all the hours there were to keep as many ships operational as possible, so catching up for a quick drink was always difficult, more often than not impossible.

Needless to say, *Damishqui* was equally hard to pin down. Michael had given up asking Anna when they might meet again. Anna being Anna, she had recovered from her in-juries in record time; refusing an offer of extended sick leave, she was back onboard *Damishqui,* chasing Hammers somewhere in the deepspace approaches to al-Jaffar planet, a pointless mission with the fingerprints of nervous politi-cians all over it.

To think, all he ever wanted to be was the command pilot of an assault lander. Climb aboard, strap in, go in hard, beat the crap out of the target of the day, come home, have a few beers with your mates, and talk shop for a few hours before turning in for a good night's sleep. Simple, straightforward, the way life should be.

Instead of which, here he sat, the biggest guinea pig of all time, the captain in command of the first ever dreadnought, a concept so new that the damn things had not even entered operational service yet.

Frustrated, he exhaled sharply, the air hissing out past tightly clenched teeth. Admiral Jaruzelska made it all sound so simple. Appoint a bright, combat-proven officer in command of ten dreadnoughts and bingo! In place of a bunch of useless hulks, the Fleet had a squadron of ships, but without all the spacers needed to operate heavy cruisers.

Michael had no problem with the theory. It was a good theory, a great theory. After losing thousands of spacers at the Battle of Comdur, Fleet had plenty of warships but not the spacers to crew them, so what else was it going to do?

Problem was, the theory had proved difficult to put into practice. Morosely, Michael sipped his coffee. Knowing his luck, tomorrow would be every bit as tough as today had been—hour after hour in the sims having endless tactical problems thrown at him, problems that would stretch a battle fleet's staff. He could only try his best, and as long as Jaruzelska had faith in him, he would keep doing everything in his power to make dreadnoughts work.

Michael set his problems aside to check the broadcast news. It had been a while, and he wondered what the Hammers were up to. Closing his eyes, he watched the familiar Federated News Network icon pop into his neuronics.

Five minutes later he shut the broadcast off, even more depressed, if that was possible. "Bloody Hammers," he grumbled. After a long period of inactivity, the bastards had detonated more antimatter warheads in Fed nearspace, two for each home planet. Apart from the usual electromagnetic pulse and some spectacular atmospheric fireworks, there was no real harm done, of course—some mership wandering around in Ashakiran farspace had been the only casualty—but that was the whole point of the exercise. The Hammers' message was brutally simple: Give them what they wanted at the negotiating table or they would reduce the Federation's home planets to radioactive slag. And just to make sure even the most dim-witted Fed politician understood the message, a Hammer spokesman—some drone in the high-necked black uniform all Hammer officials favored—had repeated the threat almost word for word. Give us what we want or you and your planets will die, he had said.

The threat was clear. Worse, despite all the posturing by the Feds' so-called allies threatening the Hammers with all sorts of retribution if they did attack the Feds—none of which amounted to a row of beans; the rest of humanspace were allies in name only—he knew the Hammers were more than capable of carrying out their threat. After being soundly thrashed in three wars by the Feds, the Hammers had come out on top thanks to their antimatter warheads and the brutal defeat they had inflicted on the Fed Fleet at Comdur. So why would the Hammers give up?

For the Hammers, success was at hand.

If Rear Admiral Perkins had his way, and the dreadnoughts did not work . . .

Friday, November 3, 2400, UD
FWSS Achernar, *Commitment planetary farspace*

The air was thick with tension, the eyes of all present locked on the massive holovid display that curtained the front bulkhead of *Achernar*'s combat information center.

"Shiiiiit," an anonymous voice said softly from the back of the compartment.

"Quiet!" *Achernar*'s captain snapped. Boris Andermak was not enjoying this operation any more than his crew was. It had been an ordeal from the word go, and the sooner it finished, the happier he would be.

The cause of all the angst filled the command holovid. Moving slowly from left to right was what any first-year cadet would identify readily as an Eaglehawk, a long-range, two-stage antistarship missile. It was an ugly brute of a thing, the backbone of the Hammer fleet's offensive missile capability. Matte black, it was big, dwarfing the space-suited handlers shepherding it away from the *Achernar,* and—to Fed eyes at least—crudely assembled and poorly finished. Not that it mattered how the thing looked. Eaglehawks might be slower and less capable than the Merlin ASSM, their Fed equivalent, but they worked and had killed more than their fair share of Fed ships over the years. The Eaglehawk was a nasty piece of ordnance and definitely not something to be taken for granted.

And that was before the Hammers went and fitted antimatter warheads to the Eaglehawk, turning it into the weapon that had snuffed out much of the Fed space fleet at the Battle of Comdur. *Achernar*'s captain was not a praying man, but he prayed now. Antimatter was the stuff of nightmares, and here he sat, meters from enough of it to vaporize him and his ship.

Andermak would be damn glad when the two Eaglehawk missiles he had been ordered to deploy cleared his ship and were on their way back to their makers. Watching the missiles, he wondered how they had fallen into Fleet's hands; he guessed they were two duds left over from the Comdur attack. But, however it had found them, Fleet refused to let on. The fact they had them at all was classified so highly that he and his crew were scheduled for selective neurowiping the instant they returned home, a process Andermak was not looking forward to.

The deployment took forever, but at long last it was done, the handlers back inboard safely. *Achernar,* sealed up, waited, ready to jump. The two Eaglehawk missiles hung in space, drifting away from the *Achernar* toward Commitment, home planet of the Hammer Worlds and seat of the Hammer of Kraa government. Slowly, the gap between the *Achernar* and the missiles opened. Andermak suppressed a shiver, not at all sure—despite all the assurances he had been given by the brass, none of whom would be within light-years of the missiles when he sent them on their way—that the damn things would work.

It took a long time, but finally the two Eaglehawks moved

safely outside *Achernar*'s antimatter blast damage radius. Andermak allowed himself to relax just a fraction.

"Ops."

"Sir?"

"Send those evil sonsofbitches on their way."

"Sir. Stand by . . . missile launch sequence initiated, missiles nominal . . . missile first stages firing . . . missiles on their way, vectors nominal."

Stiff with nervous tension, Andermak watched while the two missiles streaked away toward Commitment on thin pillars of blue-white flame, more relieved than he cared to admit. "Thank goodness for that. My money was on them blowing us all to hell. Let's go home."

"Amen to that, sir," the *Achernar*'s operations officer replied with considerable and all too obvious feeling.

Many hours after the Eaglehawk missiles had been sent on their way, the traps containing their antihydrogen payload collapsed, and the two warheads exploded in unison. In less than a billionth of a second, a bubble of gamma radiation expanded outward at the speed of light, its twin-peaked signature providing the Hammers with unarguable proof of matter/antimatter annihilation.

The Hammers would have no option but to conclude that the Feds had antimatter weapons.

Saturday, November 4, 2400, UD
Offices of the Supreme Council for the
Preservation of the Faith, McNair

"No! No, they can't have," Chief Councillor Polk croaked at last, his face ashen. "This cannot be. What . . ." His voice drained away to nothing; he sat paralyzed, staring wide-eyed at the black-uniformed man sitting opposite him.

"Sir, I'm afraid it's true," Fleet Admiral Jorge said. He

paused to steady himself. "Sir," he continued, his voice as firm as his jangling nerves allowed, "the Feds might have antimatter weapons, but they are not our equals, not after Comdur. Their offensive capability has been all but destroyed, their—"

"So you say, Admiral," Polk hissed, his face twisted into a vicious sneer, "so you say."

Fear had turned Jorge's mouth dry as ashes. He knew Polk well enough to recognize when the man was about to lose all self-control. If Polk did, he was as good as dead. "What matters is how we win," he said, keeping his voice quietly confident, "how we keep the Feds off balance, demoralized, ineffective, until we have secured our political objectives."

"Yes, Admiral, that is what matters." Polk said, bitter with disappointment. "We have to win this. If we don't, there is no future for the Hammer Worlds. And," he added, voice dripping with venom, "no future for you, Fleet Admiral Jorge."

"No, sir, there's not." Nor for you, you psychopathic dirtbag, Jorge wanted to say; wisely, he did not. "So we need to strike and strike hard," he continued. "Yes, the Feds can destroy us, but we can destroy them, too. So we won't, and neither will they. Mutually assured destruction. We might not like it, but history shows it works."

For an age, Polk stared thoughtfully at the man who controlled the Hammer's enormous military. Jorge was relieved to see the man's rage begin to subside, the angry red flush across both cheeks fading slowly. Polk's silence gave Jorge his opening. He leaned forward. "If they destroy our home planets, we'll destroy theirs, sir," Jorge said, repeatedly stabbing a finger into the desk to emphasize the point. "And why would we do that, sir? Kraa! We're not a bunch of suicidal fundamentalists."

"No, Admiral, we're not," Polk said. "That much we can agree on. So let's cut to the chase, shall we. What is it you want?"

Jorge steadied himself. "Well, sir. We cannot beat them at the negotiating table. We need to take the fight back to them. Beat them the hard way."

"And we can do that? Even if they have antimatter weapons?" Polk's face had tightened into a skeptical frown.

Jorge made sure he sounded convinced; his life depended on it. "After Comdur, we can," he said. "Antimatter missiles are just another weapon. We need to keep our nerve. We have a plan to escalate offensive operations, and we need to stick to it. It's the only way we can bring the Feds back to the negotiating table. We have the strategic advantage . . . we can force them back. We can and we will."

It was a long time before Polk replied, and when he did, his voice was subdued. "Fine, Admiral. Call me a fool, but I'm going to trust you."

"Thank you, sir," Jorge responded, trying not to sound too relieved that Polk did not want him shot out of hand, the fate all too often inflicted on the bearers of bad news.

Friday, December 1, 2400, UD
FWSS Tufayl, in orbit around Comdur Fleet Base

Vice Admiral Jaruzelska's avatar popped into Michael's neuronics. "You ready to go, Captain?" she asked.

"We are, sir. We'll be on our way when Admiral Perkins is onboard."

"Glad I caught you. Is there anything we need to talk about?"

Michael blinked. Just the one thing, not that he would be telling the admiral that. "No, sir," he said.

Vice Admiral Jaruzelska must have noticed Michael's momentary hesitation. "Perhaps," she said, her voice a touch curt, "I should make sure that the command arrangements for this mission are completely clear. Are they completely clear, Lieutenant Helfort?"

Bloody woman must be psychic, Michael decided. "Yes, sir. They are to me," he said with a confidence he did not feel. "I am captain in command. Rear Admiral Perkins is onboard strictly to observe. He is to take no part in the planning or execution of the operation. He is here to watch what we do and how we do it and report back."

Jaruzelska stared at him long and hard. "Exactly so," she said, "and you can be assured that I have made that clear in written orders, hard-copy orders"—Michael blinked; he had never known a senior officer to be forced to issue orders on paper—"to the admiral. We . . . I need to know, I must know whether or not *Tufayl* under your command can hold her own in a fight against the Hammers, and there's no way we'll know that if I have to send admirals along to hold your hand."

"Understood, sir."

"Yes, I think it is." Jaruzelska paused. "Go to it, Michael," she said with sudden warmth. "Jam it up those Hammer sons of bitches."

"I will, sir. And thanks."

Jaruzelska shook her head. "Don't thank me. Just kill as many Hammers as you can. That's all the thanks I'm looking for. If we can't put the pressure back on them, we're in serious trouble. Remember Comdur. Jaruzelska out."

"Remember Comdur," Michael responded. He stared at the blank holovid screen for a moment. He never doubted that Jaruzelska backed him 100 percent. He wished he could say the same for Rear Admiral Perkins.

Thursday, December 7, 2400, UD
FWSS Tufayl, *Faith planetary deepspace*

"All stations, command. Faceplates down, depressurizing in two. Secure artificial gravity."

The voice of *Tufayl*'s executive officer was wooden, stiff with stress. Michael sympathized. Ferreira had every reason to be nervous. The last time she had seen action, her ship had been blown out from under her; she had been lucky to escape with her life when so many of *Sailfish*'s crew had not. He glanced around the shell of *Tufayl*'s massive combat information center, the operational heart of the once great heavy cruiser. It was an unsettling sight, the huge compartment all but empty. It had been gutted, every last bit of equipment not needed for its new role as a dreadnought ripped out by an unstoppable army of voracious salvagebots.

But none of that fazed him as much as the sight of Rear Admiral Perkins: Combat space suit closed up, face inscrutable behind the plasglass visor, the man sat in back of Michael's small command team.

If he did not have enough to worry about, Perkins had already crossed the line drawn in the sand by Jaruzelska. He had been quick to say that the ops plan for the attack was fatally flawed, forcing Michael to remind him—more than once since they had departed from Comdur—that he was there to watch, not to take control of the operation. It was a bitter exchange, one that Michael had no doubt would happen again.

Needless to say, the admiral was not a happy man, and why would he be? Lieutenants did not make a habit of telling flag officers to butt out, and it could not be easy for a man with Perkins's combat record—a long and distinguished record, it had to be said—to sit back and watch a lieutenant take a heavy cruiser into battle.

Michael pushed Perkins to the back of his mind; he had better things to worry about than the man's feelings. The most important thing on his plate was getting *Tufayl* through its first combat mission intact and its crew home alive. He turned his attention back to the massive holovids that filled the forward bulkhead of *Tufayl*'s combat information center.

The threat plot was an ugly mess of red vectors, each tracking a Hammer warship in orbit around the planet Faith, the third planet of the Retribution system. Michael grimaced at the sight. Faith nearspace was not new to him. He had been there before, in *Eridani,* ironically one of a task group led by none other than the totally pissed Perkins. *Eridani* had been lucky to get back in one piece from that incursion, though that had not been Perkins's fault to be fair.

"Captain, sir. I have all green suits, ship is at general quarters, ship state 1, airtight condition zulu, artificial gravity off, ship depressurized," Ferreira said, a brave attempt at a smile visible through the plasglass faceplate of her combat space suit. "I'll be with the coxswain and the rest of the damage control crew, all one of him."

Michael chuckled; a conventional heavy cruiser's damage control team numbered in the hundreds. "Command, roger. You hang in there, Jayla. All stations, stand by to drop. Warfare. Confirm weapons free. You have command authority."

"Warfare, roger. Weapons free. I have command authority."

Michael flicked a glance at Perkins while the drop timer ran down; the man had not moved, a glowering lump of unhappiness at the back of the combat information center. A quick check confirmed that the two AIs responsible for threat assessment and operations were ready. Michael called them Kubby and Kal after the ships they came from, the long-scrapped K-Class heavy cruisers *Kuibyshev* and *Kaladima*. To maintain the illusion that they were real people, he had ordered his neuronics to integrate their whole-body avatars into his vision. The human factors wonks assured him that this would help absorb the intense stress of combat. Looking at them, two anonymous combat space-suited shapes sitting on either side of him, he was not so sure. However solid their avatars appeared, however real their space-suited figures might seem, he knew Kubby and Kal to be figments of his neuronics' imagination. Even with them, it was a small team to run a dreadnought's combat information center.

Using AIs in such mission-critical roles represented the big unknown. Brought out of retirement, they had decades of combat experience in heavy cruisers, but this was something different. Michael was surprised by their enthusiasm for their new roles as his principal advisers. Did AIs get bored in retirement? Officially, no: endless hours in Fleet's StratSim facility ensured that retired AIs stayed current, yet Michael did wonder. Anyway, what was important was that Kubby and Kal had worked well in the sims; Michael hoped they would perform as well when they faced real Hammers firing real missiles and rail-gun slugs.

But Kubby and Kal were only advisers: They had no command authority and would not be giving any orders. The biggest gamble of all remained trusting Warfare, the AI tasked with overall battle management. It was no adviser. When the attack degenerated into freewheeling bedlam— and it would—and space filled with blizzards of rail-guns slugs, missiles, and decoys, when sensors started to collapse under torrents of conflicting information dumped on them by decoys, jammers, and spoofers, the job of battle management slipped beyond the ability of humans. Only the AI had the processing power to cope; only it could make the millions of decisions needed to keep *Tufayl* safe while its enemies were put to the sword. It was a big task, and the lives of all onboard *Tufayl* depended on Warfare getting it right without the benefit of a full combat information center crew to keep an eye on things, looking for those moments when the AIs messed things up—as they always had and always would.

Tufayl dropped into normalspace with the usual gut-wrenching lurch. In an instant, things turned busy, the proximity alarms screeching to warn of Hammer ships close to the drop datum.

Michael ignored them. The Hammer ships were supposed to be close. He forced himself to wait while the ship's sensors rebuilt the threat plot, *Tufayl*'s artificial gravity pushing him deep into his seat when it came back online. Michael breathed easier; the positions of the Hammer ships had changed in the time it took *Tufayl* to microjump out-system, reverse vector, and microjump back, but not so much that the ops plan was compromised. The Hammer ships—a gaggle of cruisers and smaller warships—clustered around HSBS-261, one of the Hammer space battle stations that protected Faith planetary nearspace.

"Command, Warfare. Threat plot is confirmed." The AI's

voice was calm and untroubled, as if this were just another day in the simulators. "Executing Alfa-1."

Armored hatches opened. In seconds, hydraulic dispensers dumped thousands of decoys overboard, stubby black cylinders forming up into a huge cloud of electronic deceit driven ahead of the ship toward the Hammers by thin pillars of fire.

"Executing Alfa-2."

Tufayl leaped forward as though smashed in the ass by a giant fist. The dreadnought shuddered, accelerating hard to follow the decoy cloud toward the Hammers.

"Executing Alfa-3."

Krachov generators started spewing millions upon millions of tiny disks out into space, tiny black shapes fired ahead of the ship to form a shield to screen the *Tufayl* from Hammer sensors and diffuse antiship laser fire.

Michael struggled to breathe. He understood why Perkins was so unhappy with his plan for this operation. *Tufayl* was about to break most of the rules in the Fighting Instructions, one of which was that single-ship attacks on targets as tough as battle stations were not a good idea, but Perkins had never taken a dreadnought into battle.

"Command, sensors. Multiple Hammer missile launches. Eaglehawk ASSMs. Target *Tufayl*"—bloody AIs, Michael complained under his breath; who else would the damn target be? There wasn't another Fed warship anywhere near Faith—"time to target forty-nine seconds."

"Command, roger. Threat, warhead assess—"

Perkins's voice stopped Michael in his tracks. "This is a direct order, Helfort. Abort!" Perkins's voice rose to a near shriek. "Do you hear me? Abort now!"

"You son of a bitch," Michael whispered, "I don't need this." He shut down Perkins's com links to the rest of the ship; if the man wanted to rant, he could rant to himself. "Coxswain to the CIC!" he barked, turning his attention back to the more pressing problems facing *Tufayl*.

"Threat, what's your warhead assessment?"

"Missiles are chemex-armed," Kal replied confidently. "Hammer ships are inside the blast-damage radius for antimatter weapons, and this far inside planetary nearspace, fusion warheads are unlikely."

"Yes," Michael whispered exultantly. His gamble might pay off. He just hoped he and Kal—the AI handling threat assessment—had called it right. *Tufayl* was tough but not invulnerable. Fusion warheads could destroy even a dreadnought if they exploded close to it.

"Sir?" Bienefelt appeared in front of him, enormous in her armored combat space suit.

"Get back and strap yourself in alongside Admiral Perkins. He is not to leave his seat until I say he can. I authorize you to restrain him if you need to, using as much force as is reasonably required."

"Sir?" Understandably, Bienefelt sounded baffled. It was not every day a chief petty officer was called on to restrain an admiral.

"Just do it, 'Swain!" Michael snapped. "Make sure the admiral stays in his damn seat. If he tries to get out, sit on him. That's a direct order."

"Sir!"

Michael turned away, more unnerved by having to deal with Perkins than by the Hammer attack.

"Command, Warfare, sensors. Hammers have launched multiple rail-gun swarms. Impact in twenty-one seconds. Stand by impact assessment."

In times past, the prospect of facing a Hammer rail-gun attack would have turned Michael's stomach inside out, but not this time. *Tufayl*'s forward sections carried three times the armor of a conventional heavy cruiser, the extra mass compensated for by the tens of thousands of tons of redundant systems, equipment, landers, and spares taken out of her during the conversion. *Tufayl* would be long gone before the Hammers fired enough rail-gun slugs to penetrate her forward armor.

"Command, Warfare. Executing Alfa-4. Emergency override main propulsion!"

Tufayl's enormous mass shook as Warfare pushed her main engines to and then beyond their limits, tons of reaction mass driven out astern into thin columns of white fire

that were kilometers long. Michael forced himself to breathe
properly. This was the big roll of the dice. *Tufayl* accelerated faster than any cruiser should, and if the Hammers did
not pick it up quickly and update their targeting solutions,
the missile salvos would turn in too late to make their final
attacks. They would attack where they thought *Tufayl* should
be, not where she was. Wasted, the missiles would die a useless death in the pillars of fiery hell spewing from *Tufayl*'s
stern.

If . . .

"Command, sensors. Impact assessment. Estimate twenty
to thirty rail-gun slugs on vector for direct impact."

Michael braced himself. He had faith in *Tufayl*'s reinforced frontal armor, but thirty rail-gun slugs was one hell
of a lot of kinetic energy for the ship to absorb. Closing
at more than 800 kilometers per second, each slug would
smash the equivalent of hundreds of kilograms of TNT
onto a fingertip-size patch of *Tufayl*'s hull. The old familiar
feelings came back—stomach churning, heart racing out of
control, mouth and throat ash-dry, body slicked with a cold,
clammy sweat—returning with a rush when he remembered how bad rail-gun attacks could be.

"Threat. Hammer missile status?"

"Turning in now. Stand by . . . second stages firing . . .
vectors confirmed. *Tufayl* is outside missile engagement
envelope."

"Roger." Michael tried not to sound relieved, but he was.
He had seen enough action to know that what worked in
theory, what worked in the sims, often did not work in
practice.

"All stations, warfare. Brace for rail-gun impact."

Tufayl's close-in defenses—defensive lasers, short-range
missiles, and chain guns—did their best but failed to keep
the Hammer rail-gun attack out. Too many slugs screened
by too many decoys moved too fast, and when they hit, the
impact was tremendous, much worse than Michael had
expected. With *Tufayl*'s artificial gravity overloaded, his seat
fought—and failed—to insulate him from the shock. In a
fraction of a second, twenty-six rail-guns slugs smashed into

Tufayl's bows, the ship bucking and heaving when the slugs blew huge craters in the bows. Soon the ship disappeared behind a vast cloud of vaporized ceramsteel armor.

Tufayl shrugged off the Hammer attack. Still accelerating hard, she punched out into clear space, the Krachov shield screening them blown apart by the Hammer attack. Michael whistled in surprise; they were so close, and *Tufayl*'s attack so sudden, that he picked out the shapes of Hammer spacers working outside the battle station's enormous hull racing to get back inside to safety.

"Brace yourselves, you Hammer sonsofbitches," he murmured, "because you haven't seen anything yet."

"Executing Alfa-5. Launching missiles, lasers engaging primary target. Shutting down main engines. All stations. Stand by to jump."

Tufayl shuddered as hydraulics rammed Merlin ASSMs outboard, their first stages firing the instant the full salvo was assembled. The combat information center fell quiet, and *Tufayl* coasted on, the frantic attempts of the Hammer ships' lasers to exploit the damage to her bows ignored, her own massive antiship lasers in turn flaying the armor off two Hammer ships—the heavy cruisers *Keating* and *Persepolis*—unlucky enough to be caught stern on, both spewing clouds of reaction mass in their struggle to turn to face the attack. Michael watched in grim satisfaction when the armor of both ships failed, *Tufayl*'s antiship lasers exploiting their vulnerable sterns to bore white-hot holes into their hulls. The lasers broke through the armor and reached deep inside, probing for the ships' fusion plants. Seconds later, the lasers found their targets; in quick succession, first *Keating* and then *Persepolis* lost containment, their fusion plants exploding into balls of blue-white gas.

"Command, Warfare. Firing rail guns." *Tufayl* trembled when her forward batteries sent a full salvo of slugs on its way, timed to arrive on target seconds before the missile salvo hit home.

"Warfare, time to go."

"Stand by. Confirming ship's mass distribution."

Michael nodded. If the navigation AI jumped the ship

without an accurate estimate of the mass blasted off by Hammer rail-guns, the *Tufayl* might well end up anywhere in deepspace, including—though the odds were not high—inside something hard and unforgiving, such as an asteroid. He forced himself to sit still and watch *Tufayl*'s missile and rail-gun attack, backed up by the full weight of her forward laser batteries, fall on the heavily armored space battle station. He nodded his approval. It was a textbook attack, timed to the split second, accurate to a few meters, and focused on the station's most vulnerable point: the huge air lock doors accessing the hangars where the station stowed its air wing.

The strike dissolved into confusion. Too late, the remaining Hammer ships and the station shifted their focus from the dreadnought, concentrating their defense on hacking *Tufayl*'s missiles and rail-gun slugs out of space, their successes marked by vicious flares of wasted energy. Too few; their efforts were in vain. Michael stared at the holovid as the attack broke through the Hammer defenses. Rail-gun slugs and missiles slammed home, the battle station disappearing behind great sheets of incandescent armor blown off into space. He held his breath, cursing out loud when the station reappeared. Though its outer air lock door had been blown open, the hangar inside a blackened ruin, it seemed undamaged.

"Command. Mass distribution model is confirmed. Request approval to jump."

Reluctantly, Michael dragged his attention back to the problem of getting *Tufayl* home safely, never an easy task. *Tufayl* was jumping from inside Faith's gravity well; it was not far enough to risk the ship but far enough to make getting back to Comdur a challenging exercise in navigation. And if that was not bad enough, the ship was traveling faster than the optimum for an accurate pinchspace jump.

Quickly, Michael confirmed that the ship was ready. He said a quick prayer that they would not end up in the heart of a wandering asteroid and gave the order.

Tufayl jumped, the briefest of brief flashes of ultraviolet marking her leap into pinchspace.

Only moments after *Tufayl* departed Faith nearspace, a small red flare flickered out of the battle station's hangar air lock. In seconds, the flare grew into a raging jet, driving out into space and broadening out as it gathered power, red rapidly bleaching into white. The station shuddered, its millions of tons of mass shifted bodily planetward by the force of an explosion that spewed debris in an ugly red and black cloud. A second and a third explosion followed, their vectors perfectly aligned to push the station into a ponderous death roll out of orbit and down to the planet's surface far below.

In Faith farspace, Fed reconsats recorded the death of the Hammer battle station, the holovid transmitted by tightbeam laser through a network of relaysats to the mass tanker waiting patiently in deepspace for *Tufayl*'s arrival.

Michael allowed himself to relax only when the navigation AI—after an agonizingly long wait—finally decided where the *Tufayl* had ended up after its desperate microjump out of Faith's gravity well.

"Command, navigation."

"Command."

"Ship's position confirmed. On the screen."

Michael studied it carefully before nodding his approval, relieved that *Tufayl* would not be forced to send out a pinchcomm signal asking for help. The public admission that a ship's navigation had not lived up to Fleet's unforgiving standards was always an embarrassing business. No, *Tufayl*'s navigation AI had done well: Under the circumstances, it was not the best bit of space navigation, nor was it the worst. They had ended up a long way from where they were supposed to be, but they had enough mass for the ship to adjust vector before microjumping back to rendezvous with their mass tanker. Ordering the navigation AI to set vector, he handed the ship over to Ferreira with orders to stand down from general quarters and climbed wearily out of his seat.

He steeled himself for the coming confrontation. He was

out of time; it was necessary to deal with the problem of Rear Admiral Perkins. He made his way aft to where Bienefelt and Perkins sat.

"Thank you, 'Swain. You can carry on."

"Sir!"

Michael waited until Bienefelt left before addressing Perkins; the man had not said a word throughout the attack.

"Sir," he said, "Once you're out of your suit, I think it best if we continue in my cabin."

Without a word, Perkins climbed out of his seat. He brushed past Michael and left the combat information center. Michael watched him go. A petulant flag officer was not what he needed. He was exhausted; the adrenaline-fueled high of combat was seeping slowly away, leaving him feeling flat and wrung out.

"I'll be in my cabin, Jayla."

"Sir," Ferreira said.

Michael did not have to wait long. He had just enough time to shower and change into a fresh shipsuit before Perkins walked into his day cabin, unannounced. Without a word, he sat down in one of the armchairs. Michael took a seat opposite him.

"Something to drink, sir?"

Perkins refused to respond, his face flushed with anger.

"Well, sir," Michael said, deciding on the spur of the moment to act as if nothing untoward had happened, "any feedback on the operation?"

Perkins stared for a moment, his blue eyes flinty chips of disdain. "If you think I'm going to ignore your act of gross insubordination," he said icily, "you are very much mistaken, Helfort. It seems you have no idea what military discipline is all about."

"Sir," Michael said despairingly, hands out in a vain attempt to placate the man, "you knew the rules. We both had the order, a written order. I had absolutely no problem understanding it. None at all. The admiral's order was unambiguous. You were here to observe, sir. Nothing more. So forgive me, but I fail to understand how my actions could be considered insubordination."

Why, Michael wanted to say, would an experienced, combat-proven commander disobey Vice Admiral Jaruzelska's direct order, an order given—most unusually—in hard copy and written in language so simple that not even the most inept spacer could misconstrue it?

"Because, Helfort, there's a lot more to keeping the Federated Worlds secure than you will ever know. I don't expect you to understand. You are only a lieutenant, after all," Perkins said, his speech deliberate, his face split by a patronizing smile, "and a junior and an inexperienced one at that. For that reason, when I make my report to Admiral Jaruzelska, I am prepared to recommend that no further action be taken. Just this once."

That's real decent of you, you sanctimonious bastard, Michael said to himself, stifling an urge to remind Perkins that yes, he was an inexperienced lieutenant, but he, too, had commanded ships in combat, and successfully.

"Sir, I did not disobey the admiral's orders. I trust that you will make that clear in your report."

"Don't make things worse than they already are, Lieutenant"—Michael seethed at the insult; irrespective of his military rank, tradition required Perkins to address him as Captain or Lieutenant Helfort—"though that does seem to be one of your gifts."

Michael said nothing; if he did, he knew he would regret it. Unless he had misunderstood Jaruzelska's orders—and he knew he had not—he was not the one at fault here; Perkins would be the one trying to explain to the admiral why her orders had not been obeyed.

"That's all that needs to be said." Perkins stood up. "I'll be in my cabin until we return to Comdur. I'd be obliged if you would send my meals there."

"Yes, sir. I'll see to it."

"Be sure that you do," Perkins said dismissively.

Michael watched Perkins leave. What a prick; the man might be an admiral, but Lieutenant Michael Wallace

Helfort was the duly appointed captain in command of a Federated Worlds warship. Jaruzelska's orders had been crystal clear, and if Perkins had refused to follow those orders, that was his problem.

An hour later, he had written up his report of the incident. He sealed it for Jaruzelska's eyes only and turned in.

Friday, December 15, 2400, UD
Dreadnought Project Conference Room,
Comdur Fleet Base

"So to sum up, I think it is fair to say that the Faith operation was a stunning success. A well-conceived operation, brilliantly executed. A space battle station is the toughest target there is, and to take one out with a single ship is an outstanding result, something which no Fed cruiser has ever been able to pull off. Let's be clear. The dreadnought has come of age."

Jaruzelska waited patiently while a mix of cheers and applause ran through the crowded conference room. She understood the enthusiastic response. For the spacers present, *Tufayl*'s stunning success represented much more than a long-overdue reminder to the Hammers that the Feds were staying in the fight. More important, *Tufayl*'s success validated their commitment to an increasingly unpopular cause.

Slowly, the noise died away.

"Before I call it a day, there is one more thing. Lieutenant Helfort, I'd like you up here with me, please."

Baffled, Michael made his way to the front of the conference room.

"Right. I am pleased to be able to report that the commander in chief has issued a unit citation to the *Tufayl* and its crew for the Faith operation. My congratulations. I—"

Jaruzelska stopped, her words drowned in an avalanche of cheers, every spacer present coming to his or her feet.

It took a while, but the noise finally died away.

"Okay, folks. Thanks. Things went well at Faith, but there are always lessons to be learned. I'll release the after-action report today. Time of the follow-up review to be advised. That's all, folks. Michael, with me."

"Sir."

Leaving the conference room, the two officers walked back to Jaruzelska's office, neither saying a word. Closing the door, Jaruzelska waved Michael into a chair.

"I don't think I have to tell you why you're here."

Michael shook his head ruefully. "I'm only guessing, sir, but let me see. Does it involve Rear Admiral Perkins?"

"Yes." Jaruzelska leaned back, hands running through her hair before rubbing eyes red-rimmed with fatigue. "I'm sorry to say it does. Anyway, let's get this out of the way. I have forwarded my report on the matter to the commander in chief together with a recommendation that no further action be taken."

"Oh," Michael said. For a moment he was at a loss for words. Had he heard Jaruzelska correctly? "Hang on, sir," he said. "No further action? I don't understand. How's tha—"

"Michael, that's my recommendation," Jaruzelska said. "No further action."

"Sir! I understand that, but I'm sorry," Michael said doggedly. "The admiral disobeyed a direct order in the combat information center of a warship during combat . . . in the face of the enemy! Not my order, sir, yours. And I had to deal with it while the Hammers hurled missiles and rail-gun slugs at us"—Michael's voice started to rise—"so how can there be no furth—"

"Enough!" Jaruzelska snapped, cutting him off in midstream. "Goddamn it, Helfort, there are times . . ." She breathed carefully in and then out before continuing. "Look," she said, her voice softening, "you have to trust me on this. I don't want . . . no, that's wrong. Right now, I cannot afford to get into an open fight with the antidreadnought faction, and that is exactly what I'll get if I take any formal action in response to the admiral's . . . um . . . the admiral's behavior. Believe me, I don't, and nor do you. I spend far too much time as it is fighting to keep them in their damn box. So you get back to *Tufayl* and forget it ever happened. Okay? That's a suggestion, by the way. Don't make me turn it into an order, which," she said, her voice hardening, "I will if I have to."

Reluctantly, Michael nodded. "Yes, sir," he said. "Sorry. What happened was just . . . so wrong, sir."

"I know how wrong it was, so there's no need to apologize. I'll make sure it does not happen again." She paused. "Michael, there's something you need to understand."

"What's that, sir?"

"The day you stop trusting me is the day we—you and me—fail. I don't have another Michael Helfort, and you know as well as I do that we have to make dreadnoughts work. The Faith operation shows me we are just about there, but don't underestimate the bull—" Jaruzelska stopped herself. "Well, let's just say you're not the only one fighting the good fight. You do your bit and let me do mine."

"Yes, sir," Michael said, ashamed that he had doubted her, if only for a moment. "I trust you, sir. You must know that."

"I do. Moving on. It won't happen again because Rear Admiral Perkins will not be space riding in *Tufayl* unless I am there, too, something I don't have the time for."

"Thank you, sir," Michael said with some feeling.

"Don't mention it," the admiral replied. "One more thing. I've finally organized your Block 6 lander. Fleet will advise you exactly when, but it looks like it will arrive later this month."

Michael perked up. "Ah, that is good news, sir. Places we're going, it'll be good to have another way to get home. Attacking that battle station with just the one ship was a lonely business. If things had gone wrong . . ." Michael's voice trailed off.

"I know; sorry about that. Pity *Elusory* lived up to her name. Next time I'll task two ships for casualty recovery . . . if I can find the ships to task, that is. By the way, not aborting the operation when *Elusory* went unserviceable? That was a gutsy call, Michael. Very gutsy."

Michael nodded. More than you know, Admiral, he said

to himself. At the time, he could not shake off the awful thought he might fall back into Hammer hands; only his unshakable faith in *Tufayl* and her crew had persuaded him to push on without a ship standing by to rescue them if things went wrong.

Jaruzelska broke what had turned into a long silence. "How will you use the lander?"

"Well, sir. Without marines, it's really there as a backup ship. As for live ops, I've been running through the options. The sims have confirmed that my best choice is to deploy the lander to one of the unmanned ships prior to an attack; that way, I can use it for casualty recovery if anything goes wrong with the *Tufayl*. Diversionary attacks, decoy work, and limited ground assault operations are some of the other things I'm looking at."

Jaruzelska's eyebrow shot up. "Ah! Let me guess. If you're going to send your Block 6 into harm's way, you'll be wanting to keep the old lander," she said, "just in case. Am I right?"

"Of course you are, sir," Michael replied cheerfully. "To paraphrase an old saying, you never know when a spare lander might come in handy!"

The admiral laughed. "I don't know a spacer who would argue with that, so I won't, and I don't think Fleet will, either. I'll authorize the change to the master equipment list. Unless there's anything else . . . no? Right. I think it's time for a drink, don't you?"

"Yes, sir."

As the shuttle taking Michael back to *Tufayl* lifted off, Ferreira commed him.

"Yes, Jayla?"

"Com from Fleet, sir. Seems we are going to get our heavy lander at last."

"Ah, yes. The admiral just gave me a heads-up. When?"

"Twentieth, sir."

"Good. What about the crew?"

"I'll com you the personnel files when I get them. The command pilot is a Junior Lieutenant Sedova, Kat Sedova."

"Know her?"

"Of her, sir."

"And?"

"All good, sir. Outstanding, in fact. She'll be a real asset."

"Let's hope so."

"Well, sir. If the admiral had any say in her selection, I'd be pretty sure she's one of the best."

"I would, too. See you shortly."

Tuesday, December 19, 2400, UD
Offices of the Supreme Council for the
Preservation of the Faith, McNair

Chief Councillor Polk tilted his chair back, the better to see out of the enormous plasglass window that filled one wall of his office. The view did nothing to lift his mood. It was a miserable day, rain sheeting down, the gardens' brilliant colors crushed under a gray sky that was darkening with the approach of night. What a difference a few months made, he thought. Back in October, he believed the Kraa-damned Feds were finished, he really did.

Now he was not so sure.

He scowled for a moment before an innate faith in himself reasserted itself. Maybe he should not be so pessimistic. Maybe the Feds were history. The armistice was a farce. The Hammers still had the whip hand over the Feds, and if his military was even half-right, it was just a matter of time before the Hammer flogged them back to the negotiating table. Since the Hammer fleet had lifted the operational tempo, the Feds had found themselves in trouble right across their sphere of influence: trade disrupted, citizens close to panic at the threat of mass destruction—the concept of mutually assured destruction did not sit too well with the average Fed—all compounded by hit-and-run attacks on targets of opportunity.

Yes, it had been a good month for the Hammer of Kraa, and the Feds had floundered in responding. They had only one result: the destruction of one of Faith's battle stations after an attack so reckless that it verged on the suicidal. Polk watched the holovid of the Fed attack; he had never seen anything like it. Admiral Jorge had not been able to explain just how the heavy cruiser—*Tufayl,* that was its name—had managed to escape; by rights, the ship should have been blown to Kraa. Polk reminded himself to ask the intelligence people who the captain was; whoever it was, he was a brave—albeit terminally stupid—man.

Not that the *Tufayl* operation mattered; all it showed was just how desperate the Feds were. They would never win the war by throwing heavy cruisers at space battle stations one at a time, though he was happy to see them try. This time, *Tufayl* and the Feds had been lucky; next time they tried the same stunt, they would not be.

Yes, he decided, suddenly reenergized, he should be more positive, he really should.

His good spirits did not last long, his newfound confidence shattered by the diffident tones of his secretary.

"Chief Councillor. Teacher Calverson is here for his meeting, sir."

Kraa damn it, Polk raged, he had clean forgotten. As a matter of principle, he avoided Calverson like the plague.

"Please ask him to come in. And send in coffee."

Sour-faced, he watched the man enter his office, a black-robed specter hung with the thick gold chain and sunburst of the Hammer of Kraa's highest spiritual office.

"Good day, Teacher Calverson," Polk said, getting to his feet and going around his desk to shake Calverson's hand before waving the man to take an armchair, fixing a smile he hoped did not look totally false onto his face.

"Kraa's peace be with you, Chief Councillor," Calverson said, sitting down.

"Thank you, Teacher," Polk said, sitting down, trying not to grind his teeth. Polk despised Calverson; the man was rat-cunning, an intellectual pygmy, his mind clogged with all the superstitious nonsense spewed out of the deranged imagination of the Faith of Kraa's founder, Peter McNair. As religions went, the whole Hammer of Kraa thing was a crock of shit, yet Calverson was its chief acolyte and a powerful man, the enormous machine that delivered the teachings of Kraa to the people of the Hammer Worlds secure in his iron grip. Polk might despise him, but Calverson could not be ignored.

Polk licked suddenly dry lips. One word from Teacher Calverson and within hours a hundred thousand priests and millions of credulous primitives would be calling for his dismissal. That was why Calverson was one of the few people Polk feared. The problem was that Calverson knew it.

After the steward served coffee and left, Polk opened the proceedings. "The briefing note from my chief of staff says you want to discuss the situation on Salvation," he said with a warmth he did not feel, "but I'm confused, Teacher. It is years since the heretics on Salvation fell from the grace of Kraa. Why are we concerned about them?"

Calverson's angular face creased with concern. "Because, Chief Councillor," he said in the tones of a father speaking to a dim-witted son, "those poor souls on Salvation are still of the Faith, and it is our duty to bring them back"—Calverson's finger stabbed out—"otherwise they cannot enjoy the protection of the Faith of Kraa. They will be damned for all eternity. We owe it to them to bring them back, whether they like it or not."

What arrant, self-serving nonsense, Polk wanted to say. Wisely, he confined himself to a nod of agreement. "Yes, you are of course quite right, Teacher Calverson. There is no provision in doctrine for apostasy. But, there is the small problem of how we do that. Bring them back, I mean. Salvation is—what?—170 light-years away? That puts it well inside the Fed sphere of influence. The last time we tried to retrieve the heretics, the . . . well, let's just say the operation wasn't a complete success. In any event, I'm not sure the Worlds are in any position to carry out the operation you're asking for."

"Chief Councillor. I am but a humble priest"—with an effort, Polk suppressed a snort of derision—"but I read the strategic assessments provided by your office with great care. Even if they have antimatter weapons, I cannot remember a time when the Federated Worlds found themselves in such trouble, when our strategic advantage was so great. Our attack on Comdur dealt them a blow from which they may never recover. Am I right?" Calverson said.

"Yes, you are, Teacher Calverson," Polk conceded.

"Excellent, Chief Councillor," Calverson said, beaming. "So let's move. We must act while we can. Kraa demands it."

Polk knew defeat when he saw it, so he gave up. "Yes, Teacher Calverson, I absolutely agree with you on this. Let me talk to Councillor Jones and Admiral Jorge. When the planners have worked out how we can recover Salvation's heretics, I'll arrange a briefing for you."

Calverson's eyes narrowed. "I'll expect it a week from today," he said. "I think that should be enough time, don't you?"

"Yes, Teacher Calverson," Polk said through gritted teeth, wondering how he was ever going to justify an attack on a neutral world, never mind the diversion of Fleet assets to pursue something so pointless. For Kraa's sake! Only a narrow-minded priest would worry about a few heretics in the middle of a shooting war with the Feds.

Wednesday, December 20, 2400, UD
FWSS Tufayl, Comdur Fleet Base nearspace

"*Tufayl*, this is Comdur Command."

"*Tufayl*," Ferreira said.

"For your information, reporting the arrival in Comdur nearspace of heavy lander *PHLA-442566*, Junior Lieutenant Sedova in command, inbound from New Dawn. We've cleared *566* on a direct vector to you. Confirm ready to take tactical control?"

"Confirmed."

"Roger. Chopping tacon of *PHLA-442566* to *Tufayl*."

"*Tufayl*, roger. *Tufayl* has tacon of *566,* out. Command, copy?" Ferreira said, glancing across at Michael.

"Copied." Michael nodded, pleased to see that his new lander had made a good start, arriving on time to the second.

"Command, Warfare; *566* is on vector, cleared for direct approach. ETA 15:45."

"Command, roger," Michael said. "*PHLA-442566*, this is *Tufayl* on vidcomm channel 34, over."

"*Tufayl, 566,*" the lander's command pilot replied, "go ahead."

"Okay to talk?"

"Yes, sir. We're established on vector."

"Good. Welcome to Comdur, *566,*" Michael said, looking with interest at the latest addition to his crew, a cheerful-looking woman with an open, friendly face framed by her combat space helmet, a few rebellious strands of ash-blond hair peeking out from underneath the helmet's molded crash-foam lining.

"Thank you, sir," she said. "Junior Lieutenant Kat Sedova at your service."

"Good to have you with us. Flight okay?"

"One for the record books, sir."

"Oh?"

"Longest pinchspace flight by a vessel less than five hundred tons empty mass," Sedova said, smiling broadly. "A touch over 16 light-years. We didn't just break the record, we completely trashed it. The flight was five times longer than any previous flight by a jump-capable lander."

Michael's eyebrows shot up. "Congratulations. Impressive."

"Scary more like it, sir. Bloody scary, in fact, given the Block 6's less than stellar reputation."

"Ah, yes. Bit of a gut churner, I would imagine." Michael did not need to say any more. Sedova would have had good reason to feel nervous. Development of the Block 6 heavy lander had been a long and troubled process, culminating in the loss of the first manned pinchspace test flight. The lander had broken up when it reentered normalspace, killing the crew, a shockingly unexpected accident that drove the lander's chief designer to suicide. It took another five years and billions of FedMarks before the appallingly complex pinchspace generators squeezed into the lander's hull to create humanspace's smallest starship were certified safe to carry humans into pinchspace.

"Must admit it was," Sedova said. "But the *Ghost* did really well. The pinchspace generators never blinked. Rocksteady the whole time. No, sir, the *Ghost*'s a good one."

"Ah, yes," Michael said, "I was going to ask. So you've christened your ship?"

"I certainly have, sir. *Caesar's Ghost.*"

"You spend too much time studying ancient literature, I suspect," Michael said with a chuckle when his neuronics tracked down where the name came from.

"Something like that, sir."

"Sounds fine to me, so *Caesar's Ghost* it is. At least I won't have Fleet objecting. Anyway," Michael continued, "I'll leave you alone for the moment. We'll talk more when you've berthed."

"Sir."

Tufayl's combat information center was quiet, all eyes focused on the heavy assault lander filling the command holovid. Michael watched intently as *Caesar's Ghost* closed in. It was not an attractive sight. In Michael's opinion, assault landers had to be one of the ugliest machines ever sent into space by humankind. Brutally functional, the lander was a wedge nearly as broad as it was long, with a rounded nose and sliced flat across the stern, its matte-black shape broken by laser and rotary cannon turrets, landing gear, sensors, stub aerials, heat dump panels, and hatches, all strewn seemingly at random across its armored skin. Heavy assault landers were certainly fit for their purpose, but with the aerodynamics of a large ceramcrete block, they were neither elegant nor pretty; the fact that the machine flew at all was a tribute to the enormous power of its twin fusion-powered mass drivers.

But Michael loved them, right down to the last bolt. His

only ambition had been to be a lander command pilot. Not
that he would ever get the chance the way things were going.

"*Tufayl*, *Caesar's Ghost*. On final approach."

"*Tufayl*, roger. Approved to dock."

Sedova brought the *Ghost* to a precise stop a few meters
off the armored doors accessing *Tufayl*'s hangar. Michael
was impressed; the difference in vectors was only a few mil-
limeters per second. Reaction control nozzles flared, and the
lander drifted smoothly into the hangar air lock.

"You have the ship, Jayla," Michael said. "I'm going
down to meet our new arrivals."

"Aye, aye, sir. I have the ship."

"Welcome to *Tufayl*," Michael said, lifting his beer in
salute.

"Thank you, sir," Sedova said, raising her glass in reply.
"It's good to be here, though . . . can I be frank?"

"Of course. Shoot."

"Well, sir, I don't understand why dreadnoughts need
jump-capable landers. Our primary mission is interdiction
operations against low-level, low-density threats, acting as a
force extender. We're also good for remote, small-scale dirtside operations in support of the marines. As I understand it,
dreadnoughts are intended to take on high-level threats, targets too risky even for conventional cruisers. I cannot see
how we fit into a frontal assault on something like a Hammer
battle fleet deploying antimatter weapons, for example, nor
can we operate in high-threat missile and rail-gun environ-
ments. Assault landers are tough but not that tough. We
wouldn't last five minutes. So what exactly is our role?"

The minute Fleet approved the deployment of Block 6
landers to his dreadnoughts, Michael knew he would be
asked that question. Now he had, and by someone he suspected would not respond well to a serving of bullshit.

"Why? Well, it depends," Michael said, weighing his words
carefully, "and I am not ducking the question when I say that.
The decision made by Fleet to give each manned dreadnought a lander was politics. Pure politics"—he could not
help noticing Sedova's hastily suppressed frown—"because

Fleet was concerned that the cuts in crew size had been taken too far. So we had to increase the numbers. There are plenty of landers in our order of battle, so—"

"Why not make use of them?" Sedova interrupted with a touch of bitterness. "That's what I was afraid of."

"Steady, Lieutenant," Michael said.

Sedova's face reddened. "Sorry, sir. Excuse me."

Much as he disapproved of her bluntness, Michael understood her frustration. Nobody minded being asked to a job, however tough. But professionals did mind—rightly—being asked to undertake missions for purely political reasons.

"As I was saying, expediency and politics is where this started. But it's not where it ends."

"Oh?"

"No," Michael said with a firm shake of his head. "No, it's not. Once we knew we were getting a Block 6 lander, we started to look at how we would get the best out of it. You're right. Unless you and your crew are willing to commit suicide, there's no part for you in a conventional frontal assault. Like you say, you would not last five minutes. But for operations that take dreadnoughts deep into enemy space, operations where conventional ship losses would be unacceptably high, we will need you to get out alive. So that's one mission."

"What are you saying, sir? We're a glorified lifepod?" Sedova said. "That's it? That's all we are?"

"No, that's just the bad news. I thought I'd better get it out of the way first"—Michael was pleased to see that Sedova was still able to smile—"but given the places we'll be going to, don't be surprised if you have to fight your way out."

Sedova nodded.

"Much more importantly," Michael continued, "there is a role in taking down heavily defended targets too big for dreadnoughts alone to take care of. Asteroid-based support facilities are a prime example; there are a lot of them out there we've never even thrown a rock at. Fleet does not consider them a priority, and rightly so: too small to be worth the ships needed to get through their nearspace defenses. But dreadnoughts can, and with a lot fewer ships. *Tufayl*'s proved that. Once their defenses have been cracked, these support bases are sitting ducks. They only have platoon-sized security forces—they've never needed anything bigger—and your lander can drop more than enough marines in to finish them off after we've destroyed their space-based defenses. That's what *Tufayl* and her sisters are good at, and we can do it with far fewer ships. In many cases just one dreadnought will finish the job. But we cannot get in to finish the mission. That'll require you."

Michael waited patiently while Sedova mulled that over. "That all makes sense, sir," she said finally, "except that we don't carry marines. No point cracking open a dirtside target unless we can send the grunts in to do whatever it is they do when we're not watching."

"True, we don't. But I've talked to Admiral Jaruzelska about that. She has confirmed that we will carry marines when we need to. They won't like it much, but we can carry as many as you like in temporary living modules in the hangar. We're a long way from our mass limits."

"Still, sir, it's a long way from taking on antimatter-armed Hammer ships."

"It is. But that will be only one of our missions. Dreadnoughts are brand-new, so it will be up to us to write the tactical handbooks on how to use them. There's a lot more we can do, and Admiral Jaruzelska is not one to leave us sitting around scratching our asses. I think we'll find plenty to keep you occupied once we're let off the leash."

"I hope so, sir. I did not become a command pilot to sit around waiting for something to happen."

"I didn't think so. And guess what?"

"What, sir?"

"I didn't become captain in command of a dreadnought to sit around, either. Trust me, Lieutenant. We'll be busy, and so will you."

Friday, December 29, 2400, UD
Offices of the Supreme Council for the
Preservation of the Faith, McNair

"To summarize. The operation to return the heretics of Salvation to the Faith is scheduled for the end of January. Supported by a task group, the planetary assault vessels *Kerouac* and *Mitsotaki* will drop three marine brigades onto Salvation to secure the city of New Hope and its spaceport. Once they are secure, a DocSec brigade will round up and evacuate the heretics. We expect the operation to be completed in less than two days, enough time before the Federated Worlds can respond in force. That concludes my briefing, gentlemen. Does anyone have any questions?"

Fleet Admiral Jorge's eyes flitted across the councillors seated around the Defense Council table. "No? Chief Councillor?"

"No, Admiral. That sounds good to me. Moving along," Polk said. "Next item. Operations against the Feds. Admiral?"

"Thank you, sir. If you turn your attention to the holovid, you can see a summary of the week's operations. It has been a successful week, I have to say, an outstanding week in fact. The Feds stayed quiet, continuing their focus on defensive operations. We were more active. Coordinated antishipping operations around the Paderborn, Xiang, and Vijati reefs successfully disrupted the Fed's main trade route to Old Earth despite heavy Fed opposition. The routes to Szent-Gyogyi and Merritt's were shut by offensive mining operations around West Kent Reef that claimed the lives of six Fed merships, the pinchcomm relay station on Gok-3 was destroyed, and Fed supplies of helium-3 from mines in the Clarion system have been disrupted by the destruction of two storage facilities.

"To conserve war stocks, antimatter missile operations were limited to attacks on two Fed deepspace forward operating bases in the Panguna and Lagerfeld sectors, both destroyed. Looking at each operation in more detail . . ."

Saturday, December 30, 2400, UD
FWSS Tufayl, in orbit around Comdur Fleet Base

The eyes of all in *Tufayl*'s combat information center locked on the command holovid, the only sound the soft hiss of air-conditioning.

"Command, sensors. Positive gravitronics intercept. Estimated drop bearing Green 90 Up 1. Nine vessels. Gravity wave pattern suggests pinchspace transition imminent. Vectors nominal for inbound dreadnoughts."

"Command, roger."

Flanked by Vice Admiral Jaruzelska, Michael watched flashes of ultraviolet announce the arrival of the nine ships that made up Dreadnought Squadron One.

"Command, sensors, ships dropping. Nine dreadnoughts, drop datum confirmed Green 90 Up 1 at 30,000 kilometers."

"Command, roger."

After a flurry of laser tightbeam messages confirmed that the new arrivals really were the rest of Michael's command, Michael stood the *Tufayl* down from general quarters, leaving Ferreira to coordinate the down-shuttling of the ferry crews to Comdur.

He turned to Jaruzelska. "Big day, Admiral."

"It is, Michael," Jaruzelska said, her face grim. "And you know what? There've been times when I didn't think we'd ever get this far."

Michael nodded sympathetically. He would have to be stone deaf not to hear the growing opposition to dreadnoughts from within Fleet, opposition he suspected was encouraged—even orchestrated—by Rear Admiral Perkins, opposition that now verged on the dishonest. The Faith operation—*Tufayl*'s successful attack on the Hammer battle station HSBS-261—was portrayed by some in Fleet as a fluke, a lucky one-off never to be repeated. Sons of bitches! I'll give them a fucking fluke, Michael swore savagely. If that was not bad enough, his decision to press on with the attack without a casualty recovery ship had been turned against him. Dangerously reckless, they said, an officer willing to hazard anything and anyone to advance his own career, even if that risked the future of the Federated Worlds themselves. Worse still, the trashpress had decided that he was their next soft target, a strategy Michael had no doubt had Perkins's full support. He wondered how much longer the Hero of Hell's Moons—the trashpress's phrase, not his— would survive their growing attacks.

It was all gut-wrenchingly unfair, but he was a serving officer, and there was nothing he could do about it.

No, that was wrong. There was something. He could make dreadnoughts work. He had to, and he would. He pushed the problem away to watch the command holovid as it tracked the shuttles picking up the ferry crews.

Jaruzelska broke his concentration. "Right, Michael. I need a few more minutes of your time, and I'll be gone. Your cabin will be fine."

"Sir."

Jaruzelska looked Michael right in the face. "Right. What I'm about to tell you is classified Top Secret Mersin."

"Mersin?"

"Restricted distribution, top secret matters specific to dreadnoughts. You'll be pleased to know that you are the most junior member on the Mersin access list. I think the next most junior is a commodore, and there's only one of those."

"Oh," Michael said, wondering just how much more responsibility Fleet could load on a mere lieutenant's shoulders. "Right."

"Let me just tell you something about dreadnoughts. A bit of history. What we're doing is not the first time Fleet has experimented with unmanned warships."

Michael's mouth sagged open. "Wha . . . you're kidding me, sir."

Jaruzelska shook her head. "No, I'm not. *Tufayl* is not the first. Fleet trialed the concept during the Third Hammer war. By late '80, things were not going well for us; casualty recovery rates stayed well below what the war planners hoped for, and we struggled to crew the ships we had available. Nothing like as bad as after Comdur but still difficult. So we tried unmanned ships. Just the one to start with, the heavy cruiser *Pericles*. They didn't gut the ship the way we have dreadnoughts; they only took the crew off. To cut a long story short, it turned out a complete disaster. The ship's primary AI decided that it did not like being pushed around by someone in another ship, threw a fit, and went off on its own. It was last seen heading in the general direction of the Kalifati system— nobody knows why—before it jumped, never to be seen again. To this day, Fleet has no idea where the ship is or what it's been up to. We had a few ship sightings early on which may have been *Pericles,* and some unexplained attacks on ships, but nothing conclusive."

"Oh!" Michael said softly, eyes widening in shock. "An unmanned warship with unrestricted command authority. Tell me she wasn't carrying full missile magazines"— Jaruzelska nodded—"oh, that's not good."

"No, not good at all," Jaruzelska agreed, her face grim. "It gets worse. The *Pericles* experiment violated the Dakota System Treaty. An egregious violation was how the lawyers described it. If word leaks out, the Federated Worlds will be in a great deal of trouble given how sensitive people are about self-replicating machines. Understandably, they would see the *Pericles* as a step way too far down that road."

"I think I would, too, sir. There are a lot of smart AIs onboard a cruiser, not to mention the fabrication machines and knowledge bases to make pretty much anything they want. So that's one reason . . ." Michael's voice trailed off.

Jaruzelska finished the sentence for him: ". . . why certain senior officers are so implacably opposed to the whole idea, yes."

"Ah . . . so Admiral Perkins is cleared for Mersin material?"

"He is."

"Seems he has reason to oppose dreadnoughts, good reason."

"I hate to say it, but he does."

Michael said nothing for a while. The *Pericles* fiasco might explain Perkins's behavior, but it sure as hell did not excuse it. Orders were orders, goddamn it. "Hang on, sir," he said. "We're going to have unmanned ships with command authority. Nine of them."

"Yes, we are. Which brings me to the real point. The dreadnoughts will have command authority only while they hold biometric tokens issued by you and your executive officer, or your coxswain if either one of you is disabled. It's a fine legal point, I know, but the lawyers tell us that using time-limited tokens makes the dreadnoughts compliant with the Dakota System Treaty. The AI engineers have sworn blind that dreadnoughts can't and won't do a *Pericles* on us. So tokens it is. I'll com you and Ferreira the subroutine for your neuronics; it'll generate the tokens the dreadnoughts will need to keep operating."

"And if they don't get them?"

"Their weapons systems and fabrication machines are disabled, and they come home if they can. If they can't, they self-destruct. Right, stand by . . . Okay, you should have the subroutine. Let me see . . . Yes, you have an hour to enable your new squadron, so I suggest you get on with it. I'll be pretty pissed if I see those ships slinking back home with their weapons systems disabled. Righto, that's it. I'm off."

"Sir."

Proud of what he had achieved in such a short time, Michael watched the ships of Dreadnought Squadron One accelerate out of Comdur orbit, their first deployment as an operational unit. Jaruzelska had given him two days to prove he was able to manage ten dreadnoughts. Michael knew he had every reason to be confident; after all those hours in the sims, why wouldn't he be? The big unknown was what came next; Dreadnought Squadron One was still to receive any operational tasking.

Michael shook his head. Getting the First operational had been an enormous job, and it struck him as strange that he still had no idea what the squadron would be doing.

Not that there was a lack of potential missions. The Hammers, taking advantage of their superior numbers, were running Fleet ragged. They were hitting Fed trade hard, to the point where Fleet was considering the introduction of convoys despite the enormous costs and delays that would impose on merchant shipping. And if the Hammers were not interdicting Fed merships, they were carrying out hit-and-run attacks on forward sensor stations, pinchcomm relay facilities, deepspace support bases, and, just in the last few days, helium-3 processing plants in orbit around the gas giants Balendra-3 and Corparien-6.

Like every officer in the Fleet, Michael studied the daily summary of Fleet operations with obsessive interest, and one thing was abundantly clear to him. With the bulk of the Fleet tied up with planetary protection—thanks to the threat posed by Hammer antimatter missiles—and trade protection, there was no shortage of soft targets for the Hammers to go after. That left the Feds one step behind the Hammers, staggering around like a punch-drunk boxer trying to work out where the next blow might come from. And things would stay that way until something changed; for Michael's money, that something was the arrival of Dreadnought Squadron One. Thus, why they had yet to receive any tasking remained a mystery, though he would wager good money that Fleet politics had a lot to do with it.

"Command, Warfare. Squadron is in station, on vector. Request permission to jump."

"Command approved."

"All ships, immediate execute Kilo-2. I say again immediate execute Kilo-2. Stand by . . . execute!"

In an instant, the ten ships of the First jumped into pinch-space, leaving only brief ultraviolet flares to mark their departure.

"What?"

Brain clouded by sleep, Michael struggled to wake up, the insistent chiming of his neuronics impossible to ignore. Forcing his mind into gear, he accepted the com from the combat information center.

Sedova had the watch. "Captain, sir, officer in command, sir. Flash pinchcomm from Fleet. We've been ordered to drop into normalspace to receive new tasking."

"Ah, right," Michael replied, still groggy. "Get things moving. I'll be in the CIC in a moment. Anything to tell us what Fleet has in mind?"

"No, sir. Just that we need to drop soonest."

"Okay. On my way."

"Okay, folks. Sorry to drag everyone out of bed, but we have a mission. Operation Blue Tango." A scowl crossed Michael's face; where did Fleet get mission names from? He paused while a frisson of excitement ran through the *Tufayl*'s crew. "Right, we're going to go virtual for this so that the rest of the squadron can join in, so patch your neuronics into my conference channel."

Michael waited patiently until his crew and the avatars representing the warfare AIs of the nine other ships of the First together with those of Warfare, Kenny, and Kal came online. The virtual conference room was crowded, an air of anticipation obvious. Even the AIs—normally imperturbable—appeared interested.

"Lets go," Michael said, cutting through the rising chatter. "I'll give a quick overview before we split up to finalize the details of the ops plan. Fleet intelligence has reported the imminent departure of a major Hammer deployment out of the Fortitude system. Large task group size, mission unknown. This has left Fortitude's defenses depleted and open to attack. Clearly, the Hammers don't believe we have the assets to exploit the opportunity this deployment has given us. We also believe that they will rely on their antimatter capability to make up for any shortfall in warships left to protect Fortitude. Since dealing with antimatter threats is what dreadnoughts are for, our task is to show them the error of their ways."

There was a soft murmur, the shock obvious. The moment of truth for the dreadnoughts was at hand, and everyone knew it.

"Our mission comes in two parts," Michael said "First, an assault on this"—his hand stabbed out to identify a point in Fortitude nearspace marked in red on the holovid—"space battle station here, HSBS-372. Our aim is to draw the Hammer defenders out and force them to commit their antimatter missiles to the station's defense before closing in to destroy it. You'll understand, of course," Michael said, his face grim, "that every antimatter missile the Hammers waste on us is one less they can use on the home planets."

A quiet growl of anger ran through the room while Michael continued. "Once we have eliminated the battle station, we will jump out-system to remass"—another stab at the holovid—"here. When we've remassed, we will reverse vector for the jump back into Fortitude nearspace. Fleet believes, and I agree, that the Hammers will not be expecting us to return so quickly, so hopefully we can catch them with their pants around their ankles.

"Our target for the second run will be this orbital heavy maintenance platform, OHMP-344 here"—his finger stabbed at a red icon in Clarke orbit around Fortitude—"along with any Hammer fleet units berthed on it. Just because OHMP-344 is a maintenance platform does not mean it's a pushover. The Hammers protect them every bit as well as we protect ours, but I think ten dreadnoughts should be more than enough for the job. When we're done with them, we'll adjust vector and jump for Comdur. Any questions so far?"

The conference room was deathly quiet, and for good reason. This mission was like no mission anyone present had ever seen. Once again, Michael thought, dreadnoughts are going to tear up the Fighting Instructions before throwing them in the trash.

"No questions?" Michael asked, scanning the room. "Okay. Before we get down to the details, there are two mission constraints you need to be aware of. One is time. To place the Hammers under maximum pressure—who knows, we might even force them to recall their task group before they attack—it is crucial we launch this operation on schedule. Second, we go in cold. No loitering out in farspace building the best threat plot known to humankind, no agonizing over every sensor intercept, no analyzing every last vector. On the way in, we will rendezvous with a relaysat to download whatever intelligence Fleet's reconsats in Fortitude deepspace have been able to acquire. If that's bugger all, so be it. The space battle station's not going anywhere, nor is the maintenance platform. Okay, that's enough from me. Detailed planning teams, you know who you are, so let's get going. We'll reconvene in two hours to put everything together."

Michael offered up a silent prayer while he watched the virtual conference dissolve. The First would need all the help it could get. For a first operation, this one was an absolute doozy, and if it went even half-right, it would be a bloody miracle. A small shiver went down his spine when something struck him.

Was he being set up to fail?

Sunday, December 31, 2400, UD
Eternity deepspace

For many months, the cluster of deepspace gravitation arrays—ugly assemblies of plasteel girders thousands of meters long hung with gravity wave detectors—monitored the tiny perturbations in pinchspace caused by the passage of ships outbound from Eternity, the fourth planet of the Hammer Worlds.

Month by month, data accumulated, terabytes of numbers

recording the infinitesimal displacement of pinchspace caused by the mass of transiting starships. Over time, the data took form, and soon the arrays were able to compute the vectors followed by the Hammer ships.

Some vectors were already well known—the established trade routes between Eternity and Serhati, Scobie's World, the planets of the Javitz Union, and the Pascanici League—but one was new, a route to no place shown on any Fed chart.

A pinchcomm signal flashed across deepspace back to the Federated Worlds to report the anomaly.

Two weeks later, deepspace survey drones were dispatched to seed the mystery vector with sensorsats, spherical satellites the size of beach balls carrying a power supply, ultraviolet sensors, and a simple laser tightbeam transmitter. Working with mindless diligence, the drones laid a line of sensorsats along the mystery vector out into deepspace, the satellites strung out like beads on a thread hundreds of light-years long.

Patiently, the sensorsats scanned space for the unmistakable signature of ships dropping in and out of pinchspace, the intense, fleeting flares of ultraviolet the one transmission no ship in humanspace could suppress. Every few days, a survey drone dropped out of pinchspace to interrogate each sensorsat in turn. A handful reported ship activity. The drone dropped more sensorsats to triangulate the source. One week later, it had established the location of the ship activity: a small asteroid, not shown on any Fed survey, wandering alone in deepspace, 235 light-years out from the Hammer Worlds.

To the stealthed reconsats sent in to investigate, the asteroid's purpose was obvious: to support a small plant mining and processing the driver mass used by starships. The survey drone noted the vectors of ships leaving the planetoid after remassing. Calling for assistance, it started the process again, seeding another vector to nowhere with sensorsats.

A month after the initial report from the gravitation arrays, the survey drone found what the Federated Worlds had been searching for so desperately. Judging by the gigantic infrared signature radiated into space from massed banks of heat dumps, a substantial industrial-scale facility lay buried inside a small carbonaceous asteroid—identified on Fed charts as Mathuli-4451—deep in the heart of the confused tangle of rips in space-time marked on Fed space charts as Devastation Reef.

When analysts examined the survey drone's reports, their conclusion was emphatic. The Devastation Reef complex was the Hammer antimatter manufacturing facility, the linchpin of the Hammer fleet's strategic advantage.

Thursday, January 11, 2401, UD
FWSS Tufayl, *Fortitude planetary farspace*

Junior Lieutenant Kat Sedova's face popped onto the command holovid. The *Ghost*'s command pilot appeared nervous, her tongue flicking out across dry lips. For a moment, he wondered if he had been right to send *Tufayl*'s lander across to the *Iron Duke*. Michael pushed the concern away. Either Sedova coped or she did not. Either way, he could not worry about it. He had done his bit; it was up to her.

"All set?"

"We are, sir. This is one big ship. Kind of spooky being here on our own." She stopped. "But we'll be fine. We've simmed the mission, and we're just setting it up to run it again with a few problems thrown in. But I'm confident."

"Good. Follow the plan and you'll be fine."

"Roger that, sir. *Ghost,* out."

"Sensors. Where are we up to with the threat plot?"

"We're downloading data from the reconsats," Leading Spacer Carmellini said from the sensor management workstation. "I'll have the threat plot updated shortly."

"Roger." Michael was relieved. For some reason, the relay satellite collating data from the far-flung web of reconnaissance satellites thrown around Fortitude was not where it was supposed to be. With time running out, it had been a frantic business trying to locate it without using any active sensors; the fact that the dreadnoughts' heat dumps were radiating the prodigious amounts of waste heat accumulated in their pinchspace jump was all the advertising he was prepared to tolerate.

Michael watched the threat plot while it updated. Some update. It was time-stamped hours earlier. "Shit," he muttered. Tactical intelligence that old was worthless. It made no difference; his dreadnoughts would be going into this attack cold. The Hammers might have deployed their entire fleet across their path when the time came to attack, and he would not know it.

"Warfare. Weapons free. You have command authority."

"Roger, I have command authority," the battle management AI replied, its voice, as always, calm and measured. "All ships, Warfare. Weapons free. Execute to follow, Foxtrot-1. I say again execute to follow, Foxtrot-1. Acknowledge."

Michael listened with half an ear while the acknowledgments flowed in. It was an impressive roll call: *Orion*, the oldest ship in the squadron, proudly bearing a list of battle honors longer than that of any other ship in the Fed order of battle; *Iron Knight*, blooded in the Fourth Hammer war and sister ship to the *Iron Duke; Sina, Qurrah, Khaldun,* and *Al-Khayyam*, all sister ships to the *Tufayl*; *Rebuke* and *Rebut*, the youngest ships in the squadron.

One thing all those ships had in common was the Battle of Comdur. Far too many spacers and marines had been killed or injured in those ships, and more than ever before, the awful pressure to avenge those casualties weighed heavily on him.

Warfare gave the order. "All ships, command. Foxtrot-1, stand by . . . execute!"

In a blaze of ultraviolet, the squadron jumped, and Operation Blue Tango was under way in earnest.

A tiny fraction of a second later, the squadron erupted into Hammer space, proximity alarms screeching to let

Michael know his threat plot was seriously out of line with reality. Michael ignored them while he watched the threat plot firm up, the blazing red icon of the Hammer space battle station dead ahead of them, surrounded by a gaggle of Hammer ships. Iron bands squeezed his chest hard, making breathing difficult; he counted five heavy cruisers, supported by many times that number of smaller ships, ranging from light cruisers to heavy scouts. "Goddamnit," he murmured. That was a lot of firepower; even though his dreadnoughts were tough, this was going to be one hell of a fight.

"Command, Warfare. Threat plot confirmed."

The squadron wasted no time. Things moved so fast that the ships had to be under Warfare's direct control, the comforting—to humans, at least—rituals of order and acknowledgment giving way to laser tightbeam commands that welded ten dreadnoughts into a single offensive weapon. Truth be known, the human crews were along only for the ride, there to step in if the AIs made a mistake blatant enough for a slow-moving human brain to pick it up.

Radiating every transmitter they carried at full power— some joker at one of the planning meetings called this the "hello, please shoot at us" signal—the dreadnoughts dumped full missile salvos overboard, more than three thousand Merlin ASSMs opening out on vectors to send them far enough away to survive the inevitable Hammer antimatter attack. Deception formed no part of Blue Tango. The exact opposite, in fact. Michael wanted the Hammers to know they had a serious problem heading their way. Going in fast and loud seemed to him to be the best way to achieve that; if he could have sent a cheer squad on ahead in Day-Glo space suits, he would have done just that. He wanted to ratchet the pressure up, to force the Hammer commander to react without thinking, to make mistakes.

With the dreadnoughts now driving in hard toward the Hammers, Warfare held the rail guns back. To fire this far out meant having the dreadnoughts' missile salvo arrive long after the rail-gun slugs had arrived on target, setting a defensive problem even the dumbest Hammer commander would have little problem dealing with.

It was not easy, sitting there, *Tufayl's* combat information center silent while the ships closed on the Hammers. Adrenaline took effect. Heart thumping, Michael forced himself not to fidget, his eyes locked on the threat plot. If the Hammers did not respond soon . . .

"Command, sensors. Multiple missile launches. Eaglehawk ASSMs. No targeting assessment possible at this range. Initial salvo pattern suggests antimatter attack highly probable. Time to target 5 minutes 23."

"Command, roger. All stations. Brace for antimatter missile attack."

Michael zoomed the holovid in to focus on the incoming attack. Antimatter missiles were precious; they had to be husbanded, and the Hammers did that. To ensure that every one counted, Hammer antimatter attacks were always the same. An outer layer of sacrificial decoys and missiles carrying conventional chemex and fusion warheads led the way. They had only one task: to distract the Feds' medium-range antimissile defenses. If they made it through to their targets, that was a bonus. Following on came more missiles, some—but not all—fitted with antimatter warheads mixed with yet more decoys, the whole attack formed into a hemispherical mass. It was so unmistakable that the Hammer commander might as well have sent a message en clair telling the dreadnoughts antimatter missiles were on their way.

Michael had trouble breathing; the bands around his chest refused to ease. He checked the threat plot, looking at it the way a man watches a cobra about to strike. It was a truly terrifying sight, missile vectors fused into a single tangled mass of red that came down to a single point: the tiny bubble of space occupied by the First. The Hammers were good, very good, without exception getting their missiles away barely seconds after the squadron dropped, then accelerating away from the battle station before adjusting vectors to turn bows on to the incoming Fed ships.

Michael did not care. His ships had one target—space

battle station HSBS-372—and the Hammers essentially had left it to look after its own defense. There was a Hammer commander with altogether too much faith in antimatter missiles, he thought; Michael enjoyed the prospect of teaching the man the error of his ways.

"Command, Warfare. Hammer missiles will be inside our mission abort blast damage radius in three minutes. If they haven't fired their missiles before then, I intend to jump the squadron."

"Command, roger." Michael had no option but to agree. It would have been good to see this phase of the operation through, but not if it meant rendering his squadron ineffective. His ships were tough enough to withstand an antimatter attack, but not if the warheads blew too close. There was always nex—

Afterward, Michael would swear that the entire universe turned an incandescent white, a white beyond white, a white so bright that his eyes refused to open for many minutes afterward. An instant later, the *Tufayl* was thrown backward when its artificial gravity failed, slamming Michael hard against his safety harness. Even through the radiation-resistant layers of the armored combat space suit designed specifically for dreadnought crews, he sustained heavy bruises across his shoulders that lasted for weeks.

The *Tufayl*'s combat information center dissolved into bedlam, radiation alarms shrieking to tell Michael what he already knew—that they had been on the receiving end of a wall of gamma radiation intense enough to make a dreadnought feel like it had run into a brick wall. He breathed out with relief and shut the alarms off. He was alive, and so was the rest of *Tufayl*'s crew, even though his neuronics screamed blue murder about the amount of radiation he had received. Not that he cared; *Tufayl* carried medibots purpose-built to deal with just that problem, and he and everyone else onboard would live more than long enough to use them.

"Command, Warfare. Missile salvo one is nominal; no significant damage from antimatter attack. Launching second missile salvo. Deploying decoys and Krachov shrouds."

"Roger." Anxiously, he scanned the damage reports flowing in from the squadron. The ships had absorbed a prodigious amount of energy in a short span of time, the wall of gamma radiation blasting off hundreds of tons of bow armor before the shock wave drove into the dreadnoughts' titanium inner hull and frames. But ships and crews had survived. Not bad, he said to himself. The hundreds of design changes had done their job.

He ran down the list of ships. One of his ships had come out badly: *Iron Knight*'s starboard missile launcher rams were damaged and nonoperational, cutting her ASSM salvo capability by 50 percent. As for the rest, *Khaldun* and *Orion* suffered damage to the fusion plants supplying their antiship lasers. *Tufayl, Rebuke,* and *Qurrah,* had some damage to their starboard main propulsion. And that was it; the rest of the squadron had minor problems but none worth worrying about.

Michael turned his attention back to the command plot, making sure it tallied with the mental image of the operation he carried in his head. Things looked good. Accelerating hard, his ships were now close enough to the Hammers to deny them the option to fire a second salvo of antimatter missiles. Doing so might kill the Fed ships, but they would destroy themselves in the process. The decoys were doing the job of convincing the Hammer ships screening the battle station that they were the primary target for the Fed attack. His squadron's second missile salvo was on its way, and if Warfare's calculations were right, his ships would fire their rail guns before the Hammer ships could get their own second missile salvo away. All of that meant the Hammers' one chance of doing any serious damage was to fire a well-targeted rail-gun attack before the Feds jumped.

Edgily, Michael watched the distance close. It was the hardest thing about his job, to sit back and wait, even though that was what he should be doing.

"Command, Warfare. Firing rail guns . . . now!"

Tufayl shuddered when the forward rail-gun batteries threw a full salvo at the Hammer battle station. Michael nodded his approval; the rail-gun swarm was tightly grouped, its timing impeccable. The squadron's missiles would arrive on target seconds after the rail-gun slugs smashed home, hoping to exploit any weaknesses blasted into the battle station's armor by the slugs.

"Command, Warfare. Hammer ships turning in. Rail-gun attack imminent."

"Roger," Michael replied, trying in vain to keep his stomach under control, the sweat running cold down his spine. He swore under his breath. He would be happy never to see another Hammer rail-gun salvo ever again.

"Command, Warfare, sensors. Multiple rail-gun launches. Impact in sixty seconds. Stand by impact assessment."

"Roger."

"Command, sensors. Vector assessment on rail-gun salvo. Targets are *Sina* and *Rebuke*. Impact fifty seconds."

"Command, Warfare. All ships, stand by to jump."

"Warfare, hold. Reconfirm mass distribution models." Michael knew they had the time, so why not recheck the one thing that might really screw up the operation.

"Stand by . . . confirmed. All ships report mass distribution recomputed and nominal. Safe to jump."

"Roger. Command approved to jump when ready."

"All stations, Warfare. Jumping."

Poorly supported by the warships of a defensive screen more interested in looking after themselves, the battle station had no chance of survival. Focused, unstoppable, the Fed attack overwhelmed the station; it reeled as the massive shock of a well-timed rail-gun salvo racked its frame and fusion warheads flayed armor off by the meter, allowing missiles carrying conventional chemex warheads to punch lances of white-hot gas deep into its guts. For a while, the station hung there, seemingly untroubled, the only movement that of thin skeins of smoke boiling off into space from puddles of white-hot ceramsteel armor. It could not last; their defenses breached by Fed missiles, the station's two primary fusion power plants lost containment. A microsecond later, the unimaginable power of their explosion blew the massive armored sphere into a ball of white-hot gas seeded though with a million pieces of blast-shattered wreckage.

Phase 1 of Operation Blue Tango was over, Fed reconsats its only witnesses.

The universe twisted in on itself, and *Tufayl* dropped out of pinchspace. Michael tried to ignore jangling nerves and a protesting stomach, more interested in the flurry of activity while *Tufayl*'s crew made sure they had not dropped into the arms of a waiting Hammer task group.

"Command, Warfare. Threat plot confirmed green."

"Command, roger. Warfare. Weapons still free; you retain command authority."

"Warfare, roger."

Michael allowed himself to relax a fraction; he watched the proceedings, more than happy to see the mass tankers where they were supposed to be and relieved when the tankers dumped their passive sensor intercept logs across to *Tufayl,* confirming that no other ships were operating within billions of kilometers. He allowed himself to relax.

"Jayla, you have the ship. Stand down from general quarters. Restore ship's atmosphere and artgrav. Take us in. Oh, yes, tell our wandering lander it can come home."

"Roger, sir. They'll be pleased," Ferreira said.

"I reckon. Bit lonely over there."

Michael left the combat information center, happy to breathe ship's air in place of the moisture-laden muck that cycled around his suit over and over again, happy to get out of his combat space suit, and even happier to be able to ditch a sweat-soaked shipsuit. Back in his cabin, he stripped off, prepared his combat space suit for its next outing, showered, and was back in the combat information center freshly shipsuited in a matter of minutes.

"Sir, ship is at defense stations."

"Thanks, Jayla." Michael settled down to watch the squadron decelerate to take station on the tankers.

"Er, sir," Ferreira said.

"Yes?"

"Sick bay, sir, if you don't mind. The medibots need to take care of the radiation damage."

"Ah, yes," Michael said, embarrassed that he had forgotten.

"Thought you might have," Ferreira said, a look of stern disapproval on her face.

"Okay, okay. On my way. Just make sure you get to the sick bay, too."

"Taken care of, sir. The coxswain's there; soon as she's done, she'll cover for me."

"Good. I'll go walkabout when I'm finished."

Michael set off to the sick bay. After ten uncomfortable minutes at the hands of nano-sized medibots relentless in their determination to repair the subcellular damage caused by a fraction of a nanosecond's exposure to intense gamma radiation, he was free.

His first stop was engineering. Climbing down the ladder into the starboard engine room, he spotted the lower half of Chief Petty Officer (Propulsion) Chua. The man lay flat on his back, most of his body buried deep inside the armored casing of the main driver mass supply feed, with the rest of *Tufayl*'s engineering team huddled around him.

Michael waited patiently until Chua slid back out of the access port, his face and body black with driver pellet residue. "Any joy, chief?" he asked.

Chua shook his head. "No, sir. I think we've found the problem, though. Shock damage to one of the transporter bearing sets. Nothing fatal, but . . ." Chua stopped.

"Go on."

"Well, sir. There's a risk we might lose the whole feed if one of the bearings fails. Not a big risk, but a risk. If we're under even half power at the time, that'd probably take out the whole engine room. There's a lot of mass coming down that feeder tube."

"Fixable?"

"No, sir. Yard job. Not a big one, but it's beyond us, I'm afraid."

"Was afraid it might be." Michael masked his disappointment, though he was not surprised. The dreadnoughts' limited ability to fix battle damage was one of their biggest weaknesses. "*Rebuke* and *Qurrah*?"

"Looks to be the same problem, sir. But without spacers to crawl inside"—Chua waved a hand at the access port—"we can't be sure. Their repairbots aren't in yet."

Michael nodded. Another weakness of the dreadnought design: When it came to getting into awkward places to find out just what the hell was going on, spacers were hard to beat. "Okay. So my starboard engine is power-limited?"

"That's right, sir. You can have 90 percent if you need it and full power if the Hammers start breathing down our necks, but don't be surprised if we lose the whole starboard engine. Ten minutes at full power, tops. You can have emergency power if you override the safety interlocks, but I would not recommend doing that unless we're going to die anyway." Chua's tone of voice might be lighthearted, but underneath the dirt, his face was grim.

"Ten minutes at maximum power. Avoid emergency power. Understood." He looked in turn at the rest of the engineering department. "Any other problems? Petty Officer Morozov?"

"Well, sir, the honey pot's a bit shaken up, but apart from a bit of blowback from the crappers"—Michael winced theatrically while the rest of the engineers laughed—"which the housebots are cleaning up, we're fine."

"Pleased to hear it. Let me guess. I know the exec has nagged you guys to death, but none of you have been to the sick bay? Am I right?"

Sheepishly, the engineers nodded their heads.

"Well, guys. I need you fit and well, so get your asses up there pronto. If I can do what Lieutenant Ferreira tells me, so can you!"

"Sir," they chorused.

"Right, I'm off." Comming Bienefelt to meet him, Michael left the starboard engine room, encouraged by the attitude of the engineers and even more by the news that he could have full power if he needed it, not to mention emergency power if things turned really bad. Emerging from the engine room's armored air lock, he made his way forward through the echoing emptiness of the hangar, the backup lander—Sedova had christened it *Creaking Door*, and he reminded himself for the umpteenth time find out why—its sole occupant. Well, the place was empty only if one ignored the enormous bulk of Chief Petty Officer Bienefelt.

"Sir?" she said.

"Matti. I want to see for myself how the forward compartments survived the Hammer attack."

"I guessed that's what you wanted, sir. That's why I brought this." Effortlessly, Bienefelt waved the bulky shape of a hand-held material scanner that Michael would have had trouble lifting with two hands.

"Ah, good," Michael mumbled. "I was just going to, er . . . you know . . ."

"Let me guess, sir . . . You were going to peer at them?"

"Peer at them? Yes, I think that's the technical term," Michael said, a touch embarrassed. The idea of doing a proper survey by using a scanner capable of detecting minute cracks never occurred to him.

"Honestly, sir." Bienefelt rolled her eyes and shook her head. "What would you ever do without senior spacers?"

"Screw things up?"

"You said it, sir, not me." She grinned at Michael, the bond between them palpable. "Shall I lead on?"

"Please do, Chief Petty Officer Bienefelt, please do," Michael said with exaggerated deference, thankful, not for the first time, that he had spacers like Bienefelt to rely on, "I'm not sure I could find my way without you."

With scanner held in an enormous hand, she set off, a muted *"hmphhhh,"* her only response.

Tufayl's forward compartments were an uncomfortable sight, their rawness a stark reminder of what the dreadnought had gone through at Comdur. Not that any trace of the spacers who had died up there remained. No, it was the crude roughness with which the salvagebots had stripped the compartments, the hastily installed reinforcing to the ship's frames, and, right forward, the wall of ugly gray ceramsteel armor slabs, thousands and thousands of tons of them, cut with millimeter accuracy to fill the ship's bows right up to the original armor, the slabs secured by welds and makeshift bracing.

Michael gave the work no points for aesthetics, but that aside, the compartments were in good shape. The impulse shock from the wall of gamma radiation had left the area untouched.

"All looks pretty good, Matti," he said. "What's the scanner show?"

"We have some minor stress fractures around some of the welds but nothing that'll affect structural integrity. The bracing's good. I think the *Tufayl*'s done okay. That was one hell of a bang she took."

"It was. I'll leave you to it. Let me know if you find anything."

"I will, sir, though I'm pretty sure the engineers did it right. Certainly looks that way."

"Let's hope so. Let me know when you're done. The XO tells me the *Ghost* is inbound, so I'll be down in the hangar."

"Sir."

Reassured that *Tufayl* was okay and leaving Bienefelt to finish the survey, Michael made his way back to the hanger while *Caesar's Ghost* cycled through the air lock. Once the lander was secure, he made his way over and waited until Sedova emerged.

"How was it, Kat?" Michael said as the *Ghost*'s command pilot jumped down.

"Well, sir. To be honest, bloody terrifying." Sedova smiled, but it was forced. She unlatched her helmet and took it off, running a hand through sweat-soaked hair.

"Troops handle it okay?"

"No probs, sir. They're fine. I shut down *Iron Duke*'s artificial gravity and kept the *Ghost* in the hover until the attack was over, so we missed the impulse shock altogether, but we have a couple of radiation-induced glitches I'd like the engineers to have a look at."

"Okay. Keep me posted. To save the executive officer

having to nag you, get everyone up to the sick bay like yesterday."

"Will do, sir. Never seen my dosimeter read so far into the red. My neuronics are telling me I don't have long to live. Talk about scary."

Michael nodded. It had been. Without nanobots to repair the radiation damage, he and the rest of *Tufayl*'s crew would all be dead inside forty-eight hours. "Right. I'm off back to the CIC. Let me know when the *Ghost* is 100 percent."

"Sir."

"How are we doing?" Michael asked when he climbed back into the command seat.

"Good timing, sir. Stand by . . ." Ferreira said as the subdued rumbling of the *Tufayl*'s main engines cut out. "We're in station. The drone is launching its shuttles. Estimate squadron will complete remassing on schedule."

"Good." Quickly he scanned the threat plot—still green—before double-checking what the ship's passive sensors were picking up, pleased to see nothing out of the ordinary. Leading Spacer Carmellini had the sensor watch; Michael walked over to him and patted him on the shoulder. "Am I missing anything?"

Carmellini shook his head. "No, sir."

Michael dropped into a seat alongside Carmellini's workstation, the better to see his face. "Way I like it."

"Me, too, sir," Carmellini said with feeling.

"You okay?"

"I am, sir. The first time back in action, well . . . that was pretty hard after, you know, after . . ." Carmellini's voice faded away. "But it's better this time, though it's still tough. But tough or not, it's what we are all about," he said, recovering his composure, "so I'm happy to be here. We owe those Hammer sonsofbitches big time."

"We sure do. You're doing well, son. Very well," Michael said, pleased to see Carmellini every bit as steady as he sounded.

Graham Sharp Paul

"Thank you, sir. Remember Comdur."

"Remember Comdur," Michael replied.

He returned to his seat to watch the remassing, a slow-motion space ballet performed by chunky black boxes fitted with simple thrusters shuttling to and fro to dump their loads of driver mass pellets into the dreadnoughts' depleted bunkers.

It was a pleasant, even soothing, sight, but even though Michael was tempted to relax—with the adrenaline leaching fast out of his system, he was tired—not for one microsecond did he let his guard down. Dreadnought Squadron One was in deepspace light-years from the Hammers—so far from anything that its chances of being detected and attacked were infinitesimal—but that did not matter. Captain Constanza, *Ishaq*'s skipper, had assumed her ship was safe, and the Hammers had gone and ambushed it at Xiang Reef. Her reward? To have her ship blown apart around her, killing her along with hundreds of *Ishaq*'s crew, dumping Michael and close to three hundred other survivors into Hammer hands.

Not on my watch, he said to himself, counting the minutes down until the First returned to Faith nearspace for the second phase of Operation Blue Tango.

"Shiiiiit," Michael hissed through clenched teeth, reflexes forcing his body right back in its seat in a vain attempt to get away from the disaster bearing down on them, a disaster he could do nothing to avert.

The command holovid filled with the awful sight of a Hammer ship—the light escort *O'Connor*—closing with horrifying speed, *Tufayl*'s bows aimed right into her flank. Michael cursed his luck. *Tufayl* had dropped so close to *O'Connor* that there was no way either ship could avoid the looming disaster. A collision was inevitable. He swore again; of all the billions and billions of cubic kilometers of space *O'Connor* might have been in, it had to pick the same tiny bubble *Tufayl* would be in seconds after it dropped out of pinchspace.

"Another first for the dreadnoughts," he said sardonically, "a ramming."

"All stations," Warfare said laconically. "Brace for collision."

With nearly superhuman effort, Michael forced himself to look away. There might be only seconds before *Tufayl* was ripped apart, but he still had a squadron to think about, a squadron right in the middle of an attack on the small Hammer task group—designated Hammer-1—in loose formation close to OHMP-344, one of the orbital heavy maintenance platforms in Clarke orbit around Faith planet. Needless to say, neither the Hammer task group nor the unfortunate *O'Connor* had been anywhere near OHMP-344 when the dreadnoughts had departed from Hammer space to remass before returning for the second phase of Blue Tango. Murphy, Michael reminded himself, was very fond of military operations.

"Warfare. Status?"

"Own missile and rail-gun salvos have ten seconds to impact. Targets still turning; probability of first strike kill on *Novo City* and *Jarramshia* is high. Hammer missile salvo inbound from OHMP-344's defensive platforms, time to impact four minutes, targets *Rebuke* and *Sina*. *Iron Duke* adjusting vector to take station on *Tufayl* for casualty recovery; *Caesar's Ghost* and *Creaking Door* are at Launch 1."

"Command, roger." He had not needed to ask—Warfare's report matched Michael's mental plot of the operation—but it was never a bad thing to know for certain that nothing had been overlooked.

Turning back to look at the holovid and the relentlessly closing *O'Connor,* Michael promised himself that never, ever again would he allow the First to be thrown into an attack on the basis of old, stale intelligence. Never, and if the admirals did not like it, they could go screw themselves.

The last few seconds to impact ran off with glacial slowness. For fuck's sake, Michael swore; it was like being back in the eighteenth century! One ship ramming another. What next? All hands to boarding stations? Issue cutlasses? And if that was not bad enough, nobody could tell him whether *Tufayl* would survive what would be the first recorded collision in space combat. Michael hoped she would survive. *Tufayl* outmassed the hapless *O'Connor* by a big margin, and her reinforced bow armor should make short work of the light escort's thinly protected flanks, but that was a long way from being sure. What if the *O'Connor*'s fusion plants lost containment? What if she carried antimatter miss—

With a sickening, tearing crash that picked the ship up and shook it, *Tufayl* plowed into *O'Connor* about one-third of the way back from her bows, the impact dragged out into a series of grating crunches as *Tufayl* tore through the hapless Hammer ship, overloaded metal frames squealing in protest, bending and twisting under the stress of the collision. Horrified, Michael and the rest of *Tufayl*'s crew watched the dreadnought slice the Hammer ship apart, forcing its hull wide open, air dumped into space in a shivering, scintillating white mass of ice crystals. Nausea twisted Michael's guts into a tangled knot: The cloud wasn't just ice. It was seeded through with small, tumbling shapes blown bodily out of the ship by explosive decompression, some space-suited, most not, thin shipsuits no protection against the hard vacuum of space.

Michael shivered; *Tufayl* was not the only one taken by surprise.

Even as Michael allowed himself to hope that *Tufayl* might escape unscathed, the ship was picked up again, only to be smashed bodily to starboard, overstressed frames screeching as it was blown away from the fractured corpse of *O'Connor*. One of the Hammer ship's auxiliary fusion plants probably, Michael reckoned. Might have been worse. The *Tufayl* might not have survived if one of the Hammer ship's main propulsion plants had exploded.

Damage reports flooded in. Michael's face turned grim while he studied them. He commed Ferreira. Her face spoke volumes.

"Not looking good, sir," she said. "We don't have the spacers to deal with half the problems we're facing. And we're no longer jump-capable."

Michael nodded; he knew *Tufayl* was in serious trouble. "Can we save her?"

"No, sir," Ferreira said emphatically. "She either blows up or *O'Connor* does the job for us. Either way, chances of saving her are nil."

"I agree. I'll give the order. Get your people into *Creaking Door*." Michael did not waste any more time. There were plenty more ships to go around. It was spacers Fleet could not replace.

"All stations, command. Abandon ship. I say again, abandon ship. All hands to the lander! Command, out." Michael's space-suited finger struggled with the black and yellow cover over the abandon ship alarm, but he forced it open finally. His finger stabbed down, and the ship filled instantly with an unmistakable *whoop whoop whoop,* the combat information center filling with the lurid red flashes of emergency strobes.

Michael commed Ferreira. "Sir?" she said.

"I won't be far behind you, but if it all goes to shit, you are not to wait for me, understand?"

"Sir, I—"

"That's a direct order, Ferreira. Just do it. Captain, out."

"Command, Warfare. Have *Iron Duke* ready to receive survivors."

"Warfare, roger," the AI replied, quite unruffled by the fact that it had only minutes left to live. Michael suppressed a stab of guilt. It was just an AI, after all, and anyway, its clone and those of Kubby and Kal were all safely aboard the *Iron Duke*, ready to take over the instant *Tufayl* was destroyed. He would miss Mother, though; she was not going home, and there was no time to say goodbye.

"Command, Warfare. *Iron Duke* acknowledges. Closing on *Tufayl*. Second missile salvo away, targets Hammer light cruisers *Machuca, Fram,* and *Carlucci*."

"Command, roger," Michael said. He took one last look at the command and threat plots to make sure nothing had been overlooked and headed for the hangar, an awkward shuffling run made difficult by an uncooperative combat space suit and by what felt horribly like the imminent failure of

Tufayl's artificial gravity. He redoubled his efforts. If the ship lost artificial gravity, he would never make it. Desperately he hurled himself into the drop tube, plummeting down to the hangar deck. To his surprise and relief, he was met by Bienefelt and Carmellini on the end of safety lines rigged back to *Creaking Door*. They wasted no time. Without a word, they grabbed Michael under the arms and rushed him back to the lander, throwing him bodily through the starboard access door, Carmellini slapping the handle down to close the hatch behind them while the lander accelerated hard into space, away from the doomed *Tufayl*.

"Jeeeeez!" Michael hissed. "Jayla," he said to Ferreira, struggling to recover his composure, "tell me we have everyone."

"We do, sir. Ten souls."

"Good," Michael said, much relieved. He strapped himself in. "Who's flying this thing?"

"Sedova and her team, sir, by datalink."

"Good. Okay, back to work." He had an operation to run. He closed his eyes and switched his neuronics to the command and threat plots. A quick check reassured him that apart from the imminent loss of *Tufayl*, the operation was going well. The squadron, trailed by *Iron Duke*, bored in toward the Hammer task group, already two ships down as *Novo City* and *Jarramshia* death-rolled out of the fight, with air, smoke, and flame belching from multiple missile and rail-gun impacts. His mouth tightened into a savage snarl at the sight. The Hammer task group was not going to survive this encounter.

But the primary target, OHMP-344, was still intact. Michael had an idea. Since the *Tufayl* was well and truly in the ramming business, she ought to go out with a bang. "Warfare, command."

"Warfare."

"Set *Tufayl*'s vector to impact the platform, main propulsion to full power," Michael said, adding a silent prayer that *Tufayl*'s starboard main driver mass supply feed had held up. "Set all fusion plants to self-destruct at impact plus two seconds."

"Warfare, roger. Adjusting *Tufayl*'s vector," the warfare AI replied calmly. "Stand by . . . vector set, ship at full power."

"Command roger." The chances of *Tufayl* surviving long enough to get through to OHMP-344 were fifty-fifty at best, but it was worth the effort, if only to distract the platform's defenses. The sight of a heavy cruiser with a death wish heading right at them would attract the undivided attention of OHMP-344's defenders, that was for sure.

"All stations, warfare. Stand by Hammer missile salvo impact three minutes."

Michael urged the *Door* on; getting caught in a light assault lander in the middle of a Hammer missile attack was not conducive to a long and happy life.

"Roger. Warf—"

Without any warning, *Creaking Door* staggered, a bone-jarring bang throwing the light lander off vector, hurling the crew of Tufayl across the lander's cargo bay in a tangle of space-suited arms and legs. Michael hit the bulkhead with sickening force. He bounced off, crashing into Bienefelt's enormous bulk, his left arm—held out in a futile effort to protect himself—giving way with a dry crack when he hit. Dazed, he ignored the stabbing pain from his arm. Comming his neuronics to dump painkillers into his system, he found his feet when the *Door*'s artificial gravity came back online. He commed Sedova.

"Sitrep," he said thickly as the painkillers worked their magic, the pain receding fast but leaving him light-headed with shock.

"The *Door*'s finished. Lucky shot from an antiship laser blew out the starboard auxiliary fusion plant, I think. I'm on my way. Get the ramp down so we can take you off. We don't have much time."

"Roger that," Michael replied; he commed Ferreira to take over the transfer. He still had a battle to run. A quick check confirmed that nothing much had changed except that the clock was running down fast. Sedova would have to work quickly.

She did. *Tufayl*'s crew hung clustered around the ramp,

watching *Caesar's Ghost,* her ramp down, belly thrusters firing and decelerating savagely, come to a dead stop barely a meter away from the gaping hole in *Creaking Door*'s stern, jets of reaction mass spewing into space while Sedova realigned the lander for the run back to *Iron Duke*. A figure— Sedova's loadmaster, Petty Officer Trivedi, according to Michael's neuronics—shot across the gap, maneuvering pack on her back, trailing a thin recovery line. Nobody needed to be told what to do. Without waiting, spacers clipped in and started to pull themselves to safety.

"*Ghost,* loadmaster. That's the lot. Go, go, go," Trivedi shouted when everyone was hooked on.

Sedova did not hesitate. Leaving *Creaking Door* to tumble away into space, the timers on her self-destruct charges running, she fired the main engines in a short, sharp burst that sent the lander heading back to *Iron Duke,* spacers flailing out behind, clinging desperately to the recovery line while unseen hands inside the *Ghost* reeled them in. Trivedi's maneuvering units were spitting jets of nitrogen as she pushed from behind.

After what they had been through, the rest of the transfer turned out to be a welcome anticlimax. Once inside, Michael was more than happy to lie on the floor of the cargo bay, leaving Trivedi to push the last spacer into *Caesar's Ghost* and slam the ramp shut. He was even happier when Sedova piloted the lander inside the protective armor of *Iron Duke,* acutely aware that they had made it by a dangerously small margin.

Impatiently, he waited. Finally, *Caesar's Ghost* came to a dead stop in the *Iron Duke*'s cavernous hangar, armored air lock doors slamming shut behind them. The instant the lander stopped, he leaped out, cradling his injured arm and running hard, eyes half closed while he watched the battle unfold on his neuronics, the rest of his crew in hot pursuit.

Chest heaving from the effort, Michael burst into the combat information center, throwing himself into the command seat with only seconds to spare before the Hammer missile attack fell on the Fed dreadnoughts, fumbling one-handed to strap himself in. With the Hammer task group all but destroyed and lacking rail guns—orbital installations such as space battle stations and maintenance platforms did not carry them, only missiles, lasers, and chain guns—the platform's attack never troubled the Feds. One by one, missiles were hacked out of space by the carefully coordinated efforts of the dreadnoughts, the missiles unable to penetrate the blizzard of fire from medium-range and close-in defensive weapons, missile fusion plants, and warheads exploding in blue-white balls of flame.

It was over; barely a handful of missiles sneaked through, the damage to *Iron Duke* limited to a few patches of vaporized armor.

"Warfare, Command. Priority targets now ships of Hammer-1 and OHMP-344."

"Warfare, roger."

Michael forced himself to sit back, to assess the tactical situation dispassionately. Even though it seemed like hours, they had been in Hammer space for only a matter of minutes. The question was how much longer they should stay. Michael scanned the threat plot. The Hammers had reacted quickly to the First's incursion; a group of Hammer ships—designated task group Hammer-2—accelerated hard toward them and would be within rail-gun range soon. Their first missile salvos were already on their way, heading toward the dreadnoughts. Not long, Michael decided. The First only had minutes to finish up and get the hell out.

"Warfare, Command. We'll go for one more missile and rail-gun salvo before we jump."

"Warfare, roger."

Utterly engrossed, Michael watched the battle unfold. A swarm of rail-gun slugs joined the dreadnoughts' second missile salvo; together they fell on the ships of the hapless Hammer task group around OHMP-344—what was left of them. The Hammer ships' desperate efforts accounted for too few of the incoming missiles. In seconds, the attack slammed home, the three Hammer light cruisers reeling under the impact. Michael watched transfixed as a tear opened up across the cruiser *Carlucci*'s hull, a sinuous line, thin and impossibly bright. When the rip reached *Carlucci*'s stern, it exploded into a flare that stabbed flame out into space, and the ship staggered. An instant later, the blinding flash of runaway main fusion plants swallowed the doomed ship.

Warfare wasted no time. Missiles held back in reserve throttled up to full power, streaking in to hit the two ships in their thinly armored flanks before they could turn away. *Machuca* and *Fram* spewed reaction mass in a desperate attempt to pull out of the attack, spitting lifepods in all directions, until they, too, vanished into the hellish hearts of exploding fusion plants.

The Hammer task group was finished.

"Command, Warfare. Missiles away. Target OHMP-344. Time to target 3 minutes 15. Stand by, command . . . rail-gun salvo launched from task group Hammer-2. Time to target 2 minutes 10."

"Command, roger." The Hammers had fired early; despite the extreme range, the rail-gun swarm was big and its geometry appeared good enough to force the dreadnoughts to turn to meet the Hammer attack—taking a rail-gun swarm in the flanks was never a good idea—and ride it out if they were to get one more rail-gun salvo away.

Michael cursed some more; the Hammers were fighting smart, and things were getting complicated. The Hammers were avoiding the perennial weakness that afflicted so many of their commanders—shooting first and thinking second—and it became obvious that the salvos from OHMP-344 and the ships of Hammer-2 were timed to arrive on target to the second. Thanks to Hammer-2's arrival, the squadron was under attack from two different directions at once, something that the Fighting Instructions advised Fleet captains to avoid at all costs.

So here he was, about to be caught in exactly that position. The safest thing would be to jump the squadron clear, but that risked letting OHMP-344 off the hook. For a moment, Michael sat paralyzed by indecision before the time-to-impact counter galvanized him back into action. He emptied his lungs slowly to settle his nerves and made his decision. The Hammers were not going anywhere. He could always come back another time.

"Warfare, Command. End of operation. Adjust vectors for Comdur. Jump when ready."

"Warfare, roger."

The decision made, Michael waited for the squadron to adjust vectors for home. The Hammers were going to be pissed. The commander of Hammer-2 would have liked his chances of taking out at least a couple of the dreadnoughts. Well, he was not going to get the opportunity, and the more missiles he wasted on the doomed *Tufayl,* the better.

Satisfied that the squadron was safe to jump and with mass distribution models checked and rechecked, Warfare gave the order, and the dreadnoughts vanished into the safety of pinchspace, leaving the missiles from OHMP-344 and Hammer-2 to rip through the tangled knuckles of space-time left behind by Dreadnought Squadron One. Frustrated, the missiles attempted to turn to attack the *Tufayl,* but she was too far ahead. One by one, the missiles' second-stage engines flamed out. Unable to acquire a target, the salvo self-destructed in a spectacularly wasteful display of pyrotechnics.

But the battle for OHMP-344 was far from over.

With only one ship to deal with, the next missile salvo enjoyed the benefit of a solid target datum; they turned into the attack. As they did, *Tufayl's* antimissile defenses filled the fast-closing gap with a lethal mixture of missiles, lasers, and depleted-uranium rounds fired by hypervelocity chain guns. One after another, Hammer missiles died in fireballs of exploding warheads and failed microfusion plants, but enough survived the slaughter to press home the attack. Joined by a second rail-gun swarm from Hammer-2, a wave of missiles and slugs plunged into *Tufayl*; her bows vanished behind great roiling clouds of ionized ceramsteel armor when warheads punched deep, the doomed ship staggering under the repeated impacts, the few slugs to hit adding to the carnage.

With time to turn bows on to the rail-gun attack, *Tufayl* survived thanks to her reinforced armor, but she was left a bleeding, crippled wreck. Another missile and rail-gun attack would finish her off, but the Hammers were out of time.

Shrugging off the damage the Hammer defenders had inflicted on her, *Tufayl* closed in on OHMP-344. The platform fought to keep her out. Frantic crews labored to get the next long-range missile salvo away while close-in defenses tried to deflect the oncoming ship. *Tufayl's* hull flared white-hot as lasers probed for weaknesses in the armor, missile strikes punched gouts of yellow-red armor out into space, and chain-gun rounds speckled the bows with flashes of fierce white flame.

To no avail. With the ships of Hammer-2 unable to get another rail-gun salvo away in time, the Hammers broke and ran. All of a sudden, OHMP-344 spewed lifepods in every direction, swarms of strobes double-flashing orange pleas for help, fireflies in a desperate flight to get clear of the unfolding catastrophe.

With impressive precision, *Tufayl* smashed into OHMP-344, her battered bows driving directly into the platform's spherical heart, explosive decompression of the platform's atmosphere hurling sheets of plasteel into space, tumbling away inside an ice-crystal cloud filled with splintered plasglass, furniture, equipment, and those of OHMP-344's crew too slow to get to the lifepods.

With her hull buried deep in the platform's guts, *Tufayl's* fusion plants blew, and the ship died. The explosion ripped OHMP-344 apart, sending the smashed remains of the platform out into space, its intricate framework of girders, some with ships undergoing repair still berthed on them, twisting and buckling into a blackened mess of warped plasteel that tumbled away to nowhere.

With *Iron Duke* safely in pinchspace and ignoring the mounting pain from his arm—the painkillers were fast wearing off—Michael made it to the captain's cabin only to collapse into a chair, worn out by the aftereffects of combat but more by the certain knowledge that he had come within seconds of dying as Sedova fought to get *Caesar's Ghost* back to *Iron Duke* and safety. He sat for a long time. Not that he had much choice. Even if he wanted to move, he could not; his

legs refused to work, his arm hurt like hell, and he was beyond exhausted.

"Captain, sir." It was Ferreira.

"Yes," he croaked. "What?"

"I'm getting an alarm from your neuronics. Your vitals
are crap, and it seems you have a broken arm. Why didn't
you say something? I'm on my way."

Michael wondered if he should tell her to leave him alone
but decided against it.

The cabin door banged open, and Ferreira burst in,
closely followed by Bienefelt. The pair knelt beside him.

"For chrissakes, sir," Bienefelt said; she gently removed
his helmet. "What are you doing?"

Just having the world's biggest spacer there made Michael
feel better. "What? Can't I even have a sit-down when I want
one?" he said. "What the hell's the point of being captain
of this tub if I can't do that? Come on, you two. Help me up.
I need a shower."

"Sick bay first, sir, if you don't mind," Ferreira said.
"That arm needs fixing."

Michael started to argue, but the determined look on Ferreira's face told him that this was not the time. "Okay," he
said, resigned, "come on, get me out of this damn chair."

Thursday, January 18, 2401, UD
FWSS Iron Duke, *in orbit around Comdur Fleet Base*

"So, Michael. What do you reckon?"

"I didn't think it would happen."

Vice Admiral Jaruzelska nodded. "Did wonder myself
sometimes," she said.

"Any chance of getting the additional dreadnought
squadrons, Admiral?"

Jaruzelska shook her head. "I know we need them, but no,

none at all. Three's our lot. I had formal confirmation of that
from Fleet only this morning. So, apart from the ships held
back as operational reserves, what you see is all we get."

Inside, Michael wanted to scream out his frustration. It
made no sense. Fleet had heavy cruisers laid up in parking
orbits around every one of the Federated Worlds, fully functioning warships except for one important thing: After the
Battle of Comdur, there were no crews to take them back into
combat. Leaving them there unused at a time when Fleet
faced a resurgent Hammer was beyond dumb; sadly, there
was not a thing he—or, more significantly, Vice Admiral
Jaruzelska—could do about it.

Across the forward bulkhead of *Iron Duke*'s combat information center, the holovid flared while one after another the
ships of Dreadnought Squadrons Two and Three dropped
into Comdur normalspace, twenty converted heavy cruisers
in all, followed after a short pause by *Tufayl*'s replacement,
Reckless.

With mounting excitement, Michael watched the ships
decelerate, the shuttles tasked to remove their transit crews
already closing in. By any standard, the twenty-one converted R-Class heavy cruisers were an impressive sight.

Surely, he told himself, this was the beginning of the
end. The dreadnoughts of the First Squadron had more than
proved themselves against Hammer antimatter missiles, and
in the freewheeling chaos of close-quarters space combat,
that was the sort of fighting to be done if the Hammers were
ever to be defeated. With three full squadrons of dreadnoughts, the slow, grinding business of destroying the Hammer space fleet could get under way. Once that was done,
invasion of the Hammer Worlds could follow. For a brief moment, Michael allowed himself the luxury of imagining what
life might be like without the unending threat of yet more
death and destruction at the hands of the Hammers, a threat
hanging over humanspace for more than a century. He stifled
the idea. There was a long way to go; there was a lot more
killing to be done before that happy day arrived.

"Okay, Michael," Jaruzelska said. "I've seen enough. Let
my shuttle know I'm on my way."

"Stand by . . . It's ready when you are, sir."

"Fine. I'll see you at the squadron commanders' conference tomorrow."

"Looking forward to it, Admiral. It'll be good to get all the squadrons operational."

"It will, though I don't think the Hammers will be quite so happy."

"I hope not," Michael said with a feral grin. "I plan to make them extremely unhappy."

"I bet. Though I should remind you that we have a lot of work to be done before this lot"—Jaruzelska waved a hand at the holovid—"are up to the standard of the First."

"Just a matter of time, sir," Michael said.

"It is. I know we've set a target of three months, but you understand my concerns. We might need anything up to six, but we'll see. Before I go," she said when they had left the combat information center, "I've got a couple of admin matters for you. First, how's that arm?"

Michael waved his left arm in the air. "Good, sir. It'll be a hundred percent within a week."

"Pleased to hear it. Another wound stripe, I suppose?"

"Absolutely, sir. You know me. Too much gold is not enough."

Shaking her head, Jaruzelska laughed. "Have you heard anything from the Bachou police?"

"Yes, sir. We received formal notification this morning that the federal prosecutor's office has decided not to proceed against me, so that's that. Anna's off the hook, too. The full decision has been posted on the net if you're interested in the legal gymnastics."

Jaruzelska snorted in derision. "Oh, no, not me. I hate that stuff."

"Bit of a close thing, though," Michael said. "The bad guys might have been a bit more obvious that it was me they came for before I actually started firing, so there was an argument that the courts should be allowed to decide whether the first killing was justified or not. But get this, sir. If I'd waited until they started shooting, I would have had no case to answer at all."

Jaruzelska snorted again. "Lawyers! Anyway, I'm glad you're off the hook. You've got better things to do than waste your time defending yourself against a charge of homicide. Second, how is Anna?"

"Fine, sir. She sounded well in her last vidmail."

"Good. I think *Damishqui* missed her."

Michael laughed. "I bet they did, sir," he said, "though I'd be a lot . . ." His voice trailed away.

Jaruzelska turned to look Michael full in the face. "Don't even think it, Michael. You'll come through this, and so will *Damishqui,* trust me."

"Yes, sir."

Michael followed Jaruzelska into the drop tube that would take them to *Iron Duke*'s personnel air lock. He appreciated her confidence, but not even admirals as competent and experienced as Jaruzelska could be so sure that things would turn out okay. The Hammers had not survived by being pushovers, and *Damishqui*—along with every spacer and marine onboard—was as much at risk as any other ship in the Fleet.

Jaruzelska watched the *Iron Duke* dwindle into nothing against the stars. The arrival of the dreadnoughts brought the force up to its authorized strength; that was the good news. The bad news was that there would be no more. Once the three dreadnoughts in reserve had entered service, she would have no more ships to replace combat losses. Even convincing Fleet to release the *Reckless* had taken far more of her dwindling stock of political capital than she cared to think about.

She would need all the capital she had left. The fight inside Fleet over dreadnoughts was getting dirty. The overwhelming majority of the Fleet agreed with Rear Admiral Perkins's view that dreadnoughts were a disaster waiting to happen. If that was not bad enough, more details of the fight over the dreadnoughts had leaked through Fleet's normally watertight security; the trashpress was beginning to sniff around, looking for an angle that would allow them to make the most of the disagreement without looking unpatriotic.

She let out a long sigh: part frustration, part fatigue, part anger. The dreadnought argument long ago had crossed the line that separated rational argument from emotional slanging match—encouraged, she had no doubt, by Rear Admiral Perkins's diligent if so far covert efforts to undermine her and her ships—and that meant things were going to get a lot worse.

A depressing assessment of what that would mean for her workload was interrupted by a priority com. Closing her eyes, she read the message, then read it again to be sure.

Elation pushed depression aside. Yes, she thought, finally. After months of effort and billions of FedMarks, the Hammer antimatter manufacturing plant had been located. "Now comes the endgame," she whispered, her elation turning to anticipation. With the source of their strategic advantage gone—she had no doubts, none at all, that her dreadnoughts could bludgeon their way in close enough to destroy the plant—the Hammers were finished.

It would only be a matter of time.

She commed her chief of staff. The commander in chief had scheduled the preliminary planning conference for the next morning; she and her staff had a lot of work to get through to be ready.

Friday, January 19, 2401, UD
FWSS Reckless, in orbit around Comdur Fleet Base

"Attention on deck. FWSS *Retrieve*, FWSS *Recognizance*."

Immaculate in dress blacks, *Reckless*'s side party snapped to attention and the time-honored ritual of piping the side played out under the watchful eye of the coxswain: Bosun's calls squealed, hands snapped to foreheads in salute, the two new captains in command saluting in turn when they crossed the bow to board *Reckless*. Michael returned their salute. When the carry-on was piped, he stepped forward, arm extended.

"Captains. Welcome to *Reckless* and welcome to the Dreadnought Force."

"It's good to be here, sir," Kelli Rao said, shaking Michael's hand. "I think."

Michael smiled. "I'm sure it's a bit overwhelming, being a junior lieutenant in command of a heavy cruiser like *Retrieve*. I felt the same in *Adamant*. But you'll get used to it. Welcome," he said to Nathan Machar. "How's *Recognizance*?"

"I think you just said it, sir. Overwhelming. She's a big ship."

"She sure is. If you'd follow me. Thank you, Chief Bienefelt, impeccable as always."

"My pleasure, sir," Bienefelt replied, smiling.

Michael led the way along empty passageways. The emptiness of the place disturbed him. There was a time when *Reckless* had echoed to the sounds of hundreds of spacers and marines, their noise transforming the ship into a living thing: voices, laughter, activity, boots on decks, tools on metal, doors thudding shut, the soft hiss of air flowing through high-pressure lines, the whine of hydraulics opening and closing armored hatches. Their absence produced a quiet that was palpable, a quiet much more than the absence of noise, a powerful reminder of the changes inflicted on dreadnoughts; worse, it drained too much of the life from *Reckless* itself, leaving the ship an uncomfortable shadow of the heavy cruiser it once had been.

Shrugging aside his unease, Michael ushered the new arrivals into his cabin. Settled into a comfortable armchair, he studied his two new captains with a critical eye while the drinkbot served coffee. One thing was shockingly evident: how young both Rao and Machar were. Michael knew he was hardly a candidate for senior citizen of the year, but, those two were babies. Rao reminded him a bit of Anna: the same honey skin, a fall of fine black hair cut into a fashionable bob to frame a face dominated by pink-dusted cheeks and a firm, full nose. The similarities stopped there; Rao was much taller, heavily built, and with eyes so dark that they were almost black. Machar's bloodlines were pure African; he had the blue-black skin, height, rangy frame, whipcord muscles, and tightly-curled hair of his Nuer ancestors, migrants in the second great wave of the diaspora from Old Earth. Like most Feds, Machar was deeply proud of his links to Old Earth, links that had survived separation measured not in days and meters but in centuries and trillions of kilometers. The four small scars on his forehead bore testament to his distant roots in drought-stricken, violence-wracked Sudan.

Michael had studied their service records in detail.

Rao had seen combat in the heavy scout *Aldebaran,* Machar in the light escort *Sarissa*. They were the cream of the young officers coming out of Space Fleet College: natural leaders, technically sound, quick-thinking, and steady under pressure. Both were instinctive tacticians, their fitness for their new roles confirmed by weeks of cruelly intensive assessment under the critical eyes of Jaruzelska and her staff.

Even so, Michael wondered how they would hold up when Hammer rail-gun slugs and missiles started to tear their ships apart around them, an experience far beyond anything the sims could inflict on a spacer. Thus far, both had been lucky—though they had seen combat, their ships had come through the war unscathed, hit by not a single missile or rail-gun slug—so Michael knew he had reason to be skeptical. Rao and Machar might be fine on paper, they might be good in the sims, but they were a long way from being combat-hardened.

"Once again," Michael said, "welcome. First things first. Any issues with your ships or your crews that I need to know about? Kelli?"

"None, sir," Rao said. "*Retrieve* is 100 percent. The yard did a good job with the conversion, though it's obviously a bit rough in places. I know how much pressure they were under. All systems are nominal, we'll be fully massed within the hour, and we're provisioned for war patrol. Same goes for all the ships of the Second. We've crawled over them, we've checked every last square centimeter, and they are all operational. As to my crew, again no problems that I can see. I have a good executive officer, and my coxswain is old school, which I suspect is a good thing. The rest look good if their service records are to be believed, but I guess we'll have to see how they hold up when we get to grips with the Hammers."

"Nathan?"

"Same, sir. *Recognizance* is 100 percent, my exec and crew look good, and the same goes for the ships of the Third. We're ready to go."

"All right. Next thing. Training."

Michael tried not to laugh when Rao and Machar flicked sideways glances at each other. He understood how they felt. Not for nothing was Fleet called humanspace's largest training organization; at times it seemed to do nothing else.

"The admiral and I have finalized the training plan for your squadrons," Michael said. "Our aim is to have you combat-ready in three months"—the new captains blinked anxiously—"so you and your crews will be busy. I'm afraid all you have to look forward to is long days, not much sleep, and a lot of pressure. A word of caution, though. Given the shortage of capital ships in our order of battle, we may not have three months. If the Hammers start pulling stunts on us, Fleet may not . . . no, will not be able to leave thirty perfectly good heavy cruisers idling their time away doing endless sims. So train like every day in the sims was your last before you deploy on active service, because a few hours may be all the notice we get. Is that clearly understood?"

"Yes, sir," Rao and Machar chorused, faces tightening as the enormousness of the task ahead of them sank in.

"Good. But remember this. Dreadnoughts are Hammer killers. They're faster, tougher, better armored than anything they have in space. You've seen the records of our operations to date?"

Rao and Machar nodded.

"So you'll know what I mean. In all of Fleet history, ships have never been considered expendable. We don't throw ships away; we don't sacrifice crews. Never have. But dreadnoughts have changed that. The unmanned dreadnoughts in

your squadron are expendable, and don't you forget it. I'm
not saying waste them, but you will find you can use dreadnoughts in ways that few senior officers with all their years
of command and combat experience ever could. Something,
I might add, we have proved conclusively not just in the sims
but in combat. And that's the reason why you're the captains
of *Retrieve* and *Recognizance* instead of a pair of crusty old
four-ringers."

"Did you wonder why on Earth Fleet would give me an
entire heavy cruiser squadron to command?" Machar said.

"There's your answer."

"Explains why we have been . . . well, why . . ." Rao's
voice trailed off.

"Treated like shit is what I think you are trying to say,
Junior Lieutenant Rao," Michael said bluntly. "Why are
you surprised? If Fleet did to the rest of the fleet what it's
done to dreadnoughts, there'd be what . . . half as many officers needed? Maybe even less. It's no wonder they're unpopular. Fleet has its fair share of Luddites, and they aren't
going to sit around and let people like us change the world
any more than we can change human nature. That's just the
way it is, so get used to it."

"Yes, sir," Rao said, looking embarrassed.

"Now you know. Which brings me to what may be a more
important reason. Let me tell you about the poor old *Pericles*, the reason why dreadnoughts make some people very,
very nervous, the reason why some of those Luddites aren't
completely wrong. Now . . ."

"How did it go, sir?"

"Rao and Machar?"

"Yes, sir."

"Pretty good, Jayla, pretty good." Michael looked at his
executive officer for a moment before continuing. "But . . ."

"But what, skipper?"

"A couple of buts, I suppose. Neither of them has commanded anything bigger than an assault lander, and neither
has been on the receiving end of a really serious Hammer attack. All we know about them is what the selection process

told us—all good, of course—but how they'll go when they take their squadrons into combat, when they have to stare down an oncoming Hammer task group throwing missiles and rail-gun slugs at them, when it's time to make the hard decisions, that's another matter."

"That's not all that's worrying you, is it, sir?" Ferreira said softly.

Michael stared at his executive officer keenly. "Remind me," he said, "not to take you for granted, Jayla. No, it's not. One thing in particular bothers me. When you play war games in a sim, only your reputation is on the line. When we take the dreadnoughts into battle, everything is on the line, and I'm not talking about whether we come home alive or not. No, there'll be a lot more than that at stake."

Ferreira nodded. "The Federation and what it stands for, families, the people we love, friends, homes. Those are the stakes."

"They are."

"They don't get much bigger."

"No, they don't," Michael said. "The only reason we have dreadnoughts in our order of battle is because the Federation is screwed without them. The Hammers have more ships than us. They have more antimatter warheads. If they had the balls, they could . . . they would destroy our home planets. They beat us to a pulp at Comdur, and they can pulp us again. So we have to stop them. Despite all the crap dished out by the antidreadnought lobby, that's the only reason we have dreadnoughts. Me? I think I can handle it. But Rao and Machar? How will they go when they have to make decisions in combat knowing that the Federation might fall if they get it wrong?"

Ferreira said nothing, and the silence that followed went on for a long time.

The conference room stayed silent when the speaker paused.

"So to sum up, the concept of operations for Operation Opera envisages a battle-fleet-sized operation spearheaded by the dreadnought force"—an ugly murmur filled the air— "with conventionally crewed ships and a marine landing force following up. Their task will be the destruction of the Hammer antimatter plant."

The speaker, a young captain from Fleet's plans division, stopped again. "And let me just make this point," he continued. "Dreadnoughts are the only way to make this operation a success. That is," he said, his words deliberate, "unless you consider the loss of more than sixty heavy cruisers along with their entire crews an acceptable casualty rate. Well, I don't . . . and I suspect none of you do, either. Unless there are any questions, I would like to hand over to Warfare Division for their critique . . . No questions? Thank you. Captain al-Fulani?"

Michael wanted to stand up and cheer. Of all Fleet's staff divisions, plans—traditionally home to some of the best and brightest minds in Fleet—was the only one wholeheartedly in support of dreadnoughts, and it was good to see a staffer with the balls to stand up in public and say so. He watched Captain al-Fulani make her way to the lectern. Michael had met al-Fulani only once; it was enough. She—not to mention her division—was as implacably opposed to dreadnoughts as Plans was supportive.

"Thank you," al-Fulani said, "though regarding the reliance of the concept of operations on dreadnoughts, we would like it noted that we don't support—"

"Enough!" Fleet Admiral Kefu cut al-Fulani off, his voice

harsh. The chief of the defense force stood up. He turned to look at the assembled staffers, making no attempt to conceal his anger.

"The objections of those of you," Kefu said carefully, deliberately, "who cannot accept that dreadnoughts have any part to play have been heard . . . considered . . . and taken into account. But it seems I still have to remind far too many of you that we don't have the luxury of endless debate. If we do not deal with the Hammers and soon, we may find ourselves arguing over the ashes of dead planets. Our home planets. My home planet. My home. My family."

Kefu paused, looking hard at the officers arrayed in front of him. "I will not allow that to happen. So, for those of you a bit slow to understand what's going on, listen up, because I will not be saying this again. The role of dreadnoughts in the attack on the Hammer antimatter plant will be exactly as recommended by Plans Division. The commander in chief has made that decision. I have formally endorsed it. So stop wasting your time and mine by prolonging an argument that is over."

Kefu stood silent for a moment, face flushed with anger. "Now . . . if there is anyone here," he said with great deliberation, "who cannot live with that decision, you should leave. I will expect your resignations on my desk first thing tomorrow morning . . . Anyone . . . no takers? Good. It seems that military discipline does still mean something. I must say I was beginning to wonder."

Making an obvious effort to regain control, Kefu turned to look at al-Fulani. "Captain. How about you? You seem happy to question the decisions of your superiors in an open forum. Should I expect your resignation?" Kefu's tone was brutal.

Fascinated, Michael watched al-Fulani squirm. It was not often that Fleet officers committed professional suicide in public, but al-Fulani just had. Kefu was an unforgiving man, and he never, ever forgot. The woman was finished, her career flushed down the crapper. If she had any sense, she would resign.

"Well?" Kefu barked.

"My apologies, sir," al-Fulani replied, her face red with a mix of embarrassment, anger, and fear. "I'm in, sir," she stammered, "of course."

"I bloody well hope so," Kefu said venomously. "I have better things to do than keep insubordinate Fleet staffers in line." He turned to look at the head of Fleet's warfare division. "Admiral Chenoweth. I do not need your people second-guessing the commander in chief's decisions. Do I make myself clear?"

"Crystal clear, sir," the admiral said, his face betraying anger at the humiliation Kefu was heaping on him. "It will not happen again."

"For your sake, Admiral, I hope it doesn't," Kefu said, sitting down. "Captain al-Fulani, please continue."

"Thank you, sir, . . . er," al-Fulani said, clearly rattled by Kefu's savage response. There was an awkward pause before she recovered enough to continue. "Yes . . . Warfare Division has analyzed the concept of operations, and we believe it has the following weaknesses. First, . . ."

In the end, after hours of sometimes rancorous argument, the conference came down to a single issue. Michael watched transfixed while Vice Admiral Jaruzelska marshaled her thoughts. This conference—an initial briefing for the captains of the ships involved in Operation Opera, the operation to destroy the Hammer antimatter plant—was his first opportunity to see firsthand how the men and women responsible for the defense of the Federated Worlds worked. For Michael, one of the most junior officers present by a big margin, it was an education in itself. An unholy mix of politics, expediency, strategy, power, and ill-concealed ambition transformed the conference into a brutal contest refereed with ruthless efficiency by Fleet Admiral Kefu.

It was a long way from the dry and dusty debate he had expected, and now it was Jaruzelska's turn to enter the ring. She had a fight on her hands; sadly, if Kefu's body language offered any guide, it was a fight she was not going to win.

"Sir," Jaruzelska said to Kefu, "I have to call this the way I see it. Yes, we can launch Operation Opera within six weeks, but that would be inadvisable and imprudent."

She paused. Utterly absorbed, Michael stared not at Jaruzelska but at Kefu. The admiral's face tightened noticeably at Jaruzelska's uncompromising tone. You're going to lose this, Admiral Jaruzelska, Michael decided.

"It will be extremely tight," Jaruzelska continued, "and not just for the dreadnoughts. This is a complex operation. Logistics will be tight, as will the operations designed to draw Hammer forces away from Devastation Reef. All of that can be man—"

"Cut to the chase, Admiral, please. We don't have all day," Kefu said.

"No, sir, we don't. But to expect the follow-on dreadnought squadrons to be combat-ready in a matter of weeks is unrealistic. To throw those ships into an assault on the most heavily defended, the most important target we have ever attacked before they are ready is to invite their destruction. Not that losing ships is the problem"—she paused to look around the room—"but losing them for no good reason certainly is. To go early has no merit. The Hammer plant is not going anywhere. Delay Opera by three months and you will have an operational dreadnought force—thirty properly trained, operationally effective ships—to spearhead the attack. And that means our chances of success will be significantly greater. It's that simple, sir."

Michael watched Jaruzelska fight to turn the argument her way. The admiral's logic was faultless, but he had no doubts where the issue would finish up. The decision to go early had been made; that much was obvious from what Kefu had said, and the politicians among Fleet staff—which, in Michael's jaundiced view, was all of them—were falling in behind him. The one person who might have swung the issue—the commander in chief, Admiral Shiu—had sided with the "go early" lobby, so go early it was.

Michael tuned out of what fast became an utterly pointless argument, an argument Jaruzelska was never going to win, his mind turning to the pressing issue of how to turn two young and inexperienced officers into effective dreadnought squadron commanders in half the time he needed. Rao and Machar might have been picked after a ruthless selection process that confirmed their innate tactical brilliance, but that did not give him any guarantees that they would hold up under the severe pressure of combat, even with Jaruzelska's support and guidance.

Considering what he was expected to achieve with his dreadnoughts, Michael was strangely calm. The chances of any of the dreadnoughts surviving Operation Opera were slim—that was obvious—which meant their crews might not survive, either. There was too little time to bring the dreadnoughts up to speed, too little time to plan the operation properly, too little time to simulate the operation often enough to expose the flaws in the operational planning, too little time to rehearse.

In short, there was a good chance that Operation Opera— the one operation that had to be a success if the Federated Worlds were to survive—would turn out to be one of the great military disasters of all time.

Why the rush? Michael's guess—it was only a guess—was that Kefu had allowed himself to be steamrolled by the politicians, the real ones this time, not Fleet's part-timers, the elected ones who fancied that they actually governed the Worlds. Panicked by the Hammers' antimatter missiles, they wanted Fleet to make the problem go away. Now!

And who would be responsible for doing that? Vice Admiral Jaruzelska, of course. She was commander of Battle Fleet Lima and would be held to account for the operation's success or failure. And on whom would she rely to do the hard work to get Opera across the line? Lieutenant Michael Helfort and the ships of the dreadnought force. Who else?

Terrific, he thought, vainly trying to ignore the crushing weight of Jaruzelska's expectations. For chrissakes, how was he ever going to pull this one off?

Michael pushed back in his seat as the shuttle taking him back to *Reckless* lifted off, resigned now to his fate. He had decided that the only thing he could do was his best.

Jaruzelska had said her piece and had been overruled. She would not be the first military commander in history to suffer at the hands of politicians, and like all those before her, she would ignore her misgivings and do her duty. The way Michael saw it, Jaruzelska's job was to make Operation Opera so simple that Battle Fleet Lima could pull it off even with half-trained dreadnoughts leading the way.

There was only one problem. Making the complex simple was beyond him; it was an enormous challenge even for a combat-hardened commander such as Jaruzelska. Michael spent hours and hours looking at the Hammer antimatter plant. It sat deep inside Devastation Reef, a convoluted tangle of gravitational rips tens of millions of kilometers across, protected by every warship the Hammers had to spare, backed up by space battle stations, pinchspace jump disrupters, semiautonomous defense platforms, and antistarship minefields. Opera was not an impossible mission, but rushed planning, inadequate training, and—like every operation after the Comdur fiasco—too few ships were beginning to make it look worryingly like one.

Oh, yes, there was one more risk factor, and it was a big one—limited intelligence. The Hammers had picked the site for their antimatter manufacturing plant well. Devastation Reef was such an appalling place for starships that the Feds had never bothered to survey the deepspace around it properly—though he would lay good money down that the Hammers had—so getting in and out safely would be a challenge in itself. To make matters worse, the brass was concerned to the point of near hysteria that the Hammers might get wind of the attack. That meant no infiltration or close surveillance or covert operations assets ahead of the attack; Michael had seen the directive telling Jaruzelska to keep her reconbots well away from the plant and its approaches.

Tipping off the Hammers that an attack was imminent was not a risk she would be allowed to take. Michael understood why; he also knew who would pay the butcher's bill.

Michael had paid attention during his military history classes at Space College. Poor intelligence had doomed more military operations to failure than he liked to think about. He only hoped that Operation Opera would not be one of them.

Vice Admiral Jaruzelska was her normal brisk self, bustling in to take her seat. Not for the first time, Michael wondered how she kept going. "Morning, everyone. Seats, please," she said. "Everyone here?" she asked, turning to her chief of staff.

"Yes, sir," Captain Tuukkanen replied.

"Let's get on. Right, Captain. Let's look at the results of the latest simulations and see what they tell us about our chances of pulling this one off."

Michael sighed softly. The chances of Operation Opera succeeding? If the sims were right, they were not good, not good at all.

". . . so what we're seeing, Admiral, is consistent. Using multiple task groups to divert the Hammer defenses before the dreadnoughts destroy the plant's nearspace defenses is the only way to give the assault group—the ships tasked with actually destroying the antimatter plant—a clear run in. Any way we look at it, that is the right way, the best way . . . I think the only way."

Captain Tuukkanen paused for a moment. "We cannot assume that the Hammers will leave Assault Group alone," he continued. "This is one of the best-defended facilities in humanspace. It will be hard to crack its defenses, and anyone heading for the antimatter plant is going to get attacked.

That much we know, and that's why the sims are showing us failing more often than not. But even though they suffer heavy losses, the dreadnoughts leading the attack get through practically every time, while Assault Group does not. That leaves us in control of the space around the antimatter plant but not with the assets to destroy it. All too often, those assets are in an Assault Group that fails to get through. It foll—"

A voice cut Tuukkanen off. It was Perkins. "I cannot agree, Captain. Why should the dreadnoughts get through and Assault Group not? It does not make any sense." Perkins glanced around the room, a half smile on his face making it clear that what he had said was so obvious that it really did not need any justification.

"Sir, if I may?" Michael said. Jaruzelska waved him to continue. Perkins scowled his disapproval; Michael ignored him. "The dreadnoughts get through because they can survive attacks that a conventional heavy cruiser cannot. That's been proved not just in endless design reviews but in the sims and in combat. The data cannot be argued with. Therefore, the most likely outcome of Opera is that dreadnoughts make it through when nobody else does. That means they must have the tools to finish the job if Assault Group does not get through."

When he finished, Michael wondered if he might not have been a tad too firm given that he was arguing with an admiral. Screw it, screw Perkins, he decided. Destroying the Hammer antimatter plant was far too important to worry about the man's feelings.

"Admiral Perkins?" Jaruzelska said, a faint smile ghosting across her face.

Perkins scowled some more. "I firmly believe, Admiral, that if the dreadnoughts make it, so will Assault Group. That means we can finish the job. I think what we have here is something we've all seen before. In the end, simulations are just mathematical models, and we can pretty much make them say what we want. What we have here is just that. Too many negative assumptions producing unrealistically high probabilities of failure. Who knows why, but the sims are wrong. Assault Group will get through."

"Excuse me, sir," Tuukkanen said, glaring at Perkins, his voice choked with outrage. "Are you suggesting the sims have been rigged to make the dreadnoughts look good? If you are, sir, I strongly—"

"That is enough, Captain Tuukkanen," Jaruzelska said firmly, "I'm sure that is not what the admiral is suggesting."

"Pig's ass," Michael muttered. "That's precisely what Perkins was suggesting."

"Thank you, sir," Perkins said. "Like I was saying, we all know overly pessimistic assumptions can—and usually do—lead to more fallback planning, more resources diverted away from the mission to provide 'just in case' backup, and a loss of focus on the main game. If we make this thing too complicated, it'll fall apart just because it is too complicated. And just so we are clear, Captain Tuukkanen, I am not suggesting the sims have been rigged to make dreadnoughts look good . . . though some might think that."

Michael watched intently. Setting aside Perkins's cheap shot about rigging the sims to favor the dreadnoughts, his main point was a good one. Yes, of course Perkins wanted to reduce the dreadnoughts' role in Opera to a bare minimum—for all the wrong reasons—but some of what he said made sense. He was an experienced combat commander; he knew from firsthand experience that complexity sowed the seeds of failure just as much as oversimplification did. But keeping Opera simple by assuming that Assault Group would always make it through would be dumb. They might not; that possibility must be allowed for.

Michael was pleased to see that Jaruzelska agreed; she turned to Perkins.

"Simplicity is a virtue, Admiral," she said, "but only up to a point. To assume that either Assault Group gets through to the plant or nobody does would be a serious mistake. The sims show there is always the chance that Assault Group is interdicted by the Hammers, and if it is interdicted, the dreadnoughts must be able to complete the mission."

Michael enjoyed Perkins's response, that of a man who had just sucked a large and bitter lemon. "Admiral!" Perkins protested, "the operation is overly-complex as it is. It would be a mistake to make it even more complicated."

"I agree, I absolutely agree. So we need a simple solution to the problem, one that has no impact outside the dreadnoughts themselves, one that requires no detailed planning and that has no command overhead. Any ideas?"

There was an awkward pause. Afterward, Michael could not explain why his discussion with Sedova about the role of *Caesar's Ghost* came to mind, but it did.

"Yes sir," he said. "Assault Group's mission remains unchanged. If they get through, they will destroy the Hammer plant. If they fail to get through, the dreadnoughts will have to take over. We already carry an assault lander. Give us a platoon of marines and a demolition team. They will be a last resort, but it's better than nothing."

"Umm," Jaruzelska said. "Admiral Perkins?"

"I still believe it is unnecessary," Perkins said ungraciously, "but . . ." His voice trailed off.

"I'll assume that is a yes, shall I?" Jaruzelska said drily. "So that puts your complement up to . . . yes, up to fifty-one. Michael?"

"No problem, sir," Michael said. "Temporary accommodation modules. The marines will not be onboard long enough for it to be a problem."

"Good. You have twenty-four hours to work up a detailed proposal. Now, to other issues."

Wednesday, January 24, 2401, UD
Neu Kelheim, New Hartz Mountains, Jascaria planet

The village of Neu Kelheim might have been lifted in its entirety from Old Earth, every part of it as authentically German as Fed technology could make it, or so the public relations people said. Sadly, it was far from authentic; not one molecule of the place had ever been near Old Earth. But it was perfect, even if had ended up a theme park version of the real thing: too perfect. Not that he cared much. Fake or not, it was a pretty place: Its main street ran between bars, shops, cafés, and restaurants interspersed with guesthouses and hotels, the buildings a mix of styles under pitched roofs loaded with snow, all marked with the angular black slashes, extravagant swirls, and decorative diamond shapes of Fraktur script.

Best of all was the air: Bitterly cold under a violet sky fast darkening into night, it was generously laced with the smells of fresh bread, roasting coffee, wood smoke, beer, and a hundred other more subtle aromas from restaurant kitchens.

His senses overloaded, Michael picked his way carefully along a sidewalk covered with recent snow toward the station. With not long to go before Opera kicked off, Jaruzelska had decided a short break would do the troops good. By some miracle—Michael suspected the intervention of a higher power, namely, *Damishqui*'s executive officer—Anna had wangled a couple of days off at the same time. Michael needed a rest badly. What with planning meetings, simulator sessions, and working long hours to get the new dreadnought squadron commanders up to speed, not to mention trying to persuade Fleet to cough up the marines he needed, sleep had become an optional extra. He was bone-tired, his state of mind not helped by the awful knowledge that he would soon be throwing *Reckless* and the rest of the dreadnoughts right down the throats of the Hammers. The prospect gnawed at him. Even when he was busy, images of rail-gun-firing Hammer ships would reach down out of his subconscious to twist his stomach into a knot. When he did manage to get to his bunk, sleep came only with the help of the behavioral therapies loaded in his neuronics by Indra's postcombat trauma teams backed up by drugbots. Worst of all, the same awful nightmare had returned to torment him night after night.

"Goddamnit," he swore despairingly. It would be one hell of a weekend if he could not stay awake during the day only to thrash around escaping imaginary ships all night. Anna would not be impressed.

On time to the second, the train flowed out of the forests that surrounded Neu Kelheim and glided into the station, coming to stop with a soft hiss. Moments later, Anna fell into his arms. Michael buried himself in her neck, overwhelmed by her warmth, her smell, the feel of her skin silk-soft against his mouth, the touch of her hair across his face.

Eventually, Anna pushed him away. She looked him full in the face. "Hello, Michael," she said softly.

Michael and Anna walked out of the restaurant onto Neu Kelheim's main street. It was quiet, streetlights throwing soft puddles of light onto sidewalks blanketed with well-trampled snow under a moonless black sky thick with stars. Michael breathed in deeply and then wished he had not, his lungs seared by the brutal cold. He said a short prayer of thanks to the geniuses who had made his cold-suit while it sealed itself around him, only a small patch of his face left exposed to the bitter night air.

"Come on, slowcoach," Anna said cheerfully.

Michael suppressed a groan when they set off hand in hand. His suggestion—that it was time for bed—had been shot down out of hand. So, with a full stomach topped off with a bottle of decent Riesling, Michael followed Anna through the snow on a freezing cold night too dark to see anything not illuminated by streetlights.

Anna seemed to know where she was heading, so Michael followed dutifully across snow crunching underfoot, made brittle by the day's sun, resigned to his fate. They made their way up the main street, across the town square with its impressively large bell tower, and into Neu Kelheim's cliff gardens, hectares of geneered plants from hundreds of planets, all shapeless under heavy blankets of snow.

Just when Michael started to protest, Anna turned. "Here we are," she said, "Neu Kelheim's Pavilion of the Winds. Very famous, something you'd know if you'd done your homework." She pointed to a small pavilion, a simple structure of hand-carved timber set hard up against the cliff edge, the path to its entrance marked by a string of firefly lights.

"Bit bloody cold for this sort of thing, don't you think?" Michael grumbled past his cold-suit, trying not to think of a warm room, never mind an even warmer bed.

"Not at all," Anna said, her tone of voice making it clear that Michael did not have much say in the matter. "Come on."

When his eyes adjusted slowly to the dark, Michael saw why Anna had wanted to come to this place. The pavilion was built to screen out the light from the park behind them. A single bench ran across its open face, looking out into the void, a sheer drop falling the best part of 2,000 meters down fractured basalt cliffs into the rain forests that carpeted the foothills of the New Hartz Mountains. The air was so clear, the horizon was visible: a rough-edged black shape sawed out of the stars, the only light coming from the soft orange splashes of the towns and villages scattered over the blackness of the forest.

For a long time they sat there, unmoving, silent. "We'll be all right, won't we?" Anna said finally.

Michael swore wordlessly; talk about the 10 million Fed-Mark question.

"Think so," he said after a while. "*Damishqui* will be in the right place covering the withdrawal, and the dreadnoughts can take pretty much anything the Hammers can dish out. It's the rest of the poor bastards I worry about. Too many of them will not be coming home. But like I say, the dreadnoughts will be fine."

"I wish I believed that. I've been through the operations order, Michael. I know what you're up against. I'm worried it'll be a bloodbath."

"Listen, Anna," Michael said fiercely. "I cannot predict what'll happen any more than you can. But we have a few things going for us. The Hammers have no idea we're coming, dreadnoughts are tougher than anything the Hammers ever sent into space, and Jaruzelska is running the show. The way I see it, we have better cards than the Hammers, and if we play them well on the day, yes, we'll come through this. When it comes to the dreadnoughts, they're not indestructible; no ship is. But I've taken them into action enough times to know that the Hammers still have not worked them out. They're faster, accelerate better, turn quicker, have better armor, and I'll have twenty-nine of the ugly bastards to back me up. They can take a lot of punishment, so I really think we'll be okay."

"Like I said, I wish I believed that." Anna squeezed his hand hard. "No, that's wrong. I guess I do believe it, if only because I have to. Otherwise, what the hell's the point?" She sighed. "Come on, that's enough sightseeing. Let's get back. If it gets any colder, my nose is going to freeze and drop off."

"Can't have that," Michael said as they walked back through the gardens. "It's such a pretty nose even if it is a bit on the large—"

Whatever else Michael planned to say vanished when Anna scraped a handful of bitterly cold snow off a small wall and shoved it into his mouth.

Sunday, January 28, 2401, UD
FWSS Reckless, *Comdur nearspace*

"Captain, sir."

"Yes, Jayla?"

"The up-shuttle's just docked. The self-loading cargo's big on green shipsuits, so I think Lieutenant Kallewi and his marines have arrived . . . finally."

Michael grinned. "Pleased to hear it. It's about time. I hope we don't ever need them, but it'll be good to have them just in case. Tell Kallewi I'd like to see him when he has dumped his kit."

"Yes, sir."

"When are we embarking the demolition charges?"

"The special weapons security group has just confirmed we'll have them this afternoon: 15:00 sharp."

"Okay."

Five minutes after Michael dropped the com with his executive officer, there was a soft knock on his door.

"Come!"

It was Kallewi. Michael stood up to shake hands, the marine's thickset frame towering over him. Marines came in one of two equally lethal models: tall and heavily muscled or small and wiry. Kallewi was definitely one of the former.

"Have a seat," Michael said, "and welcome to *Reckless*. It's Janos, isn't it?"

"It is, sir."

"Right, Janos. Anything I need to know?"

"No, sir. I've got a full team, thirty regular marines augmented by an assault demolition team. We were picked because we've just completed a month's assault training together on the close-quarter combat ranges on Comdur."

"Zero g and full grav?"

"Both, sir. And they let us cook off an obsolete demolition charge on one of the deepspace firing ranges. An old Mark 34. Impressive."

"A Mark 34? What's that? Two megatons?"

"Shade under, 1.7. We have the Mark 40 now, 2.1-megaton yield. Big enough to give the Hammers a headache."

"I'd say so. Anything you need to know?"

"Well, actually, sir, there is. All we were told was to report onboard *Reckless*. I've asked why, what our tasking was, more than once, but I never did find anyone authorized . . . or willing . . . to answer the question."

Shocked, Michael felt his face twisting into a frown. "Are you telling me you don't know why you're here?"

"Yes, sir. That's exactly what I'm saying. Apart from the obvious—that something seriously big involving the Hammers is going down—no, we don't know."

"I'm sorry to hear that, Janos. Let me fix that. Operation Opera is why you're here. We will be part of Battle Fleet Lima under the command of Vice Admiral Jaruzelska, and we are going to kick the Hammers . . . hard."

Kallewi smiled, a thin, hungry smile that made Michael glad the marine was on his side. "I'll have some of that, sir."

"Okay. Let me run you through the operation as it stands at the moment." He put a schematic summarizing the operation onto the holovid screen that dominated an entire bulkhead of his day cabin. "Here's the target. It's an asteroid right in the middle of a shit-awful mess of gravitational rips called Devastation Reef; we don't know what the Hammers call it, but it's where the Kraa-loving bastards manufacture the antimatter in their missile warheads."

"Oh, shit," Kallewi hissed through clenched teeth, visibly shocked. "I guessed we were getting into something important, but nothing quite that big. Hell, that's big." The marine sounded stunned.

"It is, and they don't come much bigger. Let me run you through the time line and explain why we might need marine assault demolition teams."

An hour later, a subdued Kallewi shook his head. "I've been a marine for a while, but I have not seen anything like this. Tell you what, sir. It's going to be a pig. A real pig."

"Now that you know what you're in for, what else can I tell you?"

"The layout of the Hammer plant would be nice, sir."

"I wish," Michael said. "I've stopped asking, but the last time I did, I was told the intelligence people were being flogged hard to get something. I've not seen anything yet. It's no comfort, but I'm sure the admiral is frustrated—everyone is—that she doesn't actually know what lies underneath the surface of the asteroid. As things stand, if your team ends up with the prickly end of the pineapple, you'll have to find your own way in."

"I'm sure we'll manage," Kallewi said. "We'll have three demolition charges. Ideally, we should get them close enough to the fusion plants and hope they trigger loss of containment. That's off the top of my head, but I'm pretty sure that's how we'll have to do the job. Can you leave that with me, sir? I'll get my team onto the problem right away. I should have a first cut plan within, ah . . . twenty-four hours. Absent any decent intelligence, it'll be short on detail, but we'll do our best. That okay, sir?"

"That'll be good. I'll com the last brief I received from the admiral's staff to you: how the plant might be laid out and so on. You can use that for your training sims."

"Thanks."

"And I'd like to meet your team. Set up a time with the XO and let me know."

"Will do, sir."

Anger had been welling up inside Michael, and by the time Kallewi left his day cabin, he was seething. Buried under a mountain of more pressing matters, he had not spent much time worrying about the job Kallewi might have to do if Assault Group failed to make it through to the antimatter plant. The arrival of Kallewi and his marines had changed all that, and now he smelled a rat, a big smelly one. How the hell had three marine assault demolition teams been assigned to the dreadnought force but not told why? How could Perkins's precious Assault Group ever destroy the antimatter plant when they had no idea what it looked like?

It made no sense at all. Unless . . .

Perkins. It had to be Perkins. The man refused to believe that the dreadnoughts might have to finish the job of destroying the Hammer antimatter plant, to the point where he had decided there was no reason to brief the marines who would take over if Perkins's ships failed.

Michael commed Jaruzelska's chief of staff. He needed to know if anything important was being kept back.

Four hours later, Michael stared grim-faced at the information he had just received from Captain Tuukkanen under cover of a personal note apologizing for not supplying the material earlier. An unfortunate oversight by Assault Group's planning team, Jaruzelska's chief of staff said, for which he apologized.

Unfortunate oversight, like hell, Michael thought. Yet more deviousness from Rear Admiral Perkins, most likely. Michael shook his head in disbelief. The bloody man still acted as though Assault Group would get through to the Hammer antimatter plant no matter what. Whose side was Tuukkanen on, for heaven's sake? A good chief of staff was supposed to stop bullshit like this, to make sure the thousands of pieces that made up the Operation Opera jigsaw fit seamlessly together.

He stared at the intelligence he had been sent. It was priceless. Far from having no idea how the Hammer plant might be laid out, he was looking at schematics showing the maze of tunnels the Hammers had carved out deep below the surface of Mathuli-4451. The drawings had sat buried in the bowels of the intelligence ministry for a decade or more until a persistent analyst with a good memory dug them out. How the Federation had laid its hands on the schematics in the first place, he would never know, but looking at them, he would have bet good money on them coming from the hard-rock tunneling contractors used for the job. Not that it mattered how they had fallen into Fed hands. They had, and that meant Kallewi would have some idea at least of where he had to go.

The schematics were not everything Kallewi would have wanted: too little detail. They did not show what each tunnel was used for, nor was there anything showing what equipment went where, and nowhere was there even the smallest hint that an antimatter plant would occupy the tunnels. They described the place only as Deepspace Support Facility 27, a generic title that offered no clues to its real purpose. The intelligence analyst—in Michael's opinion, the man should get a medal—only knew he had the right place because the diameter of the asteroid shown on the drawings matched the diameter of Mathuli-4451 precisely.

Still angry, still wondering what the hell Perkins was up to, still wondering why Tuukkanen had not picked this one up earlier, Michael commed Kallewi to come to his cabin. The man would be relieved to know his marines would not have to go in blind, though he might be forgiven for wondering just what sort of lying clowns Vice Admiral Jaruzelska had doing the detailed planning for Operation Opera.

He was beginning to wonder, too.

From years of experience, Jaruzelska knew that her staff would work day and night, seven days a week, without complaint until they dropped in their tracks, utterly exhausted, so tired that even drugbots did not keep them awake. But she had learned the hard way that overwork was a trap. While it did wonders for the egos of power-drunk senior officers—of which there were far too many in Fleet for her liking—to work people to the point of collapse, it was a recipe for disaster: Staff officers who were too tired to pay attention to the details invariably compensated by cutting the AIs responsible for the nitty-gritty operational planning too much slack, often with disastrous results. She had seen it all before, and Operation Opera was challenge enough without adding AI-assisted screwups to the mix.

Her thinking showed in nearly empty offices, a handful of watchkeepers the only spacers on deck, all of them smart enough to know not to bother her while she tidied up the last of a small list of must-do items. When she left her office, she was looking forward to a much-needed workout followed by a long lunch with two of her closest friends from Space College, so the soft ping of a priority incoming com came as an unwelcome surprise.

It was her chief of staff.

"Yes, Captain Tuukkanen?" she said sternly. "This better be damned important. I have a gym session and a lunch I do not want to miss."

Jaruzelska's chief of staff shook his head. "Sorry, sir. They're off. We've been ordered to report to Fleet in person soonest. The courier is standing by. I'll have a shuttle to pick you up in five. Air lock 14-B."

"Shit!" Jaruzelska said while she started to walk as fast as age and seniority allowed. "Admiral Perkins?"

"He's on his way."

"Okay. What the hell's going on?"

"Don't know, sir. I've been promised a briefing paper before we jump. All I know is that it involves the dreadnoughts."

Jaruzelska skidded to a halt. "You're kidding me, Captain," she said incredulously.

"Wish I was, sir, but no," Tuukkanen said. "Fleet's put them on twenty-four hours' notice to deploy."

"Where are they?"

"They were on the Manovitz farspace ranges. I've ordered them back. They're in pinchspace on their way home."

"Fine. This had better be good," Jaruzelska said grimly.

With midnight long gone, Michael had sat outside Jaruzelska's office for a good hour by the time the admiral arrived. He was having a great deal of trouble staying awake. Jaruzelska's ruthless determination to make the dreadnoughts combat-ready was taking its toll; his sleep deficit was getting to a point where even the drugbots his neuronics released into his system—something he hated doing—had to struggle to keep him alert.

"Hello, Michael," Jaruzelska said. "Sorry I'm late. Had a few things to attend to. Come on in, take a seat."

Mystified, Michael did as he was told.

"Coffee, Michael?"

"Think I'd better, sir. It's long past my bedtime."

"Mine, too. How was Manovitz?"

"Tough. They whipped our asses. But we're getting there. Rao and Machar are naturals."

"Yes, they are," Jaruzelska said.

Michael struggled not to ask what the hell he was doing sitting in her office in the middle of the night swapping small talk.

After a short hiatus while the drinkbot delivered the coffees, Jaruzelska pushed back in her seat, looking at Michael across the top of her mug. He waited patiently. He knew

Jaruzelska pretty well, well enough to spot the abnormally high levels of stress and fatigue showing on her face. Something was definitely up.

"Right," Jaruzelska said eventually, sitting up straight. "Let's get on. Ever heard of a planet called Salvation?"

"No, sir," Michael said with a shake of his head, "can't say I have."

"Well, you have now. Two days ago, Fleet intelligence received a report, graded A-1, telling us that the Hammers intend to attack the planet Salvation and its settlers, a large number of whom belong to a breakaway Hammer of Kraa sect. We, and that includes you and your dreadnoughts, are going to stop them. The jokers at Fleet have called it Operation Paradise."

Unable to say a word, Michael stared at Jaruzelska.

"You can close your mouth, Michael," she said. "There's an initial briefing for you and your officers . . . Let me see, yes, at 04:00, but before that, I need to talk to you about the dreadnoughts. I have to know that they can do what's expected of them."

Despite the ungodly hour and the unremitting stress of a week spent on the Manovitz fleet battle ranges playing war games, all Michael's tiredness had vanished, washed away by the prospect of action. The intelligence analyst was just winding up his briefing.

"Thank you. That concludes my briefing. Are there any questions?"

Michael asked the question on everyone's mind. "The report's graded A-1. Has Fleet explicitly confirmed that with the intelligence providers? We need to be absolutely sure on this. We don't often see intelligence graded A-1."

"Yes," the analyst said, "we have confirmed the grading. I can also tell you that Fleet has gone back channel to the head of the Hammer desk. She's confirmed the source is impeccable. It has a good track record for being both timely and accurate. As to the intelligence itself, I can only repeat what I've already said: It is corroborated by what the Hammers are doing on the ground. Data intercepts confirm their

2nd, 18th, and 45th marine brigades have moved out of barracks to the Kerrivici marine base, which of course is one of the Hammer's planetary assault training centers.

"Until we received this report, we believed those movements were simply part of some training exercise, but we now know that to be incorrect. Doctrinal Security is also on the move; we have intercepts confirming that their 116th Shock Brigade is en route to Kerrivici"—uneasy whispers ran through the room; DocSec shock brigades were notorious for their brutal suppression of dissent—"and there's some evidence another DocSec regiment is on its way to Kerrivici, but we've not been able to confirm that. So yes, Fleet intelligence sees every reason to grade this report reliable. Are there any more questions . . . no? Thank you. The next briefer will give you a quick overview of Salvation. Lieutenant?"

"Thank you, sir," the young lieutenant said when she took her place at the lectern. "If you would turn your attention to the holovid, you can see what Salvation looks like. In a word, wet. The planet is all ocean apart from a single island . . . here . . . with one settlement, New Hope. The breakaway sect—they call themselves the Salvationists of Kraa, or Salvos for short—live in a large gated community on the northern outskirts of the town, about a hundred thousand of them. Relations with the rest of the island's population are good, mainly because they have learned the hard way to be tolerant, even to the point where they now accept AIs and geneering. Two more things to note. From a tactical point of view, the Salvos look like a soft target because they are so concentrated, but they're not. We know from previous security scares that even if we alert them to the Hammers' intentions, they will not move. They have always made it clear that they will fight and die no matter how many Hammers come after them. They are tough, they are well armed, and they are very determined. So the Hammers will have their hands full rounding them up. Second, Salvation has been declared a neutral planet under the Kalici Protocol. In theory, that binds the Hammers not to attack it, but

that's clearly a legal nicety they have no intention of re-
specting. A profile of Salvation is in your briefing notes and
we have set up an AI knowledge base for more detailed en-
quiries, so I'll stop there. Are there any questions?"

The conference room was silent. Michael glanced around;
every last spacer present sported the same look of stunned
disbelief on his or her face. He sympathized. A few hours
earlier, the crews of the dreadnoughts were looking forward
to a badly needed stand-down. Now they faced action against
the Hammers and soon, a lot sooner than anyone had ever
expected.

Jaruzelska made her way to the front of the room. "Thank
you, Lieutenant," she said.

"My pleasure, sir."

"Right. I have some late-breaking news. Fleet intel says
they have identified three Hammer stealthed reconsats in
Clarke orbit around Salvation, so I think that removes any
doubt that the Hammers are about to make their move on
Salvation."

Jaruzelska paused while a buzz ran around the room.

"I don't have to tell you," she continued, "that the next
few hours will be bedlam. We have a lot to do and not much
time to do it in. The operations planning teams are hard at
it. They'll present a first draft of the ops plan at 08:00 this
morning. I want captains and execs there for that, plus your
warfare AIs, of course. Unless there are any burning questions, that's all."

When the briefing broke up, Michael waved Rao and
Machar over. "I know you want to get back to your ships,"
he said to them, "but I think you can safely leave them with
your execs for an hour or so. We need to talk."

"Any chance of doing that over breakfast?" Rao asked
hopefully.

"Lead on," Michael said as a protesting stomach reminded
him that it had been a long time since he last had eaten.

Michael pushed his plate away and commed the drinkbot
to bring him another cup of badly needed coffee.

"It's all a bit much, I have to say," Machar said. "Salvation, eh? So much for the Kalici Protocol. Goddamn Hammers."

"My thoughts exactly," Michael said.

Machar's concern was plain to see. "Well, I don't suppose there's any point in me beating the old 'we're not ready' drum," he said. "I imagine you've done that already, and the admiral told you . . . well, she told you . . ."

"To get on with it. Is that what you were trying to say?"

"Pretty much, sir," Machar said.

"What about the 'we shouldn't do it because it might screw up Operation Opera' excuse?" Rao asked.

Michael shook his head. "That didn't fly any farther than 'we're not ready so please leave us alone' did. Look, I understand your concerns, but you need to have faith in yourselves. I know we haven't seen the plan yet, but I cannot see the Salvation operation being any more difficult than what we've just been through on the Manovitz ranges. So can we do it? Yes, we damn well can." Michael was emphatic.

"I can only speak for myself, sir," Rao said, "but I'm sure we can—"

"Sorry to interrupt, Kelli, but I am, too," Machar said, "and I didn't mean to suggest otherwise. I just wanted to be sure the powers that be understood, you know . . ."

"That dreadnoughts are still an unknown quantity?" Michael said. "Yes, they understand that, even though the First has runs on the scoreboard. Anyway, you both did well this week, so it's not such a risk. In any case, needs must. Throwing Salvation to the wolves is not an option. Think of all those bilateral security treaties that define our sphere of influence. If planets like Salvation, not to mention Kalici, New Kashmir, Bennet's World, Panguna, Covoti-B, Lagerfeld, Gok-3, Yushiro—I can go on for hours, there are so many of them—cannot depend on the Federation's promise to keep the Hammers at bay, we are in trouble. And here's one other thing you need to think about. An operation to protect Salvation might be a distraction, but I cannot think of a better way to conceal the preparations for Opera. When we make our move, any intelligence the Hammers have on our buildup for Opera will be ascribed to the Salvation operation."

Rao nodded. "One thing is for sure," she said thoughtfully. "With all the pressure Fleet's under, the last thing those scum-sucking Hammers will expect is a battle fleet operation against a tough Hammer target like SuppFac27 only weeks after having their asses kicked at Salvation . . . well, so we hope," she added.

"That point had occurred to the admiral," Michael said drily.

"But even so, sir, why use the dreadnoughts?"

"You know what, Kelli? That was my first question when the admiral told me we were tasked. The answer's simple. Fleet is under enormous pressure; it's barely holding the line against the Hammers. The dreadnoughts are the largest single tactical unit in Fleet's order of battle that is not committed to current operations. Thirty capital ships, sitting around, not fighting the Hammers like every other ship in the Fleet. Everyone knows they are committed to Opera in just over a month, but beggars cannot be choosers. They are the only warships available."

Rao and Machar both nodded, though Michael could see that neither was convinced. He was not concerned. Good officers—and his two dreadnought captains were good— always had doubts. It was only the bad ones who let those doubts stop them doing what had to be done.

"One look at Fleet's current tasking," he continued, "tells you why they need us. There is nobody else. Any way you look at it, the timing's lousy. To take pressure off our trade routes, Fleet has task groups en route to twenty major Hammer targets as we speak. Even if Fleet recalled them, they cannot get to Salvation in time to be of any use. And with resources stretched so thin, there's not a cat in hell's chance of diverting ships away from planetary defense. Unless," Michael added pointedly, "the minister issues a directive telling the commander in chief otherwise."

"Which," Rao said, "Minister O'Donnell is not going to do . . . well, not if he wants a long career in politics. The voters would tear him apart when they found out."

"That they would, Kelli. Anyway, it does not matter what reservations any of us in uniform might have. No, thanks to a ministerial directive, it's a done deal, so we just have to make the best of it. Let me tell you, guys. If our dreadnoughts cannot disrupt the Hammer attack on Salvation, nothing can. One more point. The Salvation operation will be of enormous value in getting all of us up to combat readiness. I'm not saying it'll be a walk in the park, but it is a simple operation well within our capabilities." Not like Opera, he wanted to add but did not.

"I hope so, sir," Machar said, trying to sound confident. "I've just checked the order of battle for Operation Paradise. Two planetary assault vessels have just been chopped to Admiral Jaruzelska's operational control—*Nelson* and *Tourville*—and MARFOR-3 is on standby to embark."

Rao whistled softly. "MARFOR-3, eh? That's what, thirty thousand marines? Well, that should be enough to get the job done considering that the intelligence reports say the Hammers are planning to use only fifteen thousand marines and five thousand DocSec troopers in the ground operation."

"But here's a funny thing, sir," Machar said. "Fleet's not waiting for us to get there. They're sending a small task group in under Commodore Kumoro twenty-four hours ahead of us. They leave within the hour."

Michael frowned. "I saw that. A cruiser, *Sepoy,* along with two light escorts, plus supporting units."

"Sir . . ." Machar hesitated for a moment. "It doesn't make sense. Why? That's a one-way mission. Those ships will not be coming back."

"I agree." Rao's concern was obvious. "Why send ships on a suici—"

"Don't go there, Kelli," Michael said, cutting her off. "The decision's made, so let's just leave it at that. Fleet has its reasons, and whether they are good or bad is not for us to debate. If it turns out to be a bad decision, that will come out in the after-action inquiry. So do me a favor, do yourself a favor. Leave it, both of you. Okay?"

"Sir," Rao said. Machar just nodded. Both were grim-faced, mouths pinched tight.

Not that Michael was any happier. The chances of Commodore Kumoro's task force disrupting the Hammer's attack on Salvation were at best remote. Throwing a heavy cruiser and two light escorts against a Hammer task group? It was ludicrous and meant only one thing: Fleet's decision was motivated by politics. That made it a bad decision, one spawned by Fleet's need to be seen to be doing something, even if that something meant sacrificing the lives of good spacers.

"Okay, team," Michael said. "That'll do, so I'll let you get back to your ships. I'm going to have a chat with the planners. Not that I don't trust them, but I want to make sure my dreadnoughts will be used properly. I'll see you both at 08:00. Any concerns, com me. This is not the time for surprises."

"Sir."

Michael watched as Rao and Machar left him to finish his coffee, thankful that fate—not to mention Jaruzelska's ruthless selection process—had delivered them to him. They were outstanding young officers. If anyone could make the dreadnoughts work, it was those two.

They had to. Life was demanding enough before Salvation. It was going to be ten times worse, what with the Salvation operation adding to the already intense pressure from Opera. But to his surprise, nothing about Salvation bothered him. Opera bothered him—a lot. He had spent enough time in the sims to know his chances of surviving the operation were not good, so taking *Reckless* and the dreadnoughts into action against a Hammer task group would be a welcome diversion.

And DocSec would be there in force: more than five thousand of the black jumpsuited scum. With a bit of luck, he might get a chance to blow a few of the bastards to hell.

Cheered by that prospect, Michael was debating whether another cup of coffee was in order when a soft ping announced the arrival of a com from Anna. What's this? he wondered as he accepted the call.

"Hi," he said cheerfully when Anna's face popped into his neuronics. "Thought you and *Damishqui* were on your way to Brooks Reef."

"We were," Anna replied, grim-faced, "but we had a pinch-space generator problem, so we're back. Have you checked the latest release of the Salvation operation order?"

Michael swallowed hard. This did not sound good. "No. Why?"

"Can't say. Have a look and you'll see why."

"Anna! What're you telling me?"

"Can't say," Anna said, shaking her head. "Just check the damn op order." She stared directly at Michael for a moment, eyes glittering as tears started. "I love you; remember that, Michael. I love you and I always will."

Then she was gone.

Frantically, Michael checked, and there it was. "Oh, no . . . please, no," he whispered.

Bad luck did not even begin to describe it. Plagued by main engine problems, *Sepoy* had been forced to pull out of Operation Paradise at the last minute just as the engineers had fixed *Damishqui*'s recalcitrant pinchspace generators. In desperation he commed Anna back: No link, the AI told him.

Shocked, he sat unmoving as he came to terms with the shattering news.

Anna was now en route to Salvation as part of Commodore Kumoro's task group.

Saturday, February 17, 2400, UD
New Hope spaceport, Salvation planet

With no lander movements scheduled, it had been a long night. Why would there be? Salvation was not exactly humanspace's most popular destination. That left the controller on duty at New Hope spaceport with little more to occupy his time than counting off the minutes to the end of his shift while drinking more coffee than was good for him. Moodily, the man stared out of the plasglass window:

Sprawled out in front of him was New Hope spaceport's runway, a long strip of laser-fused rock traced out of a rain-drenched night by thin lines of lights, the wind chasing silver-slashed pools of water across its milled antiskid surface. He yawned as another squall hurled rain at the windows. Tonight's storm was an unmistakable reminder that hurricane season was on its way. Not that anyone needed any prompting: Thanks to Salvation's eccentric orbit, its seasons ran like clockwork.

He yawned again. Hurricane season was a massive pain in the ass; he hated it. Spawned by fast-warming seas, huge storms ripped across the planet's ocean, driving the inhabitants underground into the safety of their bunkers. When one storm exhausted itself, the next arrived, a relentless procession of energy and raw power that stopped only when Salvation passed perihelion and started to open out from its sun. It would not be long. Hurricane Alex, the first of the year, was developing nicely on the far side of the planet. Betsy, Charlie, Deanne, and all the rest would follow when what passed for summer on Salvation arrived, a nightmare of raging winds, driving rain, and mountainous seas. So he did what he always did when hurricane season threatened: wondered why he did not move to a more congenial planet. The only people who enjoyed hurricane season were the extreme sailors, suicidal idiots whose idea of fun was surfing down mountainous waves in a ceramfiber yacht; he had tried it—once—and it had taken him weeks to recover.

Wearily, the duty controller rubbed eyes gritty from too little sleep and too much caffeine. Kraa, he was tired.

Without warning, the holovid screen burst into light to reveal Salvation's president framed by the flashing red lights reserved for the imminent arrival of a category 7 superstorm, and suddenly he was not tired anymore. What the hell? he said to himself. It was way too early for a Cat-7. Last time he had checked, Alex was a humble Cat-2 storm half a world away.

"Citizens," the president said. "This is a matter of the utmost urgency. I have just been informed by the Federated Worlds embassy that a Hammer invasion fleet is inbound.

An attack on Salvation is imminent. Help is on its way, but it may not be here in time to stop them. I fear the Hammer's target is those of you who follow the Faith of Kraa. All of you, irrespective of religion, return home, batten down your houses, and send your families into the storm bunkers. When they are safe, those of you who wish to fight—which I hope is everyone able to carry a gun—report to your neighborhood emergency station with whatever weapons you have. Team leaders will have instructions for you. Don't wait. Do it now. I will issue updates on voicecomm channel 54 when we receive more information. May God and Kraa watch over us. Thank you."

The duty controller did not hesitate. Slapping a switch to plunge the spaceport into darkness, he shut it down and raced out of the control center, an initial frisson of fear buried by fast-mounting rage. The Hammers, all arrogance and hubris, had no fucking idea what they were walking into; if they imagined the people of Salvation were going to lie down and wait to be kicked to death by DocSec, they were idiots. "Kraa damn them all," he swore, his anger replaced by an ice-cold determination to send every last Doc-Sec trooper to hell.

One hundred fifty thousand kilometers out from Salvation, space was torn apart as ship after ship dropped into normalspace, bubbles of ultraviolet racing away to announce their arrival. Aboard the flagship of the Hammer task force, Rear Admiral Tu'ivakano allowed himself to relax a fraction while the threat plot crystallized. The two light patrol ships that constituted the Salvation Fleet's entire order of battle wasted no time in running up the white flag, a single salvo of obsolete antistarship missiles the sum total of their defiance. More significantly, there were no damned Feds in Salvation nearspace.

The task force turned end for end and decelerated hard to drop into orbit around Salvation. Tu'ivakano allowed himself to relax a touch more. Things were going according to plan. By Kraa, he would be glad to see the last of Salvation.

Hanging around so deep inside the Fed's sphere of influence was something he did not enjoy.

With a thump, the flagship's main engines shut off. With well-practiced efficiency, the two planetary assault ships following Tu'ivakano's cruisers into orbit disgorged assault landers in a steady stream, their blunt-nosed armored shapes forming up into a loose cloud.

Abruptly the admiral found out why hanging around in Fed space might not be such a good idea.

"Sir," Tu'ivakano's chief of staff called, his voice tense, "Positive gravitronics intercept. Estimated drop bearing Red 70 Up 3, stand by range. Multiple vessels, designated hostile task group Foxtrot-1. Gravity wave pattern suggests pinch-space transition imminent."

"Roger."

"Shit," the admiral murmured to himself. Feds, must be. Tu'ivakano forced himself to say nothing more. His chief of staff was a competent and combat-tested spacer; he and his captains knew how to deal with the incoming Fed counterattack without any prompting from him. And Tu'ivakano's staff did know what they were doing: Ponderously, the cruisers in the task group turned to face the threat, Hammer missiles already driving away hard to meet the incoming Fed ships.

"Admiral. Drop datum confirmed. Range 15,000 kilometers. Stand by, rail-gun salvo . . . now!"

With a solid crunch, Tu'ivakano's flagship unloaded a full rail-gun salvo at the Feds. That'll make their eyes water, he said to himself, eyes locked on the command holovid, the green lines of missile and rail-gun salvos projected across the gap to intersect the drop datum, a scarlet lozenge tagged with the identity of the incoming ships: Foxtrot-1.

"Get the landers moving," Tu'ivakano said. "Don't wait. The Feds will slice them up."

"Yes, sir," the chief of staff replied.

Main engines fired; savage deceleration dropped the landers carrying the ground attack force down Salvation's gravity well like bricks. Tu'ivakano was happy to see them on

their way. The Feds would ignore the capital ships in favor of
the landers; the sooner they dropped dirtside with their precious cargoes of marines, the better.

"Foxtrot-1 is dropping, sir. Datum is confirmed. Ten seconds to rail-gun impact."

Tu'ivakano held his breath, uttering a silent prayer that
his ships had calculated their rail-gun swarm geometry
right. "Sons of bitches," he hissed. They hadn't. The swarm
sliced right through the drop datum, but the Fed ships
were too widely dispersed, a single impact on the bows of
the leading ship—*Damishqui*, a heavy cruiser—the only
payback for all that effort. But a dispersed formation was
vulnerable to missile attack, and barely seconds later, Hammer missiles accelerated to full speed, the Fed ships disappearing behind Krachov shrouds even as they dumped their
own missiles into space to take the attack back to the Hammers.

It was chaos. As Tu'ivakano expected, the incoming Feds
ignored his ships, a decision that signed their own death
warrants. Going to full power, their missiles chased after
landers plunging in desperation for the safety of the planet.
Only the Fed's rail guns—useless against small, fast-moving
landers—targeted the Hammer task group; with a time of
flight of only seconds, the Hammer ships were forced to soak
up the rail-gun swarms, the slugs' enormous kinetic energy
transformed into enough heat to blow huge craters in the
ships' bows. Tu'ivakano's body was thrown violently from
side to side as his flagship struggled to absorb the shock; his
head snapped forward onto his helmet so hard that his eyes
watered in pain.

Then the Fed's first salvo was over. Tu'ivakano, blinking
tears out of his eyes, took stock, mentally tallying losses
and gains. His lander losses, bad though they were, were
nowhere near enough to make him quit and run for home.
Only two of his ships—light escorts—had suffered mission-
abort damage, but both had survived; hulls intact, their part
in this operation was over. The rest of his task force was still
very much in the fight.

That was more than could be said for the Feds. He shook

his head: They might be the enemy, and by Kraa he hated the Feds and all they stood for, but he admired their insane bravery. With only a handful of ships, they were no match for his cruisers. His first missile salvo ripped the guts out of three heavy patrol ships and two heavy scouts, uncontained fusion plants blowing them into balls of white-hot gas in a matter of seconds, their lifepods running away in all directions.

One more salvo was enough to destroy the rest of the Feds: a carefully crafted attack that saw missiles and railgun swarms arrive on target within seconds of each other, a blizzard of close-in defensive fire marking the Fed ships' frantic attempts to keep death at arm's length. One by one, the Fed ships died, fast-expanding spheres of hot gas and orange-strobed lifepods the only things left to show they had ever existed.

Tu'ivakano grunted his approval and detached four of his heavy patrol ships to go round up the Fed lifepods. So far, the operation was textbook perfect, though he knew he had been damned lucky the Fed task force had been so understrength. He switched the command holovid back to track the lander assault. In an incandescent blaze of fireworks, the landers smashed into the upper atmosphere, the controlled violence of ballistic reentry spawning hundreds of white flares heading into the clouds of rolling gray murk that covered the planet.

Tu'ivakano switched the holovid screen to show a schematic of Salvation overlaid with lander icons. Protected by a screen of heavy ground attack landers, the marines rode their craft down until, with a precision that impressed Tu'ivakano, the attack opened out. A handful of landers headed directly for the spaceport; the rest dropped to establish a secure perimeter around the city of New Hope. Tu'ivakano switched the holovid to take the feed from the ground assault commander's lander, watching spellbound as it burst through the clouds into the leaden predawn murk. The long runway of Salvation's spaceport opened out in front of the lander's nose. Twin streams of depleted-uranium rounds from belly-mounted cannons ripped the spaceport's squat ceramcrete buildings into thousands of angry fragments, the ground on either side of the runway disappearing behind boiling clouds of mud and dirt thrown up by suppressive fire from the ground attack landers escorting the assault stream.

Tu'ivakano watched the lander's nose go up sharply, the image trembling as belly thrusters killed its forward momentum. The nose dropped, and the lander hit the runway with a crunching thud, dropped some more, and came to a shuddering halt. The ground around it filled with the ephemeral shapes of chromaflaged marines running into position, light armor already fanning out to protect the assault.

On schedule, the assault commander's head and shoulders appeared on Tu'ivakano's personal holovid screen.

"Admiral Tu'ivakano, sir. Pleased to report that the spaceport and perimeter around New Hope are secure."

"Thank you, General. We'll start down-shuttling DocSec."

"That would be good, sir," the marine said, his mouth twisting into a momentary grimace of revulsion.

Tu'ivakano ignored it; he shared the marine general's opinion of DocSec. Besides, he was pleased with the way things were going. Apart from the Feds' forlorn hope, the initial phases of the operation were running according to plan. Now the marines had to secure the streets and key buildings of New Hope. When that was done, it would be up to DocSec to go house to house rounding up the heretics and bundling them onto the landers. Knowing what lay in store for the Salvationists once DocSec's black-jumpsuited troopers laid their hands on them made Tu'ivakano uncomfortable. DocSec were the scum of the earth, and their shock brigades were the worst of a sadistic bunch.

He would hate to be a Kraa-worshipping Salvationist.

Tu'ivakano's face flushed livid with anger. "What do you mean the operation is stalled? Stalled? How can that be? These Kraa-damned Salvationists are nothing,

nothing. They're only a bunch of fucking civilians, for Kraa's sake. They don't even have an army," he shouted, struggling to control himself, white flecks of spittle collecting in the corner of his mouth. "How can the attack be stalled?"

The assault commander's face betrayed him; he was angry, frustrated, and embarrassed, all at the same time. "Well, sir," he said, "yes, they are only civilians, but they are civilians with nothing to lose, they are well armed, they understand urban combat, they know how to fight, and their damn houses are the closest things to bunkers I've ever seen. No, Kraa damn it! They are bunkers. Every one is a steel-reinforced ceramcrete fortress, mostly underground, with small windows protected by plasteel shutters, all interconnected by a tunnel network with access to the streets. I've never seen anything like it, and needless to say, we are having to take them the hard way, meter by meter, house by house."

"Wait, General," Tu'ivakano said, puzzled. "That makes no sense. Bunkers for houses? Who'd want to live in a ceramcrete bunker?"

"It's simple, sir, not that anyone considered it important enough to include in the intelligence briefings. The few prisoners we have tell us that they have storms here like nothing you've ever seen, wind gusting 350 kilometers an hour. The buildings have to be tough to survive. Problem is we didn't know that."

"Kraa damn it! Why? Why didn't we know? What's the point of an intelligence briefing that misses something this important?"

"I wondered the same thing, sir."

"Have you considered sending in the ground attack landers?"

"We tried that, sir. Doesn't help. Landers just make our job harder. Everything above the ground gets reduced to rubble, and the minute the marines go in, the heretics pop up out of their basements like nothing's happened and start shooting again."

"Kraa!" Tu'ivakano said as the seriousness of the problem

sank in. Thin tendrils of fear twisted their way through his body as he contemplated what would happen to him if he failed to carry off what was supposed to be a simple, fast in-and-out operation. "Armor?"

"Armor's no better than landers. Ceramcrete blockhouses and armor don't go well together. We end up having to blast our way through, which means more collapsed houses, more piles of ceramcrete rubble, and even more ambush sites. We'll push on, sir. It's all we can do."

Tu'ivakano nodded. "Understood. But remember, we have less than thirty-six hours to wrap this up. Finished or not, that's when we're leaving. I don't think the Fed attack this morning was an accident. Some of my staff think our operational security has been blown, in which case more Feds will be on their way."

"We're doing our best, sir."

"I hope so. For both our sakes, I hope so. Kraa, I wish we were able to nuke the damn place. That would solve the heretic problem once and for all."

The assault commander said nothing. Tempting though the idea was, Tu'ivakano knew that even the Hammers would not stoop that low.

Sunday, February 18, 2400, UD
Salvation deepspace

Coasting in at 150,000 kph, *Reckless* hung in deepspace, 4 billion kilometers out from Salvation planet. In station around her were the ships of the dreadnought force, with the planetary assault vessels *Madison* and *Nelson* and their escorts following a million kilometers behind. The virtual conference room was silent, the faces of Vice Admiral Jaruzelska's captains grim as they watched the holovid recordings of Commodore Kumoro's task group attempting to head off the Hammer attack on Salvation.

When the last Fed ship died, nobody said a word, every last spacer overawed by the insane bravery of the attack.

Except one.

Michael sat unmoving, his mind paralyzed by a gut-gnawing fear, by the ice-cold certainty that Anna must be dead, her chances of getting clear of the dying cruiser remote at best. The hurt of her loss was physical, slivers of pain stabbing into his chest, his stomach cramped into a ball of undiluted white-hot agony, his mind a maelstrom, tormented by an unruly flood of memories of Anna, always smiling, her bottomless green eyes sparkling and dancing.

The agony of her loss ignited a slow-burning rage that flared in an instant into an all-consuming fury. Why would Fleet deliberately send good ships and their crews to certain death? Why? What sort of cold, callous bastards were they?

With an enormous effort, he wrestled himself back under control.

He always knew that Kumoro's mission was doomed, but to see it fail on a holovid display, knowing that Anna and *Damishqui* were condemned, too, was pure torture. The agony was made all the worse by the fact that there was not a thing he could do—or could have done—to change the outcome.

In a matter of minutes, eleven precious ships—*Damishqui*; the light escorts *Kukri* and *Yataghan;* the heavy patrol ships *Agache, al-Badisi, Huari, Electric, Dunxi;* and *Beaumaris*; and the heavy scouts *Unukalhai* and *Tarantula*—along with far too many of their irreplaceable crew—were blown to white-hot gas. Michael did not fault the sacrifice—it was in the Fleet's finest traditions—but he did fault the commanders who had sent Commodore Kumoro and his ships to certain death, a sacrifice whose only purpose was political, an empty gesture that would tell the rest of the neutral planets in Fed space that even though they might die, they would not die alone.

The brutal fact was that Kumoro's sacrifice was utterly pointless: Only two Hammer ships suffered mission-abort damage, and only twenty-seven assault and ten ground

attack landers had been hacked out of the assault stream by
Fed missiles. Not nearly enough to stop the Hammer operation.

Jaruzelska's voice splintered the shocked hush. "You
know what we have to do."

Michael did not move.

"Skipper," Ferreira said softly, "I'm sorry . . . what can I
say? *Damishqui*—"

"You can damn well say nothing, Junior Lieutenant Ferreira," Michael barked, his voice trembling with pain and
anger, harsh and unforgiving. "Nothing, so shut your damn
mouth. What you can do is your duty. Is that understood?"

Ferreira flinched. "Aye, aye, sir . . . all stations, this is command. Faceplates down, stand by to depressurize. Secure
artificial gravity."

"Goddamnit to hell," Michael muttered, wishing he could
take back every last hurtful word. Jayla Ferreira deserved
better. He flicked a glance at her. His executive officer was
turning into one of those officers every captain dreamed of:
smart, tough, resourceful, steady under pressure, not afraid
to ask the hard questions, not afraid to admit her mistakes.
Damishqui's loss, the loss of Anna, was not her fault; he
should not take his suffering out on her. He waved Ferreira
over; he put his helmet to hers.

"Sorry, Jayla. I was out of line," he said.

"Don't sweat it, sir. I can't imagine what you must be going through. Hang in there and we'll get this done. And
there's always a chance Anna made it off. I counted thirteen
lifepods from *Damishqui*."

"So few," Michael said; Anna's chances of survival were
less than one in ten.

"I know, but there's always a chance she made it, sir."

Michael shook his head in despair even as a tiny spark of
hope burst into life before dying away. He remembered
what it had been like when *Ishaq* was destroyed, the frantic
scramble to get to a lifepod through the carnage of a dying
ship; how could he forget it when the nightmare of *Ishaq*'s
loss still haunted him most nights? Knowing that Anna had

been through the same hell was close to unbearable. Not knowing if she had made it off was . . .

He pushed all thoughts of Anna away and forced himself to concentrate. He had his own ship and crew to worry about. "Duty calls, Jayla, and Admiral Jaruzelska waits for no man, so let's get on with it," he said.

"Yes, sir . . . I have all green suits, ship is at general quarters, ship state 1, airtight condition zulu, artificial gravity off, ship is depressurized," Ferreira said.

"Roger. Warfare, you have command authority. Weapons free."

"Warfare, roger," the AI replied. "I have command authority. Weapons free. All stations, stand by to jump."

While he waited, Michael commed Rao and Machar, their AI-generated avatars good enough to betray a blend of fear and anticipation. "Okay, guys," Michael said bluntly, "let's do this right. Any last questions? Kelli?"

"No, sir. None," she said with a confidence her face did not reflect, the shock of the loss of Commodore Kumoro's task force showing in staring eyes and stress-tightened lips.

"Good. Nathan?"

"Same. Dreadnought Squadron Three is ready."

"Okay. Stick to the plan and try to bring all your ships home. I think we're going to need them for something a touch more important than poor old Salvation. I know it's an approved tactic, but no ramming Hammer ships unless you absolutely have to. I've done it, and it's not fun."

Rao and Machar glanced at each other. "Sir," they chorused.

"Good luck. *Reckless* out."

A quick glance around *Reckless*'s combat information center confirmed that all was well. Michael pushed back in his seat, and the AI tightened his safety straps securely across his space-suited body while the seat molded itself to his shape, restraints extending to cushion his helmeted head. He was ready, the familiar adrenaline rush beginning to take effect, anger and hurt fading away as discipline and duty took over.

"Command, warfare. Stand by to jump . . . jumping."

With the unmanned ships to the fore, the dreadnought force microjumped, dropping close to the Hammers, deliberately close to give the enemy ships little time to react, the dreadnoughts' massive frontal armor shrugging off missiles and rail-gun slugs while their own salvos ripped through the Hammer task group with devastating effect, ship after ship shuddering under the repeated impacts of hundreds of slugs and missiles. In a breathtaking, savage display of raw power lasting only a matter of minutes, the dreadnoughts reduced the ships of the Hammer task group to smoking, broken carcasses spiraling away into space, spewing air and lifepods, ship after ship losing the unequal battle to explode in blue-white flashes of raw energy. Stripped of their escorts, the two Hammer planetary assault vessels, their massive spherical shapes unmistakable, were left, two big, fat sitting ducks.

The planetary assault vessels were no match for the dreadnoughts. Transfixed, Michael watched the command holovid. It filled with the flame-shot wrecks of *Kerouac* and *Mitsotaki* as they tumbled through space, blazing balls spun from strands of fire, a nightmare ripped from the imagination of a drug-crazed madman, spitting lifepods in all directions.

"Command, Warfare, sensors. Assault Group dropping. Datum confirmed Red 180 Up 0."

"Command, roger."

Michael commed his two captains. What a difference being on the winning side made: Their faces spoke volumes. Rao and Machar were still on adrenaline-fueled highs, the unalloyed joy of success there for all to see. "Well done, guys," he said. "Plan the fight, fight the plan, and for once that's how it went, I'm happy to say."

"Thanks, sir," Machar said, unable to stop grinning. "That was my sort of operation. Short, brutal, and with the Hammers on the losing side."

"Mine, too," Rao said. "I hope Opera's that easy."

Michael grimaced. "Sorry, guys. I'd be lying if I said it would be," he said. His stomach did a lazy backflip at the prospect. Opera showed all the signs of turning into a blood-bath, but unlike the Salvation operation, the Feds would be doing their share of the bleeding. "Okay, that's it. Remember, it's not over yet, so stay sharp. *Reckless* out."

Michael allowed himself to relax a touch. Provided that the Hammers did not come back spoiling for a fight—part of him hoped they would—the dreadnoughts' job was largely done. He had turned his focus to the command plot tracking the incoming Fed planetary assault vessels and their escorts while they decelerated into orbit when Jaruzelska's face popped up on his personal holovid.

"Welcome to Salvation, sir," he said.

"Thanks. Nice job, Michael. Those dreadnoughts of yours certainly get the job done."

"They do, sir. That they do."

"And Michael, I'm sorry. I know what Anna means to you. You okay?"

"I am, sir," Michael said. "One of the Hammer auxiliaries was missing; I'm hoping she got clear of *Damishqui* and the Hammers shipped her out before we arrived."

"I hope so, too. Jaruzelska out."

Patched into the holocams carried by the marine tacbots that swarmed across the battlefield, Michael watched the bloody struggle to dislodge the Hammers unfold. The Hammers had not made much progress; thanks to a combination of stubborn resistance and nearly indestructible houses, their attack had ground to a halt. Queued up behind them, DocSec shock-troopers waited in sprawling groups, unable to start the job they had been sent light-years to carry out.

The Hammers faced annihilation. Trapped between Fed marines and Salvationists, unable to move forward or back, the Hammers did the only thing left to them: fight back with mindless ferocity. Not that it bothered the Fed marines. Directed by superior battlefield surveillance, coordinated by combat management AIs, and backed up by marine light armor, ground attack fliers, and combat drones, the Feds had an overwhelming tactical advantage. In the rubble of New Hope's outer suburbs, Hammer counterattacks were ripped apart before they even crossed their start lines, DocSec shock-troopers and Hammer marines dying in the hundreds alongside one another, as close in death as they had been implacable enemies in life, their bitter hatred drowned in a sea of blood.

By the time Jaruzelska ordered the dreadnoughts to head for home, Fed marines had punched huge gaps through the Hammers' perimeter, cutting them up into isolated groups. Michael watched the final stages of the ground operation as *Reckless* accelerated out of Salvation nearspace with mixed emotions. It had been a good operation for the dreadnoughts: They had survived to return home, some damaged, but none so badly that they would have to be pulled out of Operation Opera. His untested captains had dealt well with the pressure of combat, and his command team in *Reckless* had handled the responsibilities of dreadnoughts without breaking a sweat.

Oh, yes, he reminded himself. There was more news, some good, some bad. The Fed survivors from Commodore Kumoro's task group had been tracked down. Transferred to a Hammer support ship, they had been shipped back to the Hammer Worlds before the Fed attack had wiped out all the Hammer ships left in Salvation nearspace. All things considered, they had been lucky. A Hammer prisoner of war camp was better than ending up collateral damage any day.

All that was positive . . . but only if Anna had been one of those shipped back.

The bad was a small thing, a stupid thing, something every shred of common sense told him he should ignore. But he could not ignore the fact that he was leaving behind thousands of DocSec troopers alive. Not getting the chance to send one to hell burned inside him, a cold-burning flame generating anger but no heat, an anger that now reached out to encompass not only the Hammers and all their works but also the gutless scum at Fleet who would send so many good ships and spacers to their deaths. And why? To placate the politicians!

Something profound had changed, and for a moment

Michael struggled to work out just what it was. It came to him: A fleet that did not treasure the lives of each and every spacer was a fleet that deserved no loyalty. The sacred trust between commanders and commanded—to risk the lives of a spacer only when military necessity demanded it—had been broken, perhaps irrevocably.

Holding his breath, he forced the anger down. Their day will come, he vowed; their day will come.

Friday, February 23, 2401, UD
Private dining room, flag officers' mess,
Comdur Fleet Base

Vice Admiral Jaruzelska lifted her glass of wine and toasted each of the dreadnought captains in turn. "Well done, all of you. You did well," she said.

"Thank you, sir," Michael said, returning the toast, horribly aware that he might be toasting the success of an operation that had killed Anna. "Always good to remind those damn Hammers they don't own all of humanspace just yet."

"Wasn't the toughest operation of all time, though, was it, sir?" Kelli Rao said.

"No, it wasn't," Jaruzelska said, "but you guys had to start somewhere, and Salvation was as good a place as anywhere."

"Ironic," Machar said, "rescuing a bunch of lapsed Hammers. Never expected to be asked to do that."

Jaruzelska nodded. "It's one of the stranger missions I've been involved in, I have to say, but not the strangest. That would have to be the time I was sent to assist a ship attacked by pirates. It was one hell of a shock when we boarded the ship to find that the pirates had released the stars of Mister Almaghedi's Amazing Alien Circus before they left. All three hundred of them. It was absolute chaos."

The table erupted in laughter, and Machar launched into

an account of one of his father's trips to an obscure fringe world 300 light-years beyond the Delfin Confederation.

Michael let the conversation flow on around him, content to let Machar make the running. Ironically, the Salvation operation was one of the best things to happen to them. The chances of the dreadnoughts surviving everything the Hammers would throw at them while they fought to keep the Feds away from their precious antimatter plant must have improved now that his captains were blooded.

Or so he hoped. Apart from Fleet's stupidity in sending Commodore Kumoro's task group in early, Salvation had been a simple operation, an operation that should always have gone the way of the Feds.

Operation Opera would be an entirely different matter. Facing a dangerously resurgent Hammer, only a fool would try to predict how it would go, so he had given up trying. There were simply too many unknowns. Michael watched Jaruzelska, her face animated by the simple pleasure of listening to a good story well told. Assuring the security of the Federated Worlds decades into the future was a responsibility few Fed military commanders had ever been given; he wondered how she coped.

He had enough trouble coping with the demands of each day, his mind endlessly distracted by the ghost of Anna reaching for him out of a nightmare of smoke, flame, fear, and panic as *Damishqui* died a terrible death around her.

When the dinner broke up, Jaruzelska waved Michael to stay behind. "I've just had a com from Fleet," she said.

"Sir?"

"It's good news, Michael, the best," Jaruzelska said, her face split by a huge smile. "The International Red Cross has just supplied us with the survivors list from Salvation—"

"Oh, sweet Jesus," Michael hissed.

"—and Anna's on it. She's alive, Michael, slightly wounded but okay."

Michael lay in his bunk, unable to sleep, struggling to accept the fact that Anna really was alive. He had been so sure

that she had not made it off the doomed *Damishqui*, that he
would never again hold her, that he would never again bury
his face in her neck to feel her warmth, to kiss her velvet-
soft skin, to drown in the warmth and smell of her body, to
revel in her unquestioning love.

But survive she had, one of only eighty-nine spacers to
make it, a desperately small fraction of the heavy cruiser's
complement. The Hammers had reported through the International Red Cross: She had been captured, her status reported to be "Wounded—OK." The problem, as Michael
knew all too well, was how the Hammers treated prisoners
of war, fit or not, and if she had fallen foul of DocSec for
any reason . . .

He sent that awful prospect back where it came from.
He had to stop thinking that way; if he did not, it would
drive him over the edge, an edge he was already far too
close to. He had to take each day as it came, live a normal
life, and hope that Anna would get through. She was tough;
provided that she was in a prisoner of war camp run by the
Hammer Fleet and surrounded by hundreds of Fed spacers,
she would survive.

After all, he had.

Monday, March 5, 2401, UD
FWSS Reckless, *Comdur nearspace*

"Well, folks. This is it. It's come a bit later than we expected, but I've just received the warning order."

A ripple of nervous excitement ran through the spacers
and marines sitting in front of Michael.

"Operation Opera is on. There are no major changes to
the operation order, so the mission time line stands. A few
minor alterations, of course—there always are—but nothing significant. Jayla?"

"Sir?" Ferreira's face flushed with excitement.

"Battle Fleet wants us to increase our holdings of regen tanks. I agree with their thinking; if there are casualties, and there will be, we may end up carrying more than our fair share given that dreadnoughts' chances of surviving are that much higher. The authorization is on its way, so make sure Comdur's logistics people get on it right away."

"Sir."

Quickly Michael ran through the rest of a long list of things the admiral's staff wanted finished before departure. That done, he paused, eyes scanning the faces of the people he was responsible for.

"I don't think," he said at last, his voice somber, "that there is much more I can or need to say, apart from this. I give you my word that I will do everything I can to make this mission a success. We all know how important it is that SuppFac27 be destroyed. The future of the Federation rests on taking away from the Hammers the one thing that can beat us: their antimatter warheads."

An angry murmur ran through the room.

"I cannot lie to you," he continued. "Doing that may cost some, even all, of us our lives, and if that is what it takes to get this job done, so be it. But let me make this clear to you. My job is to do two things at once if I can. One, to destroy SuppFac27. Two, to bring you all home safely. And that," he said softly, "is exactly what I intend to do."

Michael paused again.

"Are there any questions . . . no? Good."

Not a word was said. The faces of some betrayed that curious mix of fear, apprehension, excitement, and anticipation common to all about to go into battle; others showed a stony indifference. Then they were all on their feet.

"Remember Comdur!" they roared, the battle cry of the Federated Worlds Space Fleet.

Michael stared at the holovid on the bulkhead. Battle Fleet Lima hung in space, motionless. The massed ranks of warships were a powerful reminder that the Federated Worlds might be down—and they were after the defeat at Comdur—but were not out. They were still a force to be reckoned with. The raw power projected by the ships struck Michael to his core, his chest tight with a nervous mixture of pride and apprehension.

Pride that for all the setbacks inflicted on the Federation, it could still send a full battle fleet into the field. Apprehension that the Hammers' antimatter plant—on which the Hammers' entire strategic advantage rested—might be a bridge too far. Suppfac27 was the Hammers' single most important strategic asset; they would defend it to the death. And if it was a bridge too far . . .

"Captain, sir."

A soft knock cut short what threatened to be a depressing review of the Fed's future if Opera failed.

"Come!"

It was Ferreira. "Lander's ready when you are, sir."

"Right, Jayla. I'll be there. No ceremonial. You've got better things to do."

Ferreira smiled gratefully. "Aye, aye, sir. As you wish."

"How do I look?" he asked.

Ferreira cast a critical eye over Michael. She nodded approvingly. "Sharp, sir. Very sharp."

Michael turned to look at himself in the full-length mirror. Ferreira was right. He did look sharp. His uniform was immaculate, the ribbon around his neck holding the Valor in Combat starburst—a slash of rich crimson—rank badges, combat command hash marks, and unit citations, all brilliant gold against the black cloth of his dress blacks, thin gold strips of wound stripes above his left cuff, the single row of medals a blaze of color across his left breast.

"It'll have to do," Michael said. "I look like a goddamn tailor's dummy."

Ferreira laughed. "Tell you one thing, sir. You have more stuff on your uniform than most senior officers I've met."

Michael knew that. What Ferreira had said might be true, but not for one moment did he like it. It made him stand out from the crowd, it provided a focus for all the resentment and anger churning around inside those less fortunate, and, worst of all, it offered the antidreadnought lobby a convenient target they were never slow to attack. He might as well walk around with a high-intensity strobe on his head; he was that obvious.

"Okay," Michael said, "tell the gangway I'm on my way. You carry on. I'll see you when I get back."

"Sir."

Deftly, Lieutenant Kat Sedova drifted *Cleft Stick*—the replacement lander for poor old *Creaking Door*—into position alongside *Seljuk,* Vice Admiral's Jaruzelska's flag a blaze of white and gold above the personnel air lock. With a gentle bump, the lander berthed.

"Nicely done, Kat," Michael said. As the saying went, a ship was known by its boats, and the old adage still applied even if it was landers these days.

"Thank you, sir. My pleasure. Give them hell."

"Don't know about that, Kat," Michael said when he turned to leave the flight deck. "Low profile for me tonight. Too much brass around for my liking."

"I'll be here when it all gets too much. By the way, sir."

"What?"

"You look sharp. Very sharp."

Michael rolled his eyes. "Oh, for heaven's sake, Junior Lieutenant Sedova! Not you, too." He shook his head despairingly. "Just be here when I need to make a run for it."

"Will do, sir," Sedova replied with a grin.

Michael dropped down the ladder and into the lander's cargo bay just as the lights over the air lock changed from red to green. The loadmaster, Petty Officer Amira Trivedi, slapped the handle, and the hatch snapped open.

"Clear to disembark, sir," Trivedi said cheerfully, her singsong intonation betraying her Nuristani origins. "You look sharp, sir, if you don't mind me saying so, very sharp."

Michael shook his head ruefully and laughed. Was this the start of a running joke? he wondered. Some had been known to follow an officer for their entire career. "Don't be so bloody cheeky, Petty Officer Trivedi, but thanks, anyway."

"No problem, sir."

Steeling himself, Michael stepped into the air lock to be greeted by the time-honored ritual that accompanied the arrival of a captain in command, no matter how junior. The side party snapped to attention, bosun's calls shrilled, and the officers assembled to greet him and the rest of the battle fleet's captains saluted. Michael paused to return the salute. *Seljuk*'s captain, a dour-looking man, his dress blacks sporting a single combat command hash mark where Michael had three, stepped forward.

"Captain," the man said curtly. He did not look happy, his perfunctory handshake a halfhearted welcome to the Fleet's latest heavy cruiser, the ship so new that it positively sparkled.

Michael forced an unwilling smile into place. Another dreadnought hater; he recognized the signs. "Thank you, sir. Pleasure to come aboard."

Seljuk's captain ignored the remark; he waved one of his junior officers forward. "Cadet Hendriksen will show you to the admiral's quarters," he said before turning his back on Michael.

Well, thanks for nothing, Michael said to himself.

"Follow me, sir," the cadet said. The boy made Michael feel a million years old. He knew he must have looked that young once, but that had been a long time ago.

They set off; not a word was said while they worked their

way through and down into the enormous cruiser. "You, too?" Michael said softly.

The cadet stopped at the two marines standing guard at the doorway into the admiral's quarters. "Here we are, sir. First door on your left."

"Thank you, Cadet Hendriksen."

His identity confirmed, Michael stepped through the heavily framed opening in the airtight bulkhead. The door into *Seljuk*'s flag conference room was open, a wave of conversation washing over him when he walked in. He plunged into the mass of black uniforms toward the only person he recognized, Vice Admiral Jaruzelska herself. She spotted him and waved him over.

"Michael," she said, "welcome. First captains' dinner?"

"It is, Admiral. All the other engagements under my command have been a bit more ad hoc. No time for formal dinners before battle."

"It's an old tradition," Jaruzelska said, "but a good one. Sadly, we don't often get the chance to do it even though it'll be one hell of a scrum fitting everyone in. The air group commander's not at all happy with what I've done to his hangar. Now"—she glanced around the crowded room—"there are some people I want you to meet."

Despite Jaruzelska's obvious support, Michael's evening got off to a rocky start and never improved. He knew how passionately the antidreadnought lobby held to its views; what he had not understood fully was how vocal it was. Except for a couple, all the officers he spoke with opposed dreadnoughts, some bitterly, and they all felt obligated to tell him why—at great length—an experience shared by Rao and Machar, as he learned when he bumped into them in the throng.

Restrained by youth, rank, and a grain of common sense, Michael refused to argue his case, resigning himself to saying no more than good manners required.

Retiring from a verbal drubbing at the hands of a vindictive Rear Admiral Perkins and two of his cronies—he had not spotted them until it was too late to escape—Michael turned around straight into the well-rounded figure of *Seigneur*'s captain.

"Oh, sorry, sir. Didn't see you there."

"Lieutenant Helfort," Captain Xiong said, shaking his hand vigorously and smiling broadly. "Good to see you again. It's been a while."

"And you, sir," Michael replied. It had been a while. The last time he had seen Xiong had been after *Adamant*, Michael's first—if brief—cruiser command, had captured the *McMullins* and *Providence Sound* and their precious cargoes of Hammer antimatter warheads.

"Let me guess," Xiong said, waving a dismissive hand, lip curling with open contempt. "Forces of darkness and re-action giving you a hard time, are they?" He smiled again, the skin around green-gray eyes wrinkling in sympathy.

Michael grimaced. "They are, Captain. It's fair enough, I suppose. They have their reasons."

"I'm sure they have, but what they ignore is simple arith-metic. Without your dreadnoughts, we could not even think about Operation Opera, much less mount it. Well"—Xiong's motherly face hardened—"not without stripping the home planets of what little protection they have left."

"That's what makes keeping quiet so hard, sir."

"I know, but it's best. Anyway, it does not matter what the naysayers think. It's what happens on the field of battle that's important. If I'm any judge of space warfare—and I should be; I've been in this business forty years—your dreadnoughts will be what gets Opera across the line. Old dinosaurs like me in our heavy cruisers cannot, and you can quote me, though please leave the 'old dinosaur' bit out."

"Thanks for the vote of confidence, sir, " Michael said with a laugh.

"Easy for me to say," Xiong said. "We won't be in the thick of it like you."

"The way Opera's looking, I reckon covering the with-drawal is the best place for *Seigneur* to be," Michael said with some feeling. "Oh! Sorry. No offense, sir," he added hurriedly.

"None taken," Xiong said, "and don't worry, I share your

sentiments. I'm too old to enjoy being shot at by the Hammers. Now, changing the subject, how's the love of your life?"

"Sorry, sir?"

"You know, that Lieutenant Cheung of yours. The lovely Anna."

Michael's face reddened. "Oh, er, fine thank you, sir . . ." he sputtered before lapsing into an embarrassed silence. He was not used to discussing his love life with senior officers.

"Relax, my boy," Xiong said with a chuckle. "My wife's one of Anna's many cousins. She's expecting an invite to the wedding, by the way."

"Oh, right," Michael said feebly. "I'll remember that. Far as I know, Anna's okay. Still no vidmail from her, but the Red Cross's monthly status reports say she's fine."

"Pleased to hear it. We were worried for a while. Bad business that. But to be serious for a moment. Opera. You and your guys ready?"

"We are, sir." Michael's face was grim. "Well, as much as we can be. The two new squadrons are good though still green, and I worry about how well they'll hold up under pressure. But they did well at Salvation, we've simmed the operation every which way, and provided we stay focused on reducing the plant's defenses, on getting through to the plant itself, we'll be fine. It'll be tough, but that's the whole point of the dreadnoughts."

"I agree. It'll be a dirty business. The shit will be flying everywhere. Just ignore it, keep going, never lose sight of the objective, and I think you'll get this done."

Michael's stomach did a couple of lazy somersaults at the prospect of facing the Hammers again. "I certainly hope so, sir," he said.

Michael had had enough. More than anything he wanted the formal dinner to wrap up so he could get back to *Reckless* to concentrate on the business of destroying the Hammer's antimatter plant. He turned his attention back to the podium, where, thankfully, Jaruzelska was winding up her speech.

". . . and finally, remember this. It's in the operation order in big black letters, but I'll say it again for those of you who don't read so well. Only one thing matters . . . destroying the antimatter plant." Jaruzelska paused to scan the faces of the captains of Battle Fleet Lima's ships. "Compared to that, nothing else does," she said fiercely. "Nothing. I don't, you don't, your crews don't, and your ships don't, so you should treat what I am about to say as a direct order.

"Every other operation I've ever been part of has gone off the rails at some point, and Opera will, too. You can count on it, especially as we know the Hammers are certain to send reinforcements; we just don't know when or how many. And when those damned Hammers start turning up, it will be up to one of you to do whatever"—her voice slashed through the air—"and I mean whatever it takes to reduce that damned antimatter plant to a ball of molten slag. Do I make myself clear?"

Silence hung heavy in the air for a few seconds before the room erupted, the sound of chairs kicked back overwhelmed by roars of support.

Unmoving, Jaruzelska waited until the noise died down. "That's all, folks. I look forward to seeing you all at the postoperation debrief. Until then . . . Remember Comdur!"

This time, the noise was deafening, the shout of "Remember Comdur" racketing across the hangar, an unstoppable wave of hate-fed energy.

Safely back onboard *Reckless,* Michael raised his mug of coffee. "Here's to us; here's to the Dreadnought Force."

Rao and Machar raised their mugs in silent acknowledgment.

"You guys all set?"

"Apart from wanting to throw up all the time, yes," Machar said with a crooked smile, his normally blue-black skin tinged with gray. "That dinner was too much. Admiral Lord Nelson has a lot to answer for."

"Tell me," Rao said. "Going head to head against a pair of Hammer light escorts in *Aldebaran* was bad, but that damn dinner was ten times worse."

"We'll come through," Michael said. "Dreadnoughts are tough. I have faith in them, in their crews, and in you. Just remember what the admiral said. The one thing, the only thing, that matters is destroying the antimatter plant. When things go to shit, and they will, if the First gets blown out of space, you guys press on. Just keep going. One of us will get through."

Michael took a sip of coffee.

"One of us will get through," he said. "We have to."

Four hours later, Battle Fleet Lima accelerated out of Comdur nearspace en route to Devastation Reef, 400 light-years distant.

Operation Opera was under way.

Friday, March 16, 2401, UD
FWSS Reckless, *Deepspace*

"Pretty awesome, sir," Ferreira said.

Michael nodded, doing his best to ignore a sick churning in his stomach. Thick clusters of green icons marked where the ships of Battle Fleet Lima spread out across space; they were a formidable sight.

"Sure is, Jayla," he said. "I just wish we had the extra dreadnought squadrons Admiral Jaruzelska asked for. I'd be a lot more confident with another thirty dreadnoughts alongside me when we go into the attack."

"Me, too, sir. Still," Ferreira said cheerfully, "if the sims are to be believed, we'll pull this one off."

"Sims are sims, Jayla; when you strip them back, they are just fancy mathematical models, and remember what you've been taught about them."

"Crap in, crap out, sir. That's the one thing I remember."

"Exactly so, Jayla. Can't say I have much confidence in them after the Hell's Moons operation. That sure as shit did not turn out the way we simmed it. You cannot simulate the arrival of Hammer task groups you don't know anything about. One thing's for certain. The second we drop in to attack, the Hammer commander is going to start screaming for help. And guess what?"

"What, sir?"

"He'll get it. The Hammers will ignore all our diversionary attacks to send every ship they can lay their hands on. They cannot afford to lose their precious antimatter plant. That's why this lot"—he waved a hand at the green icons crowding the command holovid—"are going to have to be quick off the mark when Hammer reinforcements start turning up and all that planning goes off the rails. And it will . . . which is why those extra dreadnoughts would have come in handy."

Ferreira nodded her agreement. The two of them stood without saying a word, staring at the command holovid, the space between the ships of Battle Fleet Lima busy with remassing drones shuttling to and fro, refilling mass bunkers for the coming operation.

"How's our remassing going?" he asked eventually.

"Nearly there, sir. Two more drones should see us at 100 percent."

"Good. I'm going walkabout. Let me know when we've completed remassing."

"Aye, aye, sir. I'll keep an eye on things."

Michael walked out of the gutted shell that was *Reckless*'s combat information center. Walking forward, he came to the drop tube. Without breaking stride, he stepped into it and dropped down to the hangar. The enormous space was echoingly empty, the tightly packed ranks of landers and space attack vehicles carried by a conventional heavy cruiser all gone, leaving only the lonely shapes of *Caesar's Ghost* and *Cleft Stick,* the two landers flanked by the marines' accommodation modules. When he walked over, Michael shook his head. He had not bothered to ask Kallewi's opinion of the landers' names; without exception, marines held the whole naming landers business to be unprofessional and unmilitary, a practice that reflected badly on them. Michael grinned. He had seen holovid of a marine colonel apoplectic over the prospect of boarding an assault lander called *Betty's Bouncing Ball*.

But that, of course, was the whole point. Teasing anchor-faced marines by giving assault landers outrageous names—and *Betty's Bouncing Ball* was by no means the worst of them—was one of the small pleasures that made spacers' lives bearable.

Ramp down to reveal its brightly lit cargo bay, *Caesar's Ghost* was a hive of activity. Kallewi's marines were busy off-loading all their equipment into neat piles on the hangar deck before—presumably—moving it all back again. Quite why they were doing something so pointless was not clear. Michael shook his head. He would never understand marines as long as he lived. Not all of them, though, he noticed, were involved in shifting stuff from A to B and back again. The security detail required for all special weapons not secured in dedicated magazines—marines in full combat armor, helmets on, armored plasglass visors down, assault rifles cradled across their chests—stood guard over three chromaflage-skinned boxes sitting atop maneuvering sleds. The diminutive figure of Petty Officer Trivedi, *Ghost*'s loadmaster, was fussing over the chains that secured them to the hanger floor.

The assault demolition charges appeared innocuous enough, but they had a yield in excess of 2 megatons of TNT each. Michael's pulse quickened as he imagined the damage they would inflict on the Hammer's precious anti-matter plant, their enormous power tamped into place by kilometers of rock.

Kallewi spotted him and walked over, flanked by his platoon sergeant, a burly Anjaxxian who overtopped Michael by a good fifty centimeters. Sergeant Tchiang was quiet to the point of being mute, but for all his mass, he was one of the fastest humans Michael had ever seen. He had watched Tchiang training for the assault on SuppFac27; the man was pure controlled ferocity. Michael was glad he would not be the one on the receiving end of the marine's special brand of explosive violence.

"Janos, Sergeant Tchiang. Just came to see how things were."

"Under control, sir," Kallewi said, "though I'll be a lot happier when we get this damn business started."

"You and me both. Never been good at waiting."

After a few minutes of small talk and reassured that Kallewi and his marines were as ready as they would ever be for whatever Operation Opera might throw at them, Michael made his way through the lander's cargo bay and climbed up boot-polished rungs to the flight deck.

"Welcome aboard the *Ghost,* sir," Kat Sedova said from the command pilot's seat. Flanked by the three leading spacers responsible for the lander's sensors, weapons, and systems, she appeared confident and completely in control; she had every right, after all the training sims she had been subjected to.

"Thanks. All well?"

"Yes, sir. *Caesar's Ghost* here"—Sedova patted the arm of her seat affectionately—"is ready to go. And so is the *Stick.* We've just run her up, and she's 100 percent, too."

"Good. Not long."

"Can't wait."

"That's what our tame marine said," Michael said, looking around, "and I have to say I agree with him. Glad to see you've fixed that damned fire control radar, Jackson."

"Mothering thing," the leading spacer responsible for *Ghost's* sensors said with considerable feeling, "but the new AI module has done the trick. I don't think it will let us down."

"Just hope it works," the spacer at the weapons station said. "I will be seriously pissed if I end up having to fire my cannons by eye."

"Careful what you wish for, Leading Spacer Paarl," Michael said with a grin.

"I know, sir," the woman said, returning the grin, "I know. I might get it."

"Sorry," Michael said. "Have I said that before?"

"Just a few times, sir," Paarl shot back amid chuckles of amusement from the rest of the crew.

"Yeah, yeah," Michael said. "Leading Spacer Florian."

"Yes, sir?" the engineer responsible for all the lander's main propulsion and pinchspace jump systems said.

"I know the answer to this question, but it would be good to hear it from you. You have the backup mass distribution model set up in case we have to jump without those damned demolition charges the marines are so proud of?"

"Sure have, sir. If we have to jump in a hurry, we won't need to hang around recomputing."

"Good. I plan to have *Reckless* bring us home, but you never know."

"No, sir, you don't," Florian said, her face betraying the anxiety she—and everyone else—must have been feeling.

"Right. Kat, I'm off to engineering. Far as I know, the remassing is running on schedule, so I think we'll be jumping as planned. Any changes, I'll let you know."

"Thank you, sir."

Leaving *Caesar's Ghost* surrounded by its ants' nest of marines, Michael walked aft, leaving the hangar by way of yet more empty spaces, spaces where the heavy cruiser's air group maintenance teams once had lived. The compartments had been gutted. With all nonstructural bulkheads removed along with the air group's fixtures and fittings, they were little more than large empty boxes that reverberated to the echo of boots on plasteel. Right aft, two massive doors opened through the belt of secondary armor that protected the vulnerable fusion reactors that powered *Reckless*'s main propulsion. Still moving aft, Michael found himself inside the ship's port primary power compartment. Packed with an intricately nested tangle of pipes, wiring, pumps, and control equipment, it was an enormous space, fully 60 meters high from armored deck underfoot to armored deckhead above him.

Like every warship captain who ever lived, he felt nervous in the place. Far too many ships were destroyed by enemy action because the fusion plants that powered the main engine mass drivers lost containment, blowing a ship into a huge ball of ionized gas in a matter of milliseconds. The designers did their best, of course, to protect the plants—the huge slabs of secondary armor that shielded the compartment proved that—but there were limits to how much extra armor could be packed into a ship and to what that armor could achieve. Anyway, modern missiles were more than up to the task of smashing their way in, helped by the fact that in places the armor was more holes than ceramsteel to allow pipes, ducts, power and control cables, and driver mass feeds to get in and out of the compartment.

Michael's gloomy review of the problem was interrupted by a shout from overhead.

"Up here, sir." It was Chief Chua.

"Okay."

Michael threaded his way up through the maze until he came out onto a narrow walkway, the deck below visible through the slotted metal. Surrounded by repairbots, toolboxes, and diagnostic equipment, *Reckless*'s engineers huddled around an access hole out of which stuck a pair of legs. A quick check of the main propulsion system schematics told him that the panel accessed trunking—a white plasfiber pipe fully two meters in diameter—protecting superconducting high-voltage feeds from the fusion plant to the mass driver at the heart of the port main engine.

"Chief Chua. What's up?"

"Nothing serious, sir."

Michael nodded; he already knew that. If there had been a problem, the AI controlling the ship's primary power systems would have told him already.

"We're seeing some instability in the power levels that shouldn't be there, and we're just having a look at the system to make sure it's not part of a bigger problem waiting to happen."

"Okay," Michael said. Not for the first time, he offered up a small prayer of thanks that he had engineers like Chua. More than a few he knew would have waited until the problem turned serious before doing anything about it. "Any luck?"

"Think so. Petty Officer Lim"—Chua waved a hand at

the legs sticking out of the access hole—"says it's a power controller problem. She's just checking it, and if she's not happy with it, we'll tear it out and replace it."

"And we have a spare?"

"What sort of question is that, sir? Of course we have."

The three engineers laughed. Michael knew why. Fleet, in all its wisdom, had done its best to reduce the dreadnoughts' inventory of spares to zero, arguing that there were not enough engineers to use them, so why bother carrying all that unnecessary mass? Michael's response to that argument was short and unprintable but, after editorial input from Jaruzelska, sufficiently convincing to make Fleet change its mind. Thankfully.

"Good. I'd hate not having both engines when the Hammers are breathing down our necks."

"Fucking Hammers," Chief Fodor said. "Shit, I hope we kick their asses."

"We will, chief, we will," Michael said with confidence he did not feel. "How're your fusion plants?"

"Sweet as nuts, sir, both of them. They'll not let you down."

"Good. Now. Petty Officer Morozov," he said, turning to the senior spacer standing alongside Chua, "let me see . . . yes, ship's air smells good, it's at the right temperature, oxygen levels are where they should be, trace contaminants are within limits, we have no rogue bacteria roaming around, airborne viral load is zero, the food tastes great, the water's clean, hot and cold haven't gotten mixed up, the recyclers are functioning normally, and let me think . . . what else? Oh, yes, I almost forgot. My crapper seems to be working properly at last, so am I right to assume that the habitat department is in good shape?"

"You said it, sir," Tammy Morozov said, a faint blush of embarrassment spreading across her cheeks. "Er, really sorry about your crapper, sir. The yard took out a vacuum pump they shouldn't have."

"You know what, Petty Officer Morozov?"

"What, sir?"

"I believe you," Michael said, all sincerity, "I really, really do. And on that happy note, I'll leave you all."

"Sir," Morozov mumbled over a soft chorus of chuckles from her fellow engineers.

Michael walked forward along the catwalk, passing through the upper access doors to reenter the central part of the ship on 2 Deck. According to Mother, the coxswain and the rest of the *Reckless*'s spacers—all three of them—were up forward in the final stages of checking the missile magazines to make sure that they were in as good a shape as the ship's missile AI claimed. Michael took the forward drop tube down to the hangar deck level, making his way forward to yet another massive armored bulkhead, through its double doors, and into the missile magazine lobby.

Bienefelt was inside the starboard lower missile magazine with Carmellini, Faris, and Lomidze, busy with running diagnostic routines on each missile in turn. As this magazine alone held more than six hundred missiles, it was a big job. Michael took a set of magazine coveralls from a locker and, with a final check to make sure he carried no prohibited items, stepped through the double blastproof doors and into the magazine.

The place nearly took his breath away; it always did. Racks holding the matte black shapes of Merlin antistarship missiles packed the magazine, the air rich with the telltale smell of the hydraulics that rammed missiles out of their stowages and into the salvo room, ready for launch. For Michael, this place with its mix of power and menace was what *Reckless* was all about.

"How's it going, 'Swain?"

Bienefelt stepped back from the missile she was checking. "Getting there, sir. This is the last magazine."

"Any duds in this lot?" Michael waved a hand at the racks of missiles.

"Three so far, but none that we didn't already know about. Looks like the missile AI might have its shit together for once."

Michael nodded. He could live with that. "Makes a change," he said. "The other magazines?"

"Seven duds, all known."

"Okay. How are my sensors, Carmellini?"

"All nominal, sir. Before the coxswain hijacked us—"

"Watch it, spacer," Bienefelt growled, mock serious.

"Sorry, 'Swain," Carmellini said, not looking sorry at all as Faris stifled a laugh. "All good, sir."

"Weapon systems?"

Leading Spacer Jenna Lomidze nodded at the missiles racked around her. "Apart from a few dud Merlins and number 7 chain-gun battery—the yardies are going to have to fix that—all weapons systems are online. We're good to go, sir."

"And finally, comms. Faris?"

"One hundred percent, sir."

"Good. Word in your ear, 'Swain."

Bienefelt followed Michael out of the magazine back into the lobby. "Anything I need to know, Matti?" he asked while he stripped off his coveralls.

"No, sir. *Reckless* is as ready as she can be. Troops are in good shape. Nervous as hell, most of them. Shit! I am, too, but they'll be fine."

"Carmellini?"

"He's solid. Shitting himself, of course, but I think he'll be okay."

"Good. Last I heard, we should be jumping on schedule."

"Thanks for that, Skipper. I am sick of waiting."

"Me, too. It'll be rough, Matti. You know that?"

"With you in command, sir, what else would it be?"

"Thanks for the vote of confidence," Michael said with a laugh. "I'll try not to disappoint."

"Not much chance of that."

"We'll see. I'd better leave you to it. I'll be in the CIC."

"Righto, sir."

"How we doing?" Michael asked Ferreira when he slipped back into his seat.

"*Iron Sword* managed to get herself rammed by one of the drones, but there was no damage done."

"Take more than a remassing drone to dent a cruiser's armor."

"It would, sir. Flag has confirmed we will jump on schedule."

"Good." Michael resisted the temptation to go through Opera's time line again. He had done that so many times, he knew what was supposed to happen to the second. He was glad he had done the walk-around. For all the sophistication of AI-managed information systems, for all the power of avatar software, for all the convenience of virtual meetings, there was nothing quite like seeing things for oneself. He knew captains who relied on all those things to run their ships, spending their tours of duty confined to their cabins and the combat information center.

But he was not one of those captains.

At one level, the walk through the ship told him nothing he did not already know, nothing one of the AIs had not told him already. If it had, he would have been worried. But at another level, he learned a lot, and it was all to do with the spacers and marines who would go into battle alongside him. Even if he had not been able to speak to them all, he had eyeballed every one of them, and they'd all told him the same thing.

Reckless and her tiny crew were ready for the battle to come, as ready as they would ever be. He would have one last chat with Mother—*Reckless*'s primary AI always had something useful to add—and then grab some badly needed sleep.

"You have the ship, Jayla," he said when he slipped out of his seat and headed for his cabin. "If nothing crops up, call me thirty minutes before we jump."

"Sir."

Saturday, March 17, 2401, UD
Support Facility 27 nearspace,
West Devastation Reef

In a savage flash of white light, antimatter warheads stripped out of captured Hammer Eaglehawk missiles exploded. Seconds later, a wall of gamma radiation overwhelmed the sphere of heavily armed defense platforms and pinchspace jump disrupters protecting the drop zone for ships heading for the Hammer antimatter buried deep in the heart of Support Facility 27. The radiation, ferocious in its intensity, pushed through the platforms' meager armor, forcing fusion reactors out of limits until they, too, erupted into massive balls of white-red gas, before it reached out to destroy a small Hammer task group on forward picket duty.

In less than a nanosecond, billions of cubic kilometers of Hammer space had been scoured clean, its defenses blown to incandescent gas.

Seconds later, more cargo drones dropped out of pinchspace to the north and south of the drop zone; their payloads of antimatter warheads sterilized two bubbles of space large enough to accommodate the ships of Battle Fleet Lima, the void filling with hundreds of thousands of white-hot flares as space mines were overwhelmed by gamma radiation, their directed-fission warheads going critical, stabbing jets of fire uselessly into space.

For a while, nothing happened. Slowly cooling spheres of gas expanding out into the void were the only things moving.

"Captain, sir. All suits are green, ship is at general quarters in ship state 1, airtight condition zulu, artificial gravity off, ship depressurized," Ferreira said.

Michael ignored a stomach doing somersaults as *Reckless*'s gravity disappeared. "Roger. I have the ship. All stations, stand by to drop. Thanks, Jayla."

"I'm glad it's started, sir," Ferreira said, "that's all I can say."

"Amen to that," Michael said; he meant it. The wait was killing him.

"I'll be in damage control, sir. Good luck. Remember Comdur." Ferreira spun on the spot; with a one-footed push, she glided away.

"Remember Comdur," Michael whispered while his executive officer flew effortlessly out of *Reckless*'s combat information center. The huge compartment felt uncomfortably empty, its only other occupants the anonymous combat space-suited figures of Carmellini and Lomidze strapped into their shock-resistant seats, hunched forward over consoles in front of Michael. Flanking him were the two AI-generated avatars in the operations and threat assessment seats. Kubby and Kal—their clones, to be precise; the original AIs were a small part of the diffuse cloud of gas that once had been *Tufayl*—might look every bit as solid as Carmellini and Lomidze, but they were just images spun across his mind's eye, figments of a computer's imagination. Michael did not care; it was good to have them there.

Time to commit. "Warfare, command," Michael said. "Weapons free. You have command authority."

"Warfare, roger. Weapons free. I have command authority."

Maddeningly slow, the drop counter ran off the seconds. "All stations, this is Warfare. Stand by . . . dropping."

Michael's gloved fingers dug into the arm of his seat while *Reckless* turned the cosmos inside out, the navigation AI depositing the ship precisely onto its drop datum. The rest of the dreadnoughts fell neatly into station around her.

After months of work, Operation Opera started in earnest. With a quiet prayer that he would make it out alive and that Anna would be home soon, he closed his mind to everything except the job at hand.

A crunching shudder shook the ship from end to erfd, the opening move of Operation Opera: *Reckless* and her sister ships each deployed their first salvo of long-range Merlin antistarship missiles along with their clouds of protective decoys. The missiles would keep station while the dreadnoughts added more missiles to the salvo. When the time came, and coordinated to the second, first stage engines would fire, driving the missiles toward the target in a single enormous wave, a rail-gun salvo timed to arrive on target seconds before the missiles smashed home.

Executed properly, a well-crafted missile and rail-gun attack was a brutally effective tactic, a tsunami of missiles and rail-gun slugs intended to confuse, overload, and overwhelm. Space fleets all across humanspace spent enormous amounts of time trying to get it right; Michael's dreadnoughts were no exception, and he liked to think they, too, had gotten it right.

The Hammers had more than the dreadnoughts to worry about. Running ahead of Michael's ships was Group North, a mixed task group of heavy and light cruisers backed up by fleet escorts and led by Vice Admiral Jaruzelska in *Seljuk*. Their missiles and rail guns would add to the misery to be inflicted on the Hammer ships tasked with defending the northern approaches to SuppFac27.

That was the good part.

The problem was that anything the Feds dished up, the Hammers would return with interest. Two hundred thousand kilometers ahead of Group North and Michael's dreadnoughts, the Hammer ships of task group Hammer-2 were already adjusting vectors to intercept the incoming Feds, their first missile salvo quickly deployed, with many more to follow.

It was going to be rough, and there was always the chance that the Hammers' first missile salvo would carry antimatter warheads, even if Fleet's intelligence analysts had been emphatic that they would not. The risk of collateral damage to the intricate web of fixed defenses and minefields and to the roving task groups of Hammer warships that protected SuppFac27 was too high, they argued. Michael agreed with them, not that his opinion mattered: The intelligence wonks had been known to get things spectacularly wrong, and if they had, the heavy cruisers were doomed, and so was Operation Opera.

For Jaruzelska, accepting the analysts' call had been an enormous gamble, the biggest of her long and successful career. If the analysts were wrong, she risked the future of the Federated Worlds and its billions of citizens. Michael was more than happy that Jaruzelska was in charge; it was a good time to be a lowly lieutenant, responsible for only a small part of the mind-bendingly complex business that was Operation Opera. If it all went to shit—and there was a good chance it would—it would not be his scalp the politicians came after.

"Command, Warfare. Threat plot confirmed."

"Command, roger."

Relieved, Michael whistled softly. The Hammers were where the few reconsats Jaruzelska was allowed to deploy said they would be. There were three task groups: Hammer-1, covering the central approaches to the antimatter plant; Hammer-2, 100,000 kilometers to the north; and Hammer-3, the same distance to the south. That was nice, Michael thought, a threat plot that did not turn to shit in the first few seconds of an operation, though he knew that happy state of affairs would not last. Things would go wrong, he reminded himself, the moment Hammer reinforcements started to arrive. If there was one thing certain about Operation Opera, that was it.

"Command, Warfare. Dreadnought Group established on vector. Groups North and South report launch of minefield clearance drones."

"Roger."

A quick check confirmed that Warfare had the dreadnought force in station and on vector. Michael settled back, eyes flicking between the threat and command plots. The Fed attack was developing according to a plan that for once—most unusually—was addressing a two-dimensional tactical problem rather than the three that bedeviled most space combat. That was because, buried in the heart of Devastation Reef, SuppFac27 was a difficult place to get into. Thanks to an impenetrable tangle of gravitational rips, ships approaching the Hammer plant in pinchspace were forced to come from one direction only: from the west, parallel to the galactic plane. From any other direction—up, down, north, south, or east, it did not matter—a transit through normalspace was the only way in: Tens of millions of kilometers of gravitational reef forced a long and slow transit. As one of the planners had pointed out, to come in across the reef would be to tell the Hammers a week ahead of time that an attack was on its way, ensuring that the entire Hammer fleet would be waiting to blow you to hell when you finally turned up.

All of which was why the Hammers had located Supp-Fac27 where they had, so from the west it was.

The result? The Feds would fight their way into the Hammer antimatter plant across what amounted to a flat—if invisible—surface. It was the one thing Opera had going for it, and Michael loved it; it simplified the tactical situation greatly.

There was one small problem, though. If fighting a battle on a flat surface made things easier for the Feds, it did the same thing for the Hammers.

Now the two Fed task groups drove east out of their drop zones and across the western edge of Devastation Reef; ahead of them lay the Hammer ships covering the antimatter plant's flanks. In the center, two decoy attacks—configured to look like a massive force of heavy cruisers and intended to fool the Hammers into thinking that they were the main assault force—were on vector running right up the middle, heading straight for SuppFac27.

The aim was to confuse the Hammers, to conceal the real threat to the antimatter plant for as long as possible. If Opera went to plan, the Hammers' commander would have no idea which of the Fed ships were feints and which posed the real threat to their precious antimatter plant.

To confuse them further, cargo drones spewed decoys, jammers, and spoofers into the space between the attacks until SuppFac27 nearspace was filled with an elaborately constructed torrent of electronic noise, most of it garbage. For an instant, Michael sympathized with the Hammers; he wondered what the poor sap in charge of defending SuppFac27 was thinking. Buried under an avalanche of conflicting information, flummoxed by a blizzard of electronic noise, and with attacks developing along four separate vectors, he would be struggling to sort out truth from deception, which, of course, was the whole point.

But the Hammers had one thing going for them. There was only one target, and in the end Jaruzelska's ships would have to close in on it to have any chance of destroying the plant. If the Hammers were smart, they would pull back and wait for the Feds to come to them instead of blundering around trying to sort out reality from deception. In the sims, the margin between success and failure narrowed dramatically every time the Hammers did that. When reinforcements turned up in the right place at the right time as well . . .

Happily, the Hammers were not yet doing the sensible thing. Michael was watching what might have been a "best case" simulation. As Jaruzelska's planners hoped, the Hammer ships did not wait for the Feds to come to them; they were moving out to meet and engage the incoming Feds. But the Hammers had a big problem: three task groups to interdict four Fed lines of attack. That allowed one of the Feds' decoy attacks to run unopposed right at the antimatter plant, giving the Hammer commander, Michael hoped, a severe attack of the vapors when he realized what was happening.

"Command, Warfare, sensors. Positive gravitronics intercept. Estimated drop bearing Red 180 Up 0. Multiple vessels, range 12,000 kilometers. Gravity wave pattern suggests pinchspace transition imminent. Drop datum nominal for Assault Group."

Michael acknowledged the report, relieved that Assault Group—deemed too valuable to drop with the advance guard—was on its way. The bad news was that Assault Group was under the command of Rear Admiral Perkins, a decision Michael reckoned had the fingerprints of Fleet politicians all over it. With Perkins in charge of Assault Group, the man would be in at the kill, and Michael knew full well who would take the credit for Opera's success. All too clearly, he could see what would happen. Ignoring the task forces protecting his vulnerable flanks, ignoring the dreadnoughts that had blasted the way open for him, Perkins would attribute the success of Opera to the conventional warships of Assault Group and, no doubt, to his skills as a combat commander. Sonofabitch.

Michael dismissed the Perkins problem. What mattered was making Opera a success, though he was pretty sure who would be getting the blame if Opera turned out to be the failure the analysts said it might so easily be. He would not want to be Jaruzelska if that happened.

"Command, Warfare, sensors. Assault Group dropping. Drop datum confirmed Red 180 Up 0, range 12,500 kilometers. Stand by . . . confirmed. Arrivals are Assault Group."

"Command, roger."

Michael settled down to wait. Warfare was performing flawlessly, so he forced himself to relax a touch. Space warfare, like all warfare down the ages, was a mixture of boredom and terror, invariably bucket loads of the former seasoned with occasional pinches of the latter. Opera was definitely in the boredom phase. This was as unexciting as combat got: two groups of ships hurtling toward each other across hundreds of thousands of kilometers of space, too far apart to engage, their principal task to dump missiles into space, building their opening salvos while they closed on the enemy for the inevitable. It was the bloody business of close-quarters combat, a battle of attrition as missiles and rail-gun slugs stripped armor off ships' frames, looking for a way through to the fusion plants driving main propulsion. Michael buried an image of *Reckless*'s fusion plants going up, doing his best to ignore his body's reaction to the impending fight: churning stomach, sweaty hands, hammering heart, and dry mouth.

Time dragged by with excruciating slowness, the quiet concentration of *Reckless*'s tiny combat information center crew interrupted by the routine reports of missile launches when Fed and Hammer ships dumped missiles into space.

"Command, Warfare. Update. Ships of task group Hammer-1 have engaged Decoy Group One. Expect Hammer breakaway imminent."

"Command, roger." The Hammer commander would be seriously pissed when he discovered that he had thrown one of his precious task groups into an attack on a bunch of decoys. Fed decoys were good but not good enough to mount a convincing defense once attacked. The big question was where the Hammer ships would go when they found out they had been conned.

Michael received his answer a few minutes later. The ships attacking Decoy Group One changed vector, furious jets of ionized reaction mass from maneuvering thrusters turning them end for end, the electronic and optical noise spewed out by the decoy attack ignored completely.

"Shit," Michael muttered when the Hammers' intentions became clear. They had ignored the one Fed attack they had not been able to deal with: Decoy Group Two, the second decoy attack running at SuppFac27. The Hammer commander was pulling his ships back to screen the antimatter plant, and that meant just one thing. Stopping Decoy Group Two was going to be somebody else's job. Reinforcements were on the way.

He commed the admiral's staff.

"Flag, *Reckless*."

The avatar of one of Jaruzelska's operations staff took the com, the stress on the man's face all too obvious. "Go ahead, *Reckless*."

"The Hammer ships tasked to intercept Decoy Group One are withdrawing to SuppFac27. My assessment is that reinforcements are inbound to deal with Decoy Group Two. You concur?"

"Stand by . . . yes, we concur. We're just about to update the threat plot."

"Any estimate of the drop datum?"

"Somewhere to the southeast is our best guess, but it's just a guess at the moment."

"Roger. *Reckless*, out."

Michael's worst fears were about to be realized. Reinforcements were the basis for all the nightmare scenarios they had been subjected to in the sims, and far too many of those had ended in disaster. If the Hammers dropped the right ships in the right places at the right times, even a commander as good as Jaruzelska was going to struggle.

The tactical problem was simple. Jaruzelska knew Hammer ships were on the way—that much was certain—but she had no idea how many or where or when they would drop. That meant she could do nothing to head them off. She had to wait, responding to the Hammer reinforcements as they arrived. Michael hated it—no commander liked being forced to react to events—but Jaruzelska had no choice.

"Command, Warfare. Group South engaging ships of task group Hammer-3."

"Command, roger."

Michael patched his neuronics into the holocam feed coming from the heavy cruiser leading Group South. What he saw made his skin crawl. Shrouded in clouds of decoys, Hammer missiles—arranged like a giant doughnut perpendicular to Group South's vector—had turned inward; now they plunged down onto the Fed task group, the fast-closing gap between attackers and defenders filled with the flash of missiles exploding as Group South's medium-range missiles and lasers did the grim work of tearing the Hammer attack to pieces. The battle was degenerating fast into a wretched, scrambling fight for survival, one that no Fed ship could afford to lose: A single fusion warhead, triggered by a proximity fuse to explode close to its target, released enough raw power to strip a heavy cruiser's flank armor right down to the inner titanium hull, the impulse shock violent enough to send razor-sharp splinters ripping through the ship to lethal effect.

The missiles that survived closed in, and the Feds' short-range defensive weapons joined the fight, throwing up a wall of metal backed up by lasers, clawing more and more missiles out of the attack. But missiles still made it through, relentless, unstoppable; there were too many of them. Just before missile detonation, the Hammers' rail-gun salvo arrived, slugs burying themselves deep in the frontal armor of their targets, great gouts of ionized ceramsteel armor blasted out into space, ugly clouds of white-hot gas boiling away from the ships. Seconds later, the missiles hit home, a brutally effective mix of boosted chemex and fusion warheads, lances of white-hot fire and hellish torrents of radiation putting their victims to the sword.

It was a sickening sight. Michael watched the damage reports flooding in. The ships attacking SuppFac27's southern flank had been roughly handled. Too many were beyond help, broken hulls spitting lifepods in all directions, orange-strobed specks driving away through clouds of ice and fire in a frenzied race to get clear before the ships blew, violent blue-white flashes marking the loss of one ship after another. More ships, battered and combat-ineffective, pulled out of the line of battle to reverse vector and run for safety.

The fight was not one-sided, though; now it was the Hammers' turn to suffer. The Fed ships dropped their own exquisitely coordinated rail-gun and missile salvos onto the enemy ships, flame-shot clouds of plasma erupting as rail-gun slugs and missile warheads clawed at the Hammer ships. When the clouds cleared, Michael saw that the Hammers had suffered every bit as badly as the Feds, maybe more so. Ship after ship pulled out of the line, brilliant flares flagging the death of ships when their fusion power plants lost containment.

The first phase of the engagement was over; to Michael's astonishment it had lasted only a few seconds. Now the hard slog started for Group South: The two sides closed in, trading salvo for salvo, missiles and rail-gun slugs thrown across space in a brutal war of attrition that would end when one side either ceased to exist or fled the field of battle. The Feds were relying on better salvo rates and more accurate targeting to overcome the Hammers.

Michael's mouth tightened into a thin, tight snarl of approval. Operation Opera had a long way to go, but so far, so good. It might be a bloody business, but Group South was doing what it had been sent to do: fix the Hammer ships in place, lock them into a running battle from which they could not disengage without risking destruction, keep them away from the dreadnoughts and Assault Group. It was a magnificent, tragic spectacle; while he watched, Michael tried not to think about the thousands of spacers dying to protect his ships.

"Command, Warfare. Group North missile commit in five . . . stand by . . . now."

Missile first stages fired, the Fed ships illuminated by the harsh brilliance of hundreds of thousands of thin white pillars of flame. It was an awesome sight, the missiles opening out into a ring while they flew toward the advancing Hammers, who were not slow to respond.

"Command, Warfare. Group North reports missile commit from task group Hammer-2."

"Command, roger," Michael acknowledged. His mouth dust-dry, he contemplated ending up on the wrong end of hundreds of thousands of missiles. "All stations, this is the captain. Quick update, folks. It's on. The Hammers have committed their missiles, and they'll be on us soon. So brace yourselves. It will get rough. Command, out."

Michael patched a quick com through to Rao in *Retrieve* and Machar in *Recognizance*. Their avatars popped into his neuronics, grim-faced, taut with apprehension. Michael's heart went out to them; though they had all been in combat, none of them had ever seen anything quite so daunting, quite so terrifying, as the immense missile strike heading their way.

"Kelli, Nathan. All buttoned up?"

"Yes, sir," the pair chorused.

"Good. Stick to the plan, and remember that if and when it all goes to shit, do whatever it takes to get your ships through to SuppFac27. Just go, keep on going, and get your marines into the plant."

"Sir."

"Good. See you on the other side. *Reckless* out."

Death arrived, heralded by the appalling racket of *Reckless*'s defenses when they joined with the dreadnoughts and the rest of Group North to slash missiles out of space. But there were too many to fend off. Inevitably, some fought their way through, leaving ship after ship reeling from fusion blast, missile strike, and the impact of rail-gun slugs. The Hammers had planned their attack well. Focused on the leading ships, their opening salvo ripped the guts out of Group North. Too many of the cruisers had been hit, some fatally, the telltale orange strobes of lifepods filling the space around the dying ships, the distress radio frequency filling with the urgent bleatings of automatic beacons asking for help.

"Command, sensors." Carmellini's voice was hoarse. "*Seljuk*'s in trouble, sir."

Of all the ships! Michael did not want to think what losing Jaruzelska might mean for Opera's chances of success.

He forced himself to sound calm. "Command, roger. Train a holocam on her."

The video feed from the holocam confirmed Carmellini's report. The massive heavy cruiser had been heavily punished up forward; *Seljuk*'s bows were a smoking ruin of white-hot ceramsteel armor. Worse, the full force of a pair of well-timed fusion warheads had opened up her starboard side down to the titanium frames; Michael saw right into the dying cruiser. He did not have to check the data feeds from *Seljuk;* he had seen enough damaged ships to know that she was doomed. It was just a matter of time before a Hammer missile—one of many held back, loitering behind the main attack to pick off the wounded—plunged into the ship, its target one of the massive cruiser's main fusion plants. For *Seljuk*—and Admiral Jaruzelska—Operation Opera was over.

Not having Jaruzelska in charge was bad enough.

Having Perkins in charge of Opera might be, would be, ten times worse.

A terse com from *Seljuk* confirmed his worst fears. "Command, Warfare. Message from Flag: *Seljuk* fatally damaged. Abandoning ship. Flag passes to *Seiche;* Rear Admiral Perkins has operational command. Good luck. Jaruzelska out."

"Command, roger." Damn, damn, damn, Michael raged. Without hesitation, he trusted Jaruzelska with his life. He would not trust Perkins to look after a week-old cheeseburger. Michael watched the damage assessments flood in. They made for horrific reading. But there was some good news. Largely because they had run tucked in behind the main group of Fed ships, *Reckless* and her fellow dreadnoughts had escaped unscathed, the only damage inflicted by missile debris and minor. Five minutes behind them, Assault Group drove on completely untouched.

Group North had been mauled severely: moments after *Seljuk* blew itself apart, more ships followed her into oblivion, and others started to pull out of line, but not before dumping every missile into the next attack their shock-damaged hydraulics were capable of. Relief flooded his body as he watched the next phase of the attack develop: Group North might have been battered, but it remained an effective fighting force.

Michael forced himself to stay focused, to stay objective. Hard though they might be to accept, those losses did not matter provided that the Hammer ships attacking Group North were kept away from the dreadnoughts. And the Hammers were taking a beating. Pinned in place by Group North's attack, the ships of task group Hammer-2 were being ripped to bloody shreds. It was a good result. The way things were going, none of those Hammer ships would be a threat when the dreadnoughts and Assault Group broke away for the final assault on SuppFac27.

"Command, Warfare. Stand by to alter vector in five."

"Command, roger. Advise Flag."

"Stand by . . . Flag advised."

Michael forced himself to relax. He half expected Perkins to start changing the operations plan, but thankfully, that did not happen.

Five seconds later, the dreadnoughts adjusted vector, peeling away from Group North to turn southeast to start their run into SuppFac27, 180,000 kilometers distant. At 12,500 kilometers behind the dreadnoughts, Assault Group turned to follow.

Endgame time, Michael whispered to himself, endgame time. If the Hammer commander had not shot himself in despair—or been shot for incompetence, something the Hammers were inordinately fond of doing—he would see now where the real threat to his antimatter plant lay. If Opera had been a bloodbath so far, it was going to get a whole lot worse when the Hammers focused their efforts to keep the dreadnoughts out. With fear chewing away at his guts, Michael shivered at the awful prospect of the hours still to be spent deep inside Hammer space before the job was done and they could all go home.

"Command, Sensors. Group South reports positive gravitronics intercept. Estimated drop bearing Green 60 Up 3. Multiple vessels, range 155,000 kilometers. Gravity wave pattern suggests pinchspace transition imminent. Designated hostile task group Hammer-4. Initial vector analysis suggests incoming ships tasked to intercept Decoy Group Two."

"Command, roger. Confirm vector soonest.

"Here we go," Michael whispered. With the arrival of reinforcements, the real fight had started; the tactical advantage was back with the Hammers. Keeping one eye on the battle still raging off the dreadnoughts' port side between Group North and the Hammer ships protecting the northwestern approaches to the plant, he watched the threat plot while it updated to show the incoming Hammer reinforcements.

"Command, sensors. Hammer task group designated Hammer-4 dropped. Mixed force: twelve heavy, fifteen light cruisers, ten heavy escorts, plus seven other ships. Vector nominal to intercept Decoy Group Two."

"Time to engagement range?"

"Ten minutes."

"Command, roger." Those ten minutes were precious; they gave his dreadnoughts some time to run in toward SuppFac27 unopposed, ten minutes before the new arrivals worked out that they had been suckered into another attack on a bunch of Fed decoys, ten minutes before the Hammers turned to deal with the real threat to their plant. Michael swore softly. An hour would have been better, but he would take what he could get. One thing was for sure. Hammer-4 was just the first batch of reinforcements; more were certain to be on their way. He saw it in his mind's eye: Ignoring the elaborate web of diversionary attacks staged by the Feds right across Hammer space, attacks intended to delay reinforcements for as long as possible, Hammer ships would be scrambling in a desperate race to come to SuppFac27's defense.

In stark contrast to the terrifying intensity of the battles raging to the north and south, the Hammers had ignored the dreadnoughts and Assault Group so far, their commander still too short of ships to head them off. He would be having kittens, no doubt praying to his beloved Kraa for reinforcements and soon.

The rest of Battle Fleet Lima was doing it tough. Twenty thousand kilometers to port, Group North was still slugging it out with the Hammers, exchanging missile and railgun salvos, ships either blown or dropping out of the engagement, bleeding air and lifepods into space. One hundred thirty thousand kilometers to starboard, the newly arrived Hammer ships headed for the diversionary attack mounted by Decoy Group Two. Fifty thousand kilometers beyond them to the south, the engagement between Group South and the Hammers covering the southern approaches was grinding its way to a blood-soaked conclusion, the Feds' superior missile and rail-gun launch rates giving them the advantage.

Michael scanned the damage reports and forced himself not to think of the thousands of spacers dying on the blood-drenched altars of Hammer ambition. Only one thing mattered: that Groups North and South did their jobs—running interference, keeping the Hammer defenders pinned in place and away from the dreadnoughts, their sacrifice buying Michael and his ships the time they needed to smash a path through SuppFac27's defenses, opening the way through for Assault Group.

And what a job they were doing. Ignoring their losses, the Fed ships pressed home the attack until the Hammers could take no more. One ship after another, the Hammers broke and ran.

"Command, Warfare. Group South reports Hammers withdrawing. Group North reports Hammer ships to the north also withdrawing, assessed combat-ineffective, though they expect harassing attacks from ships still operational. Flag has ordered Group North to detach all available units to support Assault Group."

"Command, roger. Units to be detached?"

"Stand by . . . heavy cruisers *Secular*, *Ulugh Beg*, *Iron Road*, *Al-Zahravi*, *Zuben-el-Genubi,* plus light cruisers and escorts."

Michael shook his head in despair that Group North could spare so few ships.

"Command, Warfare. Task group Hammer-4 has engaged Decoy Group Two. Expect Hammers to break away shortly."

"Command, roger." Michael stared at the command plot. When the ships of Hammer-4 discovered that the second decoy group was yet another Fed diversion—and it would not take them long—where would they go? They would pull back, Michael decided after careful consideration; they would pull back to defend SuppFac27. That created a new problem straightaway: Pulling back would put the Hammer ships on vector to intercept Assault Group, and Hammer-4 had enough ships to give Admiral Perkins and Assault Group a headache.

Everything told Michael that Opera was close to its tipping point. He had seen it before: the point where an operation started to slip out of control and into instability, where the assumptions underpinning the operations plan started to fall apart, where those old enemies, fear, uncertainty, and doubt began to take over, where one wrong decision was all it took to ruin an entire operation.

Michael needed to know how close they were to the moment of crisis. He commed Rao, Machar, and his AIs into a conference; together they ran the numbers.

On the Fed side, Assault and Dreadnought groups, augmented by a handful of battered survivors from Group North, were established on vector, heading right for Supp-Fac27. Between them and their goal stood SuppFac27's fixed defenses: space battle stations deployed around an inner ring of semiautonomous defense platforms—all tough and resilient but unable to move and lacking the ship-killing power of rail guns—augmented by Hammer ships pulling back from their abortive intercepts of the two decoy attacks, all supported by the SuppFac27's last line of defense: fixed missile and laser batteries emplaced on the surface of the asteroid itself.

All that was bad, but the more he studied them, the more Michael liked the odds, and so did the rest of his team.

"We can finish this," Machar said.

"Yes, we can," Rao added.

Michael agreed with them. The dreadnoughts would blow the fixed defenses aside, and their rail guns would drop a hailstorm of slugs to destroy anything and everything on the asteroid's surface. As for the Hammer ships pulling back to defend the antimatter plant, they were strong but not strong enough to withstand the weight of missiles and rail-gun slugs thrown at them by the dreadnoughts and the ships of Assault Group.

Yes, the dreadnoughts could clear the way into Supp-Fac27. Provided that nothing changed, it was game over . . . provided that nothing changed.

Michael watched and waited.

Seventy-two minutes into the operation and less than thirty minutes before the dreadnoughts smashed through the defenses around SuppFac27, Michael allowed himself to believe that the worst was over.

Then things changed.

"Warfare, Command, Sensors. Positive gravitronics intercept. Estimated drop bearing Green 45 Down 1. Multiple vessels, range 60,000 kilometers. Assault Group confirms intercept. Gravity wave pattern suggests pinch-space transition imminent. Designated hostile task group Hammer-5. Initial vector assessment suggests Hammer-5 has been tasked to intercept Assault Group. Stand by vector confirmation."

"Confirm Green 45, 60,000?" Michael said, baffled. That should not be possible. As far as he knew, the Hammer ships were going to drop right into Devastation Reef, and even Hammers were not that stupid. Their ships would be torn apart.

"Drop datum for task group Hammer-5 is confirmed, Green 45, 60,000."

"Goddamnit," Michael said, frustrated and concerned at the same time. According to the intelligence briefings, gravity rips stopped Hammer reinforcements from dropping this close to SuppFac27. But the Hammers obviously did not read Fed intelligence briefings, so there they were, a major threat he did not need. "Command, roger," he said struggling to keep his voice under control. "Confirm vector soonest."

"Warfare, Command, Sensors. Hammer-5 dropping . . . stand by . . . task group Hammer-5 dropped. Mixed force, thirty-five cruisers, sixty escorts. On vector to intercept Assault Group, time to engage ten minutes."

"Roger."

Sweat beaded Michael's forehead. The Hammers were pulling rabbits out of the hat, and they were not small fluffy ones, either. These rabbits were big, ugly, and dangerous. That many ships dropping this close to SuppFac27 constituted a serious threat. He worked through the problem: An ice-cold band wrapped itself around his chest and squeezed hard. Michael struggled to breathe. Assault Group was in trouble, and the Hammers were sure to have reinforcements inbound to help stop the dreadnoughts. All that meant Opera was in trouble. His first instinct was to turn back to help; he gave Warfare the order.

"Warfare, Command, to all ships, emergency reverse vec—"

Something made him stop. "Warfare. Disregard my last," he said, sitting back, his eyes locked on the command plot, his mind churning while he struggled to work out what came next.

One thing was becoming clear: If he followed his instincts and turned the dreadnoughts back to support Assault Group, there was a real chance he would lose most of his ships. Firing main engines to fall back to Assault Group would put the dreadnoughts beam on to the Hammers. They would not be able to fire their rail guns, and the Hammers could fire theirs right into the dreadnoughts' thin flank armor. And the most vulnerable part of his ships—their sterns—would be pointing right at SuppFac27's defenses; a well-timed missile salvo would tear the asses of his ships out. At best, they would be gutted; at worst, they would all be blown to hell. True, Assault Group would lose fewer ships, but the ones that survived would be trapped in a running battle, pinned by the incoming Hammers, unable to break away to press home their attack on SuppFac27. Chances were, the attack would stall and the Feds would not have enough assets left to press home the final assault.

Worse, the Hammers would have gained what they most needed: the time they required for more reinforcements to arrive. Michael did not know how many more Hammer ships were on their way, but they would be coming, and they would have the dreadnoughts firmly in their sights.

In the end, it came down to a simple choice. Turn back the dreadnoughts and SuppFac27 would survive, churning out antimatter for the Hammers' missiles; Opera would have failed. Press on, and there was still a chance. It was a no-brainer, the sort of tactical problem set to trip up dim-witted cadets too idle to read an operations order properly.

Any way he analyzed it, Assault Group's mission had just changed. Any chance they had of getting through to SuppFac27 unchallenged had gone. Perkins needed to forget about destroying the antimatter plant. He should pin the incoming Hammers in place, run interference for the dreadnoughts while they ran in to finish the job, and keep Hammer missiles and rail guns away from his ships.

It was the only way. But . . .

Deep down inside, something told him that Perkins and his staff might not see things the same way, so he needed to be sure. He commed Rao and Machar into conference with his AIs. Working frantically, he ran the tactical options past them. It was the work of only a minute before they reported back.

"Command, I speak for all of us," Kubby said, the operations AI's avatar grim-faced.

Michael glanced at the other AIs; the avatars nodded their agreement. "Kelli? Nathan?"

"Us, too," his two captains said.

"Fine. Go ahead."

"We've considered all the options. Realistically, there are just two. Either the dreadnoughts push on or they turn back to assist Assault Group."

"You're sure of that? I need to know I haven't missed something here."

"Those are your options," Kubby replied, its tone emphatic. "We recommend that the dreadnoughts press on. Assault Group should be retasked to deal with the latest Hammer incursion. Let me show you why."

Michael watched the AI run a quick and dirty simulation of what would happen if he turned back. It was as he feared: Opera could not succeed if the Fed attack ended up bogged down in an endless battle of attrition with a never-ending flow of Hammer reinforcements. With everything to lose, the Hammers would not hold back. They would keep throwing ships into the fight until every last Fed warship exploded into a ball of gas. Somebody had to press home the attack, and he was that someone.

"Okay," he said. "I agree. We don't have a choice. We need to push on. Warfare concurs?"

"Warfare concurs. Push on."

"Retrieve?"

"Concurs."

"Recognizance?"

"Concurs."

"Roger. Let me talk to the admiral's staff to get their approval," Michael said, praying harder than he had ever prayed that he was going to get it. "And if I don't get the admiral's approval, we're going anyway, and that's an order."

"Aye, aye, sir," his dreadnought captains replied.

"Good." Taking a deep breath—the step he was about to take had kicked his heart into overdrive—Michael commed Perkins's staff.

"Flag, *Reckless,*" he said.

"Flag." The avatar of some staff drone—a three-ring commander—replied.

"Hammer-6 will be in a position to engage Assault Group in less than ten minutes. I intend to push on to destroy the plant. *Reckless,* over."

"Stand by, *Reckless.*"

The wait was a long one; the staff officer's avatar reappeared finally.

"*Reckless.* From Flag, not approved, repeat, not approved. Dreadnought Group is to adjust vector to take station on

Assault Group. When the Hammer attack has been contained, Assault Group will res—"

"No, sir!" Michael barked. "That will not work. This Hammer attack is a distraction. If the dreadnoughts turn back to support you, we'll lose too many ships and too much time to complete the operation. We have the initiative, but we'll lose—"

"You're not listening to me, Captain!" the officer barked. "Without the support of your ships, Assault Group cannot contain these Hammer ships, so adjust vector as ordered. That's an order."

"No, Commander, you're the one not listening," Michael replied. "If we pull back, the Hammer ships inbound for SuppFac27 will get there intact. More reinforcements are sure to be on their way. Once those warships are under the protection of the battle stations and platforms, we will not have the assets to break through if we stop to help Assault Group. We'll lose too many ships. And if the dreadnoughts don't get through, that means all of this effort, all of the ships and spacers we've lost, will have been wasted. I'm sorry, I know it will be rough for Assault Group, but that's just the way it has to be. Assault Group's mission has changed. It has to change, sir. You have to run interference for us. Look at the sims; you'll see what I mean."

"Don't tell me my job, Captain," the staff commander said, his voice pure ice.

"I'm not, sir," Michael said, "but we have run the sims, and it's clear that pulling the dreadnoughts back to cover Assault Group endangers the entire operation. More to the point, it is inconsistent with Opera's prime directive."

The staff officer's eyes bulged in disbelief. He glared at Michael, visibly angry. "You leave me no choice, Captain."

"I am obliged to comply with Opera's prime directive, Commander," Michael snapped. "Sorry, sir. I will not adjust vector. Request you provide cover for my assault on SuppFac27."

"Stand by."

The staff officer's avatar disappeared, the grim face of Rear Admiral Perkins taking its place. "Listen to me,

Helfort," Perkins said, his voice shaking. "I don't care what you think. Your ships are under my command, and you'll do as you are damn well ordered."

Michael shook his head. "Sorry, sir. Under normal circumstances, of course I would. But these are not normal circumstances. If I follow your orders, Opera is lost."

"That's a matter of interpretation, Helfort, and I should not have to point out that it is my interpretation that counts, not yours." Perkins's face reddened with rage, the effort he was making to stay in control all too obvious. "Listen to me, Lieutenant, and listen well. This is a direct order. Dreadnought Group will adjust vector to take station on Assault Group. Do you understand my order?"

"I do, sir."

"Obey it!"

"No, sir," Michael said. "I can't do that. If I obey, Opera is finished. The dreadnoughts will push on. The mission's prime directive takes precedence over your orders. I'm sorry, but that's a fact . . . sir."

While Michael spoke, Perkins's face twisted with ugly rage. "Listen here, Helfort," he barked, his voice thick with fury. "Goddamn it! A direct order is a direct order. Take station on Assault Group. Now!"

"No, sir," Michael said with another shake of the head. "Sorry, I will not comply with your order, and neither will my captains. *Reckless,* out."

Michael cut the link and Perkins's avatar, mouth open, face crimson, and eyes closed to narrow slits in impotent rage, faded away. For a moment, Michael wondered just what he had done. Ignoring a direct order from an admiral in battle was bad enough. Ignoring an order with the future of the Federated Worlds at stake was a hundred times worse. Heart racing nearly uncontrollably, he forced himself back to reality.

"Command, Warfare. To all Dreadnought Group ships, immediate execute emergency speed 300, acknowledge."

"Warfare, stand by . . . all ships acknowledged, emergency speed 300."

Michael commed Rao and Machar. "You guys copy that?"

"We did, sir," Rao said.

"You with me?"

"Yes, sir, we are. The admiral has given us the same order, and we have both declined to obey it."

Michael swallowed hard. Trashing his own career was one thing; consigning officers as promising as Rao and Machar to the scrap heap was quite another. "You know what you're risking?"

"Not as much as you are," Machar said, "so don't sweat it, sir. We're in."

"Roger. Thanks. *Reckless,* out."

The die was cast; there was no going back. Michael could do nothing more. He breathed in and out slowly to try to get an unruly body back under control while *Reckless's* main engines came up to emergency power, tons of driver mass accelerated at 40,000 g pouring from her main engines in two massive blue-white plumes of plasma. Around her, the dreadnoughts followed suit, thirty ships now driving in hard toward SuppFac27.

To Michael's surprise, all of a sudden the stress, the fear, and the tension that had hung over him from the start of the operation started to slip away. With absolute clarity, Michael knew this to be the defining moment of his Fleet career. A strange calm filled his body, sharpening his senses, the terrible risks he faced visible in all their frightening detail. With a huge effort, he cleared his mind of everything but the mission, his ships, and the target. What mattered was making sure that the bet paid off.

Everything else was irrelevant.

Michael watched the command plot as the final acts of Operation Opera began to unfold. He was not going to worry about Perkins and his ships. What concerned him was the two Hammer task groups falling back to SuppFac27 after wasting their time dealing with the decoy attacks. If left unchallenged, they were strong enough to deflect his final assault on SuppFac27. Chucking yet another of the Fighting Instructions' precious rules out the window, he decided to split his forces,

"*Retrieve, Recognizance,* this is *Reckless.*"

The faces of Rao and Machar popped into his neuronics; the pressure of events was clear to see. "Sir?" they said in unison.

"Kelli. I'm detaching Second and Third squadrons under your command. Adjust vector to intercept the Hammer task groups inbound for SuppFac27. I know it's a big task, but I need you to keep them off my back while the First pushes on to deal with the antimatter plant. You must hold them up long enough for me to get through, even if it costs you every last one of your ships. Is that understood?"

"Yes, sir," Rao said.

"Good. Destroy the Hammers if you can, then take to the landers and get the hell out of here. You don't have enough time to turn your ships before they enter the southern minefield, so don't try. Okay?"

Rao said nothing for a moment. Then she nodded. "Yes, sir. I see what you want. Leave it with me; we'll do our best."

"I know you will," Michael said. "Nathan. Clear?"

"Crystal, sir. Good luck."

"We'll need it. Before you detach, I'll take two more missile salvos from your ships . . . stand by . . . right, you have targeting data."

"Roger that, sir. Launching missiles, second salvo to follow."

"See you on the other side. Remember Comdur. *Reckless,* out."

Reckless shuddered when hydraulic rammers off-loaded another missile salvo; Michael ignored the noise and scanned the command and threat plots. With the rest of the dreadnoughts under Rao's command dealing with the last of the Hammer ships, the tactical situation came down to the one defensive problem—the battle stations and defense platforms arrayed around SuppFac27—standing between him and his only objective, the destruction of the antimatter plant.

Michael briefed Warfare. His fingers tapped impatiently; he waited for the AI to translate his wishes into specific plans. One minute later, Warfare produced what he wanted:

a detailed plan to take and destroy SuppFac27's defenses, a plan that had a reasonable chance of success. And he had to succeed; if he did not, he knew that Perkins would have every right to have him shot, and he did not intend to give him the satisfaction. He would make the damn plan work.

"Command, approved," Michael said, sitting back. He had played his part; execution of the plan now rested in the hands of Warfare.

Reckless shook when massive hydraulic dispensers rammed a second full missile salvo into space, the rest of the dreadnoughts of the First following suit. The missiles opened out slowly. Two minutes later, another salvo followed, and two minutes later another, and another and another until none were left. The die was cast; *Reckless*'s missile magazines and those of the rest of the First were empty. Well, not quite. Michael kept twenty missiles back, half with fusion, half with conventional chemex warheads—they had a job, but only if and when his ships punched their way through SuppFac27's defenses.

"Now," Michael whispered an instant before Warfare gave the order that committed the missiles to the attack, tens of thousands of Merlin antistarship missiles rammed toward the Hammers defending SuppFac27 on pillars of fire.

"Command, Warfare. Missiles committed. Time to target seventy seconds."

"Roger. Update."

"*Retrieve* reports dreadnoughts have engaged. Hammer ships interdicted by preemptive rail-gun and missile attack."

"Command, roger. Nice work, guys, nice work." Michael focused his attention back on the First's salvo. He watched it smash home, the combination of missiles and rail-gun slugs overwhelming SuppFac27's defenses, space flaring white as proximity-fused fusion warheads detonated. The Hammer battle stations and platforms disappeared from view behind clouds of flaming armor.

While he waited for the battle damage assessments, Michael checked the dreadnoughts of the Second and Third squadrons, which were closing on the Hammer ships. Rao had to stop the Hammers; if she did not, Michael knew he would be attacking SuppFac27's defenses while the Hammers fired missiles up the sterns of his ships, precisely where dreadnoughts were most vulnerable.

It seemed a long wait, though it probably was not. Taking aggression to new heights, Rao and Machar threw their ships directly at the Hammers; soaking up everything thrown at them, they closed until the Hammers had nowhere left to run. The massive ships, shrouded in clouds of ionized armor blown off by the Hammers' frantic attempts to keep them out, were unstoppable. Smashing into the enemy, the dreadnoughts blew themselves apart, taking the Hammer cruisers with them, the rest of the Hammer ships falling to waves of missiles and rail-gun slugs, sheer brute force battering them into bloody wrecks tumbling away into space.

Michael frowned. Rao and Machar had done well. It was a great victory, but it had come at a terrible cost: Twenty dreadnoughts was an awful price to pay but one worth paying to give Michael's ships the clear run in he needed so badly.

"Command, Warfare. Message from *Retrieve:* Mission accomplished. Hammer task groups combat-ineffective. Own losses heavy: sixteen ships destroyed, four ships seriously damaged and combat-ineffective. Casualties: six wounded, two serious, in regen tanks. *Retrieve* and *Recognizance* abandoning ship. Kill those Hammer bastards. Remember Comdur. *Retrieve,* out."

"Command, roger. Reply: To *Retrieve* and *Recognizance,* thanks, job well done. Good luck. Get home safely. *Reckless* out."

"Warfare, roger. Message sent . . . stand by . . . missile launch from SuppFac27 ground defenses."

"Command, roger." Michael was unconcerned. SuppFac27's missile and laser batteries were well camouflaged and hard to eliminate, space battle stations were tough, and defensive platforms were expendable, but that was about all SuppFac27 had going for it. It had an Achilles' heel: None of its defenses could maneuver, which made them the sort of target every rail gunner dreamed about, and his rail guns bettered any in humanspace. His dreadnoughts would make short work of SuppFac27's defenses; millions of rail-gun slugs had already pulverized the surface of the asteroid and everything on it into a finely milled cloud of dust, the destruction systematic and unrelenting. Now his ships had to survive the Hammer missile attack pushing through his outer defensive screen of medium-range missiles at over 1,000 kilometers per second.

"Command, Warfare. Update. Assault Group reports task group Hammer-6 combat-ineffective"—well done, Rear Admiral Perkins, Michael thought acidly; you are good for something, after all—"surviving Hammer units scattering to the north, assessed no threat."

"Command, roger. And Assault Group?"

"Combat-ineffective. Heavy losses, including *Seiche*"—this was turning out to be a bad day for flag officers, Michael said to himself, trying to ignore an image of Perkins being bundled ignominiously into a lifepod, a glorious moment of unalloyed schadenfreude—"Flag has passed to *Sephardic;* Commodore Jun has operational command. Assault Group conducting lifepod recovery. Flag advises that Assault Group will withdraw on completion."

"Roger that. Request Flag to recover landers with survivors from *Retrieve* and *Recognizance*."

"Roger . . . Flag confirms landers will be recovered. Stand by, message from Flag . . . Message reads: Personal from Commodore Jun for captain in command, FWSS *Reckless*. Your actions in keeping with highest traditions of Fleet. Well done. Regret in no position to assist you. All ships combat-ineffective. Good luck. Remember Comdur. Jun out."

Michael sat for a moment, stunned. He had more friends in high places than he knew. "Send to Flag: Thanks, *Reckless* out."

Much as he appreciated Jun's vote of confidence, her confirmation that he could expect no support from Assault Group was a blow, not unexpected but disappointing nonetheless. Of all the ships committed to Opera, only his could finish what Opera had set out to achieve: the destruction of SuppFac27.

It was a lonely feeling, not least because success or failure rested on a single pair of shoulders: his.

"All stations, Warfare, brace for missile impact."

Reckless reverberated with the familiar racket of close-in defensive weapons systems fighting to keep a Hammer attack at bay, the noise underscored by a crunching thud when *Reckless* fired her rail guns, the job of reducing SuppFac27's defenses not forgotten. After the terrifying brutality of the earlier Hammer engagements, the attack launched by SuppFac27's defenses was an anticlimax: There were simply too few missiles attacking too many ships. Without the mindless violence of a rail-gun attack to break open their defenses, the dreadnoughts could focus every weapon they had on the incoming missiles while they clawed their way across tens of thousands of kilometers of space. The noise died away finally, the last Hammer missile blown apart hundreds of kilometers short of its target.

Turning his attention back to the battle damage assessment, Michael took stock. His last salvo had inflicted enormous damage but not enough to finish the job. The defensive platforms might have been scoured out of space, but the Hammer battle stations still stood; they were a much tougher proposition altogether. Though badly damaged, they had survived to launch another missile salvo, their antistarship lasers still working hard to strip the frontal armor off the inbound dreadnoughts. Enough, Michael decided, enough. What came next broke his heart, but it had to be done. He did not have the time—or the missiles—to do this the hard way.

"Warfare, command. Commit the dreadnoughts. Send them in."

"Warfare, roger."

The unmanned dreadnoughts responded. Pushing their main engines to emergency power, the ships accelerated away from *Reckless* on vectors direct for the Hammer battle stations, their defensive weapons scouring the Hammer's last missile salvo out of existence with contemptuous ease. Outnumbered, the battle stations never stood a chance. Shrugging off everything an increasingly desperate Hammer defense threw at them, the ships smashed headlong into the armored spheres, ripping them open before joining them in incandescent balls of plasma when their main propulsion fusion plants exploded.

Michael emptied his lungs in a long slow hiss of relief. The approaches to SuppFac27 lay wide open.

Reckless, the last ship of Battle Fleet Lima still engaged in Operation Opera, turned end for end and started to decelerate, its main engines firing across space toward the tiny asteroid that was home to SuppFac27, blazing pillars of driver mass reaching down to a surface scrubbed clean by the dreadnoughts' relentless rail-gun salvos.

There was one more thing to do before Michael turned his attention back to the thorny problem of destroying Supp-Fac27. "Warfare, command."

"Warfare."

"Launch *Cleft Stick* under your control. Looks to me like there'll be lifepods left in Hammer space by the main force. I want them picked up. When that's done, set the *Stick* on vector east away from SuppFac27 across the reef. We'll rendezvous with her when we leave this goddamn place. Any problems with that?"

"Stand by . . . no, none, sir. The only lifepods not recovered are drifting east away from the main force; they are well clear of any Hammer forces. *Stick* has the driver mass to pick all of them up. The Hammers are not showing any interest. They have their own problems."

"Good. Make it so."

"Warfare, roger."

Michael turned his attention back to the business at hand. "*Caesar's Ghost,* command."

Sedova's face popped into his neuronics. "*Ghost.*"

"As I'm sure you've worked out, it's up to us to finish the job, so stand by to launch. I've commed you the ops plan."

"*Ghost,* roger. Standing by."

"Command, roger. Assault Leader?"

Kallewi's avatar replaced Sedova's. "Sir?" he said.

"Well, seems like you're going to get your chance, after all. Demolition team ready to go?"

"They are, sir. Didn't think it would come to this."

"I hoped it wouldn't," Michael said, "I really did, but it has. So good luck. I'm telling you something you already know, but for chrissakes, make it fast. There are more Hammers on the way for sure, and I want to be gone before they turn up. So if you get stalled, set the charges and get the hell out."

"Roger that, sir. I hate this damn place already," Kallewi said. "Remember Comdur. Assault Leader out."

"Command, Warfare. Reconbots launched and nominal, now on vector for SuppFac27."

"Roger."

Michael turned his attention back to the command holovid, which had been switched to take its video feed from the reconbots running toward SuppFac27. The asteroid was a dismal sight, its surface ripped and scarred by rail-gun slugs fired to wipe out the radar installations, missile and laser batteries, and other surface infrastructure that protected the plant. All that remained were a few lucky buildings, spared by random perturbations in the rail-gun swarms, lonely islands of ceramcrete in a sea of shattered wreckage hurled across the asteroid's surface, the nearspace overhead filled with yet more junk thrown out into space by the appalling force of repeated rail-gun attacks, the asteroid's microgravity too weak to claw the debris back to ground.

Michael was not interested in gloating over the damage his rail guns had done. What he needed to confirm—and quickly—was the location of the main access down into SuppFac27. The schematics stolen from the Hammers showed a gaping tunnel cut down into the asteroid to allow the installation of heavy plant and equipment, and he needed to find it. The stolen schematics had identified the access as a pair of heavily armored doors framed by a massive plascrete portal, but where the hell was it?

Carmellini spotted it first, smacking a target icon on the main access a full five seconds before the optronics AI decided that yes, it really had found what it was looking for. Warfare wasted no time; the initial group of missiles fired their first stages, accelerating toward the portal. Molded into a single weapon, the missiles hit home, the plascrete framing the armored doors no match for chemex warheads blasting thin pillars of plasma deep into the asteroid, blowing enough rock away to leave a gaping crater that completely undermined one side of the portal.

Warfare sent the next missile on its way. Michael and the rest of the combat information center crew watched engrossed as it headed for the center of the crater, a gaping void bleeding thin skeins of vaporized rock back into space. With just meters left to run, the fusion warhead exploded. The flash of the blast boiled meters and meters of rock, plascrete, and armor off the portal, vaporizing hundreds of tons of mass into a massive ball of white-hot gas erupting back out into space. When it cleared, the blast had left the portal completely undermined on one side by a hellish inferno of red-hot molten rock spewing gouts of flaming gas into the vacuum.

"Aaaah," Michael hissed softly, teeth bared in a rictus of savage joy when the holocam confirmed that the armored doors had been forced wide open by the blowback of exploding gas. The access tunnel into SuppFac27 lay open.

The remaining missiles followed in a line heading right for the tunnel entrance. Michael's plan was simplicity itself. Destroying the antimatter plant by using missiles was impossible—it was buried too deep—but dropping missiles one after another as far down the main access tunnel as they would go before firing their fusion warheads would give SuppFac27's defenders one hell of a shake, to the point, he hoped, where most would decide that self-preservation was the order of the day and flee for safety, leaving Kallewi and his marines a clear run in.

An instant before the first missile disappeared into the portal's gaping blackness, Michael could not help himself. "Fire in the hole," he shouted, and its warhead exploded, a seething cloud of rock and gas veined white-red by twisting jets of flame erupting outward.

One by one, the remaining missiles followed. By the time the last missile exploded, the access tunnel had been transformed into a hellish white-hot crater hundreds of meters across, belching vaporized rock out into space. "Oh, yeah," Michael whispered, reveling in the sheer brute force of the attack. The poor bastards inside SuppFac27 would be suffering as tremor after tremor after tremor shook the rock tunnels close to the point of collapse in an unending earthquake. If that did not induce an overwhelming desire to flee in the minds of SuppFac27's defenders, nothing ever would. He knew he would not be hanging around for tea and biscuits.

"Command, Warfare. *Reckless* in station. Clear to launch *Caesar's Ghost* when ready."

Michael checked quickly. *Reckless* was in station, her enormous bulk hanging motionless less than half a kilometer above the blasted surface of the asteroid. "Command, roger." He flicked the command holovid to take the holocam feed from the reconsats.

Warfare had retasked them to keep tabs on one of Supp-Fac27's personnel access stations. Michael liked the look of what he saw. The station's squat shape—one of the few buildings to survive the dreadnoughts' devastating rail-gun attacks—spewed an ice-loaded cloud. That meant only one thing: The shock waves from the missile attack on the main access portal had destroyed SuppFac27's airtight integrity; the plant was venting humid air into space. Then a panicked flood of figures dressed in Day-Glo orange emergency space suits started to pour out of the building, bounding away in giant leaps; soon hundreds of orange blobs bounced across the asteroid's surface like a collection of demented rubber balls. Where the hell were they all going? It was such a bizarre sight that Michael could not stop himself from laughing any more than the rest of the combat information center's crew could.

"Enough, people," he said, wishing he could wipe the tears from his eyes. "*Ghost*? We have confirmation that the personnel access station's air lock is open. You ready?"

"*Caesar's Ghost* is ready to go."

"Roger, launch. Good luck."

"Thanks. Launching," Sedova replied laconically.

"Sensors."

Carmellini swung around. "Sir?"

"We're not out of the woods yet. If more Hammers come calling—and they sure as hell will—we're going to need all the notice you can give us if we're to have any chance of getting clear."

"Roger that, sir."

Caesar's Ghost cleared *Reckless* and made a long swinging turn down to the asteroid's surface before Sedova pulled the nose up sharply. She fired the belly thrusters, their efflux picking up orange blobs and tumbling them away in long, looping arcs, arms and legs flailing in desperate attempts to get back dirtside. Sedova made it look easy, the lander's massive bulk coming to a dead stop scarcely a meter above the asteroid, right alongside the personnel access station. The instant it came to a halt, the rear cargo access door dropped, and Kallewi's marines spilled out, the bulky black shapes of the three nuclear demolition charges strapped to their powered sleds close behind, a small swarm of gas-powered tacbots leading the way, the little spheres working overtime to zap the surveillance holocams that infested the place.

After a quick check of the threat plot to make sure the Hammers were not creeping up on him unannounced, Michael switched the command holovid over to Kallewi's helmet-mounted holocam. The marines were already through the outer air lock, an unwilling Hammer tethered to the largest marine in Kallewi's squad, a man even bigger than Sergeant Tchiang if that was possible. Michael grinned; the poor bastard obviously had been coerced into the role of guide. The marines paused long enough to set and fire small charges to wreck the air lock's outer doors before moving inside. The inner doors already hung open, immobilized. Inside was a large lobby, its security post empty. Ignoring the dwindling stream of survival-suited Hammers fleeing the facility, the marines flew down the central passageway; Michael was thankful to see that the facility's artificial gravity had failed and looked like it would stay that way. Kallewi's marines trained to operate in zero gravity; he doubted SuppFac27's defenders did. According to intelligence reports, only second-tier planetary defense troops protected the antimatter plant. Michael pitied them; Kallewi's marines would tear the defenders apart, something whoever had planned SuppFac27's defense clearly had never anticipated. Using planetary defense troops was a baffling decision given the plant's importance. Maybe not so baffling, Michael decided after a moment's thought; hubris and policy were the reasons. The Hammers had put altogether too much faith in the ability of their spaceborne defenses to hold off any Fed attack, and as a matter of long-standing policy, Hammer marines were never used to protect fixed installations.

Just before the next air lock—open like all the rest so far—the marines stopped before what had to be another lobby. Something was up. Kallewi waved a section forward, led by the unmistakable bulk of Sergeant Tchiang, with the marines taking up position around the frame of the lobby access air lock. Another pause. When Michael patched his neuronics into the vid feed from the leading tacbots, the problem became obvious. A plasglass-fronted security post dominated the lobby, and floating around in front of it, standard Hammer-issue assault rifles Velcroed to their chests, were ten, maybe twelve planetary defense troops, part of SuppFac27's internal security force. There were still some Hammers doing what they were paid to do; these did not look as demoralized and panic-stricken as he'd hoped.

For Kallewi and his marines, navigating their way through the maze of passageways and drop tubes that made up Supp-Fac27 with an old high-level schematic stolen from the hardrock tunneling contractor and a reluctant Hammer to show them where to go was bad enough. Doing all that while fighting their way past Hammer troopers, and pretty pissed ones at that—even if they were only planetary defense force troopers—was a complication he wanted to avoid.

Kallewi was not letting any of that worry him. The marines around the air lock erupted into action. Fragmentation grenades hurled into the Hammers exploded soundlessly in the vacuum, spalling shards of rock off the tunnel walls, and the marines fell on what was left of the defenders.

The firefight was short, vicious, and one-sided, the Hammers flailing around while they struggled to bring their guns to bear. Kallewi waved his marines on, two staying back to bag the few Hammers still living, plasfiber cocoons snapping taut with enough air to keep the occupants alive for two hours. Michael had insisted that anyone with a chance of survival be bagged, pointing out that there was a good chance the marines would be cornered somewhere deep inside SuppFac27 and that he did not want them shot out of hand for leaving wounded Hammers to die a painful death from asphyxiation. In the end, a reluctant Kallewi had agreed, but not before Michael had forced him to admit he had not volunteered for a suicide mission.

Satisfied that Kallewi had things under control, Michael turned back to check the command and threat plots. He was relieved to see nothing had changed. To the west, the tattered remnants of the Fed forces that had run interference for the dreadnoughts had cleared Hammer space, the ships of Assault Group under Commodore Jun's command the last to leave. They had done a good job recovering survivors; Michael was pleased to see that only a few wayward lifepods from the two northern task groups had slipped through the net. Beyond the Feds' reach and ignored by the Hammers, they drifted out of control into the confused maze of gravity rips to the east of SuppFac27, chased by *Cleft Stick*. It was lucky for them, he had persuaded Jaruzelska to let him keep his light lander, Michael thought. Without it, he had no way of getting them back; he had no doubt that the Hammers would have left them to die.

Michael turned back to check Kallewi's progress. He was doing well, the marines racing into the heart of SuppFac27, the Hammer opposition weak and fragmented, brushed aside by the single-minded ferocity of Kallewi's attack.

The marines stopped before another air lock door. Machinelike in their precision, they overwhelmed its security post and planetary defense troops in a matter of seconds. Leaving the medics to deal with the wounded and a handful of marines to cover their withdrawal, they were quickly on the move again.

"Command, Assault Leader. Update," Kallewi said. "One hundred meters ahead, there's a passageway to the left. According to our guide, twenty meters farther on is a drop tube that accesses SuppFac27's power distribution center, and beyond that are the primary fusion power plants. According to the schematics, the rock wall is about five meters thick. Our guide says the access doors are too heavily armored for us to shoot our way in, and I'm inclined to believe him. We've run some quick and dirty sims, and we have a 100 percent chance of breaching the plants' containment if we can get the demolition charges down there. So my plan is to do just that and get the hell out."

"Command, roger. Concur. Any sign of organized defense yet?"

"Sadly, yes. The Hammers have worked out what we're up to, but they're struggling to get their people in the right places. I suspect their c-cubed is shot to shit, they don't have any holovid coverage of our attack, and there are a lot of panicky technicians getting in their way. I've stationed marines to cover our exit route; they'll make sure we aren't ambushed when we pull back, but it's going to be tight. Estimate egress inside thirty minutes. Timers on the demolition charges will be set for forty."

"Command override on the charges?"

"Will be suppressed. There's no going back on this. Once they're triggered, they're going to blow, and we'll leave proximity-fused claymores behind to discourage the Hammers from getting too close."

Michael shivered; claymores fired down rock passages would shred any Hammers unlucky enough to get in the way. "Roger. We'll be waiting here for you."

"Hell, I hope so. There are will be some very pissed Hammers looking for a piece of my ass when this is all over. Kallewi out."

Kallewi's avatar disappeared, and Michael sat back to think things through. He hated leaving the marines with all the heavy lifting. He studied the scorched surface of the asteroid for a moment before comming Sedova. He had an idea. "You copy Kallewi's update?"

Sedova nodded. "Yes, sir. Wish I could do something to help."

"You can. See that heat dump, fine on your port bow at about 500 meters?" Michael positioned a target indicator over the remnants of a ceramcrete tower.

"Yes, sir," Sedova said. She sounded puzzled.

"Okay, this is not in the plan, but we need to take some of the pressure off Kallewi. Get your lander across there. There's bound to be a personnel access, probably a hatch, somewhere close. You have demolition charges in your ready-use lockers?"

"Yes, sir, we have."

"Good. Find the hatch, blow it open, and send your load-master across to lob a couple of charges in. I'm hoping we can persuade the Hammers that we're sending in another assault party."

"Roger that, sir."

"One proviso. Any time things start to go wrong, get the hell back here. I don't want to leave Kallewi without a lift home," Michael said. He suppressed a flicker of anxiety. Maybe dispatching *Cleft Stick* to pick up wandering life-pods had not been the smartest move he had ever made. Having a backup lander might have been the prudent thing.

"On it," Sedova said, a quick blip on the maneuvering thrusters lifting *Caesar's Ghost* off the asteroid before another burst sent the lander in a shallow arc across to the heat dump.

Something made Michael look across at Carmellini, a sudden cold shiver slithering its way up his spine. The spacer was hunched over his holovid, and his body language spoke volumes: Something was up. Michael forced himself to sit tight. Carmellini would tell him what was going on when he was ready.

"Command, Warfare, sensors," Carmellini said, his voice tense. "Positive gravitronics intercept. Estimated drop bearing Red 10 Up 5. Multiple vessels. Gravity wave pattern suggests pinchspace transition imminent. Designated hostile task group Hammer-7."

"Damn, damn, damn," Michael cursed. Another half hour

and they would have been on their way out of this godforsaken place. Not that the Hammers were so incompetent as to leave him alone for that long. Two lots of reinforcements had dropped in-system already; there would be more, and they would not be long coming.

"Command, roger. Get me a range when you can," Michael said, fingers tapping an impatient tattoo on the arms of his seat.

"Sensors, roger . . . stand by . . . Hammer-7's estimated drop datum Red 10 Up 5, range 70,000 kilometers."

"Roger."

"Command, *Ghost*," Sedova said. "You were right. There is a personnel access lock. My cannons have blown the hatch off, and Trivedi's on her way over there. I should be on my way back in five."

"Fine. I'll maintain station. You copied the drop report?"

"Did, sir."

"Well, don't hang around. I'm sure the Hammers will not be ignoring us for long. Command, out."

"Command, Warfare. Task group Hammer-7 dropping, Red 10 Up 5, range 72,000 kilometers."

"Command, roger."

Michael watched the threat plot intently while *Reckless*'s sensors analyzed the new arrivals. Things looked bad. The Hammer task group was the usual mixture of cruisers and escorts; there were a lot of them. An icy calm settled over him. The latest Hammer reinforcements were more than strong enough to reduce *Reckless*'s chances of getting away to zero. And they had dropped less than thirty minutes from him, close enough to turn *Reckless* into a ball of ionized gas five times over. He commed his AIs into conference.

"Okay, team. Shit hits fan time. Options?"

Warfare took the lead. "Three. Stay, run, or send *Reckless* out to meet them while *Caesar's Ghost* remains to recover demolition party."

"Operations?"

"Agree with the options," the operations AI said. "However, recommend *Reckless*'s crew transfer to *Ghost*. That renders *Reckless* expendable. In any event, we assess her chances of survival to be nil under any scenario."

Michael marveled at the AI's calmness in the face of its own death. "Warfare. Your recommendation?"

"All AIs concur. Off-load crew to *Caesar's Ghost,* send *Reckless* out to engage ships of Hammer-7," the AI replied. "That gives you the best chance of recovering the marines and clearing Hammer space to the east."

Michael had to agree. "Option three it is. Ops, get *Caesar's Ghost* back here. Brief Sedova while she's doing that. Warfare, give me a plan for *Reckless.* Sensors, let me know the instant the Hammers start launching missiles. And I want all your detailed records of the operation downloaded to *Caesar's Ghost.* Raw datalogs as well. If in doubt, download it. I'd rather have more than less."

"Sensors, roger."

"XO to the CIC, at the rush." With a twinge of guilt, Michael remembered he had completely forgotten Kallewi. He commed him. "Assault Leader, command. Update."

"We found the power distribution center," Kallewi said. "Charges have been placed, timers set, claymores are in, and we're on our way back. That's the good news. The bad is that a group of Hammers in the last lobby before the air lock has pushed my guys back and we're pinned down. The tacbots tell us more are coming up behind us. We can hold them off, but not forever. Oh, thanks for the diversion. We would not have made it this far otherwise. Anyway, we can't go back, we can't go forward, so I think the best thing would be for you—"

"Enough of that," Michael snapped. "I'm not leaving you. Hold the Hammers until I get back to you. Command, out." He turned to Ferreira. "Time we all left, but I have one more job for you. Take Carmellini and Lomidze with you. I want six sets of ship assault gear in the lander, plus four demolition charges."

"Six se—"

"Just do it, Jayla. I'll explain later. Get everyone down to the hangar. Go!"

"Sir." Ferreira and the rest of *Reckless*'s crew turned and ran for the lander.

"Command, Warfare. Plan's done."

"Right." Michael forced everything aside apart from how best to make use of the last card left in his hand, *Reckless* itself. He nodded his appreciation. Warfare's plan was solid. "It's good. Do it," he said. "You have command authority to execute; just keep me posted."

"Roger," Warfare said matter-of-factly.

With one last look around *Reckless*'s combat information center, Michael left, his sense of loss bitter in its intensity. *Reckless* had served him well; she deserved better. Dropping to the hangar deck, he bolted for *Caesar's Ghost* as fast as his combat space suit would allow, the hatch slamming shut behind him. After what seemed an age, the hangar doors opened. Sedova wasted no time and gunned *Caesar's Ghost* out and away from the doomed ship.

"Okay, pay attention." Michael stood at the front of the cargo bay, his crew ranged in a semicircle around him. "Right, we have precious little time. Lieutenant Kallewi and his marines are pinned down just inside the access here"—he pointed over his shoulder—"by a group of Hammers. I want six volunteers to persuade the Hammers to let my marines go. So who—"

Together, the crew of *Reckless* stepped forward. "Shit," Michael said, "weren't you dumbos taught not to volunteer for anything?" He shook his head. "Okay, Jayla, Bienefelt, Carmellini, Fodor, Lim, Morozov. Draw weapons. Go, go, go!"

Michael stopped for a second to recover. "Kat. Get the ramp down."

"Aye, aye, sir."

"Lomidze, Chief Chua," Michael snapped.

"Sir?"

"I want you to follow the XO's team in case we have casualties to recover. Take crash bags and keep your damn heads down. This is not the time for heroics."

"Sir."

A few frantic, scrambling minutes later, Michael's scratch assault team was ready. "Good luck, Jayla. Remember your close-quarters combat drills."

"You can count on it, sir," Ferreira said. "If I see a Hammer, I'll shoot the bastard. Let's go, team."

Ferreira shot out of the lander, her maneuvering pack driving her hard and fast toward the door of the personnel access facility, the spacers of her scratch assault team strung out behind her in an untidy, wavering line. Chief Chua and Lomidze brought up the rear, crash bags held tight.

Making his way up to the *Ghost*'s flight deck, Michael commed Kallewi.

"Okay. Ferreira and a team of spacers are on their way to help out. Call sign Alfa Bravo. She'll let you know when they're in place. On your mark, they'll attack the blocking force from behind. Disengage, get your guys past, and all run like hell for the *Ghost*. Ferreira will leave demolition charges to slow the Hammers down. Okay?"

"Roger that, sir. Sounds like one hell of a plan," Kallewi said, unable to conceal his relief.

"Yeah, it is. Just make it work," Michael said, dropping into a spare seat and strapping in.

There was nothing more to be done to help the beleaguered marines, so he turned his attention back to the command and threat plots. There were no surprises there. The latest Hammer task group sent to protect SuppFac27 had dropped precisely where Carmellini had said it would; now the ships were turning inward to point their bows directly at *Reckless*. Ranged around the task group hung a cloud of missiles that was growing in size with every new missile salvo dumped into space. Michael drew a long, ragged breath. It would not be long before those missiles were committed to the attack; he prayed *Reckless* kept the Hammers' attention long enough for them to get away. He tried not to think what the Hammers would do to him if he fell into their hands.

Michael commed Warfare. "All set?"

"*Reckless* is under way."

"Good luck," Michael said, realizating that when *Reck-*

less was destroyed—and she would be—he and his crew would be alone, marooned in Hammer space, deep inside an uncharted reef with only a heavy assault lander to get them home. He was no believer in miracles, but he was beginning to think he was going to need a bag of them to pull this one off. Disconsolate, he watched *Reckless* pull away, her only protection a cloud of decoys inside a Krachov shroud, rail guns her only weapons.

Michael watched sickened as *Reckless*'s massive bulk dwindled into the distance, the ship going to emergency power as soon as she was clear of *Caesar's Ghost,* accelerating away on twin pillars of flame. She was a good ship; he would be sorry to lose her and even sorrier to lose Warfare and the rest of the AIs. He had built relationships with all of them. Mother, Warfare, Kubby, and Kal might not be human, but they were characters in their own right, and it was hard not to feel a sense of loss.

He patched his neuronics into one of the tacbots covering the lobby. Kallewi's problem was obvious. A large force of Hammer planetary defense troopers had pushed back the marines Kallewi had positioned to keep his exit route clear; they now controlled the lobby, firing indiscriminately at the marines from behind the cover of the security station. To attempt to cross the lobby was to commit suicide. Kallewi was stalemated. That was the bad news. The good news was that Ferreira's team was in place.

"Assault Leader, Alfa Bravo," Ferreira said. "We're in position. Ready to go on your mark."

"Alfa Bravo, stand by," Kallewi replied. "On three, go, go, go!"

Ferreira's attack took the Hammers by surprise, grenades exploding among their tightly packed ranks with devastating effect, the carnage made worse when her team followed up with sustained bursts of rifle fire, the rounds ripping with brutal ease through troopers blown out of cover. Kallewi did not hang around to watch the slaughter. His marines broke cover in a desperate dash for the safety of the passageway leading back to the asteroid surface. They nearly made it, but a Hammer trooper managed to squeeze off a burst that took one of Kallewi's marines in the leg, spinning her out of control and into the laser-cut rock wall of the lobby a few meters short of the exit.

Ferreira did not hesitate. Emptying her rifle at the Hammer, she lunged forward, her momentum unchecked by a lucky shot that ripped through her left arm. Throwing her gun away, she grabbed the marine with her bad arm and the safety line with her good one, pulling the two of them out of the firefight and into safety, the legs of the marine's suit spewing gas, blood, and lurid green wound foam in equal measures.

"Withdraw," Ferreira shouted, "withdraw! Bienefelt, Carmellini, set those charges. And someone slap a patch on our suits before we run out of gas."

The spacers needed no encouragement. Not all the Hammers had been cut down, and reinforcements were arriving. Recovering their composure, Kallewi's marines began to fight back, pouring rifle fire into the lobby, their bullets smacking into the rock walls. Shielded by a second shower of grenades, the Feds pulled back past the hunched figures of Bienefelt and Carmellini while they packed demolition charges into the frame around the inner air lock door.

"Charges set," Bienefelt said. "Fused twenty seconds."

"Fire them and get the hell out," Ferreira said, her voice tight with pain, pushing the wounded marine at Chief Chua.

Bienefelt and Carmellini wasted no time, clearing the personnel access facility close behind Lomidze and Chua as they struggled to push the marine into the safety of a crash bag and get back to the lander at the same time. When the last spacer had crossed the threshold into the lander's cargo bay, the personnel access facility shivered, a transient cloud of smoke and flame boiling out of the doors before vanishing into space.

Sedova wasted no time closing the cargo bay ramp.

"Hold on," she shouted the instant Trivedi confirmed that everyone had made it back safely. Without any urging from Michael, she rammed the *Ghost*'s engines to full power, driving the lander in a skidding turn to place the asteroid's massive bulk between them and the Hammers before heading into Devastation Reef.

Michael patched his neuronics into the reconsats tracking *Reckless* as he made his way up the *Ghost*'s flight deck, throwing himself into a spare seat. It was a heartbreaking sight; around the doomed ship—the last of Battle Fleet Lima to fight and die that awful day—space sparkled as *Reckless* fought its final battle, salvo after salvo falling on the dreadnought, the searing heat of proximity-fused fusion warheads stripping armor off, rail-gun slugs slamming home to blow huge craters into her armor, her hull wreathed in a ghastly death shroud of ionized armor.

Michael cut the holovid feed. He could not watch anymore, so he turned his attention back to the threat plot, the latest Hammer arrivals an ugly splash of red sprawled across the screen. The big question still sat there, unanswered: Would they come after *Caesar's Ghost*?

Michael took a long, careful look at the plot. Whatever the reason, the Hammers showed not even the slightest interest in *Caesar's Ghost*. The ships of Hammer-7 focused on *Reckless;* every missile and rail-gun slug they fired had just that one target. Not that Michael blamed them: He would be concentrating on a heavy cruiser with a death wish inbound under emergency power; that much suicidal mass could inflict an awful lot of damage. The Hammers did not even bother to lock the *Ghost* up with fire control radar, nor did they send a few missiles its way. Not that worrying what the Hammers might do made any difference; if they came after *Caesar's Ghost,* there was nothing he could do about it. Heavy landers were tough but not tough enough to keep out even a small salvo of Eaglehawk missiles. Their best bet was to run, hoping *Reckless* convinced the Hammers that they had better things to do than chase after a single fleeing assault lander that was doomed to die in the uncharted wastes of Devastation Reef.

Good thing the Hammers did not know about pinchspace jump-capable Block 6 landers; if they did . . .

For Michael, postcombat exhaustion had set in with a

vengeance, the shipsuit under his space suit—as always after combat—an icy, sweat-soaked wreck. All he wanted was
a shower, clean gear, and a long sleep.

"Kat. Update."

"Roger, sir. We're . . . hold on, sir . . . the demolition
charges will blow in ten."

Michael sat up. Shit, he chided himself, how had he forgotten? "Get SuppFac27 up on holovid and let the troops
know."

Utterly focused, Michael stared at the asteroid when it
popped onto the command holovid, the ugly ball of rock a
black shape cut out of star-strewn space. He struggled to
breathe, all too aware that Kallewi's demolition charges had
to work. If they did not, he was as good as dead. Perkins
would destroy him, and maybe he would be right to.

"Stand by . . . now!"

Nothing happened.

Even as Michael began to think that the whole operation
was a bust, the appalling loss of ships and lives, the risks he
had taken, all a complete waste, the asteroid's surface, crystal clear in the holovid feeds coming from the reconsats, he
shivered. Michael was not even sure he had seen anything, it
all happened so fast. There was another tremor, much bigger
this time, shock lifting dust off the asteroid, and the black
surface of the asteroid cracked open, flaming jets of white-
hot plasma lancing out when SuppFac27's fusion plants
blew, the enormous overpressure following every access tunnel back up to the surface, the blast blowing huge chunks of
rock to tumble away into space, pursued by jets of incandescent gas.

"Oh, yeah," Sedova said, her face a snarl of pure hatred.
"Suck that, you Hammer bastards. I don't think there'll be
much more antimatter coming out of that place."

Michael choked up, but *Reckless*'s crew did not, their
cheers and shouts swamping the *Ghost*'s com circuits.

"Right, Kat," Michael said, spirits soaring as the weight
came off his shoulders before reality brought them crashing
back to ground. He was acutely aware how far from home

they all were; he hoped the cheers were not premature. For him, this mission was not over until every last spacer and marine made it home safely. "Update."

"Roger. We're at jump speed, though the navigation AI says there is way too much gravitational instability for us to get into pinchspace safely. There's still no sign of any interest from the Hammers. *Cleft Stick* has recovered lifepods from *Seljuk, Secular, Iron Bridge,* and *Darter.* She is chasing down the last of them, two from *Skeandhu.* When she's recovered those, she'll rendezvous with us."

"How long?"

"Four hours, give or take. We'll have a precise time once she's recovered *Skeandhu*'s survivors."

"Roger. Any sign of Hammers responding?"

"No, sir. Still none, and something tells me there won't be. Hammers being Hammers, they'll be more interested in lining up the poor bastards in charge and shooting them."

"My heart bleeds for the pricks. Is there a list of survivors?"

"No, not yet. The *Stick*'s AI is doing the best it can, but routine administration is not one of its strong points."

Michael chuckled softly. Assault landers were never designed to fly without a human crew; of course they could, but some of the finer points of command tended to fall by the wayside. "Fine. Ask it nicely to let us know if it can find the time. Even better, see if it can patch us through to one of the survivors. Next question: We can't go back, so where the hell do we go?"

"I was afraid you'd ask me that, sir. The bad news is that we have just one option, I'm afraid. I've checked and rechecked. Serhati is the only non-Hammer world we can reach with the driver mass and consumables we have onboard. I've done a navigation plan to get us there."

"Shit," Michael said softly with a shake of his head; Serhati did not appear on any list of friendly systems he had ever seen. "What's the transit time?"

"Not good, sir. It's . . . let me see . . . yes, a thirteen-day transit."

Michael winced; the cramped confines of a heavy lander would make for an uncomfortable trip. "Can we do that?" he said, trying not to look concerned.

"Assuming *Cleft Stick* recovers no more than 200 survivors, yes, we can . . . just," Sedova said. "Assuming 250 souls all up, consumables are the problem: We'll be out of food, our carbon dioxide scrubbers will be on their last legs, and we'll be critically low on oxygen and water. And that's even after we've stripped *Cleft Stick* bare."

"Umm," Michael said after he took a long look at Serhati's profile. "Yes, you're right. It has to be Serhati, so that's where we'll go. And yes, it'll be damn tight. But I think we can do it if we keep the troops in their bunks twenty-two hours a day to reduce oxygen consumption. The big problem is that Serhati is a Hammer client. Not officially, of course; it pretends to be a Kalici Protocol world, but scratch the surface and it's not. According to the intelligence summaries, Serhati is a covert remassing stop for Hammer ships. So I think we're in for an interesting time. Set vector for Serhati and let the troops know that's where we're headed."

"Sir."

Michael ignored a momentary flash of panic: Going to Serhati meant giving the Hammers the best chance they would ever have to get their hands on him. But what choice did he have?

"Anything else of note?" he said.

"No, sir."

"Roger. I'm going below. Keep a close eye on the Hammers. Let me know when the *Stick* has finished rescuing pods and gives us a definite rendezvous time."

"Sir."

His body saturated with fatigue, Michael dropped down the ladder into the cargo bay. He walked across to where Ferreira sat, head back, her injured arm—liberally decorated with orange leak patches and smeared black and green with dried blood and woundfoam—resting on a convenient power box. "Jayla. How's the arm?"

"Bloody sore," she said. "That fucking woundfoam is ten

times worse than getting shot in the first place. Don't care how good it is. Shit, it hurts. My neuronics say the wound's nothing serious, and anyway, I now have the combat wound stripe I've always wanted."

Michael laughed. "We have about four hours before we pick up *Cleft Stick*. You ready for a load of uninvited guests?"

"We are, sir," Ferreira said, a broad grin clearly visible through the plasglass of her helmet's faceplate. "It will be one hell of a squeeze, but we'll manage. A five-star establishment this is, and Bienefelt's agreed to be concierge while I sit around feeling sorry for myself."

"Can't see you sitting around, Jayla. Marine Mehraz, how is she? Good work, by the way, getting her out."

Ferreira's head bobbed in embarrassment. She waved her good arm in protest. "Shit, sir. Somebody had to do it. Marine Mehraz is safely in one of the regen tanks. She's in pretty bad shape; her legs took a lot of rounds, and she's suffering lung damage from explosive decompression of her suit, but the medical AI says she'll be okay until we get to Serhati."

"I hope so. As soon as we're sure the Hammers won't bother us, I'll tell Kat to get the lander repressurized."

"That would be outstanding. I am sick of this crappy space suit, and the medibots want to clean up my arm, though what I really need is a long, hot shower. How good would that be?"

Michael laughed. "Better than good, Jayla. Right, I'll leave you alone. When I'm done here, I'll be back on the flight deck if you need me."

"Sir," Ferreira said, closing her eyes and slumping back, face pale with shock.

Concerned, Michael patched into the medical AI to make sure Ferreira was better than she looked; it assured him she was, so he turned to study the *Ghost*'s cargo bay. He nodded his approval. Chief Bienefelt had wasted no time getting the place organized—loose gear stowed, bunks rigged up, fresh clothing broken out, and hot drinks laid out on a side table. He picked a beaker up and plugged it into the drinks port of his suit, grateful for the coffee's sudden lift, the grinding fatigue easing a touch. He made his way across to where Kallewi and his marines were sprawled out across the deck.

"Hi, sir," Kallewi said, setting his assault rifle aside and getting to his feet.

"No need to ask the Federated Worlds Marine Corps if things are under control."

"Sir!" Kallewi protested. "The green machine never sleeps; you should know that."

"Bloody marines!" Michael snorted. "Full of it."

"Come on, sir. You need us, and you know it."

Michael shook his head in mock despair. "Sad but true. Back to business. Jayla tells me that Marine Mehraz should be okay."

"We think so, sir. The AI says she's stable." Kallewi paused for a second. "You know what, sir?" he continued, voice soft.

"Tell me."

"We were screwed, totally screwed. All our egress routes were blocked. The Hammers had finally gotten their shit together, and there were heavy weapons squads on their way. Another ten minutes and the bastards would have overrun us. We had no chance. So thanks for sending in the cavalry. Wasn't in the plan, you didn't need to, and you probably shouldn't have. But you did. Without them we were dead meat"—Kallewi shook his head—"so tell your exec that she's welcome in any marine mess, anywhere, anytime. She did well."

"She sure did." There was a pause, and Michael reflected on the appalling risks they had all taken that day. "Okay," he said at last, "need anything?"

"This ship repressurized so we can get out of these space suits, then a hot shower, a clean shipsuit, something to eat, and some serious sack time."

"You and everyone else," Michael said, laughing, "and don't worry. You'll be sick of your rack by the time we get to Serhati."

"Sick of my rack? Never happen!"

Michael laughed, not least because he knew what Kallewi had said was true. Making his way back to the flight deck, he was relieved to see that the red icons that had infested the threat plot had been downgraded to a reassuring orange: hostile but no threat. There was no doubting it. Obviously, the Hammers had more on their plate to worry about than a fleeing lander, so he commed Sedova to repressurize the lander.

"Captain, sir, pilot."

"Yeah, go ahead, Kat."

"*Cleft Stick* is on final approach."

"Roger."

Comming Ferreira and Bienefelt to join him, Michael stood patiently at the *Ghost*'s starboard personnel air lock. After an age, a gentle bump ran through the lander, followed by a metallic *thunk* when the docking interlocks slammed home. *Cleft Stick* had berthed. Green lights came on over the air lock door, the *Ghost*'s loadmaster slapped the handle, and the door swung open and up. A short pause followed to allow the outer hatch to open with a tiny swirl of air when the two landers equalized, and there she was, Vice Admiral Jaruzelska in person.

"Attention on deck! Commander, Battle Fleet Lima," Chief Bienefelt bellowed in her best parade ground fashion.

"Thank you, Captain," Jaruzelska said, acknowledging Michael's salute. "Chief Bienefelt, good to know that you're not allowing standards to slip even though we're in the middle of nowhere."

"Thank you, sir," Bienefelt said.

"Lieutenant Ferreira."

"Welcome aboard *Caesar's Ghost,* sir."

"Glad you stayed to give us a lift. What's with the arm?" Jaruzelska said.

"Flesh wound, sir," Ferreira replied, lifting a heavily bandaged arm. "I'll live, which is more than I can say for the Hammer sonofabitch who shot me."

Jaruzelska laughed. She took Michael by the arm and pulled him clear of the procession of survivors that followed her across from *Cleft Stick,* their faces tight with fatigue and delayed shock. Michael had never seen such a sorry bunch, the strain of what they had been through etched deep.

"I know I've already said this, Michael," Jaruzelska said, "but I'll say it again, anyway. I always had faith in dreadnoughts. More to the point, I always had faith in you. You did well. About time we stuck it to those damn Hammers. Something tells me that they are going to miss that antimatter plant of theirs."

"Thank you, sir," Michael said. "They sure will. Hammer scum. But, um . . . there are a few things you need to know. We had a few, er . . . a few issues along the way."

Jaruzelska rolled her eyes. "Why is nothing ever easy with you, Lieutenant Helfort? Okay, when you've gotten rid of that ludicrously named lander of yours and we're on our way, I'll want a full brief. And when I say full," she said sternly, "I mean every last detail."

"Yes, sir."

"Well," Jaruzelska said, "Captain Tuukkanen and I have been through your report in detail, along with the records downloaded from your AIs. Way we see it, this is pretty much open and shut. So, speaking as your commanding officer, my formal response is this."

She paused, weighing her words with obvious care. "Rear Admiral Perkins will take disciplinary action against you. I don't think there's any doubt about that. However, that action will be stayed until the board of inquiry into Operation Opera finishes its work. The board will review your report of proceedings along with those of all the other commanders, along with statements from everyone else who thinks they have something worthwhile to say, not to mention every datalog they can get their hands on. Given that dreadnoughts were involved"—a hint of bitterness crept into her voice—"and, more significantly, given that you disobeyed a direct order from none other than the flag officer in charge of Opera, I think there will be plenty of people wanting to be heard. Until the board reports its findings, it would be premature to speculate any further. Suffice to say, what happens after that will depend upon the board of inquiry's findings of fact, as well as its conclusions and recommendations."

"I imagined that's how it would go," Michael replied, his stomach tightening as he sensed the nightmare that lay ahead.

"So," Jaruzelska said, her voice firm, "that's my formal response. Let me give you the informal one. Put simply, you were 100 percent right and Rear Admiral Perkins was 100 percent wrong. If you'd complied with his order, Operation Opera would have failed. It's that simple, and I intend to say so."

Relief flooded Michael's body: Even after hours of agonizing self-analysis, he still believed he had been right, but it was good to have a combat-proven vice admiral come out and say she saw things the same way. "Thanks for that, sir."

Jaruzelska shook her head. "Don't thank me. That's the only conclusion to draw from the evidence. But"—why is there always a caveat? Michael wondered—"disobeying a direct order in battle is a serious matter." She looked Michael right in the eye. "Let me tell you this, Michael. If you failed, if you'd not destroyed SuppFac27, a court-martial stacked with your best friends would have found you guilty of disobeying the admiral's order. Nobody would have asked whether or not the order was right or wrong. Failure has no friends, none at all."

"I knew that, sir," Michael said. "The moment I ignored Perkins's order, I knew I was laying my life on the line."

"And yet you still did it?"

"Well, to quote you verbatim, Admiral, if I may: 'It will be up to one of you to do whatever it takes to reduce that damned place to a ball of molten slag.' I had not forgotten. So, yes. I still did it. Anything else would have been dereliction of duty."

"It was still one hell of a big call, but one I'm glad you made. So don't worry. I'll be with you every step of the way. It'll be a bloody business, but we'll get you through it. So," Jaruzelska said briskly, "let's have a look at Serhati, a real shithole if ever there was one. Took the old *Dependent* there back in '85; the place was the pits then, and I'd be surprised if it's improved any. We're going to need a damn good plan if we're to stop those scum-sucking Serhati vermin from handing us all over to the Hammers."

"I'll second that, sir," Michael said fervently. "I think the Hammers are going to wet themselves when they find out."

Saturday, March 31, 2401, UD
Serhati nearspace

With a stomach-churning lurch, *Caesar's Ghost* dropped into normal space.

"Nice one, Kat," Michael murmured while he scanned the command plot, happy to see that they were not about to crash into some sucker entering Serhati nearspace at the same time.

"Thanks, sir. Main engines to full power . . . now. Transmitting ID and flight plan to Serhati nearspace control. Ground links will be online in seconds . . . stand by. Okay, sir, links are up."

Sedova had dropped the lander right at the leading edge of the drop zone for nonmilitary traffic, as close to Serhati as she could get it, the *Ghost*'s blunt stern facing planetward, ready for an immediate deceleration burn. Michael had crossed his fingers at that part of Sedova's plan; dropping into a strange system ass first, unannounced, and without the benefit of up-to-date traffic schedules was generally considered a bad idea. The chances of surviving an impact nose first were not great; ass first, they were nil. But survive they had.

Michael turned to Jaruzelska. "Admiral, sir. Go ahead."

"Thanks." Her eyes rolled up under half-closed eyelids while she commed the Federated Worlds ambassador to the Sovereignty of Serhati. Michael left the admiral to spoil the woman's morning cup of tea: When the poor sap had woken up that morning, she could not have known that her day was to be wrecked in quite such spectacular fashion.

The face of the Serhati duty controller appeared on the command holovid, eyes narrowed with concern. "*Caesar's Ghost,* this is Serhati nearspace control."

"Go ahead, Serhati."

"There are irregularities in your ship data. We have no record of any Federated Worlds mership matching your registration, nor have you filed any flight plan. For that we will be lodging a code violation against you. Terminate your deceleration burn immediately and adjust vector to take station on space battle station SSBS-45. Transmitting approved flight plan to you. Any deviation off vector risks use of deadly force. Acknowledge. Serhati nearspace control, over."

Sedova kept her voice noncommittal, matter-of-fact. "*Caesar's Ghost,* negative, negative. We are non-combat-effective Federated Worlds lander registration PHLA-442566, carrying wounded urgently in need of medical attention. We are also critically short of life support supplies, and our driver mass levels are dangerously low. In accordance with the Hague Convention, essential we land to receive immediate assistance. Request you designate landing field as matter of extreme urgency. Federated Worlds embassy has been advised of our arrival."

The Serhati duty controller sat bolt upright and leaned forward; he stared open-mouthed. "Ah, um . . . *Caesar's Ghost,* stand by," he said in a strangled croak. The man had never seen a problem like this before, Michael guessed. Judging from the color of his face, the excitement was a bit too much for him.

Michael glanced across at Jaruzelska, who was still deep in her com to the ambassador. The ambassador's job was to make the Serhatis believe the Feds would wipe Serhati off the face of the map if they laid a finger on the *Ghost* before it landed safely. Michael was confident she would: The Federated Worlds might not be the power it once had been, but it possessed the military grunt to destroy a pissant planet like Serhati without breaking a sweat, and he would bet good money that the Serhatis knew that.

If the Serhatis called the bluff, the *Ghost* would be forced to stay in orbit. That meant circling Serhati until the Hammers came and scooped them up. Of course, the Serhatis would protest furiously at the Hammers' abuse of their neutrality, but it would be too late by then. He would be on his way to Commitment and an appointment with a DocSec firing squad while the rest of the survivors headed for a Hammer prisoner of war camp.

Michael did the only thing left to him: He crossed his fingers and prayed hard. It was not much of a plan, but it was the best they had.

At last Jaruzelska's eyes opened.

"Done," she said. "Ambassador Sharma will do her best, so we'll keep going."

"Roger that, sir. Bet she was surprised."

"More stunned, I would say," Jaruzelska said. "I think I've spoiled her day."

Sedova did not wait for the Serhatis to decide whether to allow *Caesar's Ghost* to land. Shaking as main engines at emergency power reduced her speed for reentry, the *Ghost* started its fall dirtside, the planet's largest continent—a dark sprawling mass under scattered clouds tinged gold and pink in the early-morning sun—opening out below them. Sedova ignored the Serhati controller's increasingly hysterical bleatings of protest as she fine-tuned the lander's vector for reentry.

"Go for it, Kat," Michael said.

"Roger, sir . . . Serhati nearspace control, this is *Caesar's Ghost*. Life support status now critical. Estimate one zero, I say again one zero minutes remaining. Main engine flameout in five. Will attempt v-max reentry. Request immediate clearance into Norton Field. We don't have the driver mass to go anywhere else. Wish us luck, Serhati"—nice touch that, especially the panicky tremble Sedova injected into her voice; or maybe it was for real, Michael thought—"we're going to need it. *Caesar's Ghost*, over."

"Stand by, *Caesar's Ghost*, stand by. Out." Michael tried

not to laugh. Eyes screwed up and lips puckered into a grim slash as if someone had shoved the blunt end of a pineapple up his ass, the duty controller was an unhappy man, a man in considerable pain. He was not having a good shift.

"Main engine cut off . . . now"—the *Ghost* fell silent—"Serhati control, am committed to a v-max reentry direct to Norton Field. Request emergency services to meet on arrival. *Caesar's Ghost,* out. All stations. Visors down and make sure you are well strapped in. For those of you who've not been paying attention, we're doing a v-max reentry, so this will be rough."

Michael flipped his visor down and waited patiently until a row of green lights confirmed that he had a good suit. He commed the seat to tighten his straps as far as they could go, the crash-resistant seat molding itself around his head and body until he could barely move. Not that it made any difference to his chances of survival; if *Caesar's Ghost* broke up while traveling too fast to allow crew and passengers to eject—and there was a significant chance it would—they were all dead.

"Command, loadmaster. All suits are green, cargo compartment, casualties, and pax secured for reentry, ejection systems armed."

"Command, roger," Michael said. "Admiral, sir. We're good for reentry."

"Roger," Jaruzelska said calmly.

"Over to you, Kat."

Sedova just nodded, her whole attention focused on turning *Caesar's Ghost* nose on for reentry.

"*Caesar's Ghost,* Serhati nearspace control. Reentry approved"—yes, Michael thought exultantly. Not that it made much difference; the lander was committed, so it did not matter what the Serhatis said, but at least they were not shooting at them—"stand by reentry plan for landing at Norton Field. You are warned that any deviation . . ."

Yeah, yeah, yeah, Michael murmured to himself, tuning out; we've called that bluff. He concentrated on watching Sedova's every move. Not that he had anything to offer her. Sedova had graduated in the top 5 percent of her command

pilot class at combat flight school. If a v-max reentry was
beyond her capabilities, it was definitely beyond his. Compared to Sedova, he was a rank amateur.

Sedova pitched the *Ghost*'s nose up for reentry. Plunging planetward, the lander started to feel the first tenuous
threads of Serhati's upper atmosphere. A thin high-pitched
whistle developed rapidly into a full-blooded scream as
Caesar's Ghost ripped the air apart in its plunge to Earth,
nose and belly armor glowing first red, then white-hot as ablation started in earnest, leaving a fiery tail to mark its passing. Hands locked tightly onto the arms of his seat, Michael
prayed—hard—that *Caesar's Ghost* would get through this.
At normal reentry speeds, any lander could complete ten
reentries a week without breaking a sweat. V-max reentries
were another matter; heated by massive compression, Serhati's atmosphere would reach 13,000 Kelvin as it tore past,
too much for the lander's armor to resist, the excess heat
carried away by ablation of the carbon-impregnated ceramsteel, the lander tracing a blazing arc across the sky as it
dropped to earth.

In the end, a v-max reentry was a race to see which happened first: a successful transition to winged flight or ablation
of the armor until none was left. Without armor, *Caesar's
Ghost* would not survive two minutes before superheated
plasma broke through her inner titanium skin and she disintegrated into a flaming shower of burning wreckage.

Trailing fire, *Caesar's Ghost* plunged deeper into Serhati's
atmosphere. The lander shook violently as the aerodynamic
stress built, its artificial gravity struggling to absorb deceleration, pushing the lander's frame to its limits.

"Approaching max g," Sedova announced, her voice
calm. "Stand by pitch down. Hold on, folks."

Michael braced himself, hands locked onto the arms of
his seat. This was the most critical, the riskiest phase of the
reentry; in a v-max reentry, this was the point where the
command pilot risked her life and those of her passengers
and crew. Reducing pitch minimized the g forces acting on
the lander but exposed more of the lander's lightly armored
nose to superheated air, increasing the risk of thermal

breakthrough into the hull. When v-max reentries went to shit, it was during pitch down, and everybody knew it.

When—after a lifetime—Sedova pitched the nose back up, Michael allowed himself to breathe out. Slowly the lander's speed bled off. Maybe, just maybe, they might make it, he thought.

The rest of the flight turned out to be an anticlimax, not that Michael was complaining. He'd had all the excitement he could take. Extending the wings in small increments as the lander's speed decayed, Sedova flew a perfect engine-off approach into Norton Field, kicking the engines back into life only when the *Ghost* neared the threshold. Dropping steeply and still traveling at speed, she extended the lander's huge triple-slotted flaps, the landing gear locking down with a muffled, metallic *thunk,* then pulled *Caesar's Ghost* sharply back onto its tail in the vomit-inducing maneuver called—without any affection at all—"walking the blowtorch." With the lander now held up entirely by the power of its main engines, its nose pointing nearly vertically into the sky, Sedova rammed the belly-mounted thrusters to full power, killing the *Ghost's* speed. Crossing the threshold, Sedova eased back on the throttles and rotated the *Ghost's* nose forward and down, dropping the lander with a crunching thud onto the runway. Braking gently, she let the lander run before turning off the runway and coming to a stop. *Caesar's Ghost* was surrounded immediately by what had to be the best part of Serhati's planetary defense forces.

Sedova broke the stunned silence.

"Thank you, ladies and gentlemen, for flying Sedova Space Lines"—Michael noticed that her voice shook ever so slightly—"and welcome to Serhati. You may disembark now. And make it quick, please. I've set the self-destruct charges to blow in five minutes."

Chief Councillor Polk damned the vaulting ambition that had driven him to the chief councillorship, clawing his way up every blood-drenched step of the ladder. He damned the stupidities that had turned the Hammer Worlds into a crippled, corrupt shambles. He damned the incompetent fools he was forced to work with. He damned a military that once again had snatched defeat from the jaws of victory. He damned the Feds for wriggling out of the death grip the Hammers had on their throats.

But most of all, he damned his nemesis, a man with an uncanny ability to be there every time the Feds kicked the Hammers in the balls.

Helfort . . . Lieutenant Michael Wallace Helfort, Federated Worlds Space Fleet, may Kraa damn his evil heretic soul, the man responsible more than any other for the loss of the Hammer's precious antimatter plant.

He asked himself for the thousandth time why he was so stupid. Why had he ever allowed one miserable man to get so far under his skin? Kraa knew how hard he attempted to keep Helfort in perspective, but no matter how hard he tried, it made no difference. Not a day went by without him thinking about the man. He had even started to dream about the son of a bitch, for Kraa's sake!

Was he asking too much? No, he did not think so: He wanted the man dead, one miserable, no-account human being dead; that was all. With the full resources of the Hammer Worlds at hand, why was that so hard? Well, he decided, maybe things were going to get easier; Helfort's luck had run out . . . finally. Fate had given the Hammers the best chance they were ever going to get, and Polk intended to make sure the bungling blockheads who worked for him took it. If those useless Serhatis tried to dick him around, he would kick their Kraa-damned asses. He would give them a week to transfer the Feds back.

All being well, he decided, he would get his hands on Helfort, after all. Once the man had been tried, shot, and dumped into a DocSec lime pit—Helfort should feel right at home lying there beside Fleet Admiral Jorge and all the rest of the useless scum responsible for the Hammer's defeat at Devastation Reef—he might be able to forget him.

Thursday, April 5, 2401, UD
Hajek Barracks, Serhati

Michael stared out of the grimy windows of the barracks at the start of another stinking hot Serhati day. In the distance, the heat-battered landscape faded away into the brown haze before reappearing as the ground climbed into the Red Mountains, a hellish chain of splintered rock rising abruptly out of the narrow coastal plain that hosted the only settlement of note, Serhati City. Why the hell anyone would want to live on a planet like this was beyond him. The bits of Serhati that were not mountains were desert, and its one and only ocean was a fetid puddle so salty that the first arrivals called it, with the lack of originality that so characterized the place, the Great Salt Sea. Great Stinking Sea would have been more apt, though that would not have done much to encourage migrants.

Admiral Jaruzelska knew what she was talking about. She had said the place was a real shithole, and it was. It was not even a rich shithole. Serhati was one of far too many marginal planets scattered across humanspace, proof, were it needed, that optimism and hope beat common sense and rational thinking far too often. It had been settled by colonists riding the wave of euphoria that had driven millions of humans off Old Earth and across hundreds of light-years of space, looking for a better life; now they struggled to survive. When the first migrants found that euphoria was not enough to live on, most saw sense and left. Some stayed, settling down to an existence that was precarious in the extreme. For centuries the planet teetered over the abyss of economic collapse, its only income coming from exports of Serhati saltmullet—considered by some to be an exquisite delicacy when served raw; in Michael's opinion, it tasted like mud—and a thin trickle of tourists braving Serhati's abhorrence of customer service to gaze upon the admittedly magnificent rock formations of the Red Mountains. Even that was barely enough to maintain the fabric of civil society. In the end, all that kept Serhati out of liquidation was an annual payment from the Hammer Worlds to ensure that the Serhatis voted the way the Hammers wanted in meetings of the Humanspace Council. Needless to say, that made Serhati irredeemably corrupt.

All in all, it was a place Michael would be very happy to leave, and not just because the place was such a dump. He was interned in a Hammer vassal state, and that worried him. He knew he was dangerously vulnerable; his every waking moment was dominated by the terrible possibility that a DocSec snatch squad might break down the door and drag him away.

Heavy footsteps shook the flimsy stairs that ran up to the second floor. No DocSec this time; that could only be one person, Michael decided, turning away from the window, and it was.

"Chief Petty Officer Bienefelt. What can I do for you?"

"Briefing time, sir," she said cheerfully.

"Oh! Forgot."

"Knew you had. Come on."

Michael followed Bienefelt's enormous frame down the stairs and into the barracks mess hall. The place was packed, a soft buzz of conversation filling the room. Michael grabbed a seat at the back to see what the ambassador might have to say.

The brisk tones of Captain Tuukkanen, Jaruzelska's chief of staff, announced the admiral's arrival. "Attention on deck!"

"Okay, people," Jaruzelska said over the racket of people getting to their feet. "Please sit. Morning, all. I'd like to introduce Kayleen Sharma, our ambassador to what the locals are pleased to call the Sovereignty of Serhati. She is here to brief us on our situation. Before we start. Captain Tuukkanen. The room is clean?"

"It is, sir."

"Good. Ambassador Sharma, over to you."

The ambassador, a woman in her early thirties with thick black hair pulled back from her face into a ponytail, stepped forward. Piercing violet eyes—the product of some expensive geneering, Michael reckoned—scanned the Feds assembled in front of her.

"Thank you, Admiral," she said. "Good to meet you all at last, and I'm sorry it's taken me so long. Believe me when I say we've been busy. To business. First of all, let me say that in my time in the diplomatic service I've had plenty of surprises, but nothing like the call from Admiral Jaruzelska announcing your imminent arrival. That was one hell of a surprise, let me tell you, and I never did get to finish my breakfast." She paused to let the laughter die away. "And if you think it was a surprise for me, let me tell you that the Serhatis—forgive my crudeness, but it is the only way to describe it—the Serhatis nearly crapped themselves."

This time, Sharma was forced to wait a long time before quiet was restored.

"Anyway," she continued, "I say that not to make jokes at the Serhatis' expense but to make the point that nothing like this has ever happened to them. Now that it has, they have no idea what to do, which is where we've been helping them. Sadly, of course, the Hammers have, too, so it will take time to get the Serhatis to agree to whatever plan we come up with to get you guys safely home and even longer to make that plan happen. Bottom line is that you will just have to be patient, I'm afraid. The Serhatis' official position at the moment is this: Provided a state of war exists between us and the Hammers, you are internees, and in accordance with the rules, Serhati has the option, but not the obligation, to parole you so you can return home."

A soft groan filled the room.

"Hold on, hold on," Sharma said. "No matter what the Hammers say, I'm pretty sure we can persuade the Serhatis that it is in their interest to return you home, and that's what we are working to achieve. I will keep you up to date on our progress. One more point to make before I deal with the specific matters you have raised.

"The Hammers. They don't own this place, and the Serhatis get very angry if anyone suggests they do, so do us all a favor. Don't. You'll get your face busted, and you'll get no sympathy from me. You'll deserve to have your face busted. And don't make the mistake that many do when they first come here. Serhatis are dirt poor, and they know it. But they are tough and they have their pride, and to some extent they have a right to be proud. I doubt many Feds could make this place work even half as well as the locals have. So don't underestimate them. They deal with the Hammers because they have to, because Serhati is finished if they don't, not because they like them.

"Me? I have a lot of time for the Serhatis. They are good people deep down, and I live in the hope that one day we can wean them off the Hammer teat. But that's a discussion for another time. Right, what was I saying? Oh, yes, the Hammers. They have enormous influence, and when persuasion doesn't work, they pay to get what they want. So whatever we want to do, the Hammers will be doing their best to screw us over. We know that, and we will do our best to neutralize their efforts. I will of course keep you posted as to progress.

"Now to your issues. First, vidmail. We've finally persuaded the Serhatis to give us bandwidth, which means the embassy mail system can be accessed from your neuronics, so . . ."

Michael tuned out. Even if he wanted to send a vidmail to Anna, even if he could be sure the Hammers would pass it on, writing one was beyond him. It was not tiredness so much as a . . . he struggled to find the words to describe how he felt, and flatness—is that even a word? he wondered— came closest. Everything he had been through had crushed him flat mentally and physically, all energy, drive, emotion, appetite, ambition, hope, longing, and desire squeezed out of him like water wrung out of a rag. He was not a person anymore. He just existed, a lump of wetware whose only task was to take things minute by minute.

He let himself slip into a semidoze.

Ambassador Sharma was winding up. "So that's all from me. Like I said, updates from me will be daily at least, more often if I have anything useful to say. I'll com them straight to your neuronics along with edited highlights from the holovids back home. If you have any questions, contact the embassy directly. They'll point you to somebody who can help. Thank you all. Questions?"

After a string of questions—to Michael's frustration, mostly asked by people who had not been paying attention—the briefing disintegrated into noisy confusion. Michael stayed seated. His plan for the day was to find a quiet spot to sit out the hours, so he had nowhere better to be. With the room all but empty, Michael was still there when Jaruzelska spotted him. She waved him over to where she and Sharma stood.

"Sir?"

"Michael, the ambassador has some worrying news. Ambassador?"

"Thank you, Admiral. Good to meet you, Michael," Sharma said, shaking his hand. "Yes, I have a source inside the Serhati government. It seems that the Hammer ambassador was overheard to say that his government will agree to let the internees go home if you and one of your crew, a Lieutenant Kallewi, are transferred to them for whatever passes for a fair trial in the Hammer Worlds."

Michael's mouth sagged open. "You're kidding me, sir. Jeez! They never give up, do they?"

"It's fair to say, Michael, that they seem to have it in for you."

"And I know why," Michael said bitterly, "but Kallewi? What's that about?"

"He was the commander of *Reckless*'s marine detachment, yes?"

"Yes, he was."

"The Hammers say he shot a civilian technician during the attack on their damn antimatter plant. They claim to have vid of the incident from their security holocams."

For a moment Michael did not know what to say. Chances were that it was bullshit, of course, but in the heat of battle such things had been known to happen. "So where do we go from here?" he asked.

"Well, needless to say, there'll be no trade-offs. I think we are agreed on that. Admiral?"

Jaruzelska shook her head emphatically. "We certainly are. No trade-offs."

"Did not think there would be. So let's sit tight and see how this plays out. Okay?"

"Sir."

"One thing, though, Admiral," Sharma said, "Serhati is a poor system. Everything is for sale, and everyone has his price, including the planetary defense force troopers that guard this place, so I don't think you should leave Helfort and Kallewi alone at any time."

Jaruzelska nodded, her face grim. "We won't."

"If you're asked, you had these on you when you landed"—Sharma passed two small plasfiber-wrapped parcels across—"and they weren't picked up when you were searched."

Michael and Jaruzelska glanced at each other. The shape of a needle gun was hard to mistake. When he took his, Michael wondered how much getting them past the guards had cost Sharma.

Michael hoped his spirits would not get any lower. He was wrong.

The embassy-supplied package of news reports was the usual junk, and in particular one from World News, by a huge margin the worst of Terranova's trashpress notwithstanding its tagline: "Trusted to Inform." It was crap; the only thing he trusted World News to do was mislead. He had to fight to breathe through anger and fear as he read the headline: "Fallen Hero—How One Man's Insubordination Cost

Ships and Lives." No prizes for guessing who the man was. The detailed report that followed was a one-sided account of Operation Opera's closing stages, big on Rear Admiral Perkins's heroic struggle to hold off overwhelming Hammer forces despite the willful insubordination of Lieutenant Helfort but—strangely—not once bothering to mention the fact that *Reckless* and its crew had achieved Opera's primary military objective.

"Goddamnit," Michael swore angrily. Perkins, Rear Admiral Perkins: the lying, unprincipled sonofabitch. He had to be feeding information to the trashpress. Who else could it be?

Too depressed to watch any more, Michael was about to drop the feed when a local news item caught his eye. A Hammer heavy cruiser, *Keflavik Bay,* had dropped into orbit: The reporter took great pains to point out that the Hammer warship would stay only long enough to fix an unspecified problem with her main engines.

Here we go, Michael said to himself, the tension tightening his chest and stomach. *Keflavik Bay*'s arrival was no accident.

The Hammers had made their opening move.

Friday, April 6, 2401, UD
Hajek Barracks, Serhati

Michael was finishing his breakfast when the admiral commed him.

"Admiral?"

"Find Lieutenant Kallewi and come to my office."

"Sir."

When Michael and Kallewi reached Jaruzelska's office—a tiny cubicle tacked on to the back end of the mess hall—she waved them in.

"Take a seat, guys . . . right. I have bad news, I'm afraid," she said briskly. "The embassy has been in touch. The Hammers have lodged a request for your extradition with the Serhati government. Don't have any details yet. The police have warrants for your arrest; they are on the way to execute them. We've managed to get a lawyer to have a look at them, and the warrants appear in order. An emergency court hearing is scheduled for eleven this morning. Here's the hard part. I want you both to cooperate with the police. The ambassador is confident that we can get you out on bail, so rather than fight them here, I'd prefer to follow her advice and take them on in court, but I'd like to know what you think first."

Michael sat, sandbagged by the ambassador's news. He was not alone: Kallewi's jaw sagged, his mouth open in a small O of surprise. Michael had trouble believing it: Instead of the Hammer snatch squad he'd expected, the Hammers had resorted to the damn courts. That was a first. He forced himself to think. Stay and fight or rely on the Serhati courts? What a choice.

"Well," Michael said, finally, glancing at Kallewi. "I don't know how you feel, Janos, but I don't think two needle guns will keep the Serhati police at bay for too long."

"Not a chance," Kallewi said, his tone matter-of-fact.

"Didn't think so." Michael paused. "If the ambassador thinks she can get us out on bail, I'd be inclined to trust her on that. Much as I hate to trust anyone when it comes to the Hammers." Another pause. "Janos?"

"Even if the *Reckless* is long gone, you're still my skipper, sir, and I am a marine," Kallewi said with a lopsided smile, "so just give me the order and I'll be there."

Michael nodded. "Okay." He threw a glance at Jaruzelska. "If you think the ambassador's called it right, let's do what she suggests."

"I think she's right," Jaruzelska said; she sounded confident. "Let me talk to the Serhatis while you guys go and make yourselves presentable. I'll let you know when the police turn up."

The Serhati Superior Court occupied a tired-looking plascrete building right in the heart of Serhati City. As the busbot made its way down the ramp, loneliness almost overwhelmed Michael despite the comforting presence of Kallewi alongside him, not to mention an unnecessarily large contingent of Serhati police. If things went wrong, he was a long way from help. When they pulled up, the police hustled Michael and Kallewi out of the busbot and along a bewildering succession of well-lit corridors before pushing them into a holding cell, the door slamming shut behind them with a crash. Throughout the process, their guards said not a word.

"Jeez," Kallewi said, "don't muck around, do they?"

"Let me tell you something, Janos. After the fucking Hammers, the Serhatis are a bunch of pussies, so they can do their strong-but-silent thing all they like. Provided they don't start beating the crap out of me, I won't complain."

"Yeah. Heard about what they put you through."

"Ancient history, Janos, ancient history."

Kallewi leaned forward, his mouth to Michael's ear. "Just so you know," he whispered. "If we need to get out of here, we can. I've never seen such a sloppy bunch of amateurs."

"You sure?"

"Yup, I am. Easy. Don't know where we'd go, but breaking out of here won't be a problem."

"Well, if the bastards deny us bail, I think we might just have to exercise our God-given right to fuck off. I need some sack time, so"—Michael stretched out on one of the plain plasfiber bunks—"wake me up when something happens."

"Aye, aye, Skipper."

The courtroom was a shabby underventilated room fitted out with cheap furniture, its proceedings overseen by his honor, Superior Court Judge Corey Anderson. Michael's experience of courts was nonexistent; the endless hours of vids presented by the Court Channel back home were not something he had ever been interested in. But he was sure Fed courts were nothing like the shambolic three-ring circus he was being made to sit through. With not a legal AI in sight to keep things on track, Michael felt trapped in a time warp, shot back five hundred years.

After a lot of self-indulgent waffle by the lawyers spiced

with occasional angry exchanges, their indiscipline amply encouraged by the judge's erratic behavior, proceedings seemed to be getting to the point—Michael's lawyer was back on his feet—so he forced himself to pay attention.

". . . so once again, Your Honor, for the reasons I have outlined, there are no grounds for remanding my clients in police custody."

"Is that so, Counsellor?" Judge Anderson demanded, his voice a belligerent bark. A pained look crossed Anderson's face before he let go of a clearly audible belch. "Sorry, folks," he said, "must ease off on the chili. You were saying, Counsellor?"

"I was saying, Your Honor," the lawyer said, no less belligerently, "that there are no grounds for remanding my clients in custody."

"Yes, yes, so you say," Anderson snapped. "I heard you the first time, so sit down. I've had quite enough from you, Counsellor. And from you"—he pointed the handle of his wooden gavel at the Serhati table—"so don't waste any more of my time. Right, here's my decision. Bail is granted to respondents Helfort and Kallewi, subject to lodgment of sureties in the amount of 100,000 Serhati dollars each. Yes, yes, yes, Counsellor Markov, sit down!" Anderson barked at the Sovereignty of Serhati's lawyer when he started to stand. "Of course you don't like it, of course you want to appeal. I'm not stupid. I've known you for twenty years. You'd appeal the time of day, Counsellor"—Anderson cackled at his own joke—"yes, you would. Eh, what's that you say . . . the surety's not enough? It damn well is enough if I say it is, Counsellor Markov. Where was I? Oh, yes. Other conditions: Respondents to be sighted daily by an officer of the Sovereignty of Serhati Police, respondents to remain interned at Hajek Barracks. Now, Counsellor Markov."

"Yes, Your Honor?" the counsellor said, getting to his feet and eying the judge warily.

"Do I need to remind you that the Sovereignty has thirty days to submit its formal request to extradite?"

"No, Your Honor."

"Congratulations. You've got something right at last. Now, if you don't mind, I have better things to do than listen to you lot," the judge said, smashing his gavel down, "so this hearing is closed."

Jaruzelska was at the barracks door when Michael and Kallewi returned. "Welcome back," she said. "How were things?"

"Bizarre," Michael said.

"Entertaining," Kallewi added. "Never seen such a bunch of comedians. But the ambassador was right about bail, thankfully."

"Yes, she was, though you're not out of the woods yet. You already know the Sovereignty's appealing the decision. You still need to get through that. We've just heard; you're due back in court at 15:00 tomorrow."

Michael grimaced. "Can't wait."

"Anyway, the ambassador wants to talk to us about that in person. She'll be here soon. I'll give you a shout when she's ready to brief you."

"Sir."

Ambassador Sharma's face was troubled.

"It's not looking good, Admiral. Judge Anderson did what he was paid to do, and he did it well. Given he ruled against the Hammers, Anderson has chosen discretion over valor and is now taking an extended vacation. A prudent decision on his part, I have to say, but one that leaves us with a new problem: the judge scheduled to hear the appeal against the grant of bail, one Judge Kavaji. He's as corrupt as the rest of them, so I suspect—no, I know—the Hammers will have made it well worth his while to allow the Sovereignty's appeal."

"We can't outbid them?"

"Normally, yes. Serhati justice is simple. The highest bidder usually wins, but not this time. Judge Kavaji refuses even to talk to us. My guess is the Hammers are probably offering him hospital time if he takes our money. So unless we do something, your boys will be spending the rest of

their time here on Serhati in police custody, which I don't
like. My guess is that they will just short-circuit the whole
business by kidnapping Helfort and Kallewi."

Jaruzelska nodded her agreement. "Knowing our Hammer friends, I'd bet a month's pay on it. They are not the
most patient people. As for their commitment to legal process, I don't think they even know what legal process is.
And they have a real bee in their bonnet about Helfort."

"I'm afraid you're right. Once your two officers have been
cut out of the herd, one way or the other, it's only a matter of
time before the Hammers get their hands on them."

"Which I will not allow," Jaruzelska said. "Time for direct action, I think, don't you?"

"Funny you should say that, Admiral," the ambassador
said, trying not to look smug, "so it's a good thing I've had
my people working on a fallback plan."

Jaruzelska's eyes widened a fraction. "I think I may have
underestimated you, Ambassador Sharma."

"You might. Klera Willems, the assistant trade commissioner, is on her way. She'll brief Helfort and Kallewi on
what happens next."

Assistant trade commissioner? Jaruzelska wondered why
they bothered. The Serhatis would know perfectly well that
Willems was one of Department 24's field intelligence spooks.

Saturday, April 7, 2401, UD
Hajek Barracks, Serhati

"Okay," Kallewi whispered so softly that Michael
strained to hear him. "We're good to go. Follow me, stay
close, and move slowly. No sudden movements. Serhati surveillance gear may be secondhand, obsolete Hammer crap,
but it's not completely useless. Remember, hand signals
only, no talking, and make sure your neuronics are switched

off. They may have scanners running outside the perimeter. Ready?"

Michael nodded silently.

Carefully, Kallewi cracked open the door and eased his head out. He checked both ways and crawled out into the darkness, the night cut through—apparently at random—by the blue-white bars thrown by the searchlights. Adjusting his chromaflage cape to expose just his eyes, Michael followed, the ground under his belly still warm from another long, hot day. Slowly the pair eased their way across the expanse of dusty dirt that doubled as muster ground and futbol field, the light splashed on the ground by the searchlights coming close but never touching either of them. Despite himself, Michael was impressed. Ambassador Sharma said that everything on Serhati had a price, and she was right: Seemingly, even the bored troopers guarding the barracks perimeter could be paid to keep their searchlights off a narrow strip of darkness leading from the barracks to the wire. Michael hated to think what this little stunt was going to cost her: The troopers behind the searchlights would not be the only ones to benefit from her largesse that night.

Safely across the muster ground, Kallewi eased himself over the trip wire and paused at the single wall of interlaced razor wire that fenced the Feds' compound. Taking an agonizingly long time, he first cut away and then gingerly eased a panel of wire to one side with gloved hands. Kallewi waved Michael through and pushed the panel roughly back into place; he dropped the wire cutters—obviously homemade— beside the hole before they left.

Forty minutes later, they were well clear of the barracks, now an island of darkness flayed by bars of light, and were holed up in a culvert under the base's perimeter road. When did it ever rain enough to need culverts? Michael wondered in passing as a heavy cargobot thundered overhead. So far as he knew, it rarely rained on Serhati. More to the point, what idiot would build a culvert under a perimeter fence and then secure it with a grating a five-year-old armed with a penknife could undo? Obviously, Serhati was not a planet

that worried too much about security, and for good reason:
So far, Michael had not seen anything remotely worth
stealing.

Kallewi waved him in close. "Right," he said softly,
breathing heavily from crawling hundreds of meters on his
stomach. "That's the hard part over. Move through the culvert and crawl across the road to the clump of scrub right
opposite. Once through that, we'll be clear of the perimeter
surveillance cams and we can walk out. Two more klicks
will bring us to the road back into Serhati City. Hopefully,
we'll find Willems and the mobibot there. Questions? No?
Right, let's move out."

Two hours after Michael and Kallewi left the barracks,
the mobibot accelerated smoothly away toward Serhati
City, an orange bloom of light on the horizon. Their guide,
Klera Willems, a dark-skinned Jascarian with a forgettable
face—in Michael's opinion the sort of face well suited to a
spook—sat up front. She turned around to look at Michael
and Kallewi.

"Right, pay attention," she said. "It's a straight run into
town. This time of night, there's no traffic, and this road
takes us pretty much right to the embassy. When I give the
word, capes on, lie back, and don't move. The Serhati police have . . . well, let's just say they've got every incentive
to let us into the embassy."

Content to let Willems do all the worrying, Michael
watched the desert slide through the mobibot's headlights,
the sand broken up only by scrappy clumps of brush. It was
not long before fatigue overwhelmed him and he dropped
off to sleep.

He awoke to a steady stream of profanity from Willems.
"What's up?" Michael asked.

"Bloody Serhatis!" Willems scowled. "The problem with
corrupt places like this is the people you've just bribed immediately have something new to sell: who's just bribed
them and why. The bastards put themselves straight back
on the market for sale to the highest bidder. The embassy's
been in touch. Someone's talked, so the Serhatis know

we're coming. They are searching every mobibot going into the embassy compound, and thoroughly. Sadly, our covert people mover was written off two months ago, and I'm still waiting for a replacement, so unless we fight our way in, the embassy's not an option."

Michael's spirits crashed. "So what happens now?"

Willems flicked him a grin. "There's always a plan B, young man. You should know that."

Michael grinned back, reassured by the unassuming woman's quiet confidence. "You're Department 24, aren't you? You must know Amos Bichel."

"You should know better than to ask a girl a question like that," Willems shot back, "but since you ask, yes, I know Amos Bichel."

"Well, he smuggled me off Commitment under the noses of the Hammers, so I reckon getting us off this dump should be a breeze."

"I wish! Getting you off-planet comes later. Let me work out how we keep you two out of the Serhatis' hands first."

Michael glanced across at Kallewi. The man sat impassively; he had barely said a word so far. Happy to go with the flow, he stayed quiet, apparently unconcerned by the latest turn of events. Michael wished he shared the marine's relaxed view of things. It would be a big improvement on the near panic that threatened to overwhelm him every time circumstances reminded him that at best the Serhatis and their Hammer friends were only a few steps behind him, with a DocSec firing squad only a few paces behind them.

"Okay, folks. New plan. We'll stop short of the city to pick up supplies before we head out on Highway 2 to a place called Algal Springs"—Michael's eyebrows shot up; that did not sound promising—"which is one of the few places on this entire planet with potable surface water. A few days there and we'll move again. Where to, we'll work out later. Right?"

Michael nodded; he checked Algal Springs in his escape knowledge base, trying not to wince when an archetypal one-horse town popped into his neuronics: a single street flanked by sad, decaying buildings and a spring supplying water reputed to be packed with "health-giving" properties. But Michael saw immediately why Willems had picked it. Algal Springs backed onto a chaotic jumble of heat-shattered rocks, outliers of the foothills that climbed up to form the Red Mountains. An army could hide around Algal Springs, and nobody would know. Better, there were fresh-water springs, none big enough to support a settlement even a fraction of the size of Algal Springs but big enough to keep a small group well watered.

Satisfied, Michael closed the file and looked down the road. Serhati City was close enough to see the buildings that dominated the center of town, their lights diamond sharp in the still, cool air of early morning, the stars crystalline points of white overhead. It was a beautiful sight, the stars against—

"Oh, shit. Klera!" Michael said, his voice a half shout.

"What? What is it?"

"The Hammer cruiser. What orbit is it in?"

"Hang on," Willems said. "Yes, the *Keflavik Bay*. She's in Clarke orbit, right over the top . . . oh, shit, shit, shit." She stopped. "I've screwed up. I'd forgotten the bastard was there. Do you think they've seen us?" Willems's voice was hoarse with worry.

"Hard to say," Michael said. "Conditions are close to perfect, though: no wind, dry air, and a cooling atmosphere. Hold on, let me see what my TECHINT knowledge base says about her optronics . . . Okay, there's no chance they saw Janos and me leave the base. Too small a target, and our chromaflage capes are way too good. But the pickup vehicle, yes. Mobibots have big infrared signatures, so it would have seen that, no problem, and I'm sure they will have been watching the compound pretty closely. Why else would they sit in Clarke orbit right over the top of us? Whether the Hammers made anything of a lone mobibot, I don't know, but we need to assume they might, especially when they find out we've escaped."

Willems nodded. "Goddamn it to hell. Michael, Janos, I'm real sorry. Just to be safe, we need to get out of this mo-bibot, and . . . Hold on, there's an incoming com . . . okay.

Goddamn it. We're in the shit big-time. The Serhatis have just done a bed check. They know you're missing, so I'm pretty sure the Hammers will, too. If they haven't pinged the bot, they will when they backtrack through their holovid records. Let's have a look . . . Yes, couple of klicks up the road there's a cluster of houses and before them a park. Lots and lots of trees. Grab your stuff. When I give the word, I'll slow the bot, and out we go. Hopefully, they won't see us, and I'll program the bot to wander all over town as a decoy once it's dropped us off. Should buy us some time while we transfer to a backup mobibot. Sound okay?"

The fugitives nodded.

Michael tried to steady himself while the mobibot drove toward the park, the trees appearing as black cutouts against a night sky splashed with orange light from city street-lamps. When will it ever end? he asked himself in despair, even though he knew the answer: only when Chief Councillor Polk and the Hammer government came crashing to the ground.

Under cover of a line of scrawny trees, the mobibot slowed, but not by much. Michael knew this was going to hurt.

"Stand by. In three, go, go, go!"

With Kallewi and Willems close behind, Michael hurled himself out of the vehicle. He hit the sidewalk hard, his attempt to roll his way to a stop degenerating into a slithering, tumbling slide, the pain agonizing as the ceramcrete surface flayed clothes and skin off his right thigh and arm. "Jeez," he mumbled through agony-clenched teeth as he skidded to a halt; shakily, he climbed to his feet, relieved not to have suffered anything more serious than the loss of a few square meters of skin, or so it felt.

Willems did not hang around. "Capes on, let's go."

Ignoring the blood congealing stickily on his arm and leg, Michael set off after Willems, jaw locked against the pain as he commed drugbots into his bloodstream. He had a sinking feeling that they all faced a long day.

Two hours later, the group found itself on the outskirts of Serhati City as dawn was flushing the night sky away, life beginning to return to the streets. Willems called a halt, waving to the group. "Okay. Pickup's in ten, then it's thirty klicks to Algal Springs."

"Can't wait. I've had enough of this," Michael muttered.

"And me," Kallewi added with feeling.

Willems's head bobbed apologetically. "Sorry, guys. My fault. Never occur—"

"Don't sweat it," Kallewi said. "Stuff happens, but we're okay. Let's leave it at that."

"Thanks," Willems said. "Now, where's our lift?"

They were getting close now. Ahead, the mountains rose slowly out of the haze, a fragmented, fissured nightmare of broken rock cliffs splashed red-gold by the early-morning sun. Soon the dun-colored buildings of Algal Springs took shape, the little settlement sitting in a bay of sand beset by slab-sided rock walls and boulder falls. Wordlessly, the group readied itself, pulling chromaflage capes on over lightweight body armor and checking weapons, surveillance gear, food and water, and helmets.

"All set?" Willems said.

Michael and Kallewi nodded.

"Good, we . . . oh, crap!"

The shadow of a light assault lander blackened the road ahead, the crackling blast of its main engines shaking the mobibot bodily as it climbed steeply away. "I think we are about to be sprung, team," Willems said.

"Looks that way," Michael said. "That's a Hammer lander, and I don't believe in coincidences."

"Nor me."

Kallewi pointed to an outlying clump of rocks off to the right of the road. "There!" he said urgently. "It's our only chance. Stop!"

Willems slammed the brakes on, the mobibot skidding to a halt. "Out!" she shouted.

Grabbing his pack, Michael did as he was told. Eyes locked on the dwindling shape of the lander, he ran hard for the shelter of the rocks, his chromaflage cape blurring his image into a shapeless, rippling simulation of the desert

around him. When the mobibot sped off toward Algal
Springs, he saw that the lander was turning back. With a feeling of dread, he redoubled his efforts, goading his damaged
leg to move faster, sliding into the safe embrace of the rocks,
Kallewi and Willems piling in after him.

Without another word, Kallewi took control. "Okay, I
think they'll waste some time checking the mobibot out.
When they find it's empty, they'll backtrack through their
holovid records. Once they do, it's only a matter of time before they spot where the mobibot dropped us off. So single
file and go like hell for the hills. There"—he pointed to a
tumble of broken rock cascading down onto the sand—"if
we can get into that lot and keep climbing, the Hammers
won't be able to get behind us. If we can hold them off until
dark, maybe we'll get a chance to disengage and slip away.
Let's go."

They almost made it before Kallewi's shout drove them
into cover behind a pair of house-sized boulders. Michael
dug down into the sand with frantic desperation. The world
erupted around him as the lander's 30-mm hypervelocity
cannons fired a blizzard of depleted-uranium slugs, the appalling racket forcing Michael to dig even deeper, rock splinters tearing the air apart around him. "Oh sweet Jeezus!" he
screamed; sudden blind fear swamped him, his body shaking
uncontrollably while he ripped at the dirt, a frantic, tearing
rush to get somewhere, anywhere, safe.

No sooner had it started than the Hammer attack stopped,
the only sound the fast-fading roar of the assault lander as
it climbed away under full power.

Kallewi climbed back to his feet. "Let's go, come on.
They don't have a clue where we are, otherwise we'd be
dead, but we cannot hang around."

Nerves jangling and badly shaken by the attack's ferocity,
Michael glanced around as Kallewi led off. Banked hard
over, the lander was turning in for another run. He was relieved to see that Kallewi was right. As it steadied, Michael
saw that the lander would make its next run in front of them,
far enough ahead of the group to be a complete waste of am-
munition.

"Morons," Kallewi shouted, waving them to take cover. "They should have dropped their marines first to cut us off instead of hosing down the rocks, hoping to get lucky. Once it's finished this run, we have to get well up into the rocks. We may not get another chance to get off the sand. That gully at my two o'clock. Get in there and keep going."

Michael needed no encouragement; hands grabbing at the dirt, he ignored the earsplitting racket as the lander roared low across the ground ahead of them. Its cannons ripped the air apart. Cartridge cases—twin cascades of plasfiber flashing white in the morning sun—poured out of the turrets and into the lander's slipstream. The instant it passed, Michael was on his feet and running through the dust cloud raised by the lander's strafing run. By the time the lander climbed away, Michael had made it into the gully, its gravel bed leading up into the rocks, the air acrid with the smell of cannon-smashed stone, clouds of dust twisting slowly away in the still air. Gravel gave way to rocks, and Michael scrabbled and clawed his way across and around them in a frenzied rush to get away while behind them the lander dropped to the ground to disgorge its cargo of marines.

"Cover!" Kallewi yelled seconds before rifle fire slashed through the air over their heads. "On me."

Michael crawled after Willems to Kallewi's position, safely tucked behind a massive boulder; lungs heaving, he was happy to lie there for the moment. "Right, what they're going to do is this. Judging by where they've landed, I'm pretty sure they only have a rough idea of where we are. The marines will form a skirmish line parallel to the rocks and move in, hoping to herd us into a position we cannot"—Michael flinched as more rifle fire smashed into the rock wall above them—"retreat from. They'll use landers to move us out into the open if we look like we're getting too dug in. That, of course, is if they can ever find us, which is something I won't let happen."

Kallewi paused to catch his breath. "All we have going for us is mobility and our chromaflage capes," he continued. "Hammer marines with combat optronics will find us hard to spot."

"Surveillance drones?" Michael asked.

"Their optronics are no better. Leave them to me. I might be able to bag a few if they get close enough. The key is to move fast and smooth, and for chrissakes, don't stop in the open even if they start shooting. Remember, they probably can't see you. When in cover, take any targets of opportunity. Two shots maximum—any more and their hostile fire indicators will localize your position—then get away fast. If they get too close, we'll stop and knock a few of the bastards down. That should encourage the rest to hang back. Okay, let's go!"

Ducking and weaving, the group set off. Quickly, Michael settled into a routine—move, pause, move, pause, move—until he lost track of time, distance, and height, the group forced on by Kallewi's relentless drive. Occasionally they had the chance to fire back: a welcome break, an opportunity to give protesting legs and lungs time to recover while they reminded the Hammers they were not out for a stroll in the hills.

The day wore on, and the tactical advantage shifted slowly in their favor. The higher they climbed, the more they overlooked the Hammers and the easier it became to pick off an unwary marine. Bloodlust replaced fear. Carefully, Michael adjusted his aim until his latest victim's throat, exposed in a thin strip between helmet and body armor, sat in the center of the sighting ring in his neuronics, the rifle a seamless extension of his body. He breathed in, paused, and fired. He grunted with satisfaction when the Hammer marine fell backward. Working fast, he switched modes on his rifle and fired a microgrenade at a second who he assumed was tucked away safely behind a large boulder, the flat crack when the grenade went off rewarded by screams of pain.

"Incoming!"

Michael threw himself into a shallow cave below a boulder the size of a house. A Hammer lander howled past to unload a pattern of fuel-air blast bombs across the hillside, the latest attempt by the Hammers to blow them out of cover and, like all the rest, with too much hillside for the fleeing Feds to hide in, no more successful.

Not that Michael cared much anymore. Each attack had chipped away at his determination to keep going, and this, the latest in a long line, was closer than most. Afterward, he would swear the shock wave lifted the giant rock off the ground, its brutal power smashing into his body, the concussion so violent that he grayed out for a while. When he recovered, a frightening silence overlain by a ringing in his ears greeted him, the air in the cave filled with dust. His blast-battered brain refused to work properly. Suddenly, it was all too hard, and Michael gave up; he could not keep this up any longer. He lay there, stunned into immobility. He could not bring himself to move even though he should, he must. But he had had enough. If the damn Hammers wanted him, all they had to do was come get him. His head slumped down onto the ground.

Kallewi crawled into view. He grabbed Michael's shoulder and started to drag him out from under the boulder. "Come on, let's go. Move," he hissed. "We need to move. Come on."

Close to spent, Michael struggled to look up. Kallewi was a mess, his chromaflage cape torn, his helmet scarred by rock splinters. Michael noticed a thin trickle of blood running down Kallewi's left arm to drip onto the ground. For some reason, the blood made him angry, made him want to keep killing Hammers. Where the sudden resolve to keep fighting came from, Michael had no idea, but it was enough to get him moving.

"Okay, okay," he mumbled, crawling after Kallewi and out of the cave. "How's Willems?"

"She's fine. Let's move. I know that felt real close, and it was, but the stupid bastards still dropped their damn bombs closer to their guys than to us. It won't stop them, though. Hell knows, they've got plenty of marines to spare. Another lander's just arrived with reinforcements. Come on, we need to keep moving."

Head down, Michael forced himself to follow Kallewi

uphill to where Willems waited, tucked away at the back of a cave, her visor up as she took a drink. She, too, showed the effects of rock splinters, a massive gash across her helmet marking the path of a near miss.

Willems did not seem too bothered; she raised her canteen in mock salute and grinned at Michael. "Wondered if you made it."

"Me, too," Michael said, ducking instinctively when a storm of rifle fire howled overhead, followed by the characteristic fizzing of the lander's lasers and the shivering crack of cannon fire walking its way across the slope above them.

"Firing blind," Kallewi said laconically, untroubled by the racket, "hoping to keep us pinned down until the marines can get to us. Well, good luck to them, 'cause luck is all they have going for them. Let's go before they work out where we actually are."

They set off again, slipping through the boulder field, climbing all the time. Michael concentrated on keeping his head down while Kallewi led the way through the nightmarish falls of tumbled rock that climbed steeply ahead of them. They stopped, but only long enough to dispatch a few more Hammers—Kallewi picked off a surveillance drone that strayed too close while he was at it—before moving off again. And so it went, on and on, until Michael could think of nothing else but keeping up with the relentless pace set by Kallewi, the only breaks forced on them by the Hammer landers returning to waste yet more ordnance on the rock slope. As each attack died away, Michael said another quiet prayer of thanks to the genius responsible for marine-grade chromaflage capes. He doubted whether the Hammers had ever known precisely where they were; they would be dead otherwise.

It took a while before he noticed, but it suddenly struck Michael that the Hammers were becoming increasingly reluctant to show themselves, their skirmish line disintegrating moments after it formed, victim to the appalling terrain. Soon the marines' rate of fire dropped away noticeably, degenerating into random volleys interspersed with intermittent strafing runs from the landers that achieved very little apart from wasting prodigious amounts of ordnance in exchange for a lot of noise and broken rock.

By early afternoon, the Hammers gave up what must have been an increasingly frustrating and fruitless operation. Kallewi's pace thwarted the Hammers' repeated attempts to flank them. As they were forced to keep coming head-on, the Hammers' efforts to drop blocking forces in place were frustrated by terrain no ground attack should ever have to cross, their numbers and overwhelming firepower neutralized by never knowing for sure where their prey was hiding.

Michael watched the Hammers give up finally and start to withdraw, pleased to see an impressive number of casualties ferried away in a fleet of Serhati ambulances. Michael's opinion of the innate good sense of the locals had gone up. A large number of Serhati troops had arrived in armored half-tracks early in the battle; keeping well back, none made even the slightest effort to lend the Hammers a hand, content to watch the proceedings from a safe distance. When the Hammer landers took off and roared back up into orbit, the noise of their departure shaking the rocks, the Serhatis left, too, leaving a single half-track behind to keep an eye on things.

Even with the Hammers gone, Kallewi refused to ease up; on and on, up and up, they climbed until late into the afternoon. When Kallewi called it quits finally and waved them into a shallow cave screened by a tumbled maze of giant boulders, Michael almost cried with relief. He was a mess: hands and knees ripped and torn, his right shoulder aching after a day of firing, the skin of his shredded right arm and leg stiff with dried blood and tightening by the minute, his head muzzy with the aftereffects of fuel-air bombs dropped too close.

Sprawled across the dusty floor of the cave in silence, the group lay there for a long time. Exhausted, Michael let his mind churn through the day, a chaotic grab bag of events, places, people. And noise: the awful, bone-jarring *whuuuump* of Hammer fuel-air bombs, the whiplash of rifle fire tearing the air apart overhead, the fizzing crack of lasers, the screams of dying Hammers. Screw them, Michael said to himself. If the Hammers came knocking, he did not have enough left in him to shoot back. But tired or not, his spirits soared. He had survived. He grinned at Willems and Kallewi. They grinned back.

That said it all.

Later, Michael took his turn on watch. It was a glorious night, the sky so dark and clear that he might have been in space, with only the soft crackling of slowly cooling rock and the occasional murmur of a passing surveillance drone to break the quiet. The drones had stayed when the Hammers pulled out, even though the task of tracking marine-grade chromaflage was beyond their optronics. They flew at random across the boulder fields, hoping to get lucky. Fat chance, Michael decided as his neuronics tracked one across the sky; with an effort he resisted the temptation to hack the thing out of the air. Cradling his rifle, Michael watched the drone disappear into the night. He felt better than he had in a long time, all fear and stress purged by the atavistic pleasure of shedding Hammer blood, comforted by the knowledge that he was safe and Anna was alive.

He stared down the slope across the starlit jumble of rock, his neuronics painting it a confused mess of grays and black. From time to time, he checked the feeds from the network of tiny holocams Kallewi had set up around the cave; they, too, showed nothing but yet more rock. Nothing moved. The Hammers were long gone, and there was no sign of their coming back, though Michael could not be convinced they had just given up and gone home. If he had learned anything that day, it was that the Hammers wanted him so badly that they would waste the lives of as many marines as it took to get their hands on him. Well, let them try, he vowed; he would kill himself first.

Michael made himself as comfortable as a bruised and battered body would allow. A satcom call from the embassy told them to stay out of sight, and for the moment at least, he stood his watch, quite happy to comply.

Michael was not in good shape.

It was hot in the morning sun. It was dry. Food was running short. Water from the nearest spring was limited, its miserable flow delivering only enough to keep thirst at bay, never enough to clean up, to wash away some of the filth that encrusted his body. He stank: a sour mix of sweat, blood, burned rock, gun smoke, and dust. His body hurt, all of it. He was exhausted, his reserves of energy drained by the constant need to stay vigilant, to change their hiding place every night, to keep moving. With every fiber in his body, Michael wanted nothing more than to lie back and daydream the day away, but he would not trust the Hammers farther than he could spit. Nothing would convince him they had given up.

So he stood his watches: four hours on, eight hours off, the tumbled fall of rock in front of his position soon so deeply imprinted on his mind, he probably could draw it with his eyes closed. Bored he might be, but inattentive he was not. With scrupulous care, he scanned the approaches to their position endlessly.

For the fourth day in a row, nothing moved except dust devils and the occasional bird turning slowly in the hot morning air. Even the surveillance drones had gone home. He had not seen one for two days.

A shower of pebbles from behind him made him start; he swung around, raising his rifle, even though he knew it was Kallewi.

"Relax," the marine said, sliding into position alongside him, Willems following close behind.

"I will," Michael said sourly, "when we get off this godforsaken planet."

"Well, in that regard, I have good news. In ten hours, a

Fed task group will jump in-system, beat the shit out of the *Keflavik Bay,* and drop a marine assault force onto Hajek Barracks to recover the survivors from Operation Opera. And apparently the Serhatis will be happy to see us go, so happy that they won't be lifting a finger to stop us."

"I'm pleased to hear it," Michael said, "but what about us? I trust the plan extends to recovering us, too?"

Kallewi nodded. "It sure does. When the assault commander has the Serhatis under control, a pair of landers will be on their way to pick us up. Get the map of the local area up on your neuronics. Our exfiltration won't be easy, and we need to finalize our pickup point."

Michael's eyes narrowed. "Can't we just make our way down to the base of the rocks and wait there until the landers came?"

"That would not be smart, and I am not a trusting person. I know we haven't seen the Hammers for days, but I don't think they've given up. Their last chance to nail us is when we leave the protection of these rocks. So if I was the Hammer commander, I would have organized covert observation points"—his virtual finger stabbed down on the map—"covering all the main exit points, just on the off chance that we would be dumb enough to walk out into the open to meet whoever came to take us home."

Under the grime, Michael's face reddened with embarrassment. "Ah," he said, "that never occurred to me."

"Nor me," Willems added.

"Well, that's what you have marines for. The pickup point will be well clear to the northwest. Let me explain my thinking, and then we'd better get going. We have a lot of ground to cover. Now . . ."

For the hundredth time, Michael scanned the ground around the pickup point and the route they would follow down through the rocks and out onto the gravel pan, hunting for the shimmering blur of chromaflage capes. But even with the optronics processor embedded in his neuronics analyzing the raw optical feed, he saw nothing except sun-blasted rock, gravel, and sand.

Something caught Michael's eye. Far in the distance, a tiny speck appeared, followed by another and another until close to twenty plunged out of orbit. Michael stared. He grabbed the binoculars, and the specks swam into view. His heart raced, the relief overwhelming. The specks were Fed assault landers, and the only target of interest in that direction was the Serhati base and its unwilling crop of internees.

He called Willems and Kallewi. The pair scrambled into position alongside him. "Landers," he said, handing Kallewi the binoculars. "I think it's started."

"Not just any old landers, our landers," Kallewi whispered after a moment. "Something tells me we may not have much longer to spend on this abortion of a planet. Here, have a look"—he handed the glasses to Willems—"while I see if I can get the satcom to give us a voice link direct to the assault commander."

"When you get through, ask the marines to get a move on," Michael said.

Michael was having another look at the landers when Kallewi returned. "Okay, guys, we're on. Pickup point is confirmed, and we've got twenty minutes to get there, and the landers will not wait more than two minutes for us, so move out. Single file. I'll take point. Michael, you go last. For God's sake, keep your eyes open. I don't want us blundering into any Hammers, and always assume they're down there waiting for us. If we run into problems, we'll disengage if we can, pull back, and regroup. Neuronics off? Good. Questions? No? Right, let's go."

The group set off, the routine—move, pause, scan, move, pause, scan—now second nature; Michael's head swiveled from side to side in an unending 360-degree search for anything out of place in the chaotic jumble of broken rock and tumbled boulders around them. Slowly, they worked their way down until, with only meters to go before clearing the rocks, Kallewi's fist went up. Michael froze. What the hell?

For an age, the group did not stir. Kallewi started to inch back and to his right, every movement so slow that it took him a good two minutes to get off the line of advance. He ignored Michael and Willems, his hand working its way slowly behind his back to retrieve the satcom handset. Hard as he strained, Michael could not hear what Kallewi said. Frustrated, he stood there immobile, muscles screaming at the enforced idleness. Kallewi finished saying whatever it was he was saying. Returning the handset to its pouch, he turned slowly and eased his way back to where Willems waited. Finally, hand signals told the story: ambush, ten o'clock, 50 meters.

"Fucking Hammers," Michael said softly. "Not so dumb, after all."

Kallewi signaled them to withdraw. Michael needed no encouragement; turning slowly, he moved back up the tortuous path they had spent so much time negotiating.

Two hundred meters back, Kallewi called a halt in the shelter of a large overhang of rock protected by boulders the size of heavy landers.

"Hammer mothers," he said softly. "Ambush, up ahead. I only spotted them because their 'flage is crap. Another few meters and they'd have had us all. I think the Hammers have staked out every path out of these damn mountains for God knows how many klicks both sides of Algal Springs. Shit! You really can't take the buggers for granted."

"What happens next?" Michael asked.

"Spoke to the air assault commander. Gave him their position and ours. He's going to drop a truckload of ordnance on them, so they will not be a problem for long. But there'll be more Hammers out there, and the landers cannot carpet bomb the whole place. So here's the plan."

Michael forgot his pain-wracked body when he heard the characteristic sound of landers, the scream of fusion-powered mass drivers unmistakable.

Kallewi flicked a glance back at him. "Any second. Ready?"

"Ready."

Pushing and shoving, Michael wriggled his way as far back undercover as he could. Seconds later, he was glad he had: The rocks around him shuddered, the ground trembling, shock waves shaking the earth, blast-smashed splinters of rock screaming through the air overhead. The noise appalled him, a brain-numbing, body-shaking thunder, as the Fed landers walked a neat pattern of fuel-air bombs across the Hammers' positions.

The instant the bombing stopped, Kallewi moved. Michael leaped to his feet; heedless of the risks, he followed Kallewi and Willems in a wild, galloping run down through rocks still smoking from the attack, the air thick with powdered rock. Ahead of him, the landers made their final approach; belly thrusters blasted huge clouds of gravel-loaded dust into the air as they came into a brief hover before they dropped heavily onto their landing gear, their massive bulk blurred into black shapes by dust drifting slowly to the ground. Ramps crashed down, and marines in combat armor fanned out to take up position around the landers.

Michael ignored everything except the nearest lander's ramp, barely noticing the sudden banging of rifle fire as Hammers clear of the bomb-damaged area opened up. He drove himself on, the sudden slap-tear of bullets passing close to his head drowned out by the terrible crackling tear of the landers' lasers as they suppressed Hammer positions.

Thighs burning, lungs heaving, heart hammering, Michael had barely reached the line of marines when a giant fist smashed into his left side. An instant later, another hammered into his left leg, the shock of the two impacts enough to knock him off his feet; he hit the ground in an untidy sprawl of arms and legs and tumbled to a stop, then lay there too stunned to think, too shocked to move, his whole left side completely numb.

"Oh, shit," he whispered. He was confused. Why was he so cold? Why could he not see properly? Michael closed his eyes. Ever so slowly, he started to drift away from the light, down into darkness.

Two marines grabbed him under the arms and dragged him up the ramp. Minutes later, the belly thrusters fired, pushing the lander off the ground. The command pilot wasted no time making the transition to forward flight.

Transferring power to the main engines, he let the lander build up speed before pulling the nose up to drive the lander nearly vertically into space, closely followed by the second lander, but not before it dropped another pattern of bombs on the Hammers.

"Hello, sailor," a friendly voice said gently. "Welcome back."

Squinting against the light, Michael's eyes opened. He peered up at the face of the medic leaning over him. "Uh," he whispered hoarsely, "drink . . . drink, please."

"Here you are," the medic said, slipping a straw into his mouth.

Michael took it and drank deeply. The cool, slightly sweet liquid made him feel better immediately. "Thanks," he said gratefully. He glanced around; he soon worked out that he was lying in a warship sick bay. He had seen his share; the bloody places were all the same.

"Where am I?"

"You're onboard the *Orca*. We're twelve hours out from Serhati on our way back to Terranova. Be there in five days, give or take."

"Oh, right. What's happened to me?"

"I think I'd better get the boss. She'll explain things."

"Righto."

Orca's surgeon commander arrived promptly. "Lieutenant Helfort, morning," she said. "I'm Commander Ghella. Good to see you awake. How do you feel?"

"Believe it or not, sir, I feel pretty good. Nothing hurts."

Ghella laughed. "After all the drugbots we've pumped into you, I should hope not."

"Ah. Knew I felt too well. So what's the story?"

"Well, it's bit of a list, I'm afraid. Cuts and bruises everywhere, but nothing to worry about. You've suffered some blast damage to your brain, but it's minor. Your helmet did a good job protecting your skull, so there'll be no long-term problems, just headaches for the next few days. The big problem's two gunshot wounds, one just below and behind the armpit, the second in the upper thigh, at the back, about ten centimeters below your left buttock."

Michael thought about that for a moment before replying. "Jeez," he said, "that's okay."

Obviously baffled, Ghella shook her head. "What's okay?"

"Not getting shot in the ass," Michael said with a smile. "I'd never live that down, never. Trust me, sir. A wound stripe for being shot in the butt is not something to be proud of."

"Oh, I see," Ghella said with a look that showed she did not understand and probably never would. "The news gets better, I'm happy to say. Your body armor took most of the sting out of the first round. You have massive bruising, cartilage damage, superficial lacerations, some internal damage and bleeding, but none of that is too serious. And"—she pulled a small packet out of her pocket—"here it is," she said triumphantly, "the bullet in question, well, what's left of it. We found it in your body armor."

Michael took the packet and shook the contents into his hand: a single bullet, deformed by impact into a crumpled cylinder. "Must have been my lucky day," he said. A cold shiver ran through him; a few centimeters up and forward, and it would have been all over. The bullet would have come in under his armpit and trashed his upper chest so badly, it would have been beyond anything Fed medicine, for all its awesome power over the human body, could ever hope to repair.

"My lucky day," he said somberly.

"It was," Ghella said. "It really was. The second round did a fair bit of damage to the muscles at the back of your left thigh, in one side and out the other, tearing things up as it went. We see from your records that your left leg has been injured before."

"Yes. November '98. Shrapnel from a Hammer rail-gun slug. Sliced it up pretty badly."

"Well, it's been sliced up again, I'm sorry to say. Fortunately, no bone damage, and it missed all the major blood vessels. We've fixed up what we can with surgery and transfused nanobots to start putting it all back together again, but it will be a while before it's right. You'll be laid up for a week or so; then you should be able to get around using a legbot to support the leg while it heals."

"Terrific," Michael said under his breath. Legbots might get him back on his feet quickly, but they were a pain. "Thanks, Doc."

"Don't thank me. Thank the marines; their medics did all the hard work. So," she said briskly, "you up for visitors?"

"Sure am."

"Hang on . . . right, your XO and coxswain are on their way. I'll check on you later."

"Thanks, sir."

Commander Ghella had barely left his bedside when the pair appeared. It was good to see them. "Hi, Jayla; hi, Matti. Well, we made it, eh?"

"Yes, we did, but Jeez, you're a worry, sir," Bienefelt said with a shake of the head. "You sure Fleet is the career for you?"

"Hell, yes. I'm as sure as I can be, Matti," Michael said. "Jayla, tell me everyone made it off Serhati okay."

"We did," Ferreira said, "every last one."

"Pleased to hear it. Serhati's one place I don't ever want to see again."

Long after the last of a steady stream of visitors departed, Michael lay back exactly the way they had left him, eyes locked on a sprinkler set into the deckhead over his bed.

More focused than he had ever been in his life, he struggled to come to grips with the crisis that was on him.

He shook his head in despair.

Crisis? More like an ocean—a large ocean—of crises. Where the hell was he supposed to start? He had not received a single vidmail from Anna despite all the pressure put on the Hammers to honor their responsibilities under the Geneva Conventions. His left leg was months away from full recovery. The board of inquiry into Operation Opera had been convened, doubtless with him as its star witness. Perkins had lodged formal charges against him, alleging insubordination in combat. The Fed trashpress had picked up Perkins's line that the ship losses suffered during Opera—they preferred to call it "the Battle of Devastation Reef"—were mostly his fault. To cap it all, the Hammer Worlds wanted him dead so badly, they had started sending assault landers to hunt him down.

How much worse could things get?

Not that he cared much about himself, boards of inquiry, Fleet, the trashpress, or even the Hammers. The doctors would fix him up; the rest would sort itself out, of that he was sure. He had made the right decisions, and he had enough faith in Fleet to believe that the truth would emerge eventually. If the gutter scum producing the rivers of crap spewed out by the trashpress gave him a hard time along the way, so be it. Their day would come.

What he cared about most of all was Anna. But caring was not enough to get her back safely, and even if he did get her back, that left the problem of the Hammers doing what they did best: corrupting, killing, destroying. No, he had to resolve both problems at the same time if he was ever to shake off the ghosts of all those he had promised to avenge: the dead from the *Mumtaz, DLS-387,* and *Ishaq,* Corporal Yazdi, over whose lonely grave on a hostile Hammer planet he had sworn an oath he could never walk away from, not to mention the thousands of spacers killed in the endless wars inflicted on humanspace by the Hammers.

But quite how he was going to rescue Anna and destroy the Hammers at the same time, he had absolutely no idea.

The moon threw a thin light across the city of McNair.

The streetscape was washed of all color: flame-blackened buildings, crude barricades smashed apart in the night's fighting, smoke drifting from shops and government offices, from the wrecked cars, mobibots, and buses that littered the streets—all were painted in shades of gray splashed with daubs of black.

DocSec troopers in black jumpsuits and body armor, visors down and riot shields up, stood in small groups at crossroads, with more in front of those government offices as yet undamaged, stun guns and gas-grenade throwers cradled in their arms, assault rifles slung across their backs. Close at hand, half-tracks and troop carriers were parked in neat rows. They struck an incongruous note, their good order in stark contrast to the chaos around them.

The rioters had been forced out of the city center, harried and harassed every step of the way by DocSec; the streets were deserted. Nothing moved except smoke and ash.

The city waited, silent, still, an edgy calm settling over devastated streets.

Chief Councillor Polk stared out of the armored plasglass window of the flier while it climbed away from the brutal ceramcrete bulk of the Supreme Council building. From the air, McNair was an ugly sight. All across the city, piles of burning plasfiber spewed pillars of protest up into a gray sky, every greasy black plume of smoke a stark reminder that his grip on power might be slipping away.

He had been around long enough to know how the Hammer Worlds worked. When the unwritten contract between government and governed—prosperity and stability from the government in exchange for unquestioning acquiescence from the governed—started to unravel, it was up to DocSec to restore the status quo.

DocSec could deal with thousands of protesters: divide the mob up, kill any that stood and fought, track down those who ran, shoot some, imprison the rest, exile their families, and harass their friends and associates to remind them of the benefits of staying in line. The formula worked, as hundreds of neofascist governments had proved over the centuries. He just hoped it kept working long enough for him to die quietly in his own bed.

If the formula failed, DocSec would find itself facing millions of protesters. When it did—and Polk's instincts told him it would happen sooner rather than later—it was just a matter of time before the whole rotten edifice that was the Hammer government collapsed. Something told him that the Worlds were closer to that day than anyone was prepared to admit.

Polk dismissed the problem; if the day came, it came, and when it did, why would he care? He would be dead, left to dangle by one leg from a streetlight. He sat back as the flier cleared McNair's smoke-smeared skies. Without much success, he tried not to think about the day ahead: one meaningless public event after another, every second filmed by the holocams to demonstrate to the Hammer people that he, Jeremiah Polk, Chief Councillor of the Hammer of Kraa Worlds, was master of all the forces shaping the Worlds' destiny.

Which he was not, as anyone with half a brain knew after the fiasco at Devastation Reef.

From the largest down to the smallest, his capacity to influence events was limited, laughably so. Kraa! Despite all his pushing, the Hammer of Kraa was unable to get even one miserable piece of Fed filth off Serhati, a planet that owed its day-to-day survival to Hammer largesse. How pitiful was that? Anyway, he consoled himself, at least he could make Helfort's life miserable. That much he could and would do. Money slipped to a venal trashpress, money used to suborn Fed spacers with lavish hospitality—together they would make Helfort's life hell. Polk told himself to be patient. One day, the relentless pressure would make Helfort careless, flush him out into the open, where a Hammer hit team would find a way to get to him.

Much cheered by that prospect, Polk found to his amazement that he was actually looking forward to the rest of the day.

Monday, May 7, 2401, UD
Space Fleet headquarters,
city of Foundation, Terranova

Thanks to one of Fleet's postcombat stress teams, Michael was coping a damn sight better than he had after his escape from Commitment the last time around, but it was not easy.

The board of inquiry into Operation Opera was into its umpteenth day, and still he had not been called; he had yet to say a single word. The suspense was getting to him, though it was nothing compared with his concern for Anna; the worry was like an animal, gnawing away at his guts, hour in, hour out. True, she was alive, but she was in the Hammers' hands, and he had learned the hard way that they were never to be trusted.

If that was not bad enough, the trashpress was having a field day. His clash with Perkins was the scandal on everyone's lips; he could not say for sure who was feeding inside information to the trashpress, but somebody was. He would have bet good money it was one of Perkins's legion of dreadnought-hating supporters.

For the trashpress, it was a story they would sell their firstborn for. Apart from sex, it contained everything they wanted: the future of the Federation, age and experience versus callow youth and unthinking rashness, ambition, decisions made in the heat of battle, insubordination, death, and destruction. It could not have been much more appetizing if the whole business had been scripted to order.

Angry and frustrated, he pushed back from his desk. He commed the legbot that supported his injured left leg into life—the doctors might think the leg was getting better, but it still hurt like hell every time he moved it—before lifting himself carefully to his feet. It had been an unproductive day sitting in the offices of the Warfare Division, updating the Fighting Instructions; it was not the best place for him to be. To a spacer, the division was an implacable enemy of dreadnoughts, its staff not slow to let him know that over and over again.

He needed to get away. A few beers with the crew of the *Reckless*—like him, all posted to Fleet staff for temporary duty until the board of inquiry had finished—would go a long way to reassure him that the world was not populated completely by Neanderthal assholes.

Michael set off, limping heavily despite the best efforts of the legbot to compensate for a left thigh still a long way from complete recovery.

Three hours later, Michael found himself ensconced comfortably behind a table in one of the bars popular with Fleet spacers. Beer in hand, he was happy to let conversation wash over him, the talk ebbing and flowing over the issues that engaged most Fleet spacers most of the time: stupid politicians, amoral lobbyists, greedy defense contractors, shortsighted civilians, the pressures placed on family and friends by the demands of Fleet service, what the Hammers might do next. Around the table sat the rest of the crew of *Reckless*. Matti Bienefelt was well into a rambling account of a ship visit to a fringe planet settled by, of all things, an extreme cyborg sect so obsessed with pushing the boundaries of human geneering that their grasp of the harsh realities of world building and planetary economics was tenuous at best. Michael smiled; Bienefelt was being harassed—as tradition dictated—by Carmellini, Lomidze, and Faris every step of the way, each word sniped at the instant it left her mouth. The engineers were deep in an arcane discussion about fusion power plants Michael could not begin to understand, and Jayla Ferreira was talking landers with Kat Sedova and the crew of *Caesar's Ghost.*

"Well, well, well." A sneering voice slashed through the conversation; Bienefelt and everyone else talking stopped dead. Heads turned. The speaker was a man a few centimeters shorter than Bienefelt, with close-cropped white-blond hair and a heavily muscled body struggling to break out of clothes two sizes too small. Seven more spacers, all big enough and ugly enough to cause a lot of grief, flanked him. Michael grimaced. He had seen enough bar brawls to recognize trouble, and Snow White and his seven overgeneered— far from small—dwarves were trouble, alcohol-fueled trouble.

"So what have we here?" the man said. "The fearless crew of the *Reckless,* eh? Still trying to work out how many spacers your goddamned skipper killed? Maybe we should teach the little bastard"—Snow White jabbed a wavering finger at Michael—"which I think is you, sir, how to obey orders. Waddya reckon, team?"

A low snarl of approval greeted Snow White's suggestion, the Seven Dwarves swaying forward. Michael commed the bar manager to get the shore patrol fast. He stood up. "I don't know who you guys are, and I don't much care. So just go. That's a direct order, and I'm comming you my ID to make sure you know who I am."

"Oh, we know who you are," Snow White sneered.

"Do yourselves a favor and leave," Michael said. "Now!"

He might have been talking to himself. Snow White refused to move.

"Tell you what, sir," Bienefelt said, standing up, mashing a fist the size of a small ham into the palm of her left hand, "I've got a better idea. Leave the bastards to me. I'll move them along."

"No!" Michael snapped, "and that's an order, Matti." His voice softened. "I won't see you disrated for scum like these. Please. Just sit down"—reluctantly, Bienefelt took her seat, her face like thunder—"and you lot, go and we'll forget what's happened."

"Forget it? Forget it, after what you did? What's the matter, frightened?" Snow White taunted. "Is that why you turned and ran, you dreadnought pissants? It is; it damn well is. That's why you left so many good spacers and ships to die, you cowardly sacks of shit."

"Take that back," Bienefelt hissed, her voice pure menace as she stood up.

Michael swore. If the patrol did not turn up soon, blood would flow. Ferreira and Sedova were on their feet; Michael waved them back down. Things were bad enough without commissioned officers getting involved.

"Take it back?" Snow White's finger stabbed Bienefelt in the chest again and again and again. "Make me, you cowardly . . . gutless . . . dog turd."

"You should not have done that, my friend," Bienefelt said gently, only centimeters from Snow White's alcohol-flushed face. "You really should not have done that."

Something deep inside Snow White snapped; he and the Seven Dwarves made the mistake of throwing the first punches. In an instant, chairs went back and the crew of the *Reckless* roared to their feet, standing toe to toe with their adversaries. The bar became a shambles of swinging arms, bodies crashing to the ground, tables, chairs, and glasses going in all directions. Michael stepped back, one hand firmly locked onto Ferreira's collar, her restraint visibly crumbling in the face of the enormous temptation to give one of the dwarves a damn good kicking, the other signaling Sedova to stay seated. Spacer attacking spacer was bad enough; spacer attacking officer was a hundred times worse, an offense guaranteed to bring a long stretch in a Fleet prison, capped off by a dishonorable discharge. A well-deserved punishment, true, but better avoided if humanly possible, a lesson ground into Michael and every other cadet at Space Fleet College; spacers were expensive commodities, after all.

Egged on by raucous shouts of encouragement from the ring of bystanders, the fight ebbed and flowed across the bar, but the dwarves' greater mass proved no match for the raw fury of *Reckless*'s crew. Michael tried not to cheer while he watched, happy to see Snow White looking distinctly the worse for wear as Bienefelt's huge fists battered his face to a bloody pulp.

The shore patrol arrived in force. With ruthless, practiced efficiency, they waded in and transformed the melee into a neat row of plasticuffed, stun-shot bodies in an impressively short span of time. Michael chuckled when Bienefelt twisted her head to one side to shoot him a triumphant smile, seemingly untroubled by the blood-streaked damage to her face.

The young lieutenant in charge of the patrol waved him over. "This lot yours?" he said.

"Some of them. Not all. Don't know who they were, but they wanted a fight, they started a fight, so it's a fight we gave them."

"Yeah, yeah," the patrol officer said wearily.

"Luckily, that's what my neuronics recordings will show."

"They all say that. One of my guys will take your statement. Who's this?"

"Junior Lieutenant Ferreira, my XO. Sorry, my ex-XO."

The patrol officer shook his head despairingly. "A joker. That's all I want. I'll need your statement, too, Ferreira. And you are?"

"Junior Lieutenant Sedova."

"Ditto." The patrol officer turned to survey the wreckage. "At least the officers had the common sense not to join in, which is more than I can say for this lot."

"My guys were provoked," Michael said, "and they sure as hell did not start it."

"That's mitigation," the patrol officer said, waving a hand dismissively. "It's not justification, and you know it."

Michael nodded. The man was right; he did know it, but it was hard not to feel proud of the fierce loyalty and commitment the *Reckless*'s crew had shown. Not that loyalty and commitment would help much when the matter came to trial.

Giving his statement to the shore patrol, along with the records his neuronics had made of the incident, took an

age, and it was almost midnight before Michael made it
back to his cabin. The impersonal box—one of hundreds of
identical cabins making up the transit officers' quarters—
was as uninviting as ever. With a groan, he toppled onto his
bunk, doing his best to ignore the anger and resentment
that still simmered inside him. He knew one thing for sure.
Whatever humanspace lacked, it was not assholes, something Snow White and his seven pea-brained sidekicks
proved. Sons of bitches, he swore silently. He hoped the
provost marshal would throw the book at them; they deserved it.

Out of habit, he flicked on the holovid. When it lit up, he
wished he had not; World News was running its breaking
news segment, the ticker tape scrolling across the bottom
of the screen with the words "Fleet Hero in Bar Brawl—
Provost Marshal to Lay Charges."

"For chrissakes," Michael shouted, frustrated beyond be-
lief. "The fucking bastards."

He did not have to watch the story to know how World
News would spin it. He had been on the receiving end often
enough to know exactly how they would lay it out: heavy on
the fight—no doubt using recordings helpfully provided by
one or more of the bar's patrons—but light on who had
started it. With careful editing and without ever saying so,
they would leave the viewer with two impressions: first, that
he had been in the thick of the fight, fists swinging with the
best of them, and second—picking up the idea sown by the
ticker tape—that he had been charged. If they were feeling
creative, they probably would find a way to blame him for
starting it.

World News did that sort of thing all the time, and they
were extremely good at it, which was why they were so popular and profitable. Worse, any corrections his lawyers forced
out of them would be buried in a quick one-liner at the end of
the news a week later, by which time millions of Feds would
know—as certain fact—that he had been charged with brawl-
ing, their opinions immune to any evidence to the contrary.

Michael understood none of it. For some reason, he was

well and truly in their sights, and presumably, he would stay there until they got bored with him or a bigger sucker came along. He would talk to Mitesh in the morning. Despite the fact that his agent was just another AI-generated avatar, he had a way of getting things into perspective.

Too demoralized even to get undressed, Michael lay there until sleep overtook him.

Wednesday, May 9, 2401, UD
Offices of the fleet provost marshal, Space Fleet
headquarters, city of Foundation, Terranova

"For God's sake," Michael muttered, "how much longer do we have to wait?"

"As long as it takes, sir," Ferreira said. "The staff captain is extremely pissed, and I imagine she's had a lot to say. Not that I blame her. It's not every day she has to deal with a heavy cruiser's entire complement of senior spacers."

Michael laughed out loud. The crew of a conventional heavy cruiser included hundreds of senior spacers; he loved the idea of all of them lined up in front of some long-suffering staff captain, though he knew the staff captain would not see anything even remotely funny about the whole business.

Finally, the doors opened, and Chief Petty Officer Bienefelt emerged, leading a line of spacers out of the Fleet provost marshal's offices. Michael could not help noticing that not one of them showed the smallest sign of remorse.

"All right, chief," Michael said, shaking his head. "Tell me how it went."

Bienefelt smiled, a smile of smug self-satisfaction. "Justice prevailed, sir, as it should. Charges of common assault were dismissed, though sadly we were all found guilty of a breach of the peace." Bienefelt even managed to sound hurt.

"Well," Michael snorted, "what a surprise, considering the patrol used a stun gun to stop you from beating the crap out of . . . what the hell was the useless jerk's name?"

"Leading Spacer Rasmussen, sir. Off *Ebonite,* which wasn't within a hundred light-years of Operation Opera. Useless, scum-sucking toe rag."

"Yeah, him. And the damage?"

"Fine, stoppage of leave, loss of seniority, and we've had to kick the tin to pay for the damage to the bar."

"Oh," Michael said, "so you're still a chief petty officer?" He shook his head despairingly. "That's a fucking miracle. I think you got off lightly."

"Maybe so, sir," Bienefelt said, looking not in the least apologetic, "but let me tell you this. It was well worth it, not that Rasmussen would agree. The provost marshal threw the book at him, big-time. He's screwed, and his mates, too. My spies inside the provost marshal's office tell me they are on their way to Fleet Prison 8 as we speak."

"Good." Michael paused to look at *Reckless*'s crew. Ex-crew, he reminded himself. *Reckless* might be gone, but that did not diminish the fierce pride he had in all of them. "Well, boys and girls, I hope you've learned your lesson, though looking at you, I doubt it. I would buy you a beer to say a strictly unofficial thanks for standing up for *Reckless* and her sister dreadnoughts, but since you're all confined to barracks, I can't."

"Short arms, deep pockets, sir," Bienefelt shot back amid a soft chorus of boos and hisses. "Any excuse. Nothing changes."

"Insubordinate rabble," Michael said. "Give me a shout when they let you back into civilized society. The beers will be on me, though maybe we should try another bar. Now piss off. I've got work to do. Catch up with you later, Jayla."

"Sir."

Michael made his way through the labyrinthine corridors and drop tubes of Fleet headquarters. The place was huge, and his leg, for all the help given by the legbot, did not appreciate the workout. By the time he made it to his desk—cold-shouldered as usual by the rest of Warfare Division as he limped past—he could not have walked much farther.

He sat down, any enthusiasm generated by the unquestioning loyalty of *Reckless*'s crew evaporating fast. Updating the Fighting Instructions was important work, he knew, but only if Fleet continued the dreadnought experiment, something he had a feeling it would not. He had forced himself back to work when two pings in quick succession announced the arrival of priority mail.

His heart raced. The first message was from the Red Cross. With a silent prayer, he opened it. It was a vidmail, and it was from Anna. He breathed in sharply to steady himself and opened it.

After the usual Red Cross preamble—name, rank, serial number, followed by a certificate from the Hammers asserting the authenticity of the vidmail and giving her prisoner identity number—Anna's face popped into his neuronics. For a moment she said nothing. She seemed tired: skin washed out to a dull beige, gray bags under her eyes, her face stretched taut across high cheekbones no longer dusted with pink. But her eyes were pure Anna: an extraordinary green, alive and alert. Michael forced himself to relax. Anna was as well as any Fed could be in Hammer captivity.

"You can start," a disembodied voice said. "You have one minute."

A shiver ran up Michael's spine. The accent was pure unadulterated Hammer. The flattened vowels, chopped syllables, and staccato delivery triggered a feeling of sick dread and a flood of memories he had worked long and hard to bury.

Anna stared directly into the holocam. "Michael," she said, her voice steady and controlled, "I don't have long. As you can see, I'm okay. I had some splinter damage to my right leg, but nothing serious. The Hammer medics did a good job, it's healing well, and I now have a wound stripe. I'm not allowed to tell you where we are, but we are all safe. The loss of the ship was heartbreaking and probably the most . . . uh"—blinking, Anna's eyes filled with tears—"ah, shit . . . it was the most terrifying thing I've ever been through. I really didn't think I'd make it. Now I know how you felt when your ship went. It was horrible. Anyway, we did the interrogation thing, I told the bastar—"

"Watch it," the unseen Hammer growled.

"Sorry," Anna said, sounding anything but. "We're in a prison camp; I can't say where. It's basic but enough to get by. We're out of the rain, we get fed, and the Hammers have done the right thing by us so far. There are prisoners from other ships in this camp, so there is no shortage of advice on how to survive. The senior officer is a four-ringer. She doesn't take any shit from anyone, so discipline is tight. If I behave, I'm allowed one of these messages a month, so I'll talk to you again. You can vidmail me whenever you like. Haven't had any from you yet, so I don't know if we'll get them, but don't let that stop you from trying. Okay, have to go. Love you. Bye."

Anna's face vanished, and that was it. Michael did not know what to think; his mind seethed, a mess of mixed emotions: relief, anger, longing, and frustration, all overlaid by a blanket of raw hatred of all things Hammer. The rush of emotion triggered by Anna's vidmail was so strong, he had to force himself to push her out of his mind.

Ten minutes later, he was back in control enough to open the second message. "About bloody time," he said as he scanned it a second time to make sure he had read it right. After waiting what seemed like a lifetime, he was to get his chance to present his account of Operation Opera to the board of inquiry.

Back in his cabin that evening, Michael watched Anna's vidmail so many times that he could recite it word for word. He could not get enough of her. He watched it one more time; something nagged at him, and for the life of him, he could not put a finger on it. Becoming more and more frustrated, he watched it over and over again. He still did not get it, but there was something there. Problem was, his subconscious knew what it was but refused to let it out into the open. Michael gave up.

He would have another go at it after he had taken a shower and grabbed something to eat.

* * *

Shortly before midnight, it came to him. When it did, Anna's ingenuity left him stunned. Throughout her vidmail she blinked, but never both eyes at once. It took him a long time to understand what she was saying, but once he worked it out, it turned out to be simple. An almost imperceptible twitch of her left eyelid meant 0, a twitch of her right meant 1, generating numbers between 0 and 9. Reversing things produced numbers between 0 and 15, which wasn't helpful; Anna was always one to keep things simple.

So, thirty-two twitches gave him a sequence of binary numbers: 0001 0000 0101 0000 0101 0010 0000 1001. He shook his head in disbelief. Only a love-struck idiot would have picked it, and he was one of those; Michael was sure he was the one person in all of humanspace who would have spotted what she was doing. One of the fancier pattern recognition AIs might have cracked it, but who would have bothered?

He had a new problem. Converting the string of binary numbers to base 10 was the obvious next step; that gave him 10505209. But the longer he looked at it, the less sense it made. He was baffled. What the hell did it mean? After hours of trying, he gave up. He was getting nowhere. It was time to get some expert help, he decided.

He commed the duty intelligence officer.

Thursday, May 10, 2401, UD
Conference Room 10, Space Fleet headquarters,
Foundation, Terranova

The president of the board of inquiry, Captain Shavetz, a warfare officer with a combat record a kilometer long and medals to match, sat flanked by officers from every major specialization in the Fleet. He watched Michael take his seat.

"Lieutenant Helfort. Do I need to remind you that the oath you swore on accepting your commission as an officer in the Federated Worlds Space Fleet requires you to tell the truth at all times?"

"No, sir," Michael said, "you do not."

"Thank you. The board has studied your report of proceedings carefully. It has reviewed your report in light of statements from the *Reckless*'s crew and those of spacers from other ships together with the reports of proceedings and datalogs from the ships of the dreadnought force and the rest of Battle Fleet Lima. I have to say that your report is entirely consistent with those latter sources of information, a view that is supported by the AIs analyzing the evidence"—get on with it, for chrissakes, Michael said to himself, fuming; the way the man talked, no wonder the board of inquiry took so long—"but we have a number of issues which require some clarification."

"Yes, sir." Michael replied woodenly.

"Good," Shavetz said. He turned to a young warfare officer sitting to his left, the junior member of the board. Michael knew him only by reputation: a hotshot navigator, massively ambitious, and probably no friend of dreadnoughts. "Lieutenant Commander Grivaz?"

"Thank you, sir. Lieutenant Helfort, I have two questions. First, when *Reckless* deployed for Operation Opera, what did you understand that operation's primary military objective to be? Second, and please be precise when answering, why did you think that?"

"Well, sir . . ."

Late into the evening of a long day, Captain Shavetz glanced at each of the members of the board in turn. "Are there any more questions for Lieutenant Helfort . . . no? Good."

He turned to Michael. "Lieutenant Helfort. I think that is all. Thank you. The board secretary will advise you if we need to talk to you again. You are dismissed."

"Thank you, sir."

Michael struggled out of his seat. It had been a tough day, one of searching examination interrupted only by a short lunch break. The process had wrung him out. One after another the questions came. They never stopped, the pressure intense, the pace relentless. Not that any of that bothered him; telling things the way they happened was easy. What bothered him was the fact that even after hours of unremitting scrutiny, he had no idea what the board was really thinking.

Michael hoped they saw things his way. His future depended on it. When he limped out of the room, a chief petty officer stood in his way.

"Lieutenant Helfort?" the man asked.

"Yes?"

"Chief Tarkasian, sir. Vice Admiral Prentice's compliments. She appreciates that it's late in the day but wonders if you might spare her ten minutes."

What on earth? Michael wondered. "Vice Admiral Prentice? Yes, of course. Now?"

"I really think that might be best, sir," Tarkasian said.

Michael nodded. "Lead on, chief."

Tarkasian was right: Late in the day or not, junior officers were well advised to treat requests from senior officers, however politely phrased, as direct orders. He limped after the man, wondering what the Fleet's director of intelligence wanted. It was something to do with Anna's mysterious binary code message, of course, but what?

Five minutes later, they arrived at Prentice's office. He was shown straight in. Prentice—a severe-looking woman with thick black hair pulled back tight from an austere, angular face, penetrating brown eyes, and a fearsome reputation as one of Fleet's toughest and smartest officers, a woman for whom fools were to be stomped into the dirt—waved him into a seat in front of her desk. Almost immediately, a captain arrived, dropping into the seat alongside Michael's.

"Lieutenant Helfort. Welcome. We've never met. I'm Admiral Prentice. This is my chief of staff, Captain Cissokho."

"Sirs."

"I know this is important to you, so I thought it best if we talked face-to-face. Besides," Prentice said with a fleeting smile, "I wanted to meet the man who pulled the Federation's ass out of the fire. Opera would have been a complete dud without you, so well done." Her smile broadened. "Just don't tell anybody I said so. I'm unpopular enough as it is."

Surprised, Michael blinked. "Thank you, sir. That means a lot, more than you know."

Prentice waved a hand. "It's nothing less than you deserve. Now, to business. Bill?'

"Admiral," Cissokho said. He turned to Michael. "We followed up your analysis of Lieutenant Cheung's vidmail. You were right. She had encoded a binary message. Extremely clever of her, I must say, and equally clever of you to work it out. Anyway, it translated to 10505209. Of course, that begs the question. What does a string of eight numbers mean? It took one of my analysts a while, but I think she's cracked it. Here, have a look."

A map of the Hammer's home planet, Commitment, appeared on the admiral's wall-mounted holovid. Cissokho stabbed a marker at a point southeast of the capital, McNair. "10 degrees south, 50 degrees west is more or less where Camp J-5209 sits. That's where the survivors from the *Damishqui* are. It's the only place that fits the numbers 10505209. All the other options are either in the sea or have nothing that fits the last four numbers. It's a new camp, so we've only seen it referenced in intercepts of low-grade administrative traffic. We don't have recon vid of it, but now that we know where it is, we will. I'll let you know when it's been uploaded to the Fleet knowledge base."

"I'll be damned, sir," Michael said. "Thanks for letting me know."

"Wish it was something more exciting, but you never know. The information might come in handy one day. The Hammers never tell us where they keep our prisoners."

"Thank you, sir."

"Happy to help," the admiral said. "We'll keep an eye on things. If we hear anything about Camp J-5209, provided we can release it, of course, we'll let you know."

"Thank you, sir. Thank you both."

Michael walked away from the admiral's office feeling better than he had in a while, his body reenergized, and not just because he knew where the Hammers had imprisoned Anna. That was part of it, to be sure, but as important was the realization that despite the overt hostility expressed by the overwhelming majority of Fleet officers and the unremitting hammering he was getting from the trashpress, there were people—important people—both sympathetic and supportive.

Knowing he was not alone made a difference.

Friday, May 25, 2401, UD
Warfare Division, Space Fleet headquarters,
Foundation, Terranova

"Helfort?"

Michael glanced up from his work. It was his immediate boss. Of all the people in the Warfare Division, she was without doubt the most hostile; the woman was a festering mass of ill-concealed resentment.

"Yes, sir?

"The board of inquiry is about to release the unclassified summary of its report into Operation Opera. The director wants you to be there. Conference-5 at 10:00."

Without waiting for a response, the woman turned and left. "Thank you, sir," Michael said to her back. "Thank you so much."

The woman spun around. "Don't push your luck," she hissed, her voice dripping with venom. "It's time you got what's coming to you, Helfort. Conference-5 at 10:00 and don't be late." She started to turn away but stopped, her mouth slashed into a malicious sneer. "Oh, yes. One more thing. You might be interested to know that the provost marshal has been told to be there, too. So I wouldn't make any plans for tonight if I were you."

"Fucking cow," Michael mouthed at her retreating back, stifling an urge to rip his legbot off and hurl it at her head.

He sat unmoving, acid burning a path from his stomach up into his chest. Shit, he said to himself, finally.

The president of the board of inquiry waited patiently until the conference room, every seat taken, fell silent. Michael waited until the last minute before slipping in unseen, sitting as always at the back, well clear of the large contingent of Fleet brass that filled the front rows of the conference room, lines of black and gold flanked on both sides by holocam-wielding members of the press.

"Good morning, everyone," Captain Shavetz said, "and thank you all for coming. I am about to release our report on Operation Opera, the successful operation to destroy the Hammers' antimatter plant at Devastation Reef. The report is extremely detailed, so in deference to our friends in the press"—a subdued laugh greeted this remark; Fleet had few friends in the press, and everybody knew it—"we will present our finding of facts, a summary of what happened during Operation Opera, followed by the conclusions the board has drawn from the evidence presented to us. Our recommendations will follow this afternoon. To answer a question which I know will be asked, yes, every board member has agreed on the statement of facts, conclusions, and recommendations of this board. There is no dissenting minority report. However, one thing must be understood. We are still at war with the Hammer Worlds, so for reasons of operational security, we cannot release our report in its entirety. Some findings of fact and some of our conclusions and recommendations are classified. I'm—"

"Pantini, World News," a voice barked from the media pack. Michael shook his head. Who else but Giorgio Pantini? Why did the man bother asking questions? His often stated commitment to factually based reporting was, as one commentator so memorably put it, "a shoddy cover over a stinking pot of lies." After all Pantini had said about him, Michael had no problem endorsing that judgment.

"Yes?" Shavetz said, looking warily at Pantini.

"So, Captain Shavetz," Pantini said, "you're saying we can expect another Fleet cover-up."

"Come, come, come, Mister Pantini," Shavetz said with exaggerated deference, "that's hardly a question. That's a statement, and you know it. If you have a worthwhile question, please ask it, though I fail to see how you can have considering we haven't actually said anything yet. Otherwise, please resume your seat. We have a lot to get through."

Pantini's response died stillborn, his protests drowned out by a chorus of less than friendly encouragement to sit down and shut up, which Pantini did with petulant bad grace.

"As I was saying," Shavetz said, "for reasons of operational security, we cannot release our report in its entirety, and I hope you will bear with us on that. But I can assure you we have released all we can. More important, we have held back nothing that compromises the overall thrust of that report in any way. I would like to start with a summary of the key events drawn from the board's findings of fact. Lieutenant Commander Grivaz?"

"Thank you, sir. If you would turn your attention to the holovid behind me, I will start at the point where Opera was in its initial planning stages. In late January, the chief of the defense force, Admiral Kefu, hosted a planning conference. The objectives of this meeting were several, but the most important of them was . . ."

His voice calm and dispassionate throughout, Grivaz took more than two hours to map out the tortuous, tangled paths leading to the destruction of the Hammer's antimatter plant. Utterly absorbed, Michael followed his every word, scrutinizing everything the man said for some clue, some hint to the board's thinking. But Grivaz was either a consummate professional or well rehearsed—probably both, Michael decided on reflection—so by the time he finished, Michael knew a lot more about Opera and nothing more about his prospects. He did not enjoy Grivaz's dispassionate reconstruction of his clash with Perkins. As presented, it sounded utterly damning. Michael was not surprised. Grivaz could talk until the cows came home, and nothing he ever said would convey to the people in the room the raw terror of that awful moment when he realized he had to defy Perkins's order, that he risked the entire Federated Worlds. Even those who knew what it was like to be in combat, to be one bad decision—or one bad break—away from death, would never understand what he had gone through.

"Thank you, Commander," Shavetz said when Grivaz finished. "We'll pause for lunch now. We will start again at 13:00 sharp, so please be back here promptly. I will not wait for anyone. Not even you, Mister Pantini."

Pantini scowled when the room erupted in laughter.

Michael had no intention of joining the crowd heading for lunch: too many people asking too many questions he did not want to answer. He waited, content to hang back before slipping out to get something to eat.

He did not get the chance. To his dismay, Giorgio Pantini cut his way through the throng toward him, holocam operator close behind. For a moment, Michael toyed with the idea of making a quick break for it before common sense told him that would just make him look guilty. Stitching a look of polite interest onto his face, he waited for Pantini, sending out an urgent com for one of Fleet's PR hacks to come save him.

"Mister Pantini. Good afternoon. Can I help you?" he said, his voice loaded with confidence he did not feel, the apprehension busy turning his stomach over well concealed.

"Yes, you can," Pantini said, his tone openly belligerent. "Tell me this, Lieutenant Helfort. This morning, we saw clear evidence, unarguable evidence, that you disobeyed the direct order of a flag officer during combat. Do you agree you disobeyed Rear Admiral Perkins's order?"

"Yes, Mister Pantini," Michael said, "of course I agree. How could I not? It is a matter of record."

"So how can you live with yourself knowing that that one act of willful insubordination condemned hundreds, maybe even thousands, of good spacers and marines to death?"

In a flash, anger replaced Michael's anxiety; he struggled

to keep control. The problem was that Pantini was not all wrong. By ignoring Perkins, by leaving Assault Group to take its chances, by focusing on the antimatter plant, he had condemned good spacers and marines. But if he admitted that to a scum sucker like Pantini, he would be forever damned in the eyes of the Fed public. Clinging to the last shreds of his self-control, he stared confidently right into the holocam's lens. "Well, Mister Pantini," he said, "I don't see it that way. Operation Opera had a single objective, the destruction of the Hammer antimatter plant. I did what any Fleet officer—"

"Any officer? So you're saying that Fleet officers make a habit of disobeying orders, of needlessly sacrificing the lives of their spacers?"

Michael shook his head. "What I am saying is that I did what any Fleet officer would—"

"So you admit it? You admit sending good spacers to their deaths unnecessarily?"

A hairbreadth away from leaping out of his seat and beating Pantini to death with his own holocam, Michael kept his cool. How he did not know, but he did. He stared Pantini right in the eye. "I think, Mister Pantini, that this would be a much better interview if you actually let me finish. If you don't want me to answer your questions, if you'd prefer to do all the talking, that's fine. I'll save us all a lot of time, and I'll sit here saying nothing while you tell me—and the rest of the world—what you think."

"Please continue," Pantini said tetchily.

"Thank you," Michael said, all sweetness and light. "Here's the point. Destroying the Hammer plant was the reason—the only reason—the ships of Battle Fleet Lima were in Hammer space, and I'm sure I don't have to remind you why doing that was so important. Or weren't you here when the Hammers fired antimatter missiles at the home planets? I'd—"

"I thought you wanted to answer the question, Lieutenant."

Furious with himself for trying to score points off Pantini—he sensed Mitesh wagging his finger at him, a look of profound disappointment on his face—Michael forced himself to concentrate. "I am answering your question, Mister Pantini, if you'd let me," he said, recovering his equilibrium. "I followed my orders, and those orders were to destroy the Hammer plant. If I hadn't, that plant would still be operational, still be producing antimatter, and your home planet and mine would still be living under the threat of imminent destruction."

"Rear Admiral Perkins does not share that view with you. What will you say when the board of inquiry agrees with him?"

"We don't know that it will, Mister Pantini. I've not seen their report yet, and neither have you, so I think we should wait to see what they actually say."

And so on and on it went, around and around in circles, frustrating in all its pointless futility. By the time Michael finally rid himself of Pantini—nobody from Fleet PR bothered to turn up to help him out—it was too late to step out to grab lunch; ignoring an outraged stomach, he sat and waited for the board to reconvene.

At 13:00 promptly, Captain Shavetz brought the conference to order. When silence fell, he peered around the packed room. "Welcome back. This is what is going to happen. I will present a short summary of the board's key conclusions, absent those that are classified for the reasons I have already outlined. Then I will present our recommendations. After that, the unclassified version of our report will be available from the Fleet public relations office in the normal way. Together with the chief of the defense force and the commander in chief, I will be available for questions at a press conference at 17:00. Right, let's get on. The conclusions of the board of inquiry are these . . ."

Michael's heart started to thump when Shavetz recited the first of what would inevitably be a long list of conclusions, a process made even longer by the man's florid turn of phrase. Come on, come on, he urged Shavetz silently.

Finally Michael's moment of truth arrived.

"Conclusion 31. That Rear Admiral Perkins's order that

Dreadnought Group, commanded by Lieutenant Helfort in FWSS *Reckless,* come to the assistance of Assault Group was a legal order as defined by the Federated Worlds Code of Military Justice.

"Conclusion 32. That Rear Admiral Perkins believed his order to be consistent with the mission's prime objective, which was, to quote verbatim from the operation order, 'the total destruction of Hammer Support Facility 27.'

"Conclusion 33. That Rear Admiral Perkins issued the order to Dreadnought Group because he believed the ships of Assault Group under his command to be the only force capable of destroying Hammer Support Facility 27.

"Conclusion 34. That the Board has been unable to determine why Rear Admiral Perkins held this conviction, a conviction held despite advice given to him by all senior members of his own staff."

The conference room was silent, the attention of everyone present locked on Captain Shavetz. Hands clenched, Michael allowed a tiny flame of hope to flicker into life.

Shavetz continued. "Conclusion 35. That the evidence presented to this board of inquiry demonstrates beyond any doubt"—Shavetz stopped to look up as if to make sure everybody paid attention—"that compliance with Rear Admiral Perkins's order would have resulted in the neutralization of Dreadnought Group.

"Conclusion 36. That the evidence presented to this board of inquiry demonstrates that even with the assistance of Dreadnought Group, Assault Group's losses would have rendered it incapable of completing its assigned task, namely, the destruction of Hammer Support Facility 27.

"Conclusion 37. Noting the precedent set by *Federated Worlds v. Captain J. D. Kingsway FWSF (2315),* that the decision of Lieutenant Michael Helfort, commander Dreadnought Squadron One, of Junior Lieutenant Kelli Anushri Rao, commander Dreadnought Squadron Two, and of Junior Lieutenant Nathan Panyar Machar, commander Dreadnought Squadron Three, to disobey the order of Rear Admiral Perkins to come to the assistance of Assault Group was wholly justified."

The only sound was a gentle murmur washing across the room. Michael breathed out a long slow sigh of relief.

"Conclusion 38. That there are no grounds for disciplinary or administrative action against Lieutenant Michael Helfort or any other officer of Dreadnought Group as a consequence of their refusal to obey the order of Rear Admiral Perkins to come to the assistance of Assault Group.

"Conclusion 39. That Lieutenant Michael Helfort, Captain in Command, Federated Worlds Warship *Reckless*, and Commander, Dreadnought Group, discharged his duties during Operation Opera in a manner entirely consistent with the finest traditions of the Federated Worlds Space Fleet."

Michael slumped back in his seat, drained of all emotion. It was over.

Thursday, May 31, 2401, UD
Transit officers' quarters, Space Fleet headquarters,
Foundation, Terranova

After another mostly pointless day at his desk buried in the bowels of the Warfare Division, Michael fled to the safety of his cabin, unwilling to risk being hounded by supporters and enemies alike. Slamming the door behind him, he threw himself onto his bunk, mind racing.

Fool that he was, he had assumed that being cleared by the board of inquiry would allow him to move on, to leave Opera behind him, to convince the world that he had made the right decision.

No such luck.

The attitudes of many in Fleet were utterly impervious to the board's logic. If anything, the board's scathing criticism of Rear Admiral Perkins shocked the antidreadnought lobby into action. The response of the trashpress—never interested in either facts or logic—was no better.

Michael asked Fleet PR for a summary of the press coverage of the board's findings. When he read it, he wished he had not. True, the serious news channels had been fine, but the trashpress had not, putting a saddle on the cover-up idea floated by Giorgio Pantini and riding it for all it was worth. The headlines were terrible: "Fleet Conspiracy to Cover up Hero's Role?" "Hero's Complicity in Fleet Deaths Not Explained," "Fallen Hero—Betrayal at Devastation Reef," "Fleet Inquiry—Whitewash Alleged," "Rear Admiral Perkins—A Man Betrayed?" and so on ad nauseam. One thing was for sure: The trashpress was extracting its money's worth from Lieutenant Michael W. Helfort, Federated Worlds Space Fleet.

Michael refused any more interviews after a particularly bruising encounter with Pantini; he had come within a hairbreadth of ripping the dishonest little jerk's head off. Talking to people like Pantini was pointless. No matter what Michael said, no matter what an increasingly frustrated Fleet said, the trashpress trotted out its own warped view of the matter to the public: all selective quotations, lies, distortion, spin. Nothing was beyond them in their relentless efforts to paint Perkins as the real victim and Michael as the bad guy. His agent, the tireless Mitesh, had already launched legal action against Pantini and World News; sadly, the only result had been to goad Pantini into even more outrageous attacks.

Screw them all, Michael decided in a sudden burst of defiant energy. He'd be damned if he'd spend the rest of his life hiding out in his cabin. He would try to track down Kallewi. He might be able to persuade the big marine to spend a couple of hours in the gym; Kallewi always enjoyed showing him how little he knew about unarmed combat. Michael still had the aches and bruises from their last session to prove his ignorance, and he had a feeling that improving his unarmed combat skills might come in handy one day.

Reenergized, he started to get out of his bunk when a soft chime announced the arrival of a priority com. What now? he wondered when he accepted the call.

It was Jaruzelska. "Oh, hello, sir," Michael said. "What can I do for you?"

"Well actually, Michael, it's what I can do for you in my capacity as the ex-commander of Battle Fleet Lima," Jaruzelska said, smiling broadly. "I'm going to com you two documents. Read them carefully and com me straight back."

"Will do, sir," Michael said, mystified.

The first document popped into his neuronics. Michael read it and read it again. "Yes," he said out loud, punching his fist into the air, "thank you, Vice Admiral Jaruzelska, thank you, thank you." He sat down on his bunk, overwhelmed by the admiral's faith in him. Without any of the arguments he'd expected, she had approved every single one of his medal recommendations. Quite right; it was nothing less than the marines and spacers of Dreadnought Group deserved. He opened the second document.

His spirits sank as he read it through. He had said to Jaruzelska, as firmly as any junior officer could to one of Fleet's most distinguished flag officers, that he wanted no public recognition for Operation Opera. Jaruzelska had not tried to argue the issue with him. Stupidly, he had taken her silence for acquiescence. He shook his head. Medals might be important to some people, but he did not care about or for them. Just three things mattered to him: getting Anna back, seeing the Hammers defeated, and destroying DocSec. That was it. Fleet could throw all the tin at him they liked, and none of it would count for anything. Sadly, Jaruzelska did not agree. She attached a short covering note in which she made it abundantly clear that she would be mightily pissed if Michael declined the honors he had been awarded.

Unwilling to betray Jaruzelska's unstinting faith in him, Michael resigned himself to the fact that he would have to accept the medals. If it added more fuel to the fires raging around him, so be it. He commed Jaruzelska.

"Happy?" she said.

"Yes, sir. My guys deserve the recognition. So thanks for that."

Jaruzelska nodded. "My pleasure. They earned those medals five times over. But I notice you're not saying much about yours. Should I read anything into that, Lieutenant Helfort?"

"Er, no, sir," Michael sputtered. "No, you shouldn't. Thank you, sir. I'm honored."

"Yes, you are honored, you ungrateful tyke," Jaruzelska said. "I listened to what you said, Michael. I heard and understood every word. I know how you feel about these things, but I just cannot agree with you. You need to understand two things. First, a medal is not a piece of cheap pressed metal. It's a public statement. It shows that what you do matters enough for the Federation to take the trouble to say so, out loud, in public, for all to hear. Believe me, that's important when you're facedown in the muck and blood of combat. Second, if I don't recognize the commander of my three dreadnought squadrons, what would that tell the world?"

"That you think I was wrong to disobey Perkins's order?" Michael hazarded.

"That's right. Let me tell you, Michael, that would have been ten times worse than all the debate these medals are going to generate. Shit storm does not even begin to describe it. Understood?"

"Yes, sir. Understood."

"Good. You know something, Michael?"

"What, sir?"

"You are a good combat commander. You've proved that over and over again. But you're not a great commander . . . yet. You can be one of the greats, one of the people Fleet officers talk about in a hundred years, but only if you get your head up out of the dirt. I know it's a tired old cliché, Michael, but a great commander really does start with the big picture and work back to the details. How else can you get the small things right? Michael"—Jaruzelska's voice softened—"I know the things that matter to you, I know what you want to achieve, but don't let them make your decisions for you. Put them into context first before working out how to get them done. All right?"

"Sir," Michael said, trying not to sound mulish but not quite succeeding.

Jaruzelska sighed. "You are one stubborn son of a bitch, Michael, and that's a God-given fact," she said. "Anyway, enough of the career guidance. Fleet will be in touch about the awards ceremony. The commander in chief has agreed that all the dreadnoughts' medals be awarded at one time. Okay, that's it. Once again, well done."

"Thank you, sir."

Jaruzelska's avatar vanished, leaving Michael wondering when he would ever get one over on the admiral. Probably never, he decided as he returned to the task of locating Kallewi, as he seemed to know him better than he knew himself.

Friday, June 1, 2401, UD
Personnel Division, Space Fleet headquarters,
Foundation, Terranova

"Take a seat, Helfort."

"Thank you, sir."

Captain Selvaraj, Assistant Director, Fleet Personnel (Command Postings), studied Michael for a while before speaking. When he did speak, his voice was cold.

"Since the board of inquiry has in effect exonerated you"—Selvaraj made a point of stressing the words *in effect,* his tone leaving no doubt that there had been a serious miscarriage of justice—"we need to decide where you go next."

"Yes, sir, though if I may, sir?"

"What?"

"Well, sir. I think I should point out that the board of inquiry did not 'in effect' exonerate me, it—"

"Enough," Selvaraj snapped, eyes narrowing in anger. "How dare you . . ." He stopped, fighting to recover his composure. "I am not interested in semantics, Lieutenant. And watch your mouth. I'll not tolerate insubordination. Is that understood?"

Michael stared coolly at the man long enough to call his bluff. "Yes," he said. "Understood . . . sir."

Selvaraj's face darkened. "I've reviewed your file in detail," he said at last, "and I think what should happen next is pretty obvious. Given what you've been through, I believe you should consider resigning your commission."

Michael was not sure he had heard the man right. "Sorry, sir?" he said, confused. "What? Resign?" It was the last thing he had expected to hear.

"Yes. Resign, Helfort. I think that would be the best thing for you, for your fellow spacers, for Fleet. We think you should resign."

Anger flared inside Michael, white-hot, nearly uncontrollable. He forced himself to sit absolutely still, not trusting himself to speak. Goddamn pencil pusher, he raged. How dare he?

Selvaraj drummed his fingers on the desk. "Helfort, I don't have all day. If you've been struck dumb for some reason, if you'd like some time to think about what I've just said, we'll reschedule."

"No, sir," Michael said. "I think this needs to be resolved. Here, now. If that's okay with you, of course."

"Do not be insubordinate, Helfort," Selvaraj snapped, "even though it's the one thing you seem to be good at."

"I'll forget you said that, sir," Michael said, "even though I'd be well within my rights to lodge a formal complaint against you for saying it."

"Enough! Answer my damn question, Helfort. Resignation, yes or no?"

"Before I answer, sir, tell me something. You said 'we think' just a minute ago. Does that mean you have the director's approval for suggesting I resign?"

"Ah." Selvaraj shifted in his seat. "Yes, I think I can confirm that he has accepted my recommendation."

"Fine, sir," Michael said. "So you won't mind if I ask to see the admiral's formal endorsement of that recommendation. It would be a first, sir, I have to say. I'm a combat-proven

captain, I have more medals and unit citations to my name
than most officers three times my age"—including you,
Captain Selvaraj, you deskbound asshole, he thought—
"with more to come following Operation Opera, and yet
you want me to resign just when Fleet's screaming for all
the command-qualified warfare spacers it can get its hands
on. Sorry, sir, that does not make any sense. And if it
doesn't make sense to me, I wonder how . . . well, let's just
say I need to know that your offer has Admiral Karpovski's
formal approval . . . sir."

Selvaraj's mouth twisted into a sneer. "And if the admiral
formally approved it, would that make any difference?"

Michael shook his head. "No, sir, none at all. I am what
I am. So long as there's one Hammer left standing, I belong
in the Fleet. I belong in command of a Federated Worlds
warship. You may not like me, sir—and frankly, I don't care
whether you do or you don't—but my record has to speak
for itself. To those who will listen," he added bitterly.

Selvaraj peered at Michael for a moment. "Well," he said,
"seems we might have underestimated you, Helfort. Okay,
I cannot force any officer with your record to resign, but be
under no illusions. You are a liability. Where you go, death
and destruction follow. No"—Selvaraj's hands went up to
forestall Michael's protest—"to be fair, that's not your
fault; it's just the way things have worked out. The problem
is that it's personal. Here. Let me com you an intelligence
report we received two days ago. Perhaps you'll judge us
less harshly when you've read it."

Michael read the report carefully. When he finished, his
face was grim. He stared at Selvaraj. "The bastards," he
said. "What can I say? So the Hammers want me dead, their
chief councillor, the top dog himself, wants me dead. Shit,
sir. The Hammers want all of us dead." He shook his head.
"I don't think it changes anything."

"Maybe not, but it still leaves me with a problem. Where
I post you becomes a high-priority target for the Hammers
just because you're there. Whether you like it or not, that is
something Fleet has to consider."

"Fair enough, sir. So what's next? You must have known I'd turn down the offer to resign."

"I must admit we suspected you would," Selvaraj said with a brief smile. "So here's the deal, and"—his voice hardened—"it's the only offer you're going to get that puts you back in command . . . if you accept: captain in command of *Redwood*."

"Redwood?" Michael said, unsure what the man actually meant.

"I said that, didn't I?" Selvaraj said testily.

"Yes, sir, you did. Sorry. But *Redwood*? She's one of the reserve dreadnoughts. I understood Fleet was scrapping them."

"It should, but it can't. Too many missions for too few ships with too few spacers. It'll be the last dreadnought, but so long as it's operational, it will be in our order of battle. Fleet is also giving you *Red River* and *Redress*. They'll constitute Dreadnought Squadron Four. They are the last of the dreadnoughts, I'm happy to say, so do not waste them."

"Fine, sir," Michael said, ignoring Selvaraj's sarcasm, his mood lifting from knowing he would be back in command, and not of one dreadnought but three. "*Redwood* and Dreadnought Squadron Four it is, sir. I accept."

"Good," Selvaraj said, tight-lipped. "So noted . . . right, that's official. Let me wish you luck in *Redwood*. Nyleth-B needs you."

You bastard, Michael said to himself. He had not spotted the trap until too late; he swore under his breath when it slammed shut, with Selvaraj's sly smile of satisfaction widening into a broad grin. Michael swore some more. Nyleth-B sat about as far from the front line as one could get, so far that even the Hammers would have trouble getting to him. But so be it, he decided, so be it. If that was the best offer he was going to get, it would be up to him to make something of it.

"Can't wait, sir," he said.

"I'm sure," Selvaraj snapped. "One more thing. The crew of *Reckless* has been posted en bloc to *Redwood*. Something to do with not having to train a new crew from scratch, and that includes marines. Because of Nyleth-B's remoteness, Fleet is augmenting your marine detachment with a second platoon." Selvaraj shook his head. "Who knows why, but Ferreira, Sedova, and Kallewi have all accepted the posting without complaint, and so have the rest of the crew. The additional marines didn't get a choice."

Michael did not know what to say, so he said nothing.

"You can go," Selvaraj said, waving Michael away. "I'll get your orders posting you to *Redwood* in command. Orders establishing the Fourth will be promulgated when Fleet gets around to it."

"Thank you, sir," Michael said, deadpan. "Much appreciated."

Selvaraj's eyes narrowed. "Get out of my office, Helfort, before I kick you out."

Michael was confused. Selvaraj might be an A-grade jerk, but at least the man had given him a command. Not just any old command, either, but a dreadnought squadron command. And he was going back into space with the team from *Reckless,* Kallewi and his marines included. All that was better than good, but the more he studied it, the less attractive the deal appeared.

What worried him were the things Selvaraj had not said. Why had he been sidelined? Why the posting to Nyleth-B? It had to be the least challenging command in all of Federation space. He did not like it one bit. He wanted to be in the thick of it, somewhere he could make a difference, somewhere he could play a part in bringing Anna home, somewhere he could help to bring the goddamn Hammers to account.

With the elation engendered by the prospect of another dreadnought command evaporating fast, he set off toward Fleet operations. He needed to know a lot more about Nyleth-B.

The final bars of the Federated Worlds' national anthem faded away across the crowded lawn in front of the President's House.

Spacers and marines in dress uniform stood at ease, and the diminutive white-haired woman holding the Federated Worlds' highest office stepped forward to stand behind a simple wooden lectern.

For a moment she said nothing, looking left and then right at the two stands where families and friends were taking their seats after the formality of the Presidential Salute. She turned back to look at Michael and the rest of the spacers and marines from the dreadnoughts *Reckless, Retrieve,* and *Recognizance* standing ranged on the lawn in front of the low dais.

"Good morning, everyone, and welcome to the President's House. Or should I say, given how long I've been here, my house?"

Michael chuckled as laughter bubbled up from the crowd. Diouf was the longest serving of the Federation's many presidents; Michael reckoned she was so popular, she could make a crowd of hungover alcoholics laugh.

"In the past," she said, "I have been accused of making long-winded speeches, and yes, I will admit I have been guilty of that"—more laughter—"but not today, you will all be pleased to hear. That's because today is not about me nor is it about the office of president. It is about the men and women standing in front of me. And I do not need to say much, because what needs to be said takes just a few sentences.

"These are desperate times, and in desperate times, it is to spacers and marines that we turn. All too often, they die to protect us. They die far from home, with pain and fear their only companions. They die unseen and unheard by the people for whom they give their lives."

Diouf paused for a moment.

"By honoring those here, we honor the memories of those who could not be here, those who have fallen in battle to preserve the Federation. I ask you all to stand for a moment in silence while we remember them."

Not a word was said as the crowd stood, the quiet absolute. Michael glanced across at his parents. Both stood unmoving. Both stared into the distance as if searching for all the shipmates they had lost in their years of service, tears falling in sun-silvered lines down their cheeks. They rarely talked about their time in the Fleet, but Michael knew their long years of combat during the Third Hammer War had scarred them both deeply.

"Thank you all," the president said. "Please be seated. We now come to the day's business: presentation of medals to the spacers and marines of the Federated Worlds Starships *Reckless, Retrieve,* and *Recognizance.* These medals recognize their service during Operation Opera, a service directed by the captain in command of the *Reckless* in a manner consistent with the finest traditions of Space Fleet."

Michael had trouble believing what he had just heard. But he had not misunderstood President Diouf's intentions; her eyes had locked onto his as she spoke. She had crossed a line, and she had done it to tell the Federated Worlds that she was on his side.

Diouf turned to her aide-de-camp, his aiguillettes shimmering gold in the morning sun. "Colonel Kashvili?"

"Thank you, ma'am," the marine said. "Lieutenant Michael Wallace Helfort, Federated Worlds Space Fleet."

Michael marched briskly out to stand at attention in front of the president, his salute acknowledged with a broad smile and a quick nod of the head.

"For extraordinary leadership when in command of the Federated Worlds Warships *Tufayl* and *Reckless,* award of the Federation Command Star," Kashvili said. "For extraordinary leadership and bravery in the face of the enemy in the line of duty without regard to person throughout Operation Opera and the Battle of Devastation Reef, award of the Federation Starburst on Gold."

Taking the Federation Command Star from an aide, Diouf pinned it on Michael's left breast. The Federation Starburst was next; Diouf placed the extravagant silver spray set against a gold background on its indigo ribbon around Michael's neck.

"Congratulations, Michael," the president said warmly. "You deserve these. You've done well."

"Lucky, I guess, ma'am."

"Not sure about that. But you hang in there. We need to finish this war."

"Can't come too soon, ma'am."

"No, it can't. You be careful out there."

"I will, ma'am."

Michael took a step back, saluted, and marched back to his place in front of the crew of the *Reckless*. Standing at ease, Michael resigned himself to what was sure to be a long wait: President Diouf had a lot of medals to hand out that morning.

"Thank you, ladies and gentlemen. That concludes the medal ceremony this morning. The president invites you all to join her in the function room behind the dais. Light refreshments will be served."

The ceremony dissolved into near chaos; Michael pushed his way through the milling throng of spacers and marines to where his parents stood, two small islands of dress black in a sea of civilian color.

"Mom," he said when she folded him tightly into her arms, the scent of green-tea perfume, her favorite, triggering a surge of emotion, the feeling of security and warmth overwhelming. The embrace lasted a long time.

"Hey, hey, hey, you two," Michael's father protested, "I'm here, too, you know."

"Sorry, Dad," Michael said, repeating the process.

"How're things?" his father said, breaking what was more bear hug than embrace.

Michael shook his head. "You know. The usual. The trash-press is still on my back."

"I've stopped watching," his father said, the bitterness obvious.

"Me, too. I let Mitesh watch for me."

"Considering he's a figment of an AI's imagination, he's a gem."

"He is," Michael said, "and worth every FedMark of your hard-earned money."

Michael's mother winced. "Do not remind us. Nothing but the best, your father said, even though it cost me a year's salary."

"You exaggerate, Mom. I know how much commodores were paid in your day."

"Yeah, well," his mother conceded, "but it was worth it. Mitesh got you a big win over that nasty piece of work at World News . . . what was his name?"

"Pantini, Giorgio Pantini. Yeah, Mitesh and the lawyers did one hell of a job on him. I don't think he'll be getting his bonus this year. Or next. He's just cost World News a fortune, and it's made the rest of them ease up a bit."

"Have they paid the damages?"

"No, not yet. It's in escrow while they appeal, but Mitesh and the legal AI say they have no chance."

"What will you do with the money?"

"Me?" Michael said fiercely. "Nothing. I don't want their filthy money. I've told Mitesh it's to go straight to the Spacers' and Marines' Welfare Fund, every last grubby Fed-Mark of it. Hell, the fund needs all the help it can get after Comdur. Come, let's go inside. I need caffeine."

A welcome coffee in hand, Michael checked out the rest of the gathering. Bearing down on them was a tall, silver-haired marine colonel. "Incoming," Michael said. "The president's aide-de-camp is heading this way, so I'm guessing the president herself is not far behind."

She was. "Commodore Helfort," President Diouf said, shaking Michael's mother's hand and then his father's. "Captain Helfort. Glad you were able to make it."

"Would not have missed it, ma'am," Andrew Helfort said. "I keep telling the boy to take it easy, but I don't think he listens to me anymore. Thankless task, fatherhood."

"Children! I know what you mean," the president said with a theatrical roll of her eyes. "You both know Colonel Kashvili?"

"Certainly do, ma'am," Kerri Helfort said, shaking the marine's hand. "Let me see . . . yes, you were in *Cordwainer,* I think, the marine detachment commander?"

"I was, Commodore Helfort," Kashvili said, "a long time ago. Andrew, how are you? Last bumped into you when we were cleaning out pirates around Damnation's Gate."

"That's right. The early '70s, I think."

"Excuse me for a moment," the president said, taking Michael's arm. "I want to talk to the junior member of the Helfort military dynasty."

"Be our guest, ma'am," Kerri Helfort said. "Please try and persuade him to be more careful."

"I will," the president said, taking Michael to one side. "So, Michael. I wanted to ask about Anna Cheung."

Michael's face must have betrayed his shock. "Come on, Michael," Diouf said, "I am the president, you know, and that means I am well informed."

"Er, yes, ma'am," Michael said, embarrassed that the head of the Federated Worlds and its billions of citizens saw fit to talk to him about his girlfriend. "You are. Very."

"Well, how is she?"

"So far as I know, pretty good, ma'am. Received a few vidmails from her so far. She's tough, so she'll be fine. I just wish . . ." Michael's voice trailed off.

"I know," Diouf said. "I hate the idea of our people rotting in the Hammers' hands. You know better than most what they can be like."

"I do, though to be fair, Hammer spacers are basically okay. They tend to follow the rules of war. It's DocSec you have to worry about. They don't follow any rules at all. I'd be much more worried if she was in their hands."

"I've met the Hammer's new defense force chief, Admiral Belasz," Diouf said. "Apparently they've just shot his predecessor, something they like to do when things go wrong. Jorge, I think his name was. Sorry, Michael, I digress. Anyway, I met Belasz, a few years ago at some function or other, but I remember him quite well. For a Hammer, he's a decent man. When you are talking about Hammers, I realize that's not saying much, but we understand he is very firm when it comes to treating prisoners of war properly."

"Unlike his boss."

"Chief Councillor Polk. There's a truly evil man," Diouf said with a grimace of distaste. "Listen, Michael. Colonel Kashvili's nagging me to go to my next engagement, so I'll be quick. What I'm about to tell you is sensitive, and I'm pretty sure I should not be telling you, so I'm going to block it, okay?"

"Yes, ma'am," Michael said, utterly mystified while he enabled Diouf's neuronics block.

"Good . . . right, that's done. I just wanted you to know that we're not sitting around waiting for the Hammers to hand back our people. I'm leaning hard on the government to work with the Red Cross to arrange a prisoner exchange with the Hammers."

Michael's face must have betrayed his elation. Diouf placed her hand on his arm. "Michael, a word of caution. It's early days, and the Hammers are the most unreasonable people in humanspace. You know that. So it may well not come to anything."

"I understand, ma'am. It's just good to know that we're trying."

"We are, and I'm hopeful the Red Cross can organize it. There'll be an announcement if we make any progress, so be patient. Very patient; it's going to take a long time if it ever happens at all. Okay?"

"Yes, ma'am. And thank you."

"Don't thank me. It's a million miles from a done deal, and knowing the Hammers, there is a good chance it may never happen. I just wanted you to know we're trying."

"Thank you. I appreciate that."

"Right. Yes, yes, Colonel," Diouf said to her aide-to-camp.

"I'm coming. Good luck, Michael." And with that she left, leaving Michael to wonder how so much charisma ended up packed into so small a frame. It was no wonder she had been reelected so many times. He would be voting for her every time she cared to run.

"What was that all about?" Andrew Helfort said.

"Can't say, sorry."

Michael's father stared at him, eyes narrowed, a look of shrewd appraisal on his face. "You look happier, so I think I can guess. No, no, I won't," he said in response to Michael's look of alarm. "We want to meet your executive officer. She sounds like a real gem and a brave one to boot."

"Jayla? She's a star." Michael glanced across the crowd to where Ferreira stood. "I think she's over there with the Fleet's largest coxswain."

Andrew Helfort laughed. "Let me guess . . . Chief Petty Officer Bienefelt?"

"The same," Michael said.

"I remember her dad, though I only met him once. He was a hard man to miss. Like a small mountain on legs."

Michael rolled his eyes, wondering if there was anyone in Fleet his parents did not know. "Come on, follow me," he said wearily.

Sunday, June 17, 2401, UD
The Palisades

Beer in hand, feet up, Michael sat in the warmth of the late-afternoon sun, the only sound the comforting buzz of one of the security drones that watched over him day and night. The last thing he had wanted was leave, but Fleet had been emphatic, so here he sat, alone, slowly getting drunk and trying not to think about all the promises he had made, promises that a posting as captain in command of *Redwood* rendered nearly impossible to keep. What difference could he make, tucked away in orbit around Nyleth-B? God-damnit, what a waste of three good dreadnoughts.

Dispirited, Michael tossed the empty beer bottle into the bin and commed the drinkbot for another.

For the umpteenth time, he went through it all. After the Hammers staged their big push in May, the war settled down into a pointless series of tit-for-tat exchanges, none of which made any difference to the overall strategic situation, a badly stretched Fed Fleet holding the Hammers at bay: just. The brutal truth was that neither side had the wherewithal to force the war to a conclusion, and neither would until one side or the other won the race to get anti-matter warheads onto their missiles in large enough numbers to pave the way for a successful invasion. Michael had no way of knowing when that day might come, but it sure as hell would not be soon.

It was ironic. The Feds had the resources to weaponize antimatter but not the know-how. The Hammers had the know-how but not the resources. Either way, it was going to be years before the strategic balance shifted, and to whom it shifted . . . well, talk about the big question. One thing was for sure, though: The Hammers had as good a chance of winning the race as the Feds did.

Michael could not wait for years, he just could not. Leaving Anna to rot in some damn Hammer prison camp while he lived the rest of his life? Not a chance. Forgetting all those whose deaths he had sworn to avenge? Not a chance. Sitting around scratching his ass waiting for the Hammers to win the antimatter race? Not a chance. Sitting around praying the Feds did? Not a chance.

There was a way, he promised himself as he drained his beer. There had to be. Problem was, he had no idea what. What could he do, stuck on Nyleth-B with three dread-noughts? A lot of nothing, that was what.

In a sudden fit of frustration and anger, he hurled the empty bottle at the bin; catching the lip, it splintered into a hundred pieces. Much like his promises, Michael thought morosely as he commed the housebot to come clean up:

empty vessels, easily broken, and once broken, impossible to put back together again.

He commed the drinkbot for another beer. Since he could not work out how to keep his promises, he would do the next best thing, what losers had done since the dawn of time. He would let ethanol weave its magic and get blind, stinking drunk.

Maybe the answer would come to him.

Friday, June 22, 2401, UD
Offices of the Supreme Council for the
Preservation of the Faith, McNair

When the Defense Council meeting broke up, Polk waved the councillor for intelligence over.

"Yes, Chief Councillor?" Morris Kando said, looking warily at Polk.

"Helfort."

Kando stifled a groan. Polk's interest in the man bordered on the psychotic. "What about him, sir?"

"I've just seen the holovids of him getting even more medals for kicking us in the ass. Kraa! How many months is it I've been asking for you to terminate the little bastard? I'll tell you, Councillor. Too many, far too many."

"Sir," Kando protested, "it's not easy. We're wasting our money: Our contacts inside the Fed Fleet have nothing new to say no matter how much we wine and dine them, and bribing the Fed trashpress is not working anymore. They've found new stories to chase; Helfort is yesterday's news. He's practically disappeared. We know he is under constant security surveillance. We cannot get near him, and even the dumbest Fed crook refuses to have a go, no matter how much money we wave under their noses. They remember what happened last time."

Polk scowled. "So you've told me . . . a thousand times. Well, the way I see it, if you can't get to him, get him to come to you. There has to be a way to make him break cover, Councillor, and I suggest you find it and quickly. My patience is running out fast."

"Sir."

Friday, June 29, 2401, UD
FWSS Redwood, *Nyleth-B nearspace*

Barely a minute after *Redwood* dropped out of pinch-space into Nyleth-B nearspace, closely followed by *Red River* and *Redress,* a soft chime announced the arrival of a personal message. Michael's heart raced when he saw what it was: Anna's monthly vidmail. Busy with *Redwood*'s arrival, he decided to read it later.

It would keep.

With *Redwood* and her sister dreadnoughts tucked safely into parking orbit around Nyleth-B and an hour before he took the down-shuttle to make his duty call on the base commander, Michael found the time to watch Anna's message. His heart lurched when her face popped into his neuronics. Happily, Anna looked in reasonable shape: a bit tired and drawn but otherwise okay. It was the best he could hope for, that she would hold up until somehow the feds got her out of there.

He let the message run, happy just to hear Anna's voice, to know that she was alive. By the time the vid finished, he was relieved to know she was as well as she seemed, camp life was dull but bearable, the food was not so good but enough to live on, the regime—her code for the Hammers, he had soon worked out—was behaving itself, and she still loved and missed him.

When the message finished, Michael was on the point of

rerunning it—Anna was sure to have used her binary code trickery to pass on information the Hammers would not approve of—when her head and shoulders were replaced by someone whose face he had sworn never to forget. Not that he could.

"Oh, no, please, no," he said, his body overwhelmed with a sick dread, every fiber telling him that something terrible was about to happen.

"Hello, Lieutenant Helfort, or may I call you Michael?" the man said, the high-necked black uniform with woven silver badges unmistakably that of a senior DocSec officer.

"Do you remember me? Yes . . ."

How could I forget you? Michael thought. The man's gaunt face and pencil mustache above thin, bloodless lips were scarred into his memory, washed-out amber eyes staring at him with pitiless intensity, empty of all emotion, a short riding crop held in one hand tapping the palm of his other hand. Oh, yes, I remember, Michael said to himself; without knowing it, his fingers reached up to touch where Hartspring's riding crop had cut his face open.

". . . I'm sure you do, but just in case you've forgotten, I'm Colonel Erwin Hartspring, Doctrinal Security, Section 22. You made me look like such a fool the last time we met, so I've certainly not forgotten you. I know you think we Hammers are a bunch of clods, but we're not. So when an opportunity as good as Lieutenant Anna Cheung falls into our laps, we know what to do with it. She made a big mistake, talking about you openly the way she does."

Panic started to tear Michael apart.

"So, Michael," Hartspring continued, "we know how you feel about Lieutenant Cheung, and since we've been having such trouble getting to you what with all those damned security drones, we decided it would be much easier if you came to us. Our chief councillor is so insistent. He wants to shake your hand before we . . . well, let's leave that bit to your imagination, shall we."

Hartspring paused.

Michael struggled to breathe. Here it comes, here it comes.

"So this is what I propose, Helfort," Hartspring said, his voice hardening, "and it's nonnegotiable, so don't waste time or energy trying to wriggle out of it. You have three months to present yourself to our embassy on Scobie's World. Three months. If you're even a day late, just one, the first Lieutenant Cheung will know about this little plan of mine is when I collect her from her cozy little prisoner of war camp and hand her over to some of my more . . . let me see, how can I put this? Um . . . yes . . . hand her over to some of my more high-spirited and energetic troopers for a week of fun and games. They've seen holovids of her, and let me tell you, Michael, they are keen for the party to start. They love the way your Fed women look, all that flawless perfection, and I must say your Anna is one of the prettiest I have ever seen. They can hardly wait. And did I mention that there'll be ten of my boys at the party? No? Oh, well, now you know. Anyway, I don't think she'll look quite so attractive when the week's over, so I think I'll send her to one of my firing squads."

Hartspring paused.

"Of course," he continued, "by the time my troopers have finished with her, she'll be begging to die, so having her shot is not much of a threat, but I mention it just so you have the full picture. I think I might even command the firing squad myself. It will be fun to watch the single most important person in your life die, to watch the spark disappear from those gorgeous green eyes of hers. Ah, revenge; it is such a sweet thing. And yes, talking of watching, I nearly forgot. We'll have holocams film every minute of the last week of Lieutenant Cheung's life. I'll be sure to send you a copy. I think you'll enjoy it. I know I will. So there it is. Just so we're absolutely clear, present yourself at our embassy on Scobie's World in three months or Anna dies a death you do not even want to think about. I'll be waiting for you, so be sure to ask for me."

The DocSec colonel paused again, seemingly to make sure Michael understood fully what was required of him.

"Oh, what the hell," Hartspring added with a shrug of his shoulders. "As you know, I'm not an unreasonable man,

Michael. I know it's going to be hard for you to get to Scobie's, so why don't we say October 1? I think that's only
fair, don't you? But do not be late, d'you hear?

"Before I go, there is one last condition, so pay attention.
Do not even think about telling anyone about this little
arrangement of ours. Nobody. Because the minute we find
out you've opened your big mouth—and we will—the
deal's off and Lieutenant Cheung will be starting the party
with my troopers early. You can trust me on that, Michael.
Anyway, that's it from me. Looking forward to seeing you
real soon. Bye, now."

Paralyzed by fear, Michael sat unmoving as Hartspring's
smiling face disappeared, his mind flailing in a frantic attempt to find a way out of the Hammer's trap. He refused to
accept that there was no escape. Over and over he replayed
Hartspring's terrible message until finally it had pounded
him into submission, his defenses crumbling in the face of
its stark, callous brutality, until he had to accept the awful
truth. There was no way out, not now, not ever, and nothing
would change that simple fact.

Turn himself in to the Hammers and he would die an
agony-wracked death at the hands of Hartspring and his
DocSec thugs. Refuse and the Hammers would kill Anna.
Abandoned, betrayed, she would die a lonely death filled with
horrific pain, and he would live: his heart and soul ripped out,
his body left an empty shell wracked with bitterness, hate,
and guilt for the rest of time.

Whatever he did, he was as good as dead.